Definitely Not Mr. Darcy

Definitely Not Mr. Darcy

KAREN DOORNEBOS

BERKLEY BOOKS, NEW YORK

THE BERKLEY PUBLISHING GROUP
Published by the Penguin Group
Penguin Group (USA) Inc.
375 Hudson Street, New York, New York 10014, USA
Penguin Group (Canada), 90 Eglinton Avenue East, Suite 700, Toronto, Ontario M4P 2Y3, Canada
(a division of Pearson Penguin Canada Inc.)
Penguin Books Ltd., 80 Strand, London WC2R 0RL, England
Penguin Group Ireland, 25 St. Stephen's Green, Dublin 2, Ireland (a division of Penguin Books Ltd.)
Penguin Group (Australia), 250 Camberwell Road, Camberwell, Victoria 3124, Australia
(a division of Pearson Australia Group Pty. Ltd.)
Penguin Books India Pvt. Ltd., 11 Community Centre, Panchsheel Park, New Delhi—110 017, India
Penguin Group (NZ), 67 Apollo Drive, Rosedale, Auckland 0632, New Zealand
(a division of Pearson New Zealand Ltd.)
Penguin Books (South Africa) (Pty.) Ltd., 24 Sturdee Avenue, Rosebank, Johannesburg 2196,
South Africa

Penguin Books Ltd., Registered Offices: 80 Strand, London WC2R 0RL, England

PRINTING HISTORY
Berkley trade paperback edition / September 2011

Library of Congress Cataloging-in-Publication Data

Doornebos, Karen.
  Definitely not Mr. Darcy / Karen Doornebos.
   p. cm.
  ISBN 978-0-425-24382-4
  1. Divorced mothers—Fiction. 2. Austen, Jane, 1775–1817—Influence—Fiction. 3. Dating
shows (Television programs)—Fiction. 4. Americans—England—Fiction. 5. Chick lit. I. Title.
  PS3604.O67D44 2011
  813'.6—dc22   2010054197

PRINTED IN THE UNITED STATES OF AMERICA

10 9 8 7 6 5 4 3 2 1

To Jane Austen, may you rest in peace.

Acknowledgments

Warning: this will not be brief; writing may be a solitary pursuit, but I've had a lot of support. The good news is you don't have to read this, you can just skip to chapter one.

Before I acknowledge my fabulous agent, Paige Wheeler of Folio Literary Management, and my very cool editors, Leis Pederson and Cindy Hwang at the Berkley Publishing Group, I'd like to thank my incredibly supportive husband, Jacques, without whom this book wouldn't be possible, and my two children, Remy and Samantha, who have been a little neglected of late. In so doing, I hope I've thanked you all equally!

Thanks to my artist parents, Judie, and the late Bill Anderson, for the creative upbringing. Thanks to Barry Kritzberg, the ultimate English teacher, for the early encouragement, and Laurel Yourke, faculty associate emeritus at University of Wisconsin–Madison Department of Continuing Studies in Writing, who went out of her way to pull me aside to say I had "something."

My beta readers, who read the entire book when it perhaps shouldn't have been seen by anyone include: Kim Delich, Susan Havel, Jen Kovar, Barry Kritzberg, Kim Lutes, Alice Peck, and Katie (Meenan, at the time) Walsh.

Two critique groups helped with this manuscript, and I need to thank the first: Pat Dunnigan, Stephanie Elliot, and Elyce Rembos; and my current critique group: M. J. Bressler, Rita Chhablani, Chris Foutris, Barbara Harrison, Fredericka Meiners (writing as Ann Macela), Jan Moretti, and Sherry Weddle.

Thanks go to author and fabulous teacher Christine DeSmet; Arielle Eckstut, author of *Pride and Promiscuity*; and agent Danielle Egan-Miller, author Syrie James, Erin Nuimata of Folio Literary Management; Abigail Reynolds, prolific Austenesque author; and Maggie Sullivan of Austenblog and *There Must Be Murder* fame.

Hugs to those who put together "Young Author Outrage," a hilarious scrapbook that kept me going over the years: Michelle Burton, Liz Calby, Linda Dunbar, Gloria Gyssler, DeAnn Gruber, Anne Kodama, Audrey Korsland, Linda LaBelle, Bianca Loftus, Karen Maher, Ingrid Nolan, Kate Pennington, Jennifer Pollock, Mary Jo Robling, and Jane Wilhelm.

Other stalwart supporters include: Robin Benoy, Janan Cain, Marilyn Groble, Anne Huston, Janice Fisher, Bridget Lesniak, Cathy Louthen, Ingrid Lulich, Michelle Mendoza, Linda Roberto, Cyndi Robinson, Dorie Skiest, Cindy Vitek, and Trish Willinger. Carole and Mike Fortman, thank you for entertaining and, at times, feeding Samantha. Thank you, Jamie Anderson, for your design capabilities and Web advice, and Joost Doornebos and Laurie Gruber for believing.

Those who read pages include: Linda Dunbar, Angela Gordon, Janet Katish, Michelle Marconi, and Anne Kodama, who stopped reading because the book made her forget to pick up her child from piano, or something.

I need to thank the BBC for producing the *Regency House Party*, because, little did I know until I'd written most of the book that they had actually done a Regency reality show that is available both on YouTube and DVD. I recommend it! A tip of the hat to *The Bachelor* TV series, too.

I must come clean that my daughter named her American Girl Doll

"Chloe," and when I looked up the etymology of the name, decided to change my main character's name from "Zoe" to "Chloe." There. I said it, Samantha!

Thanks to: the Jane Austen Society of North America, Chicago chapter, and especially William Philips. Thanks as well to Romance Writers of America, especially the Windy City chapter. Barnes and Noble, Borders, the Newberry Library, Riverside Library, and Starbucks—all fueled the effort. Thanks to fellow Chicagoan, Oprah, for helping to make reading hip—I've watched you for years now, if you want to go out for coffee, just call. Thanks as well to one of my first and favorite bosses, Tim Roberts in England, and my English friends Tim and Alli Moxon.

The 1995 A&E version of *Pride and Prejudice*, and everyone involved in that production, deserves gratitude. Jennifer Ehle and Colin Firth brought a certain coolness to all things Austen and forced Janeites worldwide out of the closet. Colin Firth was consequentially typecast for the next fifteen years, but such is the price for playing Mr. Darcy a little *too* well.

Chapter 1

S he gave up pink drinks and took up tea long ago.

Chloe Parker, even after her divorce, still dreamed of a more romantic era. An age when a lady, in her gown and gloves, would, for sheer amusement, banter with a gentleman in his tight breeches and riding boots, smoldering in a corner of the drawing room.

So now that she stood deep in the English countryside, loaded down with her suitcases, at the registration desk of a Tudor-style inn, she felt as if she'd been drinking something much stronger than tea. Was she woozy from the jet lag of the eight-hour flight from Chicago to London, or enthralled with the antique furniture and aroma of scones?

A young woman in a long blue frock, apron, and ruffled cap approached and curtsied. "I'll be your maidservant during your stay, Miss Parker," she said in a monotone voice with a slight Cockney twang. "My name's Fiona."

Chloe had a maidservant? Who called her, at thirty-nine years old, a "miss" and curtsied? As Chloe's eight-year-old daughter, Abigail, would say, "This rocks."

"Pleased to meet you," Chloe said instead.

Fiona would be beautiful, were it not for the pierced hole in her pouty lower lip where her lip ring would be.

"Welcome to the set, Miss Parker," she said without a glimmer of a smile. "To Jane Austen's England. Or should I say Mr. Darcy's Derbyshire?"

Chloe would be happy to be welcomed to Mr. Darcy's pigpen, but that was beside the point.

Fiona looked Chloe over. "It looks as if you're almost dressed for the part."

Chloe wore lace-up boots, a long pencil skirt, and a poet blouse. She shopped at vintage and secondhand stores and most people noticed her quirky outfits.

Fiona took a skeleton key from behind the check-in desk. "Are you excited to join in our little charade?"

"This documentary's a dream come true for me! A chance to live in the year 1812 for three weeks? No computers, just gowns, balls, and tea parties. This is my Vegas, my—Brighton."

The ice between mistress and maidservant had been broken for a moment, because Fiona managed a half smile.

You wouldn't have to have read *Pride and Prejudice* like Chloe did at eleven years old to appreciate the magnitude of the moment. Mr. Darcy was her first love, although other Austen heroes soon followed, but Mr. Darcy loomed large in her heart for twenty-eight years—the longest relationship she'd ever had with any man, fictional or real.

She'd also never been abroad, and never to England, even though English blue blood ran thick on her mother's side and she surrounded herself with all things Austen and all things English, from BBC costume dramas to Cadbury chocolates. She had even named her daughter Abigail so she could call her "Abby" after the famed English abbeys.

Abigail, though, didn't like to be called "Abby." She took hip-hop dance classes, programmed her own apps, shot her own YouTube videos, and even filmed and uploaded Chloe's audition video for this Regency documentary.

"With all the social networking, Twittering, e-mailing, and texting I'm supposed to be doing, I'm twenty-first-century weary and twenty-first-century challenged," Chloe told Fiona. "I can't wait to escape to the 1800s and slow things down for a while."

"Right." Fiona held out her waiflike arms toward Chloe's suitcases. "It's time to go upstairs and get dressed for your carriage ride to Bridesbridge Place, where you'll be staying. Might I take your baggage?" Her outstretched arm revealed a Celtic ring tattoo around her wrist.

It occurred to Chloe that Fiona might be a little miffed that she had been cast as a servant forced to wait on the likes of her. "No thanks, I have them."

"As you wish. Follow me, please." Fiona spun around and led Chloe to a narrow wooden staircase with steps smoothed from hundreds of years of wear, and Chloe couldn't help but imagine the people who must've walked the same path over time. It was fitting that her journey would start at an inn, as inns were the crossroads of early 1800s society, where rich and poor intermingled, horses were switched out, ladies could lunch in public, and trysts in various rooms changed destinies.

Chloe tried not to bang the plaster walls with her heavy bags.

She had baggage, that was for sure. An ex-husband, a stack of overdue bills, and a house facing foreclosure, all because her antique letterpress business was tanking. Nobody paid for their wedding invitations or anything to be letterpressed and handcrafted on one hundred percent cotton-rag paper anymore.

Letterpress was a dying art, another casualty of the digital age. The bank sent her threatening letters run off on cheap paper and laser-printed in Helvetica, the font she despised the most, because it was sans serif, overused, and, to her, it heralded the reign of the impersonal.

With Chloe's failing business, Abigail's entire world was in jeopardy. That brought Chloe here, first and foremost, to compete in this documentary, to put her knowledge of Austen novels to the test and win the $100,000 prize. How else could she rally that kind of cash so quickly and generate PR for her business at the same time? Perhaps, though, even more than the cash, the documentary offered her one last chance at—everything.

Fiona looked down on Chloe from the top of the stairs. "How ever did you find out about our film project all the way from America?"

"Oh! The president of the Jane Austen Society of North America sent me the casting-call information. I'm a lifelong member and win so many of the Austen trivia contests, she thought of me right away. Once I won the audition, well, how could a lady refuse?"

Chloe might have been born two centuries too late, and in the wrong country no less, but now that she was in her ancestral England, everything was going to work out.

"Do you think you have what it takes to win the prize money?"

"Absolutely. All things Austen are a passion of mine, and that's why I decided to do this." If there was one thing she knew, it was Austen novels.

"What exactly do you intend to do with the money if you win?"

Chloe stopped on the stairs for a moment. "What do you mean 'if'?"

Fiona tapped her finger on her cheek and smirked.

"I fully intend to give as much of it as I can to charity." There. She made it to the second floor, where several closed wooden doors radiated from the landing. "But only after I set aside enough money to secure my daughter's future."

Fiona stepped back. "Daughter? Are you *married*, Miss Parker?"

"Divorced. Four years ago."

Fiona raised an eyebrow and made a flourish toward a door that, once unlocked and opened, revealed, in a corner of the room, a white floor-length Regency gown hanging from a large three-paneled mahogany dressing screen. "Your gown."

"Wow." Chloe gasped, trying to imagine herself in the straight skirting, the small puff sleeves, and the revealing neckline. She thought they'd put her in something a little more—matronly.

"I didn't expect you'd have a daughter. How does she feel about her mum being so far off?"

Chloe hadn't worn such a low neckline in a while. "Um, she actually made her own plea on my audition video, that's how much she supports my being here."

They'd had so much fun filming, along with Chloe's only employee, Emma. They shot Chloe in a hand-sewn Regency gown, sitting in a horse carriage on Michigan Avenue, sipping coffee from a white paper cup and bemoaning the plight of a modern Janeite.

But somehow, Emma's interview questions led Chloe to a rant about men who text other women while on a date or tweet breakups, who think baseball hats are fashion, and who can give a blow-by-blow account of any sporting event but are incapable of writing a love letter even if their last glimpse of the Super Bowl depended on it.

"I remember Abby said to me, 'You have to go, Mom. Who else owns a complete collection of the 'I Heart Mr. Darcy, Mr. Knightly, Mr. Tilney' blah, blah, blah coffee mugs?' She's staying with my parents, and even though they're on a fixed income, I'm sure they'll spoil her as best they can."

Fiona folded her arms. "What really brought you here, Miss Parker?" She blocked the door.

"I'm a huge Jane Austen fan, huge. But I'm here for the prize money, really. And the great PR this will bring my failing business. I'm facing bankruptcy. My ex-husband only contributes minimally, and Abigail's an advanced student, on the gifted track. I resolved a long time ago to give her the best education I could. You have no idea what it took to get her into her school, and if we have to move—"

Fiona didn't seem fazed.

"Look, I don't fit into the modern American world, but Abigail, she has an extremely bright future ahead of her. Sometimes I feel like 'Ma' from *Little House on the Prairie* with a daughter like her who's into all things futuristic and trendy. But I'd do anything for her. Anything."

"Does she know you're here just for the money?"

"I'm not here just for the money!"

"Then what else are you here for?"

"To ogle the young men in their buckskin breeches." Chloe winked.

Fiona smiled again.

"I'm here for the experience, of course! Although Abigail's under the grand delusion that I'm going to find my own Mr. So-and-So." Chloe laughed.

Fiona didn't. "And what do you think?"

The thought had crossed Chloe's mind, but, in true Regency fashion, she had repressed the idea, even after reading a sample bio they had sent her of a cast member, a certain Mr. Wrightman, a man who seemed great—Oxford-educated, an art, architecture, and travel buff—all interesting, except for that ridiculous stage name.

"You didn't come here to meet a man?" Fiona asked, confirming the vibe Chloe had picked up on.

"I think that just because a woman travels overseas, people shouldn't assume she's looking for romance," Chloe said. "I came here to dress in gowns for this documentary, to live and breathe the Regency, and use my knowledge of Jane Austen novels to win."

"Of course." Fiona turned to lead Chloe into the room.

Chloe had to sign all kinds of agreements and go through a battery of interviews and medical and psychological tests for this documentary and now her own maidservant was probing about a man, too? Why was everything always about men? She was perfectly happy without one.

Chloe stumbled, but caught her fall by grabbing onto the wooden coat tree on her way through the door.

"Mind your step." Fiona nodded toward the floor and took Chloe's bags. "Many of these old doorways have wooden thresholds."

"I never was very good at thresholds—being carried over them or otherwise."

That made Fiona laugh, and Chloe felt like she was making prog-ress with her melancholy maid and had successfully dodged the man question.

She found herself in a fairy-tale cottage of a room with a canopy bed, a scroll-armed chaise lounge, and a fire dwindling in a fireplace with a wooden-beam mantel. The dressing screen with the white gown hanging from it dominated the room, and Chloe had to won-der: Could a mom like her pull off a gown like that?

Chapter 2

"Other than your earrings, do you have any jewelry to remove? Any belly rings or the like?" Fiona asked as she closed the door behind Chloe.

"What do you think?" Chloe smiled.

"I would venture to say no."

Being a not-so-modern type, Chloe didn't need to transform too much. She washed off all vestiges of makeup, which in her case was a bit of blush, undereye concealer, and lipstick. Fiona packed Chloe's simple earrings, necklace, and understated watch into velvet drawstring bags. Time, surely, wouldn't matter for a lady of leisure in 1812.

Chloe hopped on one foot to yank off her lace-up boots until Fiona hovered, hands on her hips.

"You must get used to me doing such things for you."

"Really, it's not a problem." Chloe did everything for herself, and Abigail. It would take some retraining to have someone else to rely on.

"It's a rule once we're on set. If you'll step behind the dressing screen, I'll gather your chemise and stockings."

The room had an aroma of lavender. Behind the screen, and deep in the Derbyshire countryside, hours from London's Heathrow, and centuries away from her real life, Chloe felt more at home than ever.

She unbuttoned her blouse, because she couldn't imagine having Fiona do that for her, while her fingers skipped a few in the excitement. Maybe yesterday she'd been a stressed-out single working mom from the Midwest, almost middle-aged, and with a slightly expanding middle of her own, struggling just to get a decent dinner on the table after a long day of trying to drum up business, but today, on this June morning in England, her fantasy life unfolded before her.

The fantasy would have been even better if she'd been a few pounds lighter, but months of cheap pasta dinners had added seven pounds to her tiny frame.

"Curvy women were all the rage in the Regency era, right, Fiona?"

Fiona was smiling a lot more now and warming up to her, Chloe could tell.

One thing Chloe knew for sure: if the meals here were authentic, there wouldn't be any pasta, thank goodness. She'd had her fill.

She wriggled her black skirt past her hips. Sure, she was doing this for the business, for Abigail, but the white confection of a gown hanging in front of her enchanted her. It wasn't a froufrou Victorian with hoops, but a classic Regency with an Empire waist and—that neckline, promising escape from her modern woes or perhaps even a romp in the shrubbery.

Wait a minute, where did that come from? A lady would have to be engaged, if not married, to allow for a romp in the shrubbery, and that meant there had to be a gentleman involved. She didn't let her mind wander down that garden path, the path that led to proposals both decent and indecent, because after all, by 1812 standards, a woman her age would have one foot in the grave. No doubt her role on this show would be that of a widow in mourning. Although they didn't have her wearing a black gown, there wasn't a mourning veil in sight, and no sign of a chemisette insert or fichu to cover her cleavage either.

Regardless, any Mr. Darcy on the set would be twenty-eight years old, as he was in *Pride and Prejudice*, or twenty-three like Mr. Bingley, and both would fill their dance cards with the twenty-year-old Miss Bennets. Men just weren't on her agenda. She wanted nothing more than to enjoy this once-in-a-lifetime opportunity, answer questions about the novels, win the prize money, and get back home to Abigail.

Her new cell phone with international coverage rang, cutting into her reverie, and she sprang toward the sound of French horns echoing to the beamed ceiling. Abigail had downloaded a Regency ringtone for her. Chloe lunged for the phone, because she had told her daughter to call only in case of an emergency, and she almost knocked the pitcher and bowl off the washstand.

Chloe dug for her phone in the vintage doctor bag she used as a purse. "Cell phones. You know, Fiona, two hundred years ago, we wrote letters with quill pens and sealed them with wax. Life was so much more—romantic." She picked up without checking the caller ID. "Hello?"

Across the room, there was a knock on the door, it burst open, and three guys with spotlights on booms popped in. Chloe's blouse was completely unbuttoned and her skirt lay in a crumple at her ankles. She shimmied behind the dressing screen, clenched her blouse closed at her cleavage, and swooped down to yank her skirt back up, covering her decidedly nonthong green cotton panties.

As she looked out from behind the dressing screen, a guy with a video cam bounded in, followed by another cameraman. Lights? Cameras! What was going on here?

"Mommy? Are you there?"

Chloe forgot she was holding the phone to her ear.

"Uh—Abby? Sweetheart? Is everything okay?" Her chest thudded as she squinted into the spotlights.

"Yeah, I just have some really good news."

Chloe exhaled. "Oh, good. I want to hear all about it, but now's not a good time, okay? I'll call you right back." Grabbing the white gown to shield herself, she clicked off the phone and tossed it on the washstand. She held her hand up toward the video cameras. "Stop the cameras! What the—"

Another guy materialized with a headset over one ear, an iPhone in one hand, and an iPad in the other. All plugged in, just like her ex-husband. "Great line," the guy said in a juicy English accent. "What you said about letters. Romance. Could you say that again, please? On camera?"

Chloe stepped back, from the sheer panic of the moment, the intense spotlights, or possibly his manner of speaking. It couldn't have been his cropped auburn hair topped with a pair of sunglasses or his snug-fitting jeans. She was, after all, a raging Anglophile who could crush on any guy with an English accent, and this was the first male one she'd heard since she arrived. All this started with Disney's Christopher Robin when she was what—six?

The accent threw her, but only for a minute. "Excuse me?! What's going on?!" She clutched the white gown in front of her. It felt like a fine cheesecloth or voile, and she realized, despite her confusion and rage, that it must be muslin, that delicate Regency fabric she had up until now only read about. She softened her grip, but raised her voice. "Cut the cameras! Can't you see I'm half naked here?"

"I can see you're exactly what we're looking for. Spot-on." He extended his hand. "George Maxton. Producer. Pleased to meet you, Miss Parker. You can call me George, but once you get on location, everyone's a 'mister' and a 'miss.'"

Behind the gown, Chloe buttoned her blouse single-handedly, a skill she'd mastered while breast-feeding nine years ago. She glared at George Maxton and the crew.

He gave up on the handshake. "Brilliant. You're gorgeous."

Gorgeous? Cute, maybe. Nobody had called her gorgeous since— wait a minute. The nerve! "George, cut the cameras NOW."

He eyed her from the top of her disheveled hair to the tips of her unpolished toes. "You do realize, Miss Parker, that this is a reality show?"

Something plummeted inside her; she struggled to speak. "You mean 'immersion documentary.'"

"Documentary?" He laughed. "Now, that's the stuff I'd love to shoot. No money there." He pointed to the two cameras as he said, "This, my dear, is a reality dating program, and you're going to be a brilliant contestant."

She couldn't breathe. Her mouth went dry and her heart pounded. Was she hyperventilating? "Dating—what?! There must be some mistake—"

"No mistake. It's set in the year 1812. Cameras are on twenty-four/seven. Everything's historically accurate, Miss Parker, and I do mean everything. You will be pleased with that."

The lights blinded her. Her bosom heaved, and not in a good way. Dating show? She didn't want to date anybody—she hadn't had a date in four years! No, it was more than four years, because Winthrop, her ex-husband, was out of town so much they never could manage a date night. How could *she* be on a dating program? Not to mention the fact that she hated those reality dating things. How could this be happening?

She paced the floor, her gown dragging on the floorboards. She caught her breath and began speaking a mile a minute. "I demand some answers here! What changed between the moment I signed the contract and now?"

"Not much, really; we tweaked the concept a bit to make it more marketable, but relationships and courtship were always part of the equation. You did read the paperwork and contract we sent, correct, Miss Parker?"

"I auditioned for a public-television documentary—I'd never sign up for a dating show—I expected Jane Austen trivia contests—I certainly won't participate in any antics with hot tubs and bikini-clad massages and . . . and . . . *dates!*"

"For a person who's so above reality TV, you seem to know a lot about it," George quipped.

And he was right. "Unfortunately you can't have a pulse on this planet without knowing about reality television, especially if you don't have cable like me. Why can't you just film something tasteful?"

"Do you really think people want to watch you sit around in your gown sipping tea and taking Jane Austen quizzes for three weeks?"

Chloe felt the sting of her naïveté, and once again she lived up to her name, Chloe, which meant "young green sprout" in old Greek, and she felt grass green, despite her age.

A log fell in the dwindling fire across the room, sending sparks flying and a wisp of smoke curling into the air.

Then it hit her. "I must be cast as a doting aunt or chaperone, right? A thirty-nine-year-old in 1812 would be strictly on the shelf, not making her ballroom debut. And couples didn't date in the nineteenth century anyway."

"You're absolutely correct, Miss Parker, on two counts. Regency couples didn't 'date.' Men courted women, and that sounds so much more refined, doesn't it? Wouldn't it be wonderful to educate the public on the intricacies of Regency courtship? There weren't any hot tubs in 1812, so you needn't worry about that. To accommodate you we've bent the age rules, making you a bona fide contestant, Miss Parker. You're much too young by today's standards, and feisty enough by any standards—to be on the shelf!"

Chloe stomped her bare foot. "This can't be legal." She tried to be rational. "You misrepresented the show. Is there really any prize money? I need to call my lawyer."

"You're free to call your lawyer, but nothing was misrepresented. You will be partaking of historically appropriate tasks, in an 1812 setting. There is a one-hundred-thousand-dollar prize, and I will explain all that."

He kept checking his iPhone, and looking up when he could. "But even you, on your audition video, referred to the woes of the single American woman. During our extensive interviews with you, you said you're open to finding love and happily-ever-after. Is it true, Miss Parker, or did you misrepresent *yourself*?"

He had her there. The spotlights shone bright and hot, and she hesitated to say it on camera.

"It's true. What you said."

George smiled and looked her straight in the eye. "Say it, Miss Parker."

"I'm still hoping to find true love."

George clasped his hands.

"But not now—someday. And it'll never happen on a reality dating show."

"Don't think of it as 'dating'; think of it as 'courting.'"

"If I took this on, the only thing I'd be courting is disaster." Chloe steadied herself with a palm on the whitewashed wall. She squeezed her eyes shut. "What is the name of this atrocity?"

"The working title is *How to Date Mr. Darcy*."

Chloe's stomach churned. "You have *got* to be kidding me. If Jane Austen only knew! 'Dating' is right there in the title, it's an anachronism. Where's the courtship? Where's the class?"

"Even if the title is a little on the commercial side, the production is top-notch. Trust me."

Trust him?!

A text message beeped on her phone, and, still holding the gown in front of her, she scissor-stepped over to it. Abigail's text said "<3 u" and Chloe would never have even known that meant "heart you" had Abigail not taught her. "Hugs 4ever," Chloe texted back. She needed to call her.

Chloe sighed, phone in one hand, gown in the other, wondering what to do. If she quit this thing, would she regret it? She'd be out the money for the plane ticket, which she'd paid for with the last of her savings. She'd have to face a short sale on the brownstone, her bankrupt business, and worse, she'd have to explain to Abigail why she quit. One of the perks of doing this thing was to set an example for her daughter that a woman, even a single mom, could go to another country, hell, another era—and kick butt. But what kind of PR for her business would come out of something called *How to Date Mr. Darcy?*

Speaking of how, how could she leave England now, when she'd been dreaming of coming here her entire life? And why did the image of her on a dark-haired Mr. Darcy's arm just pop into her head?

She stared at her phone, as if it would have the answers.

"Bit of a mobile addict, Miss Parker?" George asked.

That snapped her back to—dare she think it—reality. George obviously hadn't read the bio she sent. "Oh yes, I can't get enough of modern time-sucks like Facebook, Twitter, or reality TV. Bring it on. Who would want to step back in time a couple hundred years and actually live a quality life?"

"That's the attitude, Miss Parker! So glad you're on board."

"I never said—"

His phone blared a British police-siren ringtone. "So sorry, best take this one. Whatever did we do without these things?"

"We read books and talked face-to-face. We didn't watch reality, we lived it."

George winked at Chloe. "Hallo," he answered his phone. He whispered to her, "You're perfect. Just relax. Forget the cameras. You'll make a fabulous governess."

Chloe almost dropped the gown. "Get out! I can't be a governess! I—I forgot all my college French." Being cast as a governess would be her worst nightmare. Homeschooling spoiled children in an attic somewhere? Wearing gray up to her chin? Dealing with a moody master? This sounded more *Jane Eyre* than Jane Austen.

"I'm kidding. Kidding. Of course you're not a governess. Not in that gown. Though it will tear if you step on it, I'm afraid. It's sprigged muslin."

Chloe lifted the gown and narrowed her eyes at him.

"You've just proven to me that you really do want to be a contestant and not just a—governess."

She had passed a test, and didn't even know she was being quizzed.

This time she had the questions, so many questions, and it was her turn to get some answers, but George didn't give her a chance. He left, the cameras stayed.

He slammed the door so hard behind him that something shook above her. It was swags of drying lavender. Ah, lavender. England. Regency England, where leather-bound books were treasures, where women who had a talent for drawing were called "accomplished," and where men were gentlemen—not sleazy producers.

Fiona brought over a stack of garments, placed them on the chaise, and hung the gown back up.

"Fiona, please tell George I insist on finishing our discussion."

"You're to see him after you're dressed, Miss Parker, and you can sort it all out then, can't you?"

Chloe eyed the gown. If she left, she'd be leaving this picture-perfect inn, and she hadn't even seen Bridesbridge Place yet. She slunk down on the chaise and ran her fingers over the red velvet. "I don't want to go. You can really feel the history here."

"Forgive me, miss, but it's just an inn."

"Fiona, did you know this was a dating show? What should I do?"

Fiona shrugged her shoulders. "I'm only the hired help."

"Oh, Fiona, you're much more than that, come on. What are you in the real world? A law student? Working in the financial sector?"

Fiona shook her head.

Chloe realized that Fiona wasn't going to reveal anything about her twenty-first-century self. "I guess there's no harm in trying the gown on—I'm here, aren't I?"

"You're quite lucky," Fiona said. "I know a score of charwomen and scullery maids ready to trade their lot with yours this instant."

Chloe rubbed her temples. There it was again, that flash of her and a tall, dark, and white-cravat-throated someone, this time in a ballroom under a candlelit chandelier.

The door swung open again. It was George.

"George!" Chloe called out. "We need to talk."

"We will talk. We will, Miss Parker. And not to worry. We'll edit out any naughty bits, for the American market at least. And soon as you're ready I'll explain all the rules. Cheers!" He slammed the door again behind him.

Chloe shot up. "Naughty bits? What naughty bits?!"

"I dunno, Miss Parker. Dunno."

*M*uslin turned out to be a very thin fabric, nearly sheer, and Chloe knew better than to hope for petticoats, because those had gone out of fashion by 1812.

Just as Fiona held up an equally threadbare chemise to go under the gown, Chloe's phone rang.

"See, Fiona, how modern technology interrupts our lives?"

It was Abigail. "Hi, Mom! Grandma told me not to tell you yet, but Dad took me out to lunch today."

Chloe rolled her eyes. After the plethora of times he'd been on the road, missing Abigail's school plays and hip-hop dance recitals, Chloe was out of town for the first time since the divorce, and he'd swooped in on day one.

"Dad's engaged," Abigail continued. "He's going to be married in September and the good news is I get to be a flower girl! I get to wear a pretty dress and throw the petals and ride in a limo and . . ."

Chloe leaned against the cold whitewashed wall to support herself. She didn't even know that Winthrop was dating. He hadn't even talked to her as to how to approach this with Abigail. "Are you sure about this, Abigail?" The gown loomed in front of her. White. Floor-length. Gown. The last time she'd worn one of these was . . . her wedding.

"I'll be right back, Mom. I need to look up satellites on the computer, I'm doing a mock-up for my science camp. Here's Grandma."

A cameraman stepped closer and Chloe lowered her voice to a whisper. "Mom, I don't have time now—"

Her mother plowed ahead anyway. "I just thought you should know that Winthrop wants to reopen the custody arrangement now that he's engaged. His promotion to senior VP means he won't be traveling all the time."

Chloe clutched the ruffle on her blouse and both cameramen closed in on her. Winthrop wouldn't dare put them all through another custody trial, would he? She wanted to shout, but just bit her lip for the cameras.

Fiona's shoulders slumped, she set the chemise down on the chaise, and stepped over to the fire.

Chloe's mom sighed. "You really need to win that money over there, Chloe. Now that he's promoted."

Chloe turned her back to the cameras. "Everybody's a senior vice president these days, Mom, that title doesn't mean anything anymore." The engagement and less travel would give him leverage, though.

Fiona stabbed the poker in the fire.

"I can't talk long, Mom, but take good care of Abigail, and thanks—for everything."

"Bye, dear. Here's Abigail."

"Mom, you're really going to like Dad's fiancée."

Chloe doubted that. "Mmm-hmm. What's her name?"

"Marcia."

"Marcia what, angel?"

"Marcia Smith."

No chance of Googling or finding a Smith on any social network site. She'd never felt the urge to cyberstalk someone until now.

"She's a very successful businesswoman Daddy says."

Chloe's eyelid twitched.

"She was in a magazine. She showed me."

Chloe raised an eyebrow. "What magazine?"

"It was a funny name for a magazine, like fortune cookie. Oh, yeah. *Fortune* magazine."

Of course Marcia Smith was in *Fortune.*

"She has long blond hair and does Pilates every day and she's very excited about being my other mom, she says."

Chloe made a fist. She almost growled. She thought the smoke she was smelling was coming out of her ears, but then she remembered that Fiona had stirred the fire. Chloe had never even thought of sharing Abigail with a stepmother. "She sounds nice," she said through clenched teeth. "Tell Daddy I said 'congrats.' I can't wait to see your flower-girl dress."

Wasn't Marcia fortunate enough with her long blond hair and money and her Pilates body? She could have Winthrop, but did she have to take away her daughter, too?

"Still, I don't want to call her 'Mom,'" Abigail said.

Relieved, Chloe looked into the cameras again. As Abigail recounted the dessert Winthrop and Marcia had bought her, Chloe made her decision about this show. Her mom was right, she had to win the money now.

More determined than ever, she decided to toss her bonnet in the ring.

"Sweetheart, I have to go. I'll call you soon, though, and you know I'm thinking about you every minute, right?"

"I know. You tell me every day, jeez!"

They both smooched into the phone and hung up. Chloe hurried across the room to Fiona, who was struggling with the fire. The cameramen followed her, and Chloe looked back at them, adjusting to the creepy feeling of being watched, followed, and filmed.

Fiona put another log on while Chloe took the antique red-and-gold fireplace bellows and, as if she'd been doing this her whole life, fanned the fire.

Fiona eased the bellows out of Chloe's hands. "Much obliged, but it's not your place to tend the fire. Might we get you dressed now?"

"Of course."

Chloe put her hands on her hips and spoke to the camera crew. "But only if you leave, okay?"

Not a one of them said a word.

Fiona ushered Chloe back behind the screen. "The crew cannot speak to us, only George can. They'll stay on the other side of the screen and won't film you until your chemise is on and I'm lacing up your stays, or corset, as you may know it. They'll film from the back at that point. Agreed?"

Like she had a choice? She nodded in agreement.

Chloe undressed quickly so Fiona couldn't do it for her. She relinquished her bra and green cotton panties.

"This is your chemise, also called a shift, and you wear it under all your gowns." Fiona swooshed it over Chloe's head.

It was sleeveless, grazed her kneecaps, and was so thin it almost wasn't there.

Fiona slid Chloe's arms into the stays, began to tighten the laces, and continued her narrative. "Regency women wore stays," she said with a pause.

The cameras came in on cue, and Chloe got goose bumps just thinking about being filmed in, essentially, her 1812 underwear.

"Regency stays, unlike the Victorian corset, weren't boned, and weren't meant to cinch the waist, but were intended to push the bosom up and out like a shelf."

"I'll take whatever help I can get!" Chloe said into one of the cameras, but the cameraman didn't crack a smile.

"You'll have shorter stays, too, for your more athletic pursuits, but today, posture is everything and you're wearing this longer one, with the busk."

Chloe remembered reading about busks at some point, but never really understood what they were or how they worked.

Fiona wielded the busk, a smooth, flat piece of wood, kind of like a rounded ruler, and slid it into a sewn-in pocket down the front of Chloe's stays, from the middle of her cleavage to her belly button.

"But how am I going to—"

"Bend at the waist? You won't. You'll have to bend at the hip."

Chloe was thinking more about the logistics of, shall we say, bending to go to the bathroom with a ten-inch ruler down the middle of her chest.

Fiona continued the lacing, and Chloe grew impatient, thinking she'd have to go through this every morning and night. The numerous and tiny eyelet holes were just that: holes without reinforcements. What a pain! She looked longingly at her simple bra with the hooks, folded neatly and in a plastic storage bag on the chaise.

The lacing-up gave her time to dwell on things she didn't want to think about, like the fact that she'd be in a dating show on international TV and no doubt the Internet, and, worse, that she'd have a stepmom competing for her daughter's affections. That roiled her.

"I don't understand," she said out loud. "Why aren't there reinforcements for these holes?"

"Reinforcements could only have been made of bone, and richer ladies would have them."

The money thing, again.

"There!" Fiona tied off the laces. "Let me get the mirror."

Fiona trotted back with an ornate, if slightly tarnished, floor-length mirror squeaking along on wheels.

"You don't even feel the busk, do you? And see how it creates such straight posture and how it separates to create this lovely heaving effect?"

Chloe couldn't believe what she saw. Granted, it took half an hour to lace up and she'd never be able to get the thing on or off by herself, but her boob size had gone from a 34C to a 36DD. And all because of a two-hundred-year-old bra . . . ?

The thirty-nine-year-old droobs became suddenly round, pert, and "boobilicious," as her employee, Emma, would say.

"A nineteenth-century boob job," Chloe said.

"Wait till you see how great it makes the gown look. But first, your pantalets." Fiona held up two cotton half legs with ribbons that tied around the waist in the air. They were crotchless, bottomless, scandalous.

The cameramen zoomed in on her.

"They make a thong look uptight," Chloe said. "I know Jane Austen wasn't the prim and proper type some of her relatives made her out to be, but you can't tell me she wore those."

"They were considered a little risqué at the time, but she may have." Fiona held the pantalets in front of Chloe in a "shall we?" kind of way. The ribbons danced and dangled.

Chloe figured women wore some kind of drawers under their gowns, not these things. Certainly, when she wore her Regency gown to a Jane Austen event, she wore her usual hose underneath. Austen never mentioned undergarments in her novels, and even though Chloe knew a lot about the Regency, her knowledge was by no means encyclopedic. "No drawers?"

"Drawers were newfangled, and not completely accepted until later in the Regency. Miss Austen may have done what many women did, especially in this summer heat, and you may choose to do as well."

Color rose to Chloe's cheeks. She'd never look at another period film the same way again. "I'll go with the pantalets."

With the utmost discretion, Fiona helped Chloe into the pantalets and then her white silk stockings.

"Stockings were white," Fiona said. "A woman of your station wouldn't wear pink, that would be vulgar."

Chloe began to piece together that she wasn't to be one of the "Ton," but she wouldn't be a "woman of the night" either, so maybe she'd shake out as a sort of middle-class Elizabeth Bennet?

With silk ribbon garters, Fiona tied off the stockings well above the knee, and Chloe felt suddenly sexy. Maybe, just maybe, this show could be fabulous—

Fiona plunked two lemon halves in Chloe's hands.

"You need to rub these under your arms."

Chloe cocked her head.

"Your deodorant. The staff was hard-pressed to find Regency recipes for deodorant, and most likely they rarely used it, so lemons will have to do, when they're available."

Wincing, Chloe did as she was told. Her mind drifted to thoughts of a lemon martini as she flapped her arms to dry off.

"Now for your gown. This is the best day gown you have, and even though it's a bit impractical to wear for travel in a carriage, it's important to wear your best, as you're going to a grander home than the one you came from."

Fiona lifted the gown over Chloe's head, buttoned up the back, and Chloe morphed into a nineteenth-century version of herself, all in white. She spun before the mirror. Abigail would've loved this. The high Empire waist elongated her torso, the busk kept her back straight, the neckline showed off her racked-up rack, and she felt more convinced than ever that she belonged here, in 1812, although the gown was so sheer you could see her blue ribbon garters right through it.

After Fiona slid on the shoes that had no designated left or right and resembled ballet flats, Chloe floated to the vanity, where Fiona curled and pinned her boring brown hair into a seductive Regency updo that somehow camouflaged the few gray hairs she had. Brown tendrils of hair skimmed her face.

Fiona clasped an amethyst necklace around Chloe's neck as Chloe pursed her lips in the mirror. She knew only prostitutes would wear lipstick, but getting anyone to woo her without it would be a challenge.

Fiona rubbed crushed strawberries on Chloe's cheeks, but that didn't seem to do much other than make her cheeks feel tight and sticky, kind of like her underarms with the lemon. The only suitors this might attract would be flies.

"When we have special occasions, I'll do your eyes up with candle soot," Fiona said.

"That *is* something to look forward to," said Chloe.

"But for now we have elderberry stain for your brows."

The elderberry just seemed to bring out the dark circles under her eyes. "I don't know if I can face a world without undereye concealer and lipstick."

She might've been better off in an eighteenth-century dating show, with her face painted white like Marie Antoinette, covering up the undereye circles and filling in the beginnings of crow's-feet. Of course, that white face paint proved to be full of lead and poisonous, even fatal, to women of the time. Still. No makeup was a bit too revealing.

Chloe padded over to her vintage bag, cameramen behind her, in search of her concealer, and came across the foil-wrapped strip of condoms Emma had slipped her at the airport.

*W*ith all those hot Englishmen in tights you might need these," Emma had said.

"They won't be wearing tights, Emma. That would be seventeenth century."

"Bummer."

"Anyway, I'm not going there for the men, and sex before marriage was a real taboo in Regency England. Have you not heard of Lydia Bennet?"

Emma dangled the condoms in front of her. "They're strawberry-margarita flavored," she singsonged.

She handed Chloe the condoms.

Chloe pushed them away. "What do you think? I'll be having a quickie in the back of a chaise-and-four?"

"I hope so, for your sake!"

Chloe tossed her head back. Resistance was futile. Emma tucked the condoms into Chloe's bag.

"It's your first trip without Abigail, and I think you should be going to Key West, not repressed England. Take them just in case, okay?"

"All right. And just for the record, I have no desire to ever go to Key West."

* * *

She knew she couldn't possibly bring such contraband with her, and as if she read her mind, Fiona made it clear.

"The crew searched all your bags and suitcases, Miss Parker, and only one item qualifies to go with you; everything else will go under lock and key for three weeks."

Was she more shocked by the fact that they searched her bags or that she could only bring one thing? It was hard to tell.

"You can bring this." Fiona held up a red velvet bag and pulled out Chloe's diamond tiara, a family heirloom and her good-luck charm. "It'll be perfect for the ball."

"So there will be a ball?"

"Yes, of course."

Fiona handed the velvet bag to Chloe.

"My grandmother gave it to me for my seventeenth birthday." Chloe had worn it in the audition video, as well as the Jane Austen Society balls she'd attended, but she'd never danced in it.

"It's beautiful, and will fit in your reticule. Now, if you will simply hand me your purse."

Chloe handed over her purse, minus her phone and charger.

Fiona held out her palm.

"What?"

"Everything is historically accurate, Miss Parker. You know you can't bring your phone. Regardless, there isn't any electricity."

Chloe couldn't even process the thought of no electricity. "No phone? Not even just for texting or e-mailing?"

Fiona put a hand on her hip, or what would've been her hip if she had any. "It'll be here, safe under lock and key."

Chloe sank down on the chaise, but the busk kept her from slumping over. "I can't do this. I need to talk with Abigail."

Fiona smiled. "Not to worry. Everyone has a direct line of communication through George for any emergency, day or night. Your family has George's phone numbers. Send her a text that you'll write. You said yourself you're keen on writing by hand. She can write you back. It'll be—sweet."

Chloe keyed in a last message to Abigail: "Will snail mail u. Snail back. Can't take phone. Call George Maxton in emergency. Love u. B good."

She hadn't felt it till now, but she really was across the ocean, thousands of miles from home.

Fiona zipped the phone in a plastic bag, just like all the rest of her things, as if Chloe were going to jail. The zip sliced through the air and the sudden silence of the room closed in as Fiona whisked the bag away.

Then the phone rang inside the bag, breaking the silence.

Chloe got goose bumps. What if it was Abigail and what if she couldn't bear not to be in touch with her mom and what if she wanted her to come home—

"Wait! Stop!" Chloe hustled after Fiona, her boobs jostling in her stays and the cameramen jostling after her.

Fiona stood at a metal safe, closing the door, turning the key.

"Stop, Fiona! I need my phone! Give me my phone!!"

Chapter 3

"Miss Parker," George said as he raked his auburn hair with his hand, "A call from your daughter asking if she can go to a pop concert does not constitute an emergency."

Chloe had hunted George down and found him in his production trailer, which was set up in a green behind the inn. Thankfully, he'd instructed Fiona to retrieve Chloe's phone, and he allowed her to return the missed call from Abigail. Abigail had called merely to ask if she could go to a concert with Winthrop and Marcia, and reluctantly Chloe acquiesced. The competition for Abigail's affections had begun in earnest with Chloe half a world away and incommunicado.

Coffee permeated the air of George's trailer, good coffee, the kind Chloe didn't get on the eight-hour flight.

George stood in front of three high-def TVs mounted to the wall, dividing his attention between Chloe and his iPhone.

"It's not an emergency to you, George," Chloe said. She covered his iPhone screen with her hand for a moment. "She's not your daughter. At her age I was reading *The Secret Garden*. I didn't go to my first concert until I was a teenager. It took a lot of thought for me to say yes."

Chloe, still shaken, and stirred, propped herself up against the floor-to-ceiling wine refrigerator. "I guess I overreacted to having my cell phone confiscated for three weeks. I've never been out of touch with her like this. I'm a single mom—" She looked straight into the camera filming her, sucked in her cheeks, and edited herself to become more restrained and guarded as a single woman of the era should be.

"Are you sure you're strong enough to forgo modern technology for more than a fortnight?" George asked.

Fortnight. She loved that word.

She was happy to leave everything but her cell phone. Her pantalets, she noticed, were sticking to her thighs. "Of course."

"Did you really read all the fine print in the contract you signed? Because this shouldn't be such a surprise to you."

The lemon deodorant failed as a bead of sweat dribbled down her side. She was so thrilled to have won the audition that she really didn't take the time to read every single word in that giant stack of paperwork they'd sent, and couldn't afford to pay a lawyer to go through it with her. Had she once again donned her rose-colored glasses and seen only what she wanted to see in the contract? Legalese, math, science—these were not her forte; she was much more of a big-picture person.

"You are aware, for example, that you agreed we could film you twenty-four/seven upon arrival, and that anything you do is fair game not only for the final program but for any social networking site, Twitter, or blog entry, or any streaming video on the website and any YouTube video we produce?"

Chloe sucked on her lower lip to keep herself from saying anything a lady might regret, but her stomach churned. She'd signed up for a rock-bottom reality show in period costume and she would've been better off in Vegas sunbathing topless, guzzling pink martinis, and gambling her last dollar in hopes of winning it big.

"Your antics, such as storming my trailer, will be posted on You-Tube," George said. "We're going for heaving bosoms and bulging breeches here, not ladies lunching."

Chloe buried her head in her hands.

"Throw in an eligible, handsome, and rich bachelor for good measure."

"What do you mean 'an' eligible bachelor? There's only one? I thought this was a dating show."

"It is! There are two bachelors, really, one infinitely wealthier than the other, so he is more desirable, naturally—"

"And how many women are there?"

"Several."

Chloe couldn't take it anymore. "Jane Austen would be horrified. This is a mockery of everything women have accomplished in the past two centuries!"

"Some people find true love on these kinds of shows, and I think Jane Austen would approve of *that*. Besides, during the Regency, women outnumbered men because so many men had died in the Napoleonic Wars or were on active duty. Many others were out in the East Indies, trying to make their fortune."

He folded his arms. "Do you realize how many women were competing for the same country squire? It would be historically inaccurate to arrange a party of, let's say, ten men and ten women. Surely a stickler for historical detail such as yourself can't argue that point."

He handed her a piece of paper. "Here's Mr. Wrightman's bio. I'm sure they e-mailed this to you in Chicago. Did you read it? He's our most eligible bachelor."

She'd read it more than once. Now it made sense that they only sent one man's biography instead of the entire cast or an array of bios of other possible suitors. It would be her and a gaggle of other women pitted against one another to snare the wealthy Mr. Wrightman.

At least he looked good on paper. If Chloe could believe the bio, the Oxford-educated Jane Austen fan valued honesty, was ready to start a family, but also loved to travel. She and he seemed compatible in every way, but her hopes had been crushed before.

"Yes, I read it." She turned her back on the TVs, handed George the bio without even looking at it, and paced the floor. The camera followed.

A gangly girl dressed in black sauntered out of a room in the back of the trailer to the Miele espresso maker.

George checked his iPhone again. "Chin up, Miss Parker. You're an American heiress come to summer here in the English countryside. I fully expect you to take on that role."

Did he say "heiress"?

"Heiresses don't need to win a man." She walked back over to him.

He handed her a thick black hand-bound book with *Miss Parker's Rulebook* embossed in gold script on the cover. "Tell Janey what kind of coffee you take."

"Double espresso skinny latte, please. If you can't, then just a regular—"

George interrupted. "An heiress would not concern herself with whether the hired help can or can't do her bidding. It's not her problem." He finally set his iPhone aside, picked up a remote, and aimed it at the three TV screens. "You're going to love doing this show. It's a once-in-a-lifetime opportunity. Check it out. Here's what's going on throughout the estate."

A young woman in a bonnet fed chickens on one screen, on another a cook chopped herbs. And, on screen three, a dark-haired guy paused near a copper bathtub, untying his cravat while light from a window behind the tub gave him a silhouette quality. A butler removed his waistcoat and pulled the loose linen shirt over his head. The guy's shoulder blades popped. Was that him? The Mr. Wrightman she was supposed to win over?

She pretended to fan herself. "Be still, my beating heart. Oh, George, is that my future husband?"

George eyed the young woman feeding the chickens while he talked. The swooshing of the milk frother on the espresso machine almost drowned out his voice. "Rule number one. Sarcasm will not be tolerated. Rule number two. You don't have a daughter on this program. Not a word of it, and Fiona's been instructed not to speak of her with you, nor to say anything about it to the rest of the cast."

Janey gave George his coffee in a black mug and handed Chloe her latte in a white paper cup, complete with plastic lid and cardboard sleeve. "Thank you," Chloe said, noting the significance of the fact that hers was a to-go cup.

Without a word, Janey slunk back to wherever she came from.

Even through the cardboard sleeve, the coffee burned Chloe's hand and she set it down on the table littered with gossip magazines.

George finished off his coffee. "It's all very celeb of you, being a single mum in the twenty-first century, but you don't have a daughter here. That would be very uncool unless you're a widow, and that just wasn't sexy enough for us, quite frankly. Here you're an American heiress eager to secure a place in society—and fast. This may be your last chance, considering your age."

Chloe said nothing.

"You need to marry a man of society and save your American family from ruin. They can only afford to keep you here for three weeks."

Chloe turned her back to the camera. "Why would an heiress need to marry up?" She whispered, "It sounds a little desperate."

"We do our best to base everyone's stories on their current circumstances."

"What is that supposed to mean?"

He looked at the camera then turned away from it, lowering his voice. "You come from a blue-blood English family on your mother's side, but you've fallen on hard times. Your business is about to go belly-up and you can't rally the cash to afford your home or your daughter's private school. You depleted your savings just to fly over here. Am I right?"

The air conditioner blew cold air on her bare back. The camera panned around her. The trailer closed in and felt too small for four people. He sure did his homework. She was a girl without a fortune, a damsel in financial distress. She gravitated to the wine refrigerator. She needed a drink. Or two. "Miss Parker may need financial security by marrying a certain gentleman, but *I* don't. I've got lots of irons in the fire."

"I'm sure you do." George smirked. "Think of this as another iron. Get him to propose and you've won our little Regency love match. A hundred thousand dollars. How can you resist?"

"Ugh. I have to get him to propose to win the money? Please."

"Certainly you, of all contestants, would know that the only way a Regency woman of your stature could acquire such a sum would be to marry into it. Women couldn't work to amass their fortune, you know that."

Chloe sighed. "This might be more realistic than I'd bargained for."

"Who knows? Perhaps you'll fall in love with Mr. Wrightman."

On TV number three, the man, who she was convinced must be Mr. Wrightman, was now in the tub, and bowed his dark-haired head while his servant poured pitchers of steaming water over him. Chloe gaped at his broad shoulders, which glistened in the sunlight. What if he was The One? As soon as the question shimmered through her, she thought of how her employee, Emma, might react if she quit and came home.

"Let me get this straight," Emma would say. "The guy was good-looking and rich. And you came home because—?"

Chloe had nothing to lose—except her dignity.

"If I can do this, you certainly can," George said. "Come here so I can wire you for sound."

She folded her bare arms over her shelflike bosom, and that wasn't easy.

"You belong here, Miss Parker. You drive your college intern batty with your four o'clock teatimes, you take carriage rides in the city instead of taxis, although I doubt you can afford that indulgence now, and you don't have cable TV. Do you think the average American eight-year-old even knows who Jane Austen is? Your daughter does. Think of how disappointed she'll be if you go home now."

She'd thought of that already. "You're a rake, George. Isn't that what they'd call you in 1812? An absolute rake."

He smiled. "I've been called worse. This is my business, Miss Parker. Reality."

"Hook me up, then—with the mike, that is."

He laughed and clipped the wireless translucent microphone pack to the back of her gown, then draped a silky shawl over her shoulders. "Mr. Wrightman handpicked you. You! Out of eight thousand applicants—"

Chloe interrupted. "Eight thousand?"

She felt flattered, and already enamored of the kind of man who would participate in such an elaborate Jane Austenesque scheme in the hopes of finding his true love—if she were to believe all this.

"You're the only American contestant."

She didn't like the sound of that. It had a competitive, Olympic-type feel to it, as if she alone were representing the entire United

States, and she hardly qualified to represent the typical American woman.

"Rule number three," George said. "Stay in character. No talking about the Internet and jobs and iPods."

"I think we're up to rule number five now. But not to worry about me babbling on about modern life. I'm ecstatic to be away from it."

"Every day there will be a task, some tasks will take only a few hours, others will be ongoing, but each small task will be worth five points. Larger tasks and competitions will be worth fifteen. You'll acquire these 'Accomplishment Points' by completing challenges such as trimming a bonnet and seeing a few Regency craft projects through to completion.

"For every twenty-five Accomplishment Points you accumulate, you win time with Mr. Wrightman. There will be various competitions, including archery and a foxhunt. Winning will be to your advantage. And, in order to be invited to the ball, you'll need to survive the Invitation Ceremonies. At every Invitation Ceremony, somebody, sometimes several women, get sent home. Oh, and the audience, via phone and Internet, rates you during your stay as a service to Mr. Wrightman. You have three weeks to win *How to Date Mr. Darcy*."

Chloe was rendered speechless at such a delicious array of Regency experiences soured by the odious reality-show points system, popularity contests, and jockeying for a marriage proposal. She didn't really understand how the scoring worked and she hated the thought of it. She squinted at George, but her eyes widened when, on the screen behind him, she got a flash of what must've been Mr. Wrightman's taut butt as he stood up in the tub, just before the servant wrapped a linen sheet around his dripping body.

"He's got a great ass, don't you think?" George asked, looking at the screen side by side with her.

Chloe propelled herself toward the trailer door.

"I'm glad to see you exhibit the proper modesty of a Regency heroine. You must behave at all times as if you are a lady of quality in 1812. As a Jane Austen fan, you should know what you can and can't do, but just in case, your rule book details everything. Any modern behavior and you risk expulsion."

She bit her lip.

"Now for the fun part. Accessories." George guided her toward an open wooden trunk.

"Your purse, or 'reticule.' Inside you'll find your tiara from home to wear to the ball." He hung a slip of a crimson silk bag from her arm and the golden tassels dangled as she moved.

It looked like one of Abigail's toy purses. "Women really did have a lot less baggage back then," she said.

"Vinaigrette." He opened a silver perforated case, smaller than a matchbox, and waved it under her nose. Vinegar and—lemon? He tucked it into her reticule. "A lady would open her vinaigrette to avoid rank smells, say in the streets of London. Or to keep herself from fainting."

"I never faint. And what could possibly smell rank out there?" Chloe looked out the trailer-door window at the lush English countryside.

"Fan." With a crinkle, George opened the fan to reveal a painted scene of a woman in a flowing gown playing a lute.

"It's gorgeous."

George slipped it into the reticule. "Calling cards." He opened a silver case the size of a cigarette tin and revealed a cream-colored stack of cards. *Miss Chloe Parker* had been printed in black script and hand-set on a letterpress printer. She ran her fingertip along the script and felt the debossed letters sinking into the paper. "They're letterpressed."

* * *

eel this," she'd said to Winthrop when she finished printing up menus for one of their fund-raising dinner parties.

"Okay. So I can feel the letters."

"That's why the slogan for the business will be 'Make a great impression.'"

"Cute." He tossed the menu on the table. "But if you're going to open your own business, don't you think it should have something to do with the Web? I mean. That's where the money is."

"You don't get it. My future's in the past and I'm going to do handmade. Hand-set type. Cotton-rag paper. Hand-stitched books. It's what the world needs right now."

He got that fuzzy look in his eye that told her everything she needed to know. Then he pulled his BlackBerry out of his jeans pocket to check his e-mails.

eorge tipped the calling-card case into her reticule. "I can see you approve of the calling cards. I told you everything is historically accurate here. Just look at these gloves, for example. A lady never leaves home without them." He gave her a pair of light gray gloves that she glided onto her arms with a strange familiarity, as if she had been wearing them all her life. They reached just past her elbows, almost touching her cap sleeves, but they became a little loose and bunchy just at her biceps. So sexy! She thrilled at the feel of the leather.

"Whenever you're outside, shade yourself with a parasol. Tanned skin was only for farm girls. Any infractions of these rules and Accomplishment Points will be deducted. Serious digressions mean you'll be sent home." He handed her a fringed white parasol. "Congratulations. For the next three weeks, Miss Parker, you're no longer a working girl."

"But you still want me to work it, right?"

He set the rule book in the crook of her arm. "Rules, Miss Parker. Please read them."

"What about a little pin money, Mr. Maxton? In case an heiress sees a new chapeau she must have at the haberdashery?"

"There are no haberdasheries where you're going, Miss Parker. This isn't a costume flick. We could hardly afford to set up an entire town. You'll be confined to your lodgings and the gardens at Bridesbridge Place—"

"What about London? Won't we be going to London?"

George laughed. "And just how would we pull that off? London in 1812 on our budget?"

"Bath? Brighton?!"

"You'll visit Dartworth Hall, and you're invited to explore the reflecting pond, hedge maze, and grotto. Just remember, you're surrounded by a five-thousand-acre deer park, and a lady wouldn't find herself trudging through the thicket in search of a fancy coffee or hackney coach to Brighton, now, would she?"

Chloe was beginning to like George. He placed a bonnet with a straw rim and slate silk top on her head. He tied the ribbons under her chin, just like she used to tie Abigail's winter hats on when she was little and never left her mother's side. The bonnet, like the pantalets, felt a little ridiculous.

"You'll find a turban and some bandeaux in your wardrobe, but Regency ladies would never be seen outside without a bonnet. Never."

The brim narrowed her view, the straw scratched the back of her neck, and Chloe wanted nothing more than to yank it off. Even when she went to her Jane Austen Society galas in costume, she didn't wear a bonnet, but chose a tiara or a turban. She tugged at the ribbon under her neck.

George stepped back to look at her. "I find it very interesting to see who has the strength of character to throw themselves into the time period and who doesn't."

"I'm all about rules," Chloe said. "That's half the fun of it. Regency manners and etiquette."

He smirked and opened the trailer door. "And no cell phones."

Sunlight fell upon them. George put his aviator sunglasses on. "Shall we? The carriage awaits." He offered his arm.

She looked back over her shoulder at her untouched latte sitting on the coffee table. The copper tub on TV number three had been emptied, upended, and propped against the wainscoted wall. Chloe put her arm in George's. He'd won this round, after all.

The vista from the top of the trailer steps softened her. The grass in England seemed greener, the trees more gnarled, and the sheep more picturesque, with horns and long wool. Of course, there were no such things in Chicago. The sheep bleated as Chloe and George ambled past the inn, which must've dated from the Tudor era. They passed a cabbage-rose garden, a crumbling stone wall, and a stream along the lane, and Chloe took it all in. They approached the carriage from behind, and Chloe noticed a stack of weathered wooden trunks strapped to the back of it.

"In these trunks," George said, "you'll find your wardrobe for the next three weeks. Everything—your gowns, wraps, shoes—has been custom-made for you, all in your favorite colors. Green, yellow, red. What the people of the day would call 'pomona,' 'jonquil,' and 'cerise.' I hope the lady approves."

Chloe looked down at her shoes. They might've been flimsy, and entirely without modern arch support or heel, but they fit her size-seven-and-a-half foot perfectly. She hadn't even thought that they had to tailor-make everything for her. "Thank you. I didn't realize—"

"Quite all right." He made a flourish with his arm toward the gleaming carriage. "Mr. Wrightman sent one of his carriages to collect you. Not even an heiress could afford a carriage like this."

The open carriage, on four wheels with spokes, shone glossy black in the sunlight, complete with brass fittings and a golden family crest featuring a W, a hawk, and an arrow. A driver in a red coat tipped his three-cornered hat and four horses stamped their hooves.

"Wow." Chloe ran her gloved hand along the side. "I've never really been into cars, but I can tell a barouche landau from a gig any day. It's gorgeous."

A footman who couldn't be a day over eighteen held out his white-gloved hand to her, opened the half door, and handed her into the red velour interior. She perched on the tufted seat, crossed her underwearless legs, set her parasol and rule book in her lap, and looked down on George. She actually felt like an heiress.

George propped his sunglasses atop his head for a moment. "Your chaperone, Mrs. Crescent, will be waiting at Bridesbridge Place—"

Chloe's shoulders slumped and the shawl slid behind her. "Chaperone—?" She knew chaperones were de rigueur, but not for someone her age, surely. "Aren't I too old for a chaperone?"

"Thirty-nine is not as old as you think, Miss Parker, you are a single woman, and it would be unseemly to have you go alone. Your chaperone is a few years your senior, and it's your duty to treat her with respect. Read your rule book along the way. It's nearly a four-mile drive through the deer park."

He pushed his sunglasses back down and he looked—good. He rested his hand on the carriage. "Good luck."

The bonnet shaded her eyes from the sun. "Thank you, George, for everything. Really."

"You'll see me out there with the camera crew. But they're strictly forbidden to interact with the participants. Good day, Miss Parker." He bowed and slapped his hand on the carriage door. He shouted to the driver: "Drive on. To Bridesbridge Place! Good luck, Miss Parker!"

Surely she would be better behaved than some American heiresses are wont to be. The carriage lumbered forward, crushing the mike on the small of her back into the velour. She eyed the camera on the ATV beside the carriage and, with her gloved hand, gave George the royal wave and a clipped smile. He gave her the royal wave back. She'd miss him—the cad. Something about him intrigued her.

The horse hooves clomped and gunned her forward. She felt as if she were leaving something behind, something important, like her cell, for one thing. She looked away from the camera with a feigned disinterest as any heiress would. Ancient and storied trees laced into an archway overhead. The sky seemed bluer in England, the sun brighter. Of course, she didn't have sunglasses on because they hadn't been invented yet.

Sunlight dappled in a clearing far from the road, and when Chloe squinted her eyes she saw two men, one dark-haired in a white shirt open to his chest, in breeches and boots, jogging with two logs atop his shoulders, and the other brawny and bald, who clapped and cheered and yelled. The dark-haired man hurled the logs onto a cart, then ran back for two more. The bald man put his hands on his hips and shouted at the guy. Chloe looked back at the footman behind her on the coach, wanting to ask, knowing it would be improper.

The footman spared her. "Training." That was all he said.

Chloe nodded. It was the Regency term for working out. Was it Mr. Wrightman? Only a gentleman would be able to afford a trainer. Whoever it was, she admired the fact that this guy was so into the Regency that he even stepped up his workout to a nineteenth-century routine.

He flung two more logs onto the cart and she heard the impact all the way out on the road. He turned his head toward her carriage and shielded his eyes to see her.

She wanted to wave, but didn't, especially when she thought she saw him smile. The trainer turned his head toward the carriage, then pointed toward the logs and shouted until the dark-haired man lifted four logs.

It was her first real glimpse of Regency life here on the estate, not to mention her first glimpse of a man in an unbuttoned shirt and snug pants in a while. He looked as if he had just burst from the cover of a Regency romance novel and it took serious willpower not to turn and stare long after the carriage had passed. If the rest of the people on the show were as gung ho as that guy, this could be "cool," as Abigail would say. Really cool.

She cracked open the rule book in her lap and ran her fingers along the thick pages that had been hand-cut. She brought the book up to her nose to breathe in the smell of paper pulp and ink. Then she settled back to read.

> *Miss Chloe Parker, you are thirty-nine years old, an American heiress who may be without a fortune due to unforeseen circumstances in your family's business. You have one foot in the States and another one firmly planted in your mother's native England. A projected income of five thousand pounds a year is yours, provided you land Mr. Wrightman, a husband of the English gentry, thus securing your family's social status. Your parents and your younger sister, Abigail . . .*

Chloe stopped there. Abigail. She squeezed her eyelids shut for a moment.

> *. . . and your younger sister, Abigail, depend upon your success. Mrs. Crescent, your chaperone, will introduce you to English society. Best of luck.*

The table of contents included chapters on "Archery Rules," "Ballroom Behavior," "Your Chaperone," "Dinner Etiquette," and "Sexual Protocol." Hmm. Chloe paged over to that very short chapter:

A lady would never engage in sexual relations with a gentleman until after marriage. So doing would compromise her reputation, her position in society, and her eligibility to marry someone her equal or above. One wrong move and a lady could be ousted from society and plunged into a life of poverty and depravity, doomed to remain an outsider. A lady may be kissed only when she is properly engaged. Before engagement, a gentleman does not touch a lady, except to hand her into a carriage, dance at a ball, or escort her on a walk in the garden with her chaperone. He may only touch her in extreme circumstances, in emergency, if the lady finds herself in trouble.

Chloe looked back, toward the inn, the trailer, and George, but she couldn't see any of it anymore. And suddenly she felt a million miles from American men, work, TVs, computers, phones—Abigail.

The rule book slid off her lap. She leaned over, struggling to pick it up despite the busk restricting her movements. The cameraman on the ATV eased back to get a good shot of her boobs, no doubt. She wrapped the shawl tighter around her shoulders.

The carriage lurched to the top of a hill and stopped. Dust rose from the dry road and Chloe coughed, digging into her reticule for her fan.

The driver turned around, tipping his hat. "There it is, miss."

Chloe tossed the fan aside, put her hand over the brim of her bonnet, and, awestruck, stood up. Tucked in a valley off in the distance, rising out of the greenery, was a Queen Anne stone mansion, complete with a four-columned portico and stone urns on all four corners of the roof.

She collapsed back in the carriage seat. "Is—is that his estate? Mr. Wrightman's?" Chloe asked.

"No, miss." The driver laughed. "That'll be Bridesbridge Place, that. Where you'll be staying with the ladies."

Chloe had never imagined she'd be staying in such luxury. She had pictured—a cottage. She fell back farther in her seat and fanned herself, shocked and jet-lagged all at once.

"Mr. Wrightman's—Dartworth Hall—that's almost a mile beyond Bridesbridge," said the driver. "You can't see it from here." He snapped the reins and the carriage rolled ahead.

The sky widened above her as the trees thinned out. The air smelled of fresh rain and cowbells clanged in the distance. Pastures dotted with sheep and cows yielded to glistening grasses, as pastoral as a John Constable painting. The dirt road became pea gravel as the carriage approached the ocher-colored gates of Bridesbridge Place.

"Bliss," she whispered to herself.

A shot rang out. The carriage lurched forward, then toppled to one side. Chloe screamed, the cameraman fumbled. The horses snorted and kicked as she, the cameraman, and the driver stumbled from the lopsided carriage onto the soft, spongy grass.

"Excuse me," said a sexy female English voice from behind the carriage. Through blinding light and dizziness, Chloe made out a tall woman dressed in an ankle-length red walking dress and red turban, wielding a clunky pistol. The cameraman, despite a bloody nose, continued filming, and the cameraman on the ATV joined the fray.

The sexy woman spoke, looking briefly at Chloe and then past her, at the camera. "Seems I've nicked your carriage wheel with my target practicing."

The wooden wheel lay on the ground, broken in half, spokes blown off.

The woman cocked the pistol against her hip.

Chloe checked herself for blood. Her legs shook. She straightened her bonnet.

"I'm Lady Grace—of the d'Argent family. And you must be the

American girl." Grace switched the pistol to her left hand and held out her right to Chloe.

Chloe didn't shake. "You could've killed us!" Not to mention the fact that Grace should be wearing a bonnet.

"Killed you? With this silly thing?" Lady Grace leaned over and whispered in Chloe's ear, turning her back to the camera: "You Chicago people. Think everyone's Al Capone. That's where you're from? Chicago?" Still, she didn't look at Chloe, but past her, at the cameras. "Did you smuggle in any cigarettes? A mobile phone?"

Chloe opened her mouth to speak, but nothing came out. Suddenly everything went dark around the edges, like the end of a silent movie, where the circle closes in on itself.

Chapter 4

Chloe opened her eyes. A light grew brighter and brighter, taking a rectangle shape while a piano played downstairs, something Baroque.

"Mr. Wrightman? She's awake," Fiona said.

The rectangle became a floor-to-ceiling window draped in yellow silk and tassels. Fiona's face came into focus, then a video camera. Chloe tried to sit up, but didn't have the strength. One of her biceps hurt, so she tried to look at it, but stopped to focus on the two faces staring at her. One was Fiona and the other—the light from the window shaded his face. She collapsed back again.

Chloe felt for Fiona's hand and touched an embroidered cover. She must be in a bed. A lumpy bed that crunched. "Mr. Wrightman? Mr. Wrightman's here?"

Fiona patted Chloe's hand. "Yes, yes, he carried you in. Quite endearing, that was, miss."

Chloe sighed, and an image of herself, in her white gown, draped over Mr. Wrightman's strong arms, her head against his broad shoulders, his dark wavy hair grazing her bonnet, popped into her head. He had been forced to do the forbidden and touch her—carry her in. She'd have to wait till it came out on DVD. She squinted at the light and struggled to move.

"Mr. Wrightman's been tending to you the entire time," Fiona said.

"Miss Parker," said a deep voice in an English accent.

Chloe melted just a bit. His voice was enough to make a girl forget she'd been shot at.

"Can you see clearly?"

"Yes, I can," she lied. The blur of a man looking down at her so intently, with so much concern, came through clearly, even if his features didn't. "My arm hurts. Did a bullet graze me or something?"

Fiona stifled a giggle.

"You fainted," said Mr. Wrightman. "I'm going to put some smelling salts under your nose now. It will smell rancid and sting a bit, I'm afraid—"

"Ooooo! What the—" Chloe snorted and sneezed simultaneously, and she sprayed droplets into Mr. Wrightman's face. "Excuse me," she said, trying to regain composure.

The first thing she really saw was Mr. Wrightman's lips curving into a smile, a very sexy smile, as he handed her his handkerchief. He wore a brown cutaway coat with tails, an upturned white collar tied with a ruffled cravat, a waistcoat, and cream-colored breeches tucked into buckskin boots. Still, he didn't look like the guy in the bathtub or out in the field. Instead of dark wavy hair, he had dirty-blond straight hair, with a couple strands falling into light brown eyes. He was pale with round wire-rimmed glasses. Despite his seductive smile, he looked more like a librarian than the local Mr. Darcy.

"The smelling salts really clear the senses after a fainting spell," he said. With a large but gentle hand he pressed a cool cloth on her forehead.

The cloth felt great, but what if it smeared her elderberry-painted eyebrows? "Fainting spell? I don't faint."

"Of course you don't." He stepped back and let Fiona hold the cloth to Chloe's forehead.

She wasn't the fainting type. But this was England, after all, and people fainted in England. She handed the handkerchief back to him, but he didn't take it. Her thumb grazed the blue embroidered *HW* in the corner. "Well, I've never fainted before."

"I suppose it follows that if one has never fainted before, one never will. When a lady doesn't faint, as you clearly haven't, I recommend a brief rest in her boudoir."

Chloe's head spun. She thought sarcasm wasn't allowed. The nerve of him to spar with a person who'd supposedly just fainted. But—boudoir?

"Did you say 'boudoir'?" Chloe dropped the handkerchief in the folds of the bedspread and looked around from under the cool cloth at the floral molding, yellow walls with painted-grapevine border, Empire writing desk, high marble fireplace topped with a gilded mirror, and the mahogany four-poster bed she'd been propped up in. Boudoir. Bridesbridge Place! She couldn't wait to explore it, so she sat up, the cloth slid off her forehead, the room spun, and Mr. Wrightman, with a firm hand, settled her shoulders back against the bumpy pillows.

"Fiona," Mr. Wrightman said. "Please fetch Miss Parker a cordial water."

"How cordial of you," Chloe said. She looked forward to something that smacked of alcohol.

"Standard protocol for a woman who has *fainted*," he replied.

"You gave my Fifi and me a most dreadful scare, Miss Parker," said a gorgeous, probably eight-months-along pregnant woman as she bustled through the doorway in a periwinkle gown and lace cap. The gown complemented her pregnant shape. She carried a pug dog under her arm. "I'm Mrs. Caroline Crescent, your chaperone at Bridesbridge. This is my boy, Fifi."

Chloe hated small, hyper, bug-eyed dogs. And who would name a male dog Fifi? She scooched up on her good elbow. "You're my chaperone?" Mrs. Crescent was not only pregnant, but probably a year or two older than her. Tops.

"We did arrange a more suitable welcome," said Mrs. Crescent. "But you fainted."

Chloe opened her mouth, then shut it.

"Very ladylike. The fainting bit," whispered Mrs. Crescent. "Well done." She patted the panting pug's head as if he had something to do with it. "I see you've met Mr. Wrightman."

Chloe felt a ripple of disappointment until Fiona waved in two footmen carrying Chloe's trunks. They set them on the floor near a great mahogany wardrobe.

Across the room, Mr. Wrightman opened another drapery and light gushed in. "It may well have been hysteria," he said. "The pistol incident and all."

Everything came back to Chloe in a flash. "'Pistol incident'? That woman practically killed us!" She sat up and her left arm, for some reason, felt strange. "Where is that b—"

Chloe stopped herself, but Mr. Wrightman coughed.

"Blanket?" Mrs. Crescent interjected. She covered Chloe's stocking feet with a tasseled blanket.

"Yes, blanket. Thank you."

Chloe took a large gulp of cordial water and Mr. Wrightman raised an eyebrow. She barely managed to get it down. Who knew it would taste like mouthwash? Fiona offered it again but Chloe shook her head. "I'm quite refreshed, Fiona. Thank you." Fiona whisked the drink away.

Chloe's arm must've fallen asleep. She turned her head slowly, trying not to start the room spinning again, but someone had tied a leather strap around her biceps. She quickly untied it. On her night-stand, next to the silver candlestick holder, was a jar with something slithering around in it. What was it? Maggots? Then it hit her. They were leeches. Leeches for sucking the blood from sick people, be-cause that was what they did back in the 1800s. The leather strap? A tourniquet. The leeches squirmed around in blood and she bolted upright. Did he bleed her or what?!

She wanted to scream. To rant. To possibly crash the Wedgwood washbowl atop Mr. Wrightman's head. Instead, she cleared her throat. "Excuse me, Mr. Wrightman?"

He was packing up his black medicine bag without a care in the world.

"You didn't by chance, say, bleed me with leeches, did you?" She dangled the tourniquet in front of her.

He stepped back, folded his arms, and took his glasses off, look-ing, suddenly, not so librarian-like. If she hadn't been so steamed she might even consider him attractive in a tall, pale, and blond kind of way.

She let her arm with the tourniquet fall. How could *he* be in-sulted? The gown might be exquisite, the boudoir charming, but she didn't come all this way to get shot at and bled to death just to hook up with someone who wasn't a Regency buck but some sort of blood-sucking vampire with glasses.

She swung her legs out to stand. "Well. It was a pleasure meeting everyone, but I do believe I should go back home. Fiona, call the carriage for me, please." She stood in her stocking feet, but her knees weakened as she remembered the money, and the glimmer of possible love, although that was fading fast. The man in the tub, the man in the field, was he a stable hand, or perhaps a favored gardener's son? If so, then Chloe, in all her heiressness, wouldn't even be allowed to talk to him.

Mr. Wrightman guided her back to the bed, settling her on the mattress, which seemed to be stuffed with hay.

Mrs. Crescent came and sat so close to Chloe that the pug licked her arm. Chloe scooched away.

"Mr. Wrightman did not bleed you, my dear. Look at your arm. Do you see any open wounds?"

She checked both arms. "No."

Fiona swung open the wardrobe doors and hung a yellow gown, then a green one, and then another white, each one more exquisite than the last.

Chloe bit her lip and stared at the leeches, slurping and slithering in blood, gorged and happy as caffeine addicts after a few triple espressos.

"Whose blood is that, then?" she asked as politely as possible as she slid to the side of the bed farthest from the jar.

"It's pig's blood," said Mr. Wrightman. He picked up the jar of leeches as if it were a glass of red wine. "I'll take them away."

"Why did you tie my arm, then?"

"It's what any apothecary would do when a lady who didn't faint pushes away the smelling salts. But luckily, it wasn't necessary to do a bleeding. This time." He winked at her.

She clenched her fists. The pug was now in the bed with her, nudging her arm with his slimy nose to get her to pet him.

Mr. Wrightman held up the jar to the camera. "Don't you find it fascinating, Miss Parker, how leeches cure everything from melancholy to deadly fevers?"

"I find it fascinating you diagnosed me with a fainting spell when in fact it may have been something much more serious, considering the gunfire. And what am I, some sort of guinea pig? How could you even pretend to bleed me with leeches? As if I'm part of some kind of experiment here?"

Mrs. Crescent rubbed her pregnant belly and whispered to Chloe. "Mr. Wrightman is a doctor at the finest hospital in London, dear. Truly, you were never in any danger."

The piano downstairs stopped.

Chloe looked over at him leaning against the doorjamb. "Oh," she said.

He put the leeches into his medicine bag. "The carriage ran into a rock and the wheel broke at the very moment that Lady Grace happened to fire her pistol—in the opposite direction."

Chloe wanted to believe him.

He bowed. "If you will excuse me, Miss Parker, you seem to be quite recovered. All that's required now is a bit of rest. If you need leeching, or any other medical assistance, I'm happy to oblige. Pleasure meeting you, welcome to Bridesbridge." His coattails swished behind him.

Something sank inside her when he swooshed out the door. She hadn't even thanked him. Worse, she implied that he was incompetent. Worse yet, she didn't even let him know how happy she was to be here, despite the gunfire and leeches. But come on, he feigned bleeding her with leeches.

A woman laughed in the hallway. "Really, Mr. Wrightman, you flatter me." Grace sauntered into Chloe's room without knocking, chin in the air. "He's such a good man," she said. "So observant. So intelligent. So kind of him to even notice, much less compliment, my pianoforte playing while he has a patient in the house."

Fiona and Mrs. Crescent curtsied while Chloe glared.

"Don't bother curtsying on my account, Miss Parker," Grace said. "Are we feeling better?"

Chloe looked at the camera. "Infinitely. Much obliged that her ladyship would inquire."

"You do look rather piqued. Fiona, do get us some tea and a proper meal. I'm starved. And no doubt Miss Parker and Mrs. Crescent are, too."

True, Chloe was famished.

Fiona waited until Chloe nodded in approval.

Grace lounged on Chloe's settee in front of the window. "With all this fuss over you, Miss Parker, it seems the staff entirely forgot our breakfast."

"The audacity. Perhaps they'll whip up a bullet pudding in your honor for dessert tonight."

Grace looked confused and her blond sausage curls bounced as she slid the turban off her head.

Chloe smiled. Grace didn't get the obscure reference to the festive Regency parlor game in the guise of a dessert that included a real bullet and Chloe made a mental note to have it served up here sometime very soon.

Mrs. Crescent anchored herself in a scroll-armed chair beside Chloe's bed, hand on her belly, Fifi curled at her feet.

"I'm here to make amends," said Grace as she looked outside. "I do apologize, even though it was a misunderstanding. It seems a bullet never hit your carriage. Your wheel crashed into a rock."

Chloe leveraged herself out of bed and stood strong this time, smoothing her gown over her legs.

"Can you manage it, dear?" Mrs. Crescent asked, and Fifi lifted his head.

"Yes, I'm fine."

She slid on her shoes.

"Miss Parker, you really should have Fiona put your shoes on for you," Grace said. "What would we do without servants after all? Life here would hardly be tolerable. Thank God for that brilliant Mr. Wrightman. Any minute that I'm not with him seems like an eternity."

"Really?" Chloe asked. Grace was catwalk stunning; she seemed a little beyond Mr. Wrightman's league.

"Mr. Wrightman is an amazing man," Mrs. Crescent said. "Charming. Why, I truly was touched when he confided in me . . ."

Mrs. Crescent launched into an anecdote about how much Mr. Wrightman admired mothers like her and how he wanted to be a father. One of his cousins recently had a baby and named it after him, and the moment he held that baby he knew he was ready. Ready to fall in love, marry the woman of his dreams, and have children.

Fiona stepped in carrying a tray with a Wedgwood teapot, teacups, and some sort of bread piled high and set the tray on a table near Mrs. Crescent.

Chloe couldn't believe a maidservant was serving her tea in her boudoir, and she leaned in to admire the teapot's design. Both sides of it had been hand-painted with the ruins of an abbey standing in a field of yellow flowers and green grass.

Grace sprawled in a chair Fiona had pulled up for her. "Well, there is one other thing that makes it exciting. But when you've been here for weeks as we have without—"

"Wait a minute. Did you say you've been here for—weeks?" Chloe pulled her own Empire chair to the table.

"We've been here, what, three weeks now, Mrs. Crescent?"

Mrs. Crescent nodded. Chloe plopped down in her chair, rattling the teacups in their saucers. "Three weeks?!" She lowered her voice. "I mean—really?"

"Really." Grace took a skeleton key from her lap, unlocked a wooden box on the tea tray, and scooped tea leaves into a strainer over the teapot.

The cameraman turned his camera on Chloe. The mike dug into her back, her stomach roiled, and her ears burned, she was so upset. The rule book said a Regency lady must never go to emotional extremes. She should never be too happy, too sad, or too angry. Suddenly she didn't even want tea. She gaped at Mrs. Crescent, who was buttering her bread. Fifi scuttled over to the table, wagging his curl of a tail. George had warned her of surprises, but this? How many Accomplishment Points had the other women garnered in all that time? And they obviously had already gotten to know Mr. Wrightman. She felt the urge to hurl a teacup into the camera. "Mrs. Crescent, will you pass the knife, please?"

Mrs. Crescent looked up from her plate.

"The butter knife, please. And the butter." Chloe buttered her bread with vigor then stabbed the butter knife upright into the butter dish. Her first English tea in England—ruined. Still, she realized that she hadn't eaten since the breakfast on the airplane. And sheer excitement had kept her from eating then. So she hadn't eaten in more than twenty-four hours and really was starved. The bread tasted grainy, though, and too floury, which indicated that the food, too, would be historically correct.

Mrs. Crescent spoke first. "Miss Parker. We've been here three weeks and several women have come and gone. Last week, my former charge, Miss Gately, had to leave due to a family emergency, and that's why you were chosen to join us. Miss Gately made the most amazing things out of bits and bobs, didn't she, Lady Grace?"

"Oh yes," said Grace. "She was so talented. So accomplished. She took a rather insipid bonnet of mine and made it quite attractive, really. Pity she had to leave."

The tea was watery and Chloe looked into her cup. Had she come all this way to drink weak tea and play second string in a posse of women vying for Mr. Wrightman's attention?

"Something wrong with your tea, dear?" Mrs. Crescent asked Chloe.

"No. Yes. It's so much different from what I had expected. You can imagine."

"You will come to like it, as I have," Mrs. Crescent said. "Fiona, please put some sugar in Miss Parker's tea."

Fiona took a tongslike tool and cut off three lumps of brown sugar from a mound in a dish on the table. She dropped the lumps into Chloe's tea and stirred for her.

"Tea is very expensive, what with the Napoleonic Wars," Mrs. Crescent explained.

Fiona dropped Chloe's teaspoon on the floor. "Sorry. So sorry, miss," she said.

"It's fine. No worries—not to worry."

Grace yawned and covered her mouth. "It's so quiet here one quite forgets all about the wars."

Fiona was holding on to the fireplace mantel as if to brace herself.

"Are you all right, Fiona?" Chloe asked.

Grace locked the tea caddy. "One great thing about war. All those gorgeous men in red coats."

Fiona hurried out. Chloe stood to go after her, but Mrs. Crescent patted the chair for her to sit down. "Since tea is expensive, it's kept under lock and key here," she continued. "Perhaps you don't do that in America. The highest-ranking lady—that would be Lady Grace here at Bridesbridge—holds the key to the tea caddy."

Grace hooked the tea-caddy key to a bejeweled thing dangling from the side of her waist.

"Do you quite like my chatelaine?" she asked Chloe. "Only the lady of the house carries one. See? There's my watch on one chain. My seal on another. And the tea-caddy key. It really is quite clunky with this thing clanking around all the time. But it is a status symbol, I suppose."

"I'm glad I don't have to lug one around," Chloe said.

Mrs. Crescent cleared her throat. "Often, to conserve supply, we brew the tea weak. Very weak indeed. In lesser houses, tea leaves are reused."

The tea did taste better with sugar, and all this talk of tea would've been more interesting if Chloe had not been so angry that this thing started three weeks ago and they'd obviously added her only to amp up the drama.

Grace stood to leave. "It's a shame that you can't shoot pistols with me, Miss Parker. Only titled ladies can shoot. It would be such a diversion." With that, she spun to the other side of the room.

Chloe turned to Mrs. Crescent with a smile. "Now, that *does* sound diverting. But I'm sure we can arrange a duel at dawn with swords or something." She lowered her voice. "What have I done to her, anyway?"

"Nothing, dear. You're new, and fresh."

Chloe hadn't considered coming in late to the game an advantage until now.

Fiona returned, looking as if nothing had happened, and with a clanking of china and silver, cleaned up the tea things.

Chloe gathered the silverware for Fiona until Mrs. Crescent tapped her wrist and shook her head.

Grace sauntered back over to Chloe. "You don't have titles in America, do you?"

"Well, my father always called me 'princess.' Which I believe ranks higher than a lady."

Grace rattled her chatelaine. "We might practice archery together. You needn't be titled for that."

Mrs. Crescent curtsied and it took Chloe a while, but she did bow her head. Nevertheless, as Grace turned to walk down the hallway and the cameraman followed, she pretended to shoot her in the back with a bow and arrow.

"Might I have a word?" Mrs. Crescent brought a handkerchief to her sweaty brow. She whispered, "I'm glad to see you're a fighter. I've never seen anyone handle her quite like that. We have a chance at winning, you know. A big chance!"

"What do you mean 'we' have a chance at winning?" Fifi nuzzled his head under Chloe's arm and Chloe edged away.

"We're in this together! Of course you know your father hired me to find a suitable match, and if we get Mr. Wrightman to propose to you, I get five hundred pounds."

Chloe's real father didn't have an English pound to spare, so this must've been part of the script. It rang true, because Chloe knew chaperones were often hired by eager fathers during the Regency, and the chaperone would be paid a predetermined amount when she married off her young charge.

This gave Mrs. Crescent a real stake in Chloe's winning.

Mrs. Crescent whispered, "I get five hundred pounds from your father and ten thousand from the show itself if we win, and I really need to win. That's all I'll say about the game for now." She looked crushed. "You wouldn't know how it is when you're a mother—you don't have children."

Chloe looked down at her ballet-flat shoes. Abigail used to take ballet, before she switched to hip-hop.

Another camera came in; this time it was a camerawoman.

Mrs. Crescent changed her tone and spoke up. "So, I have four children, and another on the way." She patted her pregnant belly. "Our five-year-old son needs surgery, the physician said."

Fifi licked Chloe's arm and Chloe rubbed it off. "For what?"

"To remove a lump in his neck. He's always been sick and we have no more means to pay. The local physician has a long wait list, and we want to get it done as soon as possible, which means we have to go into town, which is going to cost us."

Did Mrs. Crescent's son have a medical issue in real life? Or was this just part of the chaperone's character sketch? Chloe knew that socialized medicine meant often getting wait-listed for a procedure and thought maybe the Crescents wanted to hurry everything up and pay for it to be done in a private clinic. She tried to catch Mrs.

Crescent's eye, but the worried mother looked away wistfully, toward the window.

"I'm counting on that money." Mrs. Crescent put her hand on Chloe's knee. She looked Chloe in the eye. "My whole family's counting on it."

Her story had to contain some element of truth. "What's your son's name?"

"William," Mrs. Crescent said, without hesitation. She opened a locket hanging around her neck and pointed to a miniature portrait of a boy with blond hair and curls.

"He looks like a little Cupid."

Mrs. Crescent closed the locket, rubbing it with her fingers. "He is a love. It's hard to be away from him for weeks on end. You can't imagine."

Sweat dribbled down Chloe's back. "It must be hard."

Mrs. Crescent stood and waddled toward the door. "Having children changes your priorities forever. Right. Tonight you'll meet the rest of the women, but for now, Fifi and I can show you Bridesbridge Place."

Chloe wanted to know more about little William, but she soon got swept up in the tour of Bridesbridge. She gushed over everything, from the drawing room and its pianoforte to the kitchen garden thick with dill, lavender, and basil.

"Might you show me the—water closet, Mrs. Crescent? All that weak tea seems to have gotten to me."

Without a word, Mrs. Crescent guided Chloe to her boudoir, where, like a statue, she pointed to the bottom shelf of a credenza. On the shelf, atop a linen towel, sat a china pot, shaped like a gravy boat, only slightly bigger. Chloe lifted it by the handle even as her heart sank.

"A chamber pot?"

"Yes."

"There must be a water closet somewhere."

"You'll find a basket of rags under your bed. The chambermaid will take care of everything when you've finished."

The poor chambermaid!

"I'm going to take a little nap." Mrs. Crescent rubbed her belly. "I get so tired these days. Settle in. We'll spend the next forty-eight hours working on your accomplishments. Dancing. French. Pianoforte. We have much to catch up on, and the task of the day is mending pens."

Chloe had to chuckle at the reference to the scene in *Pride and Prejudice* where Caroline Bingley offers to mend Mr. Darcy's pen. What fun that would be, but how horrifying the thought of a chamber pot was. She set it on the floorboards. First a chamber pot, then Lady Bootcamp. They were trying to break her, to make her crack on camera, to become the crazy, crying girl that was so good for ratings.

"Come, Fifi." Mrs. Crescent left.

A cameraman filmed Chloe staring into the chamber pot until she shut the door on him. He must've been her designated cameraman because he always seemed to be the one who followed her when she went off on her own. He was a lanky guy, in his late twenties maybe. Like the other camera crew, he never said a word.

She set the chamber pot back down under the credenza. The whole thing reminded her of potty-training Abigail. "There's got to be a bathroom here somewhere," she said out loud.

She opened the door, and the cameraman followed her as she dashed through Bridesbridge, checking every door. The rooms she had found so charming earlier, with the neoclassical clocks and Oriental vases and silver epergnes whizzed by in a blur. Some doors were locked and she was convinced one of them was a bathroom. Grace floated by just as Chloe yanked on the last ornate silver doorknob of the last locked door.

"Looking for something, Miss Parker?" Grace asked in a flat voice.

"You wouldn't happen to have a key to a water closet, would you?"

Grace smiled, fingering her chatelaine. "I have heard of some extremely wealthy houses installing newfangled water closets, as you say, but I cannot imagine you are used to such luxuries in America. We don't have anything of the sort at Bridesbridge."

Chloe let the doorknob go. She didn't want to pee in her pantalets. She flew to the staircase and took two marble steps at a time, nearly colliding with the butler, who was carrying letters on a silver salver.

"Letter for you, Miss Parker."

If she didn't have to pee, this would've been such a memorable moment. The butler handed her an actual letter, sealed in an envelope. Not an e-mail, not a text, not a tweet.

"Thank you," she said as she whisked the letter away from him. She bounded up the stairs, knocked her door shut with a sway of her hip, tossed the letter on her writing desk, and straddled the chamber pot. Hoisting her gown and bending to the best of her abilities with the busk, she untied and stripped her pantalets and squatted as if she were in the woods. Never in her life had she felt so unladylike. And the rags—ugh. Carefully, she carried the chamber pot back to the credenza and draped a towel over it. Thank goodness she hadn't been cast as a chambermaid. Washing her hands in the bowl on the washstand, she discovered what must be the soap, a white ball no larger than a candy Easter egg. After the eight-hour flight, a dusty carriage ride, the chamber pot, and sweating in this house without air-conditioning, she needed a shower—er—bath. She rang for Fiona and eyed the letter on her writing desk. It couldn't be from Abigial. Not only was it too soon for that, but there was no postage. It simply said *Miss Parker* on it in handwriting with great flourishes. The back of the thick envelope had been sealed with an elegant red wax *W*, for Wrightman, no doubt. Chloe fingered the *W*, then with a bronze letter opener and trembling hands, she sliced open the envelope, leaving the *W* intact.

Dear Miss Parker,

I would like to take this opportunity to welcome you to Bridesbridge Place and Dartworth Hall, both of which my eldest son currently oversees. I live at the seaside now, as it is better for my health. My son is a wonderful man who I'm convinced will, through this experience, find his true life partner. I'm very excited for him and I very much look forward to meeting you in future. .

Wishing you a pleasant stay,
Lady A. Wrightman

This woman certainly seemed much nicer than Chloe's ex-mother-in-law. Of course, Mr. Wrightman's mother came from a polite, well-bred, titled family, and clearly, she wanted the world for her son, as any mother would. Mr. Wrightman's father was extremely rich as Mrs. Crescent had said, but untitled like Mr. Darcy's father. It made Chloe feel guilty that she needed to win over Mr. Wrightman for the money first and foremost. Phew, it was warm upstairs.

She opened her casement window to let in the cooler air. Looking out the window past the Bridesbridge gardens, she saw a pond shimmering in the midday light. At the moment she'd give anything just to dangle her feet in it for a few minutes.

The chambermaid knocked, opened the door, and beelined toward the chamber pot while the cameraman followed.

"Excuse me," Chloe asked, "might I have a bath?"

"Bath will be on Sunday, miss." The chambermaid picked up the chamber pot and basket of used rags.

Chloe pulled back the draperies to get a better look at the pond. "But—today's Monday."

"That's right, miss. Only one bath per week."

This took Chloe a minute to absorb.

"As you know, the servants have to pump the water, then heat it and carry it in buckets up the stairs. Bath will be Sunday."

"Ugh," Chloe blurted out.

"What was that, miss?"

"Might I have more soap and water, then?"

"The soap ball needs to last you two weeks when the Irish soap monger will be coming by again. I'll have a footman fetch fresh water." She bowed her head and took the pot away. Where? Chloe wondered. The cameraman followed the chambermaid. Apparently Chloe's chamber pot was more interesting than Chloe herself.

Chloe fixed her eyes again on the water that was glistening in the distance. She paced in front of the yellow draperies, trying to put a positive spin on this. So there wasn't any plumbing. There would be time to paint, there would be a ball, and candlelight dinners in Dartworth Hall.

She stopped and buried her head in her hands. Come on, she was almost forty and a mom. Why couldn't she grow up and give up the fairy tale? No bath till Sunday. Chamber pots. No phone to call Abigail. Bullets. Leeches. Psycho-housemate Grace. Ready-to-pop-a-baby chaperone. And a Mr. Wrightman who foiled her expectations. She imagined him as dark-haired and brooding, or at least standoffish, and was taken aback that he seemed approachable and caring, if a bit left-brained for her taste. Still, how could she win over any man without being able to bathe for six days? If she wanted to win this thing, she had to be proactive, and she had to, at the very least, smell good.

Something wet nuzzled against Chloe's leg.

Fifi was nudging his way under her gown, sniffing and licking. Chloe pulled on her walking half boots, snatched the soap ball, a linen towel, and had gotten as far as the hallway when she remembered her bonnet. Bonnet, parasol, and gloves retrieved, she scampered down the servants' staircase, almost missing a step in the darkness.

Chapter 5

*H*er white stockings hung from a nearby branch and swayed in the breeze while she waded in the pond. She had rolled up her pantalets, lifted her gown to her knees, and washed her legs and arms with the soap ball when what she really wanted to do was just pull off her gown and dive in. Not only would that have been inappropriate, but she wouldn't want anyone to see her stark naked unless they'd had a few drinks and she was illuminated by candles. Candlelight was one of the perks of nineteenth-century living for an aging spinster like her.

The water around her ankles cooled her entire body, and even though it wasn't a shower, she felt cleaner. She convinced herself that any lady worth her salt would do the same for the sake of personal hygiene, and after all, she did leave word with a servant to tell Mrs. Crescent that she would be right back. According to the rule book, as long as she didn't leave Bridesbridge property unchaperoned, she should be okay.

She looked back toward Bridesbridge, but couldn't see it through the trees. Something, probably a deer, moved among the greenery. She'd better get going. Mrs. Crescent would be waking from her nap soon. Chloe forced herself to head back toward the bank.

Atop a hill, in the distance, stood a Grecian temple with a green dome and six columns. Just above the dome, an airplane sliced through the sky and the rumble of the airplane engine cut through her.

Chamber pots and weekly baths aside, she really didn't want to go back to the modern world. She had gone in worse places than a chamber pot in her lifetime. Porta-Potties. A parking lot once or twice during the college years. In a plastic cup at the OB when she was pregnant. Then there was Mrs. Crescent's poor son William, who seemed to have some kind of medical condition. And Abigail, who looked up to her mom and expected her to succeed. Mr. Wrightman may not have looked like her vision of a Mr. Darcy, but her second impression, after the leech incident had been cleared up, was good. Certainly Grace and Mrs. Crescent considered him a paragon.

She'd better get back to the drawing room—pronto.

A horse whinnied on the other side of the water, she lost her soap ball in the water, and her hem fell into the pond.

"How's the water?" The male voice was English-accented. Unfamiliar. It came from behind the chestnut tree.

Everything went numb, even her lips. The water turned icy, sunlight broke through the trees, and the water went translucent. A man in a green riding coat emerged from behind the tree. He stepped onto the embankment in black riding boots and breeches, a gloved hand holding on to the reins of a white horse. Two greyhounds flanked him.

It could've been a scene right out of a Jane Austen adaptation— tall, dark, and handsome hunk of man appears in forest out of nowhere—except, of course, the heroine wouldn't be knee-deep in pond water, her stockings hung in a tree.

He lifted his hat and bowed his head of slightly unruly black hair.

He had dark eyes and broad shoulders in the well-tailored riding coat, and he had to be the man she saw working out with the logs in the field. "Pity we haven't met formally, Miss Parker, or we'd be free to converse. And I could, perhaps, escort you out of the water."

How did he know her name? Her stockings floated in the breeze and her ability to speak simply floated away.

"I have been most anxiously awaiting your arrival, and now I can see why."

She flinched.

"Not to worry. I won't report this infraction. Not yet, anyway. Luckily, I gave my cameraman the slip for the moment. You're on Dartworth property unchaperoned, you know. You'd be asked to leave. And I wouldn't want that, I can tell you." He moved toward the pond's edge, the dogs panting at his side.

She didn't think the pond could be on Dartworth land! She had to get out of here. Then it occurred to her that she was alone in the woods with a man she didn't know, her stockings hanging in a nearby tree.

"Just who are you?" Chloe asked.

"Don't you know who I am?" He laughed.

Now, that was pretty egomaniacal even if he was gorgeous.

He shaded his eyes with his hand and tried to get a better look at her. This *was* the guy from the field, from the bathtub. She could see that now. She stepped back. Maybe this was a trap. A man wasn't supposed to see a woman's bare legs or ankles until after marriage. Chloe's ankles were well hidden under the water, and she decided not to move until he left.

But he just kept staring at her as if she were the only woman left in the world, and it made her—uncomfortable.

"Since we haven't been properly introduced, I'm going to have to ask you to leave," she said.

He cocked his head, stepped off the boulder, and a look of hurt came over his face. She instantly regretted the remark, but had to play by the rules, especially since she had already accidentally broken one of them. He mounted his horse, tipped his hat. "Good day, Miss Parker." She curtsied. And he galloped off, his horse's tail twitching, his dogs bounding after him.

Whoever he was, he'd probably report her infraction and she'd be on the next flight home. As she trudged toward the bank, a strange noise came from behind. She whipped around. A group of frogs was croaking on the opposite side of the pond, their throats puffing with air. Something slithered around her ankle. She fumbled up the embankment and scrambled toward her linen towel. As quickly as she could with a linen towel, she dried off her legs and feet. The sound of hooves pounded around the far edge of the pond. Flickerings of a man on horseback appeared through the trees. He'd come back! She rolled down her pantalets and reached for her stockings.

Chloe turned to say something—anything—to him. But . . . it wasn't him. It was Mr. Wrightman, who dismounted his black horse even as it was moving.

She didn't think his appearance was mere coincidence. Her every move was probably tracked on a GPS chip in her microphone pack. She slid into her stockings and fumbled with the ribbons. Finally, she tied them off, though they were much slouchier than when Fiona had done them.

He took off his hat and bowed. "And here I was hoping you'd emerge from the pond in a wet shirt."

Despite herself, Chloe laughed at the Colin Firth *Pride and Prejudice* reference, but she kept herself from saying anything out of character and determined to get back on Bridesbridge property right away. She hurriedly pulled on her shoes.

"I suppose you weren't swimming. You were—trimming your bonnet? Do you want to be asked to leave?"

"No! I love Bridesbridge. It was—the chamber pot. And the one-

bath-a-week thing. I'm over it now. I've got to get back to Bridesbridge." She yanked on her gloves.

"Just now, when I saw Sebastian, and he told me you were here at
the frog hatchery, I—"

"His name is Sebastian? And this is a frog hatchery?" She'd
washed off in a frog hatchery?!

"It's one of my conservation projects. A mere two hundred years
from now, in the twenty-first century, more than half of the global am-
phibian population will face extinction."

He was spewing factoids at a time like this? She plopped the
bonnet on her head and spun toward the pond, seeing now, for the
first time, just how many frogs were scampering around. Her soap
had disappeared. She eyed the boulder where the dark-haired so-
called Sebastian had appeared with his dogs and horse, but she didn't
dare ask about him. No doubt Mr. Wrightman would find it all very
improper.

He grabbed her fan and parasol and handed them to her.

His gallantry surprised her. She scampered toward the footpath,
looking back as she spoke. "I'm much obliged to you, Mr. Wrightman,
for helping in the preservation of the Miss Parker species."

"My pleasure. It's a specimen we really wouldn't want to lose." He
untied his horse and caught up with her.

She spoke as quickly as she could. "And I apologize for my bad
reaction to the leeches. I just don't appreciate being put under the
microscope. But . . . I have to hurry back. I didn't want to break any
rules, I just needed to wash up."

"I understand. It's better that you go back alone, and to get on
Bridesbridge property sooner, you should go that way." He pointed to
the north side of the property. "Watch out for the ha-ha. Do you
see it?"

"The what?"

She knew quite a bit about the Regency, but this was a new one, and she always loved to learn something new, although now might not be the time.

"It's a four-foot drop in the land to keep the sheep and cows from grazing in the gardens. It's reinforced by a stone wall and a low fence that you can hardly see. I'll tell you all about it when we have more time. You don't want to run and fall into the ditch. See it now?"

She said yes even though she couldn't see it. What she could see was that Mr. Wrightman was a knowledgeable and thoughtful man, and his little lecture had piqued more than her interest. She liked the way strands of his hair fell into his eye, and she almost reached out to brush them away for him.

"Once you hit the ha-ha, you're on Bridesbridge property, and safe." He bowed. "Hurry."

She curtsied, hiked up her gown, ran across the field, and stopped dead in her tracks when she hit the edge of the moatlike ha-ha. A cow looked up at her from across the ditch and mooed. She made a running jump and crossed it. Mr. Wrightman had saved her.

Winthrop, too, had saved her all those years ago. That was how they met. She'd fallen into the water during a party on a Lake Michigan dock and he dove in, rescuing her. She waited months to tell him she ranked second on her high school swim team.

She brushed past the kitchen garden at Bridesbridge and the scent of dill permeated the air. The sound of women laughing and talking was coming from just around the water pump, and she stopped, not wanting them to see she had been out on her own. But a feathered shuttlecock flew over the shrubbery and a young woman in a pastel-yellow gown and bonnet came pouncing after it with what looked like a primitive badminton racket. The shuttlecock landed almost at Chloe's feet. Swooping down to pick it up, she handed it to the woman, who seemed to be at least ten years younger than her.

"Here. Toss it to me!" the woman said, readying her racket. At that moment a camerawoman emerged from the shrubbery.

Chloe tossed the shuttlecock and the woman hit it underhand over the shrub, and more laughter ensued.

"You must be the heiress from America." She didn't wait for a reply. "I'm Miss Julia Tripp." She gave a quick and jaunty curtsy.

Chloe curtsied back.

"Come and meet everyone."

Everyone?

Julia spun the racquet in her hand and led Chloe around the shrubbery, where four women sat under their parasols on a picnic blanket eating miniature sandwiches. Clearly, she'd missed lunch— or "luncheon," she should say. Another cameraman stood off to the side and filmed.

"Ladies, this is Miss—"

"Chloe Parker. Pleased to meet you." Chloe opened her parasol.

Julia retrieved the shuttlecock and began hitting it straight up into the air over and over while the women stared at Chloe. The only sound was the *swoosh* of the racket and the *poing* of the shuttlecock on the racquet's strings.

Then Chloe remembered to curtsy and the women introduced themselves. They chattered in their various English accents and they all seemed so poised and lively. Most of all, though, they struck Chloe as young and carefree. Here for the sheer fun of it. There was Miss Kate Harrington, who had a very red nose and puffy eyes and sneezed a lot. No doubt the poor woman suffered from a cold or allergies and couldn't take her meds here. Miss Becky Carver, the only African-English girl in the group, proudly announced she'd just celebrated her twenty-first birthday at Bridesbridge yesterday. Miss Gillian Potts bemoaned the fact that Miss Parker had an amethyst necklace and she had just a silver cross. And why didn't her parasol have fringe like Miss Parker's and Lady Grace's? But it was Miss Olive

Silverton who noticed Chloe's soaked hemline. "Miss Parker, whatever happened to your gown?"

Julia still batted the shuttle around.

"Oh. That. Was an accident. If you will excuse me, I have a letter to attend to. Pleasure meeting everyone." She curtsied and turned toward Bridesbridge.

"A letter?" Chloe heard Gillian say. "She just got here. I haven't received a letter in weeks!"

*B*ack in her boudoir, Chloe sat down at her writing desk to write Abigail and Mr. Wrightman's mother. She untied a red ribbon that bound a stack of handmade writing papers and plucked a quill from the penholder. Her eyes settled on the bottle of black ink and then moved toward her white dress. When she was in art school, she had used pen and India ink and remembered just how messy that became. Art school. She had been what—twenty-one? The tender age of the lovely Miss Becky Carver?

Chloe fanned her face with the writing paper. She couldn't believe Mr. Wrightman would pick her and a twenty-one-year-old in the same fell swoop. It didn't seem to make sense. Either you like more mature women or you like jailbait. How could a thirty-nine-year-old compete with girls in their early twenties? How old was Mr. Wrightman anyway? Not old enough to make her a cougar. Not that she was a cougar anyway—yuck. But Becky was actually closer in age to Abigail than to Chloe!

She set the quill down. Her head throbbed and jet lag hit her again.

There was a quick rap on the door and Fiona came bursting into the room.

"No time for writing now, miss. Time to dress!"

Fiona dressed her in a green—pomona—evening gown, which

reminded Chloe of frogs and Mr. Wrightman, who saved her from falling into the ha-ha. Then her mind turned to a certain dark-haired man whom she had insulted at the pond.

"Jeez," she said out loud.

"What is it, miss?" Fiona asked as she clipped the mike to the back of Chloe's dress.

Chloe rubbed her temples with her fingers and closed her eyes. "I just have a headache."

"I can prepare a cloth soaked in vinegar, salt, and brandy. It'll decrease the inflammation of the brain."

"Forget the cloth. Skip the vinegar and salt. Just bring on the brandy."

Fiona smiled and pinned up stray strands of Chloe's hair. She didn't bring the brandy.

But Fiona could provide answers, Chloe thought. "Fiona, I saw a man from the window—dressed in gentleman's clothes—with dark hair and a white horse. Do you know who he is?" She knew better than to ask about him by name, as that would indicate she'd met him inappropriately.

Fiona pulled a thin yellow ribbon from the dressing-table drawer. "That would be Mr. Wrightman."

"No, it wasn't Mr. Wrightman. It was someone else. With dark hair. Tall?"

Fiona cracked a smile. "Oh, it *is* confusing. There are two Mr. Wrightmans. They're brothers." She wove the ribbon through Chloe's hair.

"Brothers?" Chloe slid her tiara out of her reticule. The tiara was broken. Cut in half! Chloe gasped. It must've happened when the carriage tipped over.

Fiona examined the tiara. "I'm so sorry, miss. You'll need a good silversmith to fix it. Mr. Henry Wrightman does a right good job of fixing things."

Chloe tried to piece it together, to see if anything was missing. In eight years it would be Abigail's. "I can't have someone around here fix it." She put it down gently on the vanity. It looked like a broken heart.

"Suit yourself. But if you change your mind, miss, I can have it sent to Mr. Henry Wrightman. He's quite talented in that way."

"Henry. Is he the one who—who almost bled me with leeches?"

Fiona nodded her head yes. "Yes, but—"

"If he's one of the brothers, then who's the other one?"

Fiona continued to braid the ribbon through Chloe's hair. "Sebastian, but you haven't met him yet, miss. He's dark-haired, and rides a white horse. He stands to inherit the estate, as the eldest of the two. Mr. Henry Wrightman, the blond, with glasses? He must marry money, as he's the younger brother and will inherit very little."

Chloe shot up, half the ribbon dangling down her back, and snatched both halves of the tiara in hand. Fabulous. Not only had her crown broken, but she switched up the brothers and totally insulted Sebastian, the man whom she needed to propose to her in less than three weeks. Worse, she couldn't e-mail or call him to apologize and she couldn't write him a letter either, because a couple had to be engaged to do that.

She stomped toward the drawing room and a footman opened the double doors for her. For a moment she lost some of her huff. She wasn't used to footmen opening doors for her.

And the drawing room, with its two-story ceiling, scrolled-arm Grecian couches, and window treatments more elaborate than the train of a wedding dress, helped her remember her heiressness, as did the cameraman behind the pianoforte.

Mrs. Crescent, who was playing whist with another woman in a white cap at the game table near the fireplace, homed right in on Chloe's dangling ribbon and broken tiara. "Where have you been, dear? You cannot go ambling about outdoors without my consent."

Just as Chloe gathered the composure to speak without yelling, a bell rang. Mrs. Crescent and her cardplaying companion stood and hurried toward the double doors. Everybody knew what it meant except her.

"That's the dressing bell," Mrs. Crescent said. "Time to get dressed for the evening."

She'd just *gotten* dressed. Fifi wagged his tail at her.

Chloe sidestepped away from the pugly thing, setting her halved tiara on the game table next to the queen of hearts. "Excuse me, Mrs. Crescent. My diamond tiara broke in the carriage 'accident,' and oh, by the way, why didn't you tell me that Henry's the wrong Mr. Wrightman? That Sebastian's the right Mr. Wrightman?" Fifi rubbed up against her leg and she gently pushed him away with her foot.

Mrs. Crescent stood to tuck the dangling ribbon into Chloe's hair. "My dear, I thought you knew Henry was the younger brother."

It turned out that Mrs. Crescent was very forgetful. She thought she'd told Chloe there were two Wrightman brothers while she was giving her the tour of Bridesbridge.

*W*inthrop would forget to tell her things, too, after Abigail was born. He'd forget to tell her little things like "I'm working late tonight" and big things like "I canceled our vacation because something came up at work." After that big argument, he suggested she check her e-mail more than once a week and he began sending her e-mails about the big, the little, and everything in between. Chloe agreed. She didn't realize that he'd never call her from work anymore, he'd just e-mail. Or CC or forward her own e-mails. Which would've been fine during work hours, but since he was a workaholic, she'd get an eight o'clock e-mail instead of an eight o'clock phone call. When he was on the road and Abigail was older, he would send Abby e-mails, too. He was in Hong Kong on business for a week and that was when Chloe forgot. She forgot what his voice sounded like.

O
f course Henry's not *the* Mr. Wrightman. You're not ready to meet *him* yet," Mrs. Crescent said to Chloe.

If she only knew.

"You need to be groomed to meet a man of his caliber." She stood back and eyed Chloe from head to toe. "We'll need to smooth off the rough edges."

Chloe folded her arms and smirked. She was so thrilled that Sebastian was the real Mr. Wrightman, not even that remark could bring her down.

"Still, Fifi and I are so glad to see you so passionate about Mr. Sebastian Wrightman. That means you'll want to win!"

"Oh, I want to win, all right."

"Wonderful! We'll start by learning how to mend a pen for five Accomplishment Points."

"But Mr. Darcy prefers to mend his own pen."

"Mr. Wrightman, however, may not. One must be prepared."

Chapter 6

After the pen-mending lesson that involved a goose quill, a penknife, and considerable patience, Chloe, from sheer exhaustion, had conked out, missed dinner, and slept right through to the next morning. Still, she earned the five Accomplishment Points for the task. When she woke, she found Henry's handkerchief crumpled under the quilt next to her, and she chucked it into the drawer of her washstand.

Maybe today she could get with the program, the one with Mr. Sebastian Wrightman as the star. She and all the women sat at the table in the robin's-egg-blue breakfast room dressed in their morning gowns. Chloe looked around and determined that she was the oldest, the Anne Elliot of the crowd.

"Ladies . . ." The butler discreetly interrupted the chatter.

The women had been talking about "Mr. Wrightman," Sebastian, of course. Nobody spoke of Henry. Each girl had some glowing thing or another to say about Sebastian, and they all tried to read between the lines of his actions and discern his feelings for them. From what Chloe had gathered since her arrival, and coupled with the bio she had read back in Chicago, she began to piece together his character.

She knew the type. He was upper-crust, intelligent, and reserved. Proper, but probably a softy underneath, and perhaps in need of a bit of reform, like Mr. Darcy himself. Clearly, he hadn't met the right woman yet, and he might be a tough one to crack, but a fun, smart American woman like herself was up to the task. She couldn't wait to meet him officially and figure him out for herself.

"We have an exciting day lined up for you at Bridesbridge Place," the butler continued. One camera focused on him while another filmed the women.

Chloe had to smirk at the staginess of this butler-as-host thing. She pushed her cold beef and dry toast around on her plate. The women had been quick and used up what little butter there was while she was still getting her food at the sideboard. Butter proved scarce, as the kitchen maids had to milk the cows and churn it by hand, and Chloe felt for them and all of the staff. But, just like Fiona, most of the staff went home at night. They were, for the most part, Mrs. Crescent told Chloe, aspiring actors, and they couldn't compete for Mr. Wrightman or the prize money, but they got to sleep in their own comfortable beds at night, enjoy the pleasures of plumbing, and eat a decent breakfast.

Chloe made a mental note to come down earlier in the mornings and score some butter. Writing those letters to Abigail and the woman she now knew was Sebastian's and Henry's mother with quill had taken longer than she anticipated and the ink stained her fingers. Of course, she'd left her soap behind at the pond, and she only had room-temperature water to wash with.

Julia, who sat next to her at the table, was bouncing her knee up and down. She seemed an unlikely girl to dress in a gown, though the cap sleeves did show off her biceps. Even her hollow cheeks had muscles that were visible when she chewed.

Grace yawned. "I certainly hope we won't be painting another landscape—outside, of all places."

Chloe held back a laugh.

The butler cleared his throat. "In preparation for the upcoming archery tournament and the ball, you will be split into two groups to facilitate rotation between the dance mistress and the archery range. One group will consist of three women, and the other group will have four. Your chaperones will join you. But, to graduate from one activity to the next, you must meet certain prerequisites. If you start with archery, you must shoot three bull's-eyes in a row to progress to dancing. If you start with dancing, you must successfully complete a dance selected by our dance mistress."

Chloe thrilled at the thought of archery and Regency dancing all in one day, for so many reasons, including getting to wear two other gowns in addition to the day dress she had on. Maybe at some point during all this, she'd get to officially meet Sebastian. She didn't even care to drink any more watery tea she was so anxious.

"You'll love them both," Julia said to her.

"Love both of what?" Chloe asked.

Grace dropped her knife on her plate with a din.

"Dancing and archery. They're both really great exercise."

The butler smiled for the cameras. "And—I have a letter from Mr. Wrightman." He paused so the cameras could pan the table for the women's reactions. Chloe might not have had butter for her bread, but the drama was spread on pretty thick, that was for sure.

The butler lifted a creamy envelope from a silver salver and broke the red wax seal with a dramatic flourish. Chloe was, however, suitably impressed with the envelope and picked it up to examine it after he set it on the table. It too had been sealed with a red wax W, now broken in half. Fingering the seal, she wondered who might be behind details like this.

Inside her writing desk she had discovered historically correct drawing paper, charcoal, and paints. Did George think of it? Someone on the production crew? Set design? She found the attention to such details enchanting and figured it would have to be a woman or a gay guy. Unless Sebastian himself was responsible. After all, he made the effort to work out as if he were living in the nineteenth century.

"Most likely the invitation will be for you," Julia said to Chloe. "You're the newest girl, and he probably wants to get to know you."

Chloe raised her eyebrows . . . and her hopes.

The butler unfolded the letter. "Dear—Lady Grace." He stopped for a moment while the tableful of women did their Regency best not to react too emotionally one way or the other, but a general sigh was audible. Chloe hadn't prepared herself for the sting of rejection, but then again, Sebastian hadn't even really met her yet.

"Oh," Julia said.

Kate sneezed.

Grace dabbed the corners of her mouth with a cloth napkin, drawing attention to her Botoxy smile. Grace, though very attractive, was definitely not twenty-one. Still, she didn't look like she was facing the big four-O yet either.

The butler continued. "'Would you, Lady Grace, be inclined to accompany me on a horseback outing this afternoon? Please leave word with my footman. I will be at Bridesbridge at three o'clock to collect you if you are so kind as to accept. Sincerely, Mr. Wrightman.'"

When it was put that way, so eloquently, on paper, Chloe felt a twinge of—jealousy. And not just because of the prize money.

The other women whispered among themselves.

"Tell the footman I accept, of course," Grace said.

The butler folded the letter before he spoke. "Aside from her ladyship's obvious charms, winning this invitation may have something to do with her high number of Accomplishment Points." He looked down at Chloe. "And Mr. Wrightman's choice may have been influenced by some . . . peccadilloes of others in the party."

Chloe remained stoic.

Gillian stood and put a hand on her hip. "I have two hundred and ten Accomplishment Points. I'm sure I'm due for another outing with Mr. Wrightman, too."

But what really set the room atwitter was the butler's announcement that Mr. Wrightman and his brother, Henry, would be practicing their fencing on the east lawn.

"First dibs on the telescope!" Chloe heard Gillian say amid the din.

Chloe, embarrassed for the entire female gender, slumped in her chair. Mrs. Crescent poked a finger between her shoulder blades. "Posture, Miss Parker. Posture."

*I*t took longer for her, with Fiona's help, to change out of her green archery dress and into her day gown than she had spent on the archery itself. The lady's lancewood bow with linen bowstring and green velvet grip was exquisite, and the brown suede archery gloves lovely, but she was no Robin Hood, that much was clear. Still, despite a dismal start, she had completed the task of scoring three bull's-eyes in a row, and was allowed to progress to dancing lessons with a total of ten Accomplishment Points to her name.

When the contestants walked into the drawing room with their fans in hand, ready to dance, the servants scrambled. Nobody had told them that another group would be dancing and they had already set the furniture back when the first group had finished. Quickly, the servants moved the furniture, hauling it to the periphery of the room, and rolled up the French Aubusson carpets. Chloe wished she could help, especially when she saw the beads of sweat gather on their red faces. The footmen, even in this heat, had to keep their heavy livery coats on, and a hint of body odor permeated the air, despite the open windows. Chloe thought she might need her vinaigrette, the tin with the lavender-scented sponge, after all. No doubt it would've been useful at a ball where hundreds of people crushed together, many of them dancing, and very few of whom had likely bathed that day.

Julia, Becky, Grace, and their chaperones wandered in.

Lady Martha Bramble, Grace's chaperone, cleared her throat, organized her sheet music at the pianoforte, and batted away a fly that had flown in through the open window.

Lady Martha struck up the pianoforte, and Chloe was spellbound. She couldn't wait to learn the dances that had looked so elegant on TV and the big screen.

Grace fanned herself and her blond curls bounced as she sprawled on a settee. She looked at Chloe, then past her, at Mrs. Crescent. "Must I move? Really?" Away from the camera, she added, "Pity we can't tweet here. I'm sure my people miss me."

Chloe wondered why Grace had bothered to audition for this thing. "Are you familiar with an author named Jane Austen, Lady Grace? She wrote *Sense and Sensibility*."

"I know what she wrote. I absolutely adore Jane Austen."

Chloe leaned in to whisper, knowing, as she did, that in 1812, the only Austen novel to have been published was *Sense and Sensibility*. "I'm curious. Which is your favorite?"

"*Pride and Prejudice*," Grace whispered back. "The one with Keira Knightley."

Chloe cringed. Not her favorite adaptation. It was historically inaccurate, for one thing. "I mean which book do you like the most?"

"Oh. I love all of Jane Austen. But I've never read her books."

Chloe looked at her askance. This explained everything.

Julia twirled into the room with her chaperone behind her.

Grace put her chin in the air. "Truly, Miss Parker, I cannot understand why you Americans obsess over all things British. Jane Austen is ours." She lowered her voice to a whisper. "And so are the Beatles. James Bond. Mr. Sebastian Wrightman. Hands *off*."

Chloe sat next to Grace. "I'm the first to admit I'm a proud Anglophile, but with an attitude like yours, it's no wonder we staged the American Revolution. And won. Can you say 'Boston Tea Party'?"

"Shoulders back." Mrs. Crescent poked Chloe in the shoulder blades.

Grace nodded in agreement. "Unlike in your savage America, it's all about the propriety and manners here, Miss Parker."

"Please. It's not about the manners. It's about the man," said Chloe.

"Or maybe it's about the money?" Grace whispered behind her fan.

Mrs. Scott, the dance mistress, clapped her hands three times and the room, now crowded with various servants to serve as extras in the dance, went silent. A tall woman, probably in her early fifties, Mrs. Scott had a fabulous figure and wore a purple gown with a tall purple feather sticking out of her turban.

Mrs. Scott stared at Chloe, Grace, Becky, and Julia with piercing blue eyes. Without thinking, Chloe straightened her posture and visualized a book on her head. *Persuasion*.

Mrs. Scott moved to the center of the room. "Far be it from me to draw attention to myself, because this is all about you young ladies, surely." She brandished her lace fan, sashayed her hips. "But allow me to demonstrate some steps as a female dancer in 'Mr. Beveridge's Maggot.' *Maggot* means 'whim,' as you all well know. I find this particular dance so—dramatic." She clapped her hands and the hodgepodge of servants, footmen, and even the cook from downstairs, who was simply known as "Cook", stepped forward and created two lines facing each other. "Mr. Reeve?"

A young footman hurried over to Mrs. Scott, his face still red from hoisting sofas.

Mrs. Scott hid her face behind her fan. "I'm young. I'm the belle of the ball. Ask me to dance."

Grace rolled her eyes.

Chloe sat on the edge of her seat, enraptured.

Mr. Reeve bowed. "Excuse me, miss. Might I have this dance?"

Mrs. Scott peeked out from behind her fan. "Hmm. I do believe I am available." She batted her eyelids and curtsied. With a snap of her fingers, she cued Lady Martha, and the music began. Moments after the first chords were struck, Chloe was transported back to the 1995 TV adaptation of *Pride and Prejudice* with Colin Firth and Jennifer Ehle.

Grace checked the watch on her chatelaine.

Julia tapped her fan in her hand to the rhythm.

Becky smiled.

Mrs. Scott announced the moves. "Both couples turn by right hands." Chloe, entranced, did everything she could to memorize the steps. "Left hands. Ones cross and cast down." But she kept getting swept away by the music and a vision of Sebastian in his coat and riding boots at the pond. "Ones dance back-to-back and faceup."

At first, Mrs. Scott paired Chloe with Julia, and the two proved to be a great match. Julia danced with a bounce in her step and always looked her dance partner in the eye and smiled; maintaining perfect posture and poise, she was an inspiration.

After just a few dances, Mrs. Scott moved Julia down the line and set Grace across from Chloe. "Your ladyship, might you dance the male role with Miss Parker? I want to watch her form."

Grace sneered. She stood a full head taller than Chloe. For the first time in a long time, Chloe missed her heels. She never wore stilettos, but even her chunky heels would've helped. Lady Martha started in on the pianoforte. Grace bowed while Chloe curtsied. The two stepped toward each other, to grasp hands and turn. Chloe stretched out her hand and Grace recoiled.

"Ugggggh! Whatever is that all over your hands, Miss Parker?"

Lady Martha hit a wrong note on the piano and stopped.

"It's ink. Dried ink." Chloe held out her hands. "From some letters I wrote."

"That happens to me every time I write," Julia said. "It takes aeons for it to wash off."

Grace tossed her head back. She must've worn her hair long in the real world, as tossing her hair seemed part of her repertoire, but when it was pinned up, the head toss didn't have the same effect. "I can't tolerate it."

Chloe put her hands down at her sides. She had to wonder about Grace. Was she a born socialite or did she actually do something for a living? Fashion designer? Manscaper? Personal trainer from hell?

Cook, who stood next to Chloe in the line, held her hands out. They were very rough and chapped from all her work, no doubt. "You're not alone, Miss Parker."

Chloe took Cook's hands in hers and gave them a little squeeze. "Oh, Cook. What would we do without you?"

Mrs. Scott pulled the bell and moments later Fiona ran in, out of breath, set a scrub brush and bucket down at the door, and curtsied.

Mrs. Scott didn't even look at her. "Do fetch Miss Parker and Lady Grace's dancing gloves. Hurry now." She clapped three times.

Chloe cringed at seeing her maidservant treated so rudely.

"Mrs. Scott," Grace said in the same whiny voice Abigail used when she wasn't the center of attention. "Much as I would love to be the man in Miss Parker's life, I do want you to know that Mr. Wrightman will be coming to collect me very soon. I need to change into my riding habit."

Chloe shot a look at Mrs. Crescent, who turned toward Fifi, fast asleep atop a rolled-up carpet.

Fiona dashed in with the gloves, and the pianoforte and dancing resumed. Chloe, dizzy and thirsty from the dancing, counted the steps as she turned around Grace, as Grace turned her, and as they cast down to the end of the line of dancers. Grace knew all the dance steps, because she had been here for three weeks, so she threw zingers at Chloe every chance she got.

"What kind of perfume do you have on, Miss Parker? Eau de algae?"

Chloe concentrated on the figures and whispered to herself, "Right-hand turn, left hand. Cross, and cast down. Bounce on your toes."

"I heard about your little foray into the frog hatchery. I can understand sneaking a pinch of snuff or taking a nip of the Madeira, but dipping into the frog hatchery? Well, naturally your little adventure has cost you. As you know, Mr. Wrightman and I will be riding off into the sunset together. You haven't even met him yet, have you? Wealthy English gentlemen are not that accessible to the likes of you—from America. I do hope you realize your place."

Grace was not "in" with the other girls. Nobody seemed to like her, and Chloe suspected her of having some kind of hidden agenda—but what? Did she join the show to launch an acting career? Was she just after the money or was it more complicated than that? Chloe continued to mouth the dance moves to herself. "Face up, take hands, elbow forms a W, in a line of four. Forward three steps—"

Grace stopped in the middle of the line and put her hands on her hips. "Lady Martha, if you please."

Lady Martha stopped playing.

"Miss Parker will need private dance coaching. She has made entirely too many mistakes."

Chloe folded her arms. "I may have made mistakes, but they have nothing to do with dancing."

Mrs. Scott adjusted the feather in her turban. "Ladies. I have changed my mind. Let us break from dancing for a moment. I want to work on: fanology. The art of sending messages to your love without a word. You can say 'I love you' or 'kiss me' or 'I wish to speak to you' all with a flick of your fan. I realize it's a bit old-fashioned and now used mostly at court, but I find it delicious."

Chloe sighed. "How romantic."

Grace slumped over in a chair.

"Your fans, ladies? Lesson one." Mrs. Scott dropped her fan. Chloe picked it up for her.

"Tsk, tsk, tsk, Miss Parker," Mrs. Scott said. "When a woman drops a fan, or a glove, or a book, you must allow a man to retrieve it. Again."

She dropped her fan again. Nobody picked it up, because all the footmen had bolted when they'd had the chance.

"Your ladyship, pray tell me what it means when a lady drops her fan."

"It means 'we will be friends.'"

Mrs. Scott's fan, splayed upon the floor, seemed much larger than Chloe's, and more ornate, with tortoiseshell sticks and black lace. Grace's fan sticks glistened in the natural light streaming in from the windows. Her fan seemed to be made of mother-of-pearl with little mirrors embellishing the tips, and an elaborate scene of two young people dancing had been painted on it. Chloe's fan had wooden sticks. The scene on her fan depicted a woman, classically clad, playing a lute, alone.

When Abigail was in preschool, she went through a phase where she folded fans out of paper. Pink, purple, and yellow construction-paper fans of all sizes were all over the place. Those were the days when business was brisk, when people were spending money on letterpress-printed invitations, business cards, menus, and booklets. Then, as suddenly as it began, the fan folding ended, and so did the brisk business.

"Miss Parker. Are you paying attention to me? What could possibly be more interesting than learning to flirt without saying a word? Mrs. Crescent, your charge has offended me most deeply by not paying attention, and I will not tolerate it." She swooped up her fan, put the back of her hand to her forehead, and fell back into the fainting couch. Mrs. Crescent frowned and Fifi got up on all fours.

"I am sorry, Mrs. Scott," Chloe apologized.

"It's too late for apologies. I'm hurt. Wounded. My lady? You know the fan language so well. Would you do me the honors of reviewing it with Miss Parker?"

"My pleasure." Grace stood, looking down on Chloe, her free hand on her hip. She let the fan rest on her left cheekbone. "This means 'no.'"

She opened and shut the fan. "This means 'you are cruel.'"

She drew the closed fan through her hand. "This means 'I hate you.'"

She twirled it in her left hand. "This means 'I wish to get rid of you.'" She waited for Chloe's reaction.

Chloe's ears burned, her hands shook and so did her fan. The cameras were on her. She fanned herself, quickly, and an idea came to her. She could bend all her fingers down and leave the middle one. "Do you know what that means, Lady Grace?" She would say, shoving her middle finger toward her, just for emphasis. But instead she just continued to fan herself. "How kind of you, Lady Grace, to teach me all this. But I'm sure there must be something positive you can say with your fan, is there not?"

Grace dropped her fan.

Chloe looked down at it. "Dropping your fan means 'I'd like to be friends.' And of course, I'd love to. The pleasure's all mine."

Mrs. Scott lifted her vinaigrette to her nose. "Oh my, oh my. How can I bear it? I do regret that the lovely Miss Gately had to leave! You two are like oil and water." She breathed into her vinaigrette. "Miss Tripp?"

Julia was practicing the dance steps off to the side with her chaperone, who looked quite worn-out and happy to sit down.

"You will resume Miss Parker's fanology lesson in your spare time."

Grace sighed. "Thank goodness. If you will excuse me, ladies, I really must get dressed for my excursion with Mr. Wrightman. I see the stable boy has already brought our horses, Lady Martha." She nodded toward the window.

Mrs. Scott crossed her arms. "Ahem. There will be a fanology test soon. I expect everyone to know the terms."

A chestnut Thoroughbred and a creamy mare shook their manes in the courtyard.

Lady Martha pressed the sheet music against her dress with a crumple.

Chloe stepped toward the door, but Mrs. Crescent yanked her back. "The woman of highest rank always enters and exits a room first," she whispered in Chloe's ear.

"Perhaps they don't have such customs in America," Grace said. "From all accounts I hear, Americans seem quite wild. It's no wonder we're at war with them."

Chloe put a hand on her hip. She was surprised Grace would be smart enough to reference the war of 1812. "It's war, all right. And the Americans declared it against the English on June eighth—just a few weeks ago. The gauntlet has been thrown down. I wonder who will win?"

America won, and Chloe was sure Grace knew that, too.

Grace turned her back on Chloe, bustled out of the drawing room, and Lady Martha scuttled after her.

Mrs. Scott sat up, snapping her vinaigrette closed. "Miss Parker, I'm not done with you yet. You will dance with me these next three hours. You need to learn this dance to earn your Accomplishment Points, and so you're all mine."

Chloe pressed her ink-stained fingers against the window, looking out on the horses tied to the post in the courtyard. If she had known that this was going to be boot camp in ball gowns, she might not have enlisted. Just half an hour ago she was all about dancing, but Grace had ruined that for her.

Beyond the courtyard, past the sculpted shrubs, along the country lane curving in the distance, Mr. Wrightman, Mr. Sebastian Wrightman, rode in on his white horse, galloping toward the house, his greyhounds barreling behind him. He wore a black hat, a tan cutaway coat, a cravat in a ruffle at his throat, and riding boots. He moved up and down in the saddle in a slow, rhythmic pulse. Chloe clenched her fan in her left hand.

"Ah," said Mrs. Scott, fully recovered. She came to the window. "Carrying the fan in the left hand means you desire his acquaintance."

Chloe felt color rise to her cheeks.

"Yes, but it's going to take more than a morning of archery practice and a few dance lessons to earn an introduction," Mrs. Crescent said.

Earn an introduction?

Mrs. Crescent looked at Chloe as if she were a schoolgirl. "First impressions are so very important, don't you agree, Mrs. Scott?"

Mrs. Scott nodded her head. "Oh yes. Absolutely, dear. Crucial. There has to be that spark—that je ne sais quoi—right from the beginning."

Chloe's shoulders slumped. If Mrs. Crescent was depending on a good first impression, well, they were screwed.

Alongside Sebastian, the film crew rode in an ATV, cameras rolling. Hanging off the back of the cart, in his blue jeans, sunglasses, and baseball hat, was George.

"George," Chloe whispered. Her mind flitted back to Abigail, the money, the modern world. She really wanted to dash out there and ask him if he'd heard anything from home, but that, of course, would not be the ladylike choice.

Mrs. Crescent, obviously sensing Chloe's urge to see George, hung on to the ribbon tied behind Chloe's Empire waist, and that, too, held her back.

"Don't go out there. Think of William," Mrs. Crescent murmured.

"I think of him more than you know."

Mr. Wrightman dismounted and took off his cutaway coat to inspect one of the horseshoes on his horse.

"I daresay," Mrs. Scott said from behind her lace fan at the window, "that must be quite a 'whore pipe' Mr. Wrightman sports under his inexpressibles."

Chloe laughed. She didn't know much Regency slang, or "vulgarian," as it was called, but it didn't take a rocket scientist to figure that one out. She covered her mouth with her gloved hand.

"Shocking!" Mrs. Crescent gaped at Mrs. Scott.

"You know I was an actress, years ago, Mrs. Crescent. Not as well bred as you, I'm afraid."

Mrs. Crescent tightened the reins on Chloe. "Miss Parker, Mrs. Scott, I beg you to be discreet. Consider—"

"Consider they'll never see us behind these draperies," Mrs. Scott said. Mrs. Scott wore a marquis-cut wedding ring, but her blue eyes sparkled even more than the diamond. She really charmed Chloe with her dramatics. "Consider we're rather man-depraved around here. I'm quite overcome. Oh, to be young again!" She lifted her hand to her heart.

George directed the camera crew around the front door. He spotted Chloe in the window and lowered his sunglasses down his nose. She raised her eyebrows. Then he seemed to wave her over toward the front entrance. Mrs. Crescent released the ribbon, and Chloe stepped on Fifi's paw.

The dog yipped and growled. "Sorry, Fifi. Sorry, Mrs. Crescent, I didn't mean to—"

Fifi bolted.

"Someone catch him!" Mrs. Crescent shouted.

Chloe ran after him, with Mrs. Crescent's voice trailing behind her. "He's going to run out to the stables again and get trampled!"

Hot on Fifi's trail, Chloe pulled off her gloves and flung them on the silver salver on the hall table. She swooped down to grab the dog, but he wriggled away. Fifi charged down the hall and skidded in the front foyer, where the footmen were just opening the front doors. Just before the dog made it to the threshold, Chloe grabbed him single-handedly, and she bumped right into—Sebastian. She conked right into his ruffled cravat and snug waistcoat. She pressed her hand against his chest and pushed herself away. He glanced at her ink-stained hand, then his waistcoat.

Fifi barked.

"Excuse me," Chloe managed to say, holding the pug in her arms. "I had to stop Fifi from running outside."

Sebastian smiled. "Miss Parker? I presume?"

"Uh—yes." She curtsied. It was the tall, dark, and handsome rich English gentleman who had the power to change her destiny. The one she insulted at the pond. But they couldn't acknowledge each other until they had been properly introduced.

Chloe stood on her toes, just for a minute, to look for George. Only a single cameraman stood on the portico filming; the ATV was gone. She turned her attention back to Sebastian, who stared deeply into her eyes. His pupils seemed to grow bigger.

"You seem—different from the others," he said under his breath.

Good different or bad different? Chloe wondered. Still, he had noticed she stood apart from the other girls, and he was right.

"I'm afraid we have not been formally introduced, yet, sir," she said. Mrs. Crescent would have her head if she knew they were talking.

"I will have to secure that introduction, and fast." Sebastian lowered his voice. "Perhaps you're more—intelligent than the rest? More multifaceted? Independent? With a sense of humor? Entertaining to talk to?"

Chloe was smitten, but her ink-stained hands were tied.

Fifi growled at Sebastian's greyhounds. They didn't even look at Fifi.

"Fifi. Stop." Chloe petted the dog. Sebastian bowed.

Chloe felt herself—swoon. Fifi flailed in her arms, Chloe had to catch him from jumping out, and she and Sebastian butted heads.

"Ow," Sebastian said, rubbing the cleft in his chin.

"So sorry," Chloe said, and curtsied. "I don't mean to keep—bumping into you like this."

He laughed and stepped closer. "I quite like a girl who can make me laugh."

She whispered, "I'm sorry about what I said at the pond, too. Really."

"Oh, that? My apologies as well, for invading your—privacy." He bent forward just enough for her to appreciate his smile.

"Why, Mr. Wrightman," Grace said from the landing on the staircase behind them. In her slate riding dress with half boots and a so-very-tight cropped riding jacket, she stopped for a moment, smiling, and stared down on Chloe. Grace looked quite the seductress in her black riding hat, a scaled-down version of a man's hat with a sheer black ribbon tied in a knot under her chin, and a riding crop tucked conspicuously under her arm. "I didn't know you had been introduced to our latest arrival from the Colonies."

Chloe turned toward Grace. "They're not colonies anymore. It must be some time since you've read the newspaper. Like maybe thirty-six years?" It had been thirty-six years since the American Revolution, and Grace knew it.

Sebastian covered his mouth as he laughed.

Grace fluttered her eyelashes. "I daresay I'm not even thirty-six years old."

"Really? You seem so—mature."

Sebastian cleared his throat. "Pleasure to see you as always, Lady Grace." He bowed in her direction. "I haven't yet had the pleasure of formally meeting our newest guest."

"Pity," Grace said as she descended the stairs with her maidservant carrying the train behind her riding dress. She brushed past Chloe in a waft of lavender water.

Sebastian took Grace's arm and led her to her horse, but he did look back at Chloe and gave her a meaningful, lingering stare.

Grace nudged him. "Are you quite ready for our ride?"

"Quite." He bowed to Chloe.

Chloe curtsied, her mouth dry. Sebastian set a mounting block next to Grace's horse and handed her up into the sidesaddle. Lady Martha nudged past Chloe and the stable boy helped her into the saddle of her horse. Fifi had settled down and was now licking Chloe's arm.

Chloe didn't see George anywhere. A bee buzzed through the front doors and into the foyer.

"Excuse me, miss," one of the footmen asked. "Will you be going out?"

She wanted nothing more than to either continue watching Sebastian or run out and ask George if he'd heard anything from anyone back home. "Out? Oh. No, thank you."

When the footmen shut the doors, she set Fifi down and he scampered back to the drawing room. Chloe got a glimpse of herself in the silver-leaf entry-hall mirror. She looked, in a word, disheveled. Grace, in her riding habit, was so put together.

Still, Sebastian had spoken with her, and made her feel so good about herself.

She fell into a reverie, of Sebastian kissing her, of his hands tracing her curves, of him crushing up against her.

Someone tapped her on the shoulder and she gasped.

It was Mrs. Scott, her blue eyes beaming. "Shall we dance?"

Three hours later, Mrs. Crescent was sparkling with hope. "Thank goodness you won your Accomplishment Points for the day. We're up to fifteen now. You're almost as accomplished a dancer as Miss Gately, that wonderful charge of mine, was. A shame that she had to leave. But you have her level of talent, nearly."

"Well, that *is* a compliment," Chloe said, collapsing onto a settee. She craved a bottle of ice-cold water. When was the last time she craved water? The dancing made her thirsty, dizzy, and sweaty. Mrs. Crescent rang for tea.

Chloe whispered, "Tell me more about William. The lump is benign, right?"

Mrs. Crescent rubbed her pregnant belly. She eyed the camera and dropped her newspaper. The headline read THREE HANG ON THE GALLOWS AT NEWGATE. When she bent over to pick the paper up, she whispered back, "That is our hope, but it won't be properly biopsied until it's removed. Now. Not a word more of it."

Fiona came in, spotted the newspaper headline, and just as quickly looked away. "Ladies, a messenger has arrived from Dartworth Hall and your presence is requested in the parlor, if you please."

This would've all been very exciting were it not for thoughts of William losing his curly hair and Abigail with a new stepmom, not to mention the haunting image of three people hanging from the gallows.

In the parlor, a minty-green room with chairs and tables that dotted a heavily carved marble fireplace, Grace, back from her excursion, was looking out the window through a bronze telescope. Her chaperone darned stockings at the table. And, in a chair by the fire, a young redheaded woman, younger than Grace but older than the rest of the women, sat reading a book of poems. She looked up from her book with big green eyes and stood, smiling at Chloe.

Mrs. Crescent made the introduction. "Miss Parker, I'd like you to meet Miss Imogene Wells and her chaperone, Mrs. Hatterbee. Mrs. Hatterbee just returned from London."

Imogene offered her hand. "Pleased to meet you, Miss Parker."

Chloe shook, but her hand went limp. Was this woman the latest recruit? And London? What was up with that?

"Surely I told you about Miss Wells." Mrs. Crescent lowered herself into a neoclassical chair.

"No doubt you did." Chloe leaned against the chair opposite. She was trying to be as nice as possible about this because Mrs. Crescent's son was sick.

"Miss Wells took to her room these past few days. Indisposed."

Chloe's brows furrowed. "But I opened all the doors—"

"My door was locked," Miss Wells said.

Chloe could see that Imogene was using one of Sebastian's calling cards as a bookmark. A corner of the card was folded down, and that meant he'd come calling for her in person, instead of sending a messenger.

"During *that* time of month, a woman must be confined to her room. There is no other way to manage."

Chloe tried to do the math. When was she supposed to get her period?! Not anytime soon, she figured. Imogene brought the count up to eight women duking it out for Sebastian. Chloe put her hands on her hips. "Mrs. Crescent, are there any more beautiful single women locked up in this house—perhaps in the attic?"

Fifi, by some gymnastic feat, managed to jump into what was left of Mrs. Crescent's pregnant lap. "You two ladies have common ground," said Mrs. Crescent. "You both like to paint."

"I'm so glad to be back," Imogene said. "My time here at Bridesbridge means so very much to me."

At that moment the rest of the women and their chaperones spilled into the parlor, chatting and laughing. Chloe looked Mrs. Crescent in the eye, careful to couch this properly for the cameras. "It seems most unfair—eight unattached ladies and only one eligible gentleman."

Mrs. Crescent patted Fifi. "You may not be aware, Miss Parker, that here in England, and London in particular, many women find themselves without homes, without husbands, and very poor. We're experiencing a great shortage of men at the moment. Some of our men are away in the West Indies seeking their fortunes. Others are at war on the Continent, or in America, many of them getting killed in combat, it's most unfortunate."

Chloe'd never given much thought to this dark side of the glittering Regency.

Fiona, who had been arranging lemonade and buns on the sideboard, dropped a plate on the floorboards and it shattered. The hum of women chatting stopped, and everyone turned to Fiona, who looked ready to cry.

Chloe popped up to help, but Mrs. Crescent grabbed her by the elbow. In no time several servants appeared to sweep up the china shards, but Fiona had disappeared.

Mrs. Crescent shot Chloe a look, but Chloe went after Fiona just the same, and a camerawoman followed her. Chloe found Fiona in the hall, leaning up against the floral wallpaper.

"Fiona, what is it? You can tell me. You know a secret about me. Whatever your problem is, maybe I can help you. Are they working you too hard? Are you getting enough to eat?"

"It's not that. You can't help." Fiona hid her hands in her apron.

Chloe leaned forward and gave her a hug. Fiona sobbed on her shoulder like Abigail would after a bad day at school.

"It's my fiancé. He's stationed in the Middle East."

Chloe hugged Fiona tighter and rubbed her back. Now she understood why Fiona got so emotional anytime the Napoleonic Wars were mentioned.

"I thought this would be a distraction for me until he's back." Her whole body shook with crying.

"When does he come home?" Chloe asked.

"September."

Fiona was right, Chloe couldn't help, but she could offer her support and a shoulder to cry on, at the very least.

Fifi tugged at Chloe's hemline. Mrs. Crescent stood at the doorway, hands on her hips. "Miss Parker! Get back into the parlor immediately."

Fiona wriggled away and dashed down the hall.

Mrs. Crescent and Chloe knew she shouldn't have been caring about, much less hugging, a servant. Chloe decided to help Fiona out as much as possible by doing little things like making her own bed and such. When she stepped into the parlor, the women stopped talking and stared at her, except for Imogene, who smiled.

Grace tapped a bronze telescope in the palm of her hand. She held it up to her eye and extended it toward the window. "Finally. The messenger's here."

Imogene slid over on the neoclassical bench and patted the empty space for Chloe to sit. When Imogene closed her book and set it on the bench, Chloe picked it up. It was a leather-bound edition of *Sense and Sensibility, Volume I*. At last, a true Austen fan.

"Would you like to read it when I'm done?" Imogene asked.

"I'd love to. For the fourth time." Chloe smiled.

"It's my third, and I discover something new every time."

A footman knocked at the door. "Invitation from Dartworth Hall." He bowed and presented the butler with the now-familiar creamy envelope closed with a red wax seal.

Chloe didn't expect this invitation would be for her either. She watched as the butler cut the envelope open with a bronze letter opener and read the invitation aloud for the cameras:

"'Dear Mrs. Crescent—'"

Mrs. Crescent winked at Chloe. Fifi wagged his tail.

The butler continued. "'I would like to invite you and your charge to join me for a brief excursion to see the old castle ruins here on the estate. Perhaps you could be ready to join me in the carriage at half-past ten tomorrow morning? Please apprise my footman of your decision. Yours truly, Mr. Sebastian Wrightman.'"

Mrs. Crescent all but squealed. Chloe had to smile at the prospect of ambling around castle ruins—with Sebastian.

Grace stood with her hands on her hips. "But she hasn't earned twenty-five Accomplishment Points yet. And the castle ruins! Humph!"

The women all turned to look at one another.

Chloe looked at Imogene.

"I'll tell you later," Imogene whispered.

"Mr. Wrightman is exercising his prerogative to override the Accomplishment Points rule. You may inform Mr. Wrightman," Mrs. Crescent said to the footman, "that I graciously accept his invitation and my charge and I will be ready." She pushed herself up from the settee. "Much to do, Miss Parker. We must excuse ourselves—"

"Excuse *me*, Mrs. Crescent," the butler interrupted. "But there is another envelope here." The footman handed over another creamy envelope with a red wax seal.

Mrs. Crescent sat down with a huff and Grace stifled a laugh.

The butler opened the second envelope, and as he read it aloud, the women sat on the edge of their scroll-armed seats.

"'Dear Ladies of Bridesbridge Place, you are all cordially invited to dinner at Dartworth Hall tomorrow evening. My carriage will arrive at four o'clock. I very much look forward to the pleasure of your company. Sincerely, Mr. Wrightman.'"

Chloe didn't quite know how to take this news. It seemed to almost cancel out her morning excursion with him.

Which may have been why the edge of Grace's mouth curled into a smile. "You may tell Mr. Wrightman that I accept," Grace said.

"Surely we all accept, don't we?" Mrs. Crescent looked at the women and their chaperones. Everyone nodded.

As the women fell into discussion, Grace put the telescope on the side table next to Chloe and leaned over. "Prepare yourself for the Invitation Ceremony before dinner tomorrow," she whispered.

"What?"

"It happens before every formal dinner at Dartworth. Fourteen women have been sent home already. He's very cutthroat. He only keeps a woman here if he can envision her as his future wife. Unless your outing with him goes extremely well, he'll send you right back to the hole you crawled out of."

Chapter 7

"T he gall of that woman," Chloe whispered to Mrs. Crescent as they took a turn in the rose garden with Chloe's cameraman in front of them.

Mrs. Crescent snapped her fingers. "Gall! That reminds me. We can get ahead on a task right now—your task for day after tomorrow is to make your own ink."

"And the connection to gall is—?" Chloe did her best to navigate her chaperone's thought patterns, but there didn't seem to be a pattern she could discern yet.

"Galls. Oak apples?"

Chloe was truly lost now.

"You know the globular growths underneath oak leaves? You'd do well to spend this time collecting them, as they contain gallic acid, the tannins needed for the ink recipe. There's a ladder, should you need it, but you might be able to find them on the ground over there." She pointed to a cluster of trees just beyond the formal gardens. "I'm afraid I must get out of this heat and put my feet up.

Please, Miss Parker, don't go beyond the oak trees. Gather five or six galls and report back to me, without any tarrying. I shan't expect you to be long!"

Chloe nodded, happy to get ahead in a task, to break away from Grace for a while, and thrilled to be making her own ink! The cameraman followed her as she bounded, in her day gown and half boots, toward the trees.

She found a few oak branches on the ground, but only discovered four galls. Propping the wooden ladder against a sturdy tree trunk, she climbed up in her flimsy-soled boots. When she looked down at the cameraman, she saw he'd set his video cam down and was talking on his cell in the kitchen garden!

As she reached for the galls she'd spotted, she realized that, already, she was thinking less and less frequently about the prize money, and worse, didn't think as often about Abigail. What was happening to her? Her head swirled with thoughts of an excursion with Sebastian.

Then, as if she'd conjured him, he appeared on horseback, riding toward her, or more accurately, toward Bridesbridge Place. From her vantage point on the ladder, she had a bird's-eye view of him, in his dark hat, broad-shouldered black cutaway coat, and ruffled cravat, breeches, and riding boots.

He did look the part of a Jane Austen hero on horseback. The pounding of the hooves seemed to move the earth beneath her and she steadied herself on the ladder, wondering whether she should climb down or just stay here and Watch. Him. Ride. His. Horse.

Before she knew it, he reared up his horse right below her, because the horse would've crushed the video cam otherwise.

The horse neighed, and she froze as Sebastian looked around for the cameraman and then spotted her on the ladder.

He tipped his hat and, gentleman that he was, made no comment about her so obviously ogling him from her perch.

Chloe realized this was probably not the most flattering of ways to be seen—with her butt hovering above him, but she found herself unable to move. The galls slipped out of her hand and tumbled to the ground.

He dismounted and tied his horse to a nearby tree. "I see your cameraman has disappeared, and I've outrun mine for the moment."

He picked up the galls from the ground and stared at them in his hand. "Whatever are you picking here, Miss Parker?"

A real gentleman obviously didn't have to make his own ink.

Looking at him from above, she couldn't help but notice a bulge in his buckskin breeches, and a thought rang through her head: *Balls.* Where was all this coming from?! Why couldn't she just focus on winning money? Luckily, she didn't say it. "Galls. For making ink."

He offered his hand to help her down.

She hesitated.

"The cameramen aren't here, it's quite all right. I know we haven't been formally introduced, but please, let's take this opportunity. I want to know everything about you—everything."

She took his gloved hand, and when she stepped onto the ground, he didn't let go. He just looked at her, taking her in.

He had a woodsy aroma about him, but that could've been the trees they were standing under.

Heat radiated between their hands, although it was summer, and they were both wearing gloves.

"You came all this way, from America, and you're like a breath of fresh air. I so look forward to getting to know you. I debated for a long while over what we should do on our outing tomorrow. We both love art, and for a while I thought perhaps showing you the galleries at Dartworth Hall would be best, but you'll enjoy the castle ruins on a gorgeous summer day more, I'm sure."

He still held on to her hand and Chloe wanted to hold on to this image of him, in the dappled late-afternoon light, so intently focused

on her. She looked over both her shoulder and his, afraid a cameraman would capture them.

"You're right to be on the lookout, Miss Parker, because even
though your cameraman appears to be gone, mine will be here any
second, the scoundrel." He made a slight bow. "Until tomorrow. If
I could've managed our excursion any sooner, I would have. I just
want you to know that."

Normally so talkative and quick, Chloe found herself unable to
say anything. But then again, she wasn't to speak to him until formally introduced.

He stepped closer, and the woodsy aroma turned out to be him
after all.

"You have a beautiful face." His dark eyes moved toward her
heaving bosom, set off in her square-cut neckline. "Your profile in-
trigues me. I should like to capture your silhouette."

Chloe just wanted to capture—him. "I'm sure you can arrange for
that to happen." An image of darkness, him, and candlelight flickered in her head. She was really getting into this, into him! Wait a
minute. She couldn't forget about the money. But maybe the best
way to win the money would be to surrender to these early feelings
for him? She wasn't sure.

He ran his thumb across her knuckles, released her hand, poured
the galls into it, untied his horse, and mounted. "It will happen, Miss
Parker, it will." He tipped his hat and trotted off, his timing impeccable, as his camera crew caught up to him instantly on their ATV.

He rode away from Bridesbridge, leading her to believe he must've
come expressly to see her and tell her that he'd wanted to arrange
their first outing sooner. And he spoke of her love of art within
the very first breaths of his conversation.

Her hand was still warm from his touch.

Her cameraman lumbered back from the gardens, hoisted his
camera, and aimed at Chloe.

"Miss Parker? Miss Parker?!" It was Mrs. Crescent calling from the rose garden. "You won't score any points kicking about in the leaves, I'm sure!"

*T*hat evening, just before sunset, Imogene and Chloe were sitting outside, sketching the facade of Bridesbridge in their leather-bound sketchbooks. The cameraman, bored with their chatter about books and architecture, had left in search of more dramatic footage. Their charcoal sticks made swooshing noises on the thick drawing paper as they roughed out the features of the building.

Chloe, trying not to think too much about, or too much of, the encounter with Sebastian, imagined this was what it must've been like for the ladies of quality who had no work to do in the nineteenth century. They had time to pursue their passion for the arts. Some of the girls at Bridesbridge seemed quite bored with this free time, but Chloe and Imogene took advantage of the opportunity, and even talked of the place as being like their own artists' retreat, for after all, everything, including the cooking, the laundry, the cleaning, was done for them.

Chloe noticed that Imogene's drawing style was looser, more abstract than her own. Chloe's was more romanticized.

They'd been comparing notes on Grace.

"She tries to psych everyone out, not just you," Imogene said.

As they sat under the green bower on a stone bench, Imogene confided her suspicions about Grace quickly, before another cameraperson appeared. According to Imogene, Grace wanted to win not just the money and Mr. Wrightman, but the land the Wrightmans owned as well. Imogene had overheard several conversations between Grace and her chaperone. From what she could piece together, Grace's great-great-grandfather had lost significant tracts of land on a drunken gambling bet, and much of that lost land was now owned by the Wrightman family. The castle ruins stood on part of that land. Grace wanted to stake her family's claim. The Wrightmans and Grace's family were distant relations and both members of the peerage at one point in time, but now only the Wrightmans retained their status.

To pursue a man for his land seemed so—nineteenth century to Chloe. Then again, were her reasons any less mercenary? No doubt most of the women had their eye on the $100,000 prize money, too. Chloe wanted to talk more, but when Imogene's chaperone, Mrs. Hatterbee, settled down with her needlework nearby, their conversation had to turn.

Just as Chloe was putting the finishing touches on her sketch, she felt someone peering down on her work.

"You've forgotten the stone urns on the cornices of the house."

Henry's voice startled her, and his breath smacked of crushed mint leaves. She dropped her charcoal stick, and without a word, he picked it up and handed it back.

She composed herself and looked up at Bridesbridge's facade. He was right, she had forgotten the urns. "It's only a sketch," she said.

Imogene looked over at Chloe's sketchbook.

"Yes, but details make all the difference." Henry scrutinized Imogene's sketch. "Details can help you make that leap of faith that Aristotle spoke of in the dramatic arts. Don't you agree, Miss Wells?"

Imogene smiled. "I do."

"I like both of your drawing styles," Henry said. "I'll be curious to see how the final drawings work out, ladies." He bowed.

Chloe frowned at her sketch. What did she care about his opinion?

"Good evening, Mrs. Hatterbee." Henry bowed to Imogene's chaperone and moved toward Bridesbridge's front entrance.

"And just what are you doing here at Bridesbridge at this late hour, good sir?" Mrs. Hatterbee asked.

"A footman arrived to tell me Miss Harrington has fallen ill." Henry held up his medicine bag.

Kate's allergies ensured Henry of frequent visits to Bridesbridge.

"Ah. Poor girl." Mrs. Hatterbee went back to her needlework. Chloe watched Henry take the stairs two at a time.

Imogene whispered, "I honestly don't know which of those two brothers I like more."

"What?" Chloe asked.

"Sebastian's an enigma and very attractive, but I find Henry just as intriguing."

"You do?" None of the other women ever even mentioned Henry, but then again, none of the other women were like Imogene.

"Absolutely. He has a brilliant personality and he looks really good without those glasses."

Chloe raised an eyebrow.

"Last week we watched Henry and Sebastian fencing."

"Mmm-hmm." Chloe leaned in toward Imogene and whispered, "Henry's great. But I'm all about Sebastian, myself. Of course, I know George better than I know Sebastian at this point. It's too soon to tell about Sebastian, really. You're going to laugh, but I have to admit, there is something about George that I like, too."

"George? You can't be serious," Imogene whispered back.

Mrs. Hatterbee cleared her throat.

"Well—"

"George is married."

"He is? Not to—to Janey?"

Imogene shook her head. "His wife and two kids live in London while he shoots all over the globe."

"But he doesn't act married. He doesn't even wear a wedding ring."

"No, he doesn't, on both counts."

Chloe slumped over her sketchbook. "This isn't *really* the nineteenth century, is it?"

"Even the nineteenth century wasn't the nineteenth century," Imogene said.

Chloe didn't want to believe that. If Imogene had a flaw, maybe it was her occasional cynicism.

A raindrop fell on Chloe's sketch and smeared the charcoal. The air had cooled, and in the time it took them to close up their sketchbooks and gather their charcoal sticks, it had begun to rain heavily. The English rain seemed to arrive with no warning and disappear just as quickly, and with such frequent watering, it was no wonder the grass looked greener here. It was.

Mrs. Crescent waved them in at the front door. "Miss Parker! Another gown soaked? It'll need to hang for at least two days now."

The footmen closed the doors behind them and Chloe and Imogene stood dripping in the foyer until Fiona and Imogene's maidservant arrived with linens to dry them.

Mrs. Crescent put her hands on her hips. Fifi stood by her side. "And must you use that charcoal? Look at your hands. If you get that on your gown, the scullery maid will never be able to get it out."

Imogene cracked a smile at Chloe.

Mrs. Crescent picked up Fifi. "Why you can't amuse yourself with playing cards like the other girls is beyond me."

That night, in the candlelight, as Chloe stooped over her washbowl and sprinkled tooth powder on her toothbrush made with swine's-hair bristles, she stopped and looked at herself in the mirror hanging above her washstand.

She wondered if Abigail missed her. She wanted nothing more right now than to be brushing her teeth next to Abigail, then sitting on Abigail's bed, reading to her, breathing in the aroma of her hair and neck, and kissing her good night. She missed the good-night kisses most of all. And when would a letter arrive from her, Emma, or her lawyer? Her impatience surprised her. The days seemed infinitely longer without the phone, e-mail, and the Internet. She couldn't believe it was only Tuesday night. In just two days so much had happened.

She poured water over the tooth powder, making it into a kind of paste. Cringing, she stuck the brush in her mouth. The powder felt like chalk dust and tasted worse than baking soda. No wonder everyone's breath smelled horrible except for Henry, who no doubt carried mint leaves with him everywhere. Chloe made a mental note to pick some from the kitchen garden before her outing with Sebastian tomorrow.

Certainly the Jane Austen Society would be impressed by the historical accuracy of this project, but they would look askance at the reality-show gimmicks. Female contestants hidden behind locked doors, Invitation Ceremonies, Accomplishment Points, ancient vendettas. What could possibly be next? Girls in gowns dueling at dawn over Mr. Wrightman and his vast estate?

She spit into a bowl on the side. Still, despite everything she missed from home, she felt like she belonged here.

She carried the candlestick to her bedside table, climbed into her lumpy bed, and blew out the candle. Smoke and grease permeated the air. Grace had beeswax candles that smelled much better and burned much slower than the cheap tallow candles Chloe had been given. She found out the tallow candles were made from mutton fat. No wonder they reeked, and spattered, too. Still, she wasn't a scullery maid scrubbing the floors and the servants' chamber pots. She wasn't at the bottom of the rung, but she wasn't at the top either. Her place was somewhere in the middle.

The problem was she needed to be number one.

*T*he next morning, Chloe wanted to have Fiona wash her hair before the excursion with Sebastian, but Mrs. Crescent insisted that it wouldn't dry in time. This was life before blow-dryers. She'd have to wait until the afternoon, before the dinner at Dartworth.

So for once, the must-wear-bonnets-outside rule worked in her favor. Mint leaves in her reticule and dressed in her blue day gown, she waited with Mrs. Crescent in the parlor while the other girls were busy getting ready for tonight's dinner. Grace was having her hair washed.

"I wonder," Grace had said to Chloe, "if you'll have enough time to prepare for tonight. It simply takes forever to dress for a formal gathering."

"I'm willing to take that risk." Chloe smiled.

When at last the sound of hooves clomped on the gravel circular drive and the landau came into view, Chloe's heart throbbed as if she were in high school all over again. One cameraman preceded her to the door and another cameraman followed.

Sebastian wore buckskin breeches, brown boots, white shirt, ruffled cravat, and a black riding jacket. He took off his black riding hat and bowed, sending dark hair cascading onto his forehead. His eyes sparkled with what looked like mischief.

"Mr. Sebastian Wrightman," Mrs. Crescent piped up from behind. "I'd like you to meet my charge, Miss Chloe Parker."

Chloe curtsied.

"She comes from a very well-to-do family in America." What Mrs. Crescent neglected to say was that Chloe's family made their fortune from trade, and that put her in a distinctly lower class, the nouveau riche, as opposed to inherited wealth. Regardless, the family fortune had been lost.

"Pleased to meet you at last," Sebastian said.

"And you. I was beginning to wonder if you truly existed."

Sebastian smiled, but Mrs. Crescent nudged her from behind.

"Shall we?" He extended his arm and she linked her arm in his. When he handed her into the landau, he took her hand in his, and even though she had gloves on, never had a touch been so deliberate, so meaningful to her, and it rendered her speechless. Was it just her competitive streak? She really hardly knew the man. No, it was the opportunity that this afforded her—to live her dream, to win the money—and to consider the man.

The cameras were on her, Mrs. Crescent was next to her with Fifi, and she had to curb her tendency to lead a conversation, as this was frowned upon. Not that it mattered, as not one witticism came to her.

Sebastian sprawled in the carriage seat across from them, with his arm stretched across the top of the seat. He was the silent type.

Finally, she couldn't restrain herself any longer. "This must be quite a summer for you."

Lady Crescent elbowed her.

His eyes laughed. She'd hooked him.

"It is exciting, yes, I have to admit." And then he began to say how he had looked forward to this excursion. He asked how she liked England. Were the lodgings to her liking? Was there anything miss-ing, or anything that needed remedying?

"Everything is perfect," Chloe said. "Better than I could've imagined."

Just when she thought things couldn't get any better, the carriage rounded a bend and above them, atop a kelly-green hill, stood the ruins of a red-brick wall with three massive Gothic windows. Sun streamed through the arched frames where glass once might have been. It was the most picturesque date she had ever been on and she felt a tinge of Austen's Mr. Henry Tilney wrapped up in a Mr. Darcy package for a fleeting moment.

"Here we are," Sebastian announced. "The ruins of Dartworth Castle. Mrs. Crescent. Will you be joining us as I escort Miss Parker up to the castle keep? Or would you rather stay in the comfort of the carriage?"

Mrs. Crescent eyed them both. "I will stay here, Mr. Wrightman. But you must both remain in my line of sight at all times."

Sebastian handed Chloe out of the carriage. "Not to worry," he said.

It wasn't as if they would be alone, what with the two cameramen on them.

Chloe had never seen anything like the castle ruin before, but Sebastian had grown up with it, and might've even played here as a boy. Chloe drank it in. Here was ground more ancient than Bridesbridge, and the crumbled walls looked more than five feet thick.

"Amazing," Chloe gushed.

Sebastian looked smug. "Why, thank you."

"I'm referring to the castle, Mr. Wrightman. I've only just met you! When was it built?"

"The earliest pieces of it date from about the year 1130, I think, but it was added onto sometime in the thirteenth century, and then again later."

As they passed under the remains of the archway in the gatehouse, Chloe could imagine the noble families that must've passed through this spot all those centuries ago, with their flowing robes, thick gold jewelry, and royal headdresses.

But Sebastian was asking her a question. "How are you getting along with the rest of the women at Bridesbridge?"

Chloe had to stop and think of something, anything, witty or even interesting to say. It was hard to conjure anything amid such enchanting surroundings.

"I'm getting along with them," she said. "But not all of them are getting along with me." She stepped away from the cameraman, and stepped up onto what must've been an old wall partition. Could this have been the great hall? Grass grew in what would've been the stone floor.

"It must be difficult," Sebastian said. He walked the perimeter of a crumbled wall until it ascended and he stood in one of the Gothic window openings. Chloe would not soon forget the image of him with his black coattails against the blue sky as he took off his hat to wave it toward Mrs. Crescent. He looked like he was born to wear breeches and boots. He smiled down at Chloe, who steadied herself near a freestanding fireplace with a partial chimney.

He stepped down from the window and leaned against the chimney. "Is there anyone in particular causing you trouble? Do tell."

"Lady Grace," Chloe said. She smiled at the cameras. "Seems rather preoccupied with making me miserable."

Sebastian laughed. "Does she, now?" Under his breath, he added, "I do find her rather tedious myself."

That was to his credit. She had to wonder, then, why he didn't send her home.

As if he read her mind, he leaned into her as he whispered. "I'm supposed to humor her because of this land issue. Very touchy, that."

Chloe was shocked that he knew about the land thing, and even more shocked that he confided in her about it with the cameras rolling. "You know about the land?"

"Know about it? Well, her family's been trying to claim a portion of our land as theirs for almost two hundred years."

"It must get a little—old."

Sebastian laughed. "Now, *that* was good." He looked into her eyes, and she felt him taking her in. First her eyes, then her face, her breasts, her legs. He pressed against her arm and his breath warmed her cheek. "I need to spend more time with you. You're just the tonic I need."

Her breathing became heavier and her body ached to get closer.

One of the cameramen angled in, as if to capture her agony.

"You know where to find me," Chloe said. "I'd be much obliged to you to take me away from my needlework and bonnet trimming."

Sebastian clasped his hands behind his back. "Now then. I have a little task for you. See if you can find the castle keep. I've hidden something there for you." He folded his arms, leaned against the chimney, and watched her intently, as if he wanted nothing more than to be here, with her, watching her.

"A scavenger hunt? What fun!" Chloe spun around. She was enthralled. He had thought of a gift. He had taken the time to hide it here, in this enchanting spot.

"You have to hurry. Of course, the benefit for me is that I get to watch you run."

"Ladies aren't supposed to run."

"Really?" He pulled out his watch fob. "You have exactly two minutes to find it and bring it back here. Ready? Go!"

She lifted her gown, and with the cameras behind her, she ran on the soft grass toward the keep, a crumbled tower in the far northeast corner of the property. The keep had a small entry, like a cave, and it was very dark, but just inside, atop a stone ledge, was something wrapped in a gold cloth, and she grabbed it, lifted her gown, and ran back, laughing.

"Just in time." Sebastian wasn't even looking at his watch. His eyes were on her. He walked toward her and they met in the middle of the green, surrounded by the jagged fortress wall, where they were drenched in sunlight. "Go ahead. Open it."

Her fingers fumbled in the excitement. It was a packet of painting paper, period-correct oil paints, brushes, and a freshly picked pink cabbage rose. Chloe heard herself say, "How lovely of you. Thank you!" as if she really were English.

For a moment she felt transported to another place and time and she breathed in the perfume of the rose. How thoughtful of him. But she couldn't kiss or hug him, so instead, she looked at him as if she had just finished kissing him.

He raised his hands as if to take her in his arms, but let them fall and cleared his throat. "Unfortunately, we really must get back, or Mrs. Crescent will give me a chiding."

"You're right." Chloe pressed her paper and paints to her chest.

Sebastian beamed. "I'm glad you like the gift. But, listen. Feel free to come to me, to talk to me if Lady Grace ever crosses the line with you. I'm not sure how much longer I can tolerate her." He guided them toward the carriage. "I so look forward to seeing you again tonight. It's refreshing to have someone with intelligence and wit to talk to. And you will get a laugh when you see who I have to sit next to all night. If only I could sit next to you!"

And with that, they were at the carriage, where Mrs. Crescent checked the time on her chatelaine. Chloe looked back at the ruins, wondering what had just happened. She hadn't learned a thing about the castle, but she did learn something about Sebastian. He was thoughtful, playful, sexy, attracted to her, and, most importantly, he saw right through Grace. He wasn't swayed by her good looks, and that pointed to his intelligence. It gave them common ground to be in cahoots against her, too. Sebastian didn't seem as reserved around Chloe as he did with the others; she had gotten him to loosen his starched cravat, and that was exactly what she had intended to do. He had given her a meaningful gift, yes, but in just a short window of time he had given her something more, much more, and that was the hope that she could desire, and perhaps even love, once again.

Fiona washed Chloe's hair in a washbowl with a sticky mix of rum, eggs, and rose water. Chloe cringed every time her maid poured a pitcher of cold water over her head to rinse her hair. To help get through the ordeal, she thought of Kate, who had accidentally eaten a nut in one of the luncheon dishes, broken out in hives, and had to spend the day with her face covered in a paste of melted lard and crushed brimstone that Henry had whipped up. Brimstone, as in sulfur.

Fiona set out a paper-thin chemise and new stays for Chloe. The stays seemed more like lingerie and Chloe's breasts showed through the sheer fabric. Mrs. Crescent burst in with Fifi. She set down a fresh washbowl, plunged her hands in, and proceeded to press her hands against Chloe's thinly covered boobs.

"Aggggh!" The camerawoman had filmed Chloe's chest and she tumbled back into her dressing table, spilling the mashed strawberries meant to be her blush. "What *are* you doing?!"

"What every other right-minded chaperone does to attract the men to her charge. I'm dampening your stays. Now hold still."

Chloe shuddered. It was the nineteenth-century equivalent of a wet T-shirt contest.

Fiona pushed the mashed strawberries back into the china bowl. Mrs. Crescent shook her wet hands at Chloe, sprinkling lavender water on her corset. "When a lady has such assets as yours, Miss Parker, she must take advantage. Many a Regency girl does this."

"What about the impeccable Miss Gately? Did she dampen her stays?"

"Yes," Mrs. Crescent said.

"Well, a lot of good it did her."

"She wasn't asked to leave. There was a family emergency. Surely I told you that?"

She had. Lightning struck outside and rain pummeled against the single-pane windows and Fiona lit the candles. She had laced Chloe's hair with a string of beads, stained Chloe's cheeks with strawberries, and used candle soot as eyeliner to fabulous effect.

Mrs. Crescent clasped her hands. "Mr. Wrightman couldn't take his eyes off you this morning, and I intend full well to keep it that way. I've never seen him so animated. And he's never given any of the other girls a gift."

Chloe's creamy silk, and now slightly wet, gown clung to her breasts as she descended the staircase. Grace, who sat in the foyer on a cushioned bench as if it were her throne, glared at her, a result of her dampened stays, no doubt.

Fiona guided her to a bench next to Imogene. "With the rain, miss, we'll need to strap on your pattens." She strapped what looked like roller skates without wheels to Chloe's evening slippers.

Imogene explained. "We wouldn't want to get our slippers caked in mud." She clunked around on the black and white hall tiles, lifting her powder-blue gown to her ankles.

The pattens took Chloe some getting used to as they elevated her four inches off the ground.

Even Grace the fashionista couldn't pull these things off. She frowned at them under her gold lamé gown as her maidservant draped her shoulders in a fur capelet.

"I quite like your headdress," Mrs. Crescent said to Grace. "You look very exotic."

Grace toyed with her gold-and-pearl necklace. "Why, thank you."

"Your pelisse," Fiona said to Chloe. Chloe slid her arms into an ankle-length slate-colored satin coat, tight fitting on the top.

The great doors opened and a footman stepped in, rain dripping from his trifold hat. "Carriage is here for the first group."

Becky, Gillian, Olive, Julia, and Kate descended the stairway to get fitted with their pattens. Becky, billed as an heiress from Africa, looked radiant in a white silk gown and white headdress. Her dark complexion didn't need any makeup, and out of all the women, she looked the best.

"You all look gorgeous," Chloe said. "Especially you, Miss Harrington. All the hives are gone."

Kate smiled. "I know. It was worth breathing in the smell of rotten eggs all day. I wouldn't be here right now if it weren't for Mr. Henry Wrightman."

Chloe tried to arrange it so that she didn't sit near Grace in the chaise-and-four, but with the rain pelting down and the teetering on her pattens, when all was settled, Grace sat right next to her and Mrs. Crescent across from her. Imogene sat at the far end of the carriage next to Mrs. Hatterbee.

The women's wet gowns and stockings stuck to the leather seats and the windows of the carriage steamed up.

"I'm sure we all have dampened stays now," Chloe whispered to Mrs. Crescent, who motioned her to be quiet. She pointed to a mike hooked up inside of the carriage.

The rain cascaded on the roof of the carriage, lightning flashed, a rumble of thunder jolted Chloe, and for a moment she missed her car. At least when you were in a car, with the rubber tires, lightning wouldn't strike you. She felt for the poor driver and footman outside, getting soaked through.

After the carriage got stuck in the muddied road and the footman managed to get the wheels moving again, Mrs. Crescent wiped the condensation off the window with her glove. "Can you see it, in all this rain, Miss Parker? From the vantage point of this hill, Dartworth Hall is quite remarkable."

Chloe looked out the window, squinting, and she couldn't take her eyes off it. Even in the rain and lightning, the edifice, of Anglo-Italianate design, two-story windows, and a massive neoclassical triangular pediment atop three-storey ionic columns shone. It wasn't ornate, but classic and strong. It had to be at least two or three city blocks end to end. A lake curved along the west end of it, and if it were sunny, the estate would be reflected in the water. She could almost hear the French horns resounding in her head. Like some sort of drug, or at least the feeling of euphoria she got while watching the 1995 BBC version of *Pride and Prejudice* for the umpteenth time, the vision of Dartworth in the distance washed over her, putting a new gloss on everything.

"It's Pemberley," Chloe mumbled.

Grace laughed and the spell almost broke. "It's as big as Pemberley—I should say as grand as Chatsworth or Lyme Park. Better yet, a real, live man owns it."

The man that could choose from any one of eight beautiful, and a few intelligent, young women.

Just as quickly as the vision of Dartworth appeared, it disappeared in the condensation that soon re-formed over the window as the carriage descended into the valley.

Grace crossed her legs, one of her pattens knocking against Chloe. "I'm curious, Miss Parker. Do you fancy Mr. Wrightman any better now that you've seen his vast estate? Or did you like him before you knew how much he was worth?"

Chloe took some satisfaction in noticing that Grace's elderberry eyebrow makeup had smeared. "I liked him from the moment I knew he enjoys architecture, bird-watching, and reading. How he's looking for true love. I just didn't realize—"

"You didn't realize just how much you fancied him until now."

Chloe squirmed in her seat. "I'm not like that."

"Of course not. None of us are like that," Grace said. "If you enjoy reading and bird-watching, I should introduce you to the hermit on Dartworth grounds. He's very attractive. Very brainy. About your age. Fortyish, I should say. And an artist, too. Into nature. You would adore him. He just so happens to live in a hut he fashioned from scrap wood himself. The hermitage."

"He sounds perfectly charming. I'd love to meet him."

Mrs. Crescent snapped open her fan. "The hermit is here for our amusement only, Lady Grace. He is not suited to marry a lady's companion—much less Miss Parker."

"Marriage? I'm never getting married ag—" She almost said "again."

Grace raised an eyebrow at her. "Just why are *you* here, Lady Grace?" Chloe asked, sliding closer to the window. "Maybe it's the footmen. They always seem willing to do anything you ask." She lowered her voice to a whisper. "And I do mean anything."

"So many footmen." Grace smiled. "So little time."

Imogene cut in. "I do hope we'll have time to read poetry again tonight. That was so wonderful when we did that a couple of weeks ago."

It took them more than five minutes just to climb the staircase at Dartworth in the pattens, in the rain. The stone stairs and landings reminded Chloe of entering a museum.

"Welcome, ladies." The Dartworth butler ushered them in from a marble foyer the size of the entire first floor of Chloe's brownstone, to a three-story domed hall. The rooms emanated melting beeswax. With all these candelabra and chandeliers, the candles alone must've cost a fortune. Blue sky, sun rays, and white clouds adorned the dome ceiling overhead. This beat any McMansion Chloe had ever been in. Grace, Imogene, and the rest of the women seemed unfazed, but they had been here before.

A maid came and whisked away Grace's wet fur capelet, guiding her to a sofa by the hall fireplace to unstrap her pattens. The white ostrich feather in her headdress drooped. More maids appeared, taking everyone's wet outerwear and helping the women with their pattens. Chloe admired the massive oil painting above the fireplace, wondering if it was a scene from Dartworth grounds. The foyer and hall struck her as elegant and rich, but not overdone.

She stood under a life-sized portrait of a man and boy that hung across from the fireplace. Judging by the man's ponytailed white wig and the boy's trifold hat, the portrait had been done in the late 1700s. The boy's dark eyes mesmerized her.

Imogene joined her. "Isn't he adorable? He's the Wrightmans' great-et-cetera-grandfather. One of the maids told me he was well known in this part of the country for being very generous and up-standing."

Chloe sucked in her bottom lip, because this wasn't just a game, just a chance for her to win money and flirt around. Sebastian came from a long line of aristocratic ancestors, a heritage that seemed to have little to do with a letterpress printer from Chicago.

Lightning flashed in the semicircular fanlight window above the great doors in the foyer.

"The gentlemen await your arrival in the south parlor," the butler announced.

This time, Chloe allowed Grace to lead the procession along with one of the cameramen. A camerawoman stayed in back of the group, filming Chloe. The butler guided them through the hall, past a library so vast that Chloe had to stop and stare.

It was a bibliophile's dream. Floor-to-ceiling mahogany bookcases loaded with leather-bound books covered all walls. A wooden globe in a stand, an antiquated drafting table, and a book stand that held an open birding book with color illustrations stood at various spots around the room. On the walnut secretary, a stick of red sealing wax and a quill knife anchored a pile of paper, and a quill held upright in a silver stand attached to the inkwell made it seem as if Mr. Wrightman had only just written to someone. A book of Cowper's poems lay open. Could it be possible that by seeing a man's office, or in this case, his library, you could fall for the man himself?

The firelight flickered on the gold lettering of the hardbound books, and in an instant, Chloe remembered the law library, in college, when she was dating a law student. She hadn't thought about him in years. Decades, even. They had been flirting and studying all night when he challenged her to look something up, and there, in the back of the stacks, he closed the book in her hands, slipped it back in the bookcase nearest her hip, and pressed himself against her, opening her mouth with his. Her back pressed up against the bookcase as he slid her skirt up slowly to her waist and a thrill zigzagged through her. Maybe it was the excitement of doing something illicit. Maybe it was the books. She remembered unzipping his jeans—

"You really are such a bluestocking, aren't you?" Grace asked.

"Oh yes, all I ever think about are books."

What had stirred to life within her?

"We have an eight-course dinner and a gorgeous man awaiting us, but you're gushing over the *library*."

"You're right. Nothing interesting ever happens in a library."

Imogene laughed.

"Come along, dear," Mrs. Crescent said.

Chloe shook off the memories. It was like seeing a cut from a movie you had watched but forgotten all about.

"Look at this solarium," Mrs. Crescent said. It soared to two stories high with palm trees, singing canaries in wooden cages, and unpainted wicker furniture, but Chloe couldn't blot the library from her brain. They reached another domed hall. The butler stood in front of twin mahogany-paneled doors, each flanked by a footman, and the camerawoman came closer to Chloe.

"Ladies, take a moment," said the butler. "As soon as we pass through these doors, we will be in the crimson drawing room. A carriage awaits outside. Five of you will be offered invitations to dinner. Three of you will not be invited. Those three will be asked to leave Bridesbridge.

For once, Chloe didn't have a wisecracking thought in her swirling brain. She didn't want to go—and not just because of the money either. Beyond just lusting for Sebastian, she actually wanted—no, needed to be with him, to talk with him and learn more about him.

The footmen opened the mahogany doors. "Ladies." It was George, dressed in a butler's coat, his auburn hair coiffed to Regency perfection, with a curl tumbling down his forehead and into his eye. He was a player. Why hadn't Chloe seen it? She leaned in toward him, hoping for a message from home, but there wasn't one. The footmen shut the mahogany doors behind George.

"Before we enter the hall, I'd like to take a moment to review everyone's Accomplishment Points." He pulled a black leather-bound book from his pocket. "Lady Grace d'Argent leads with three hundred and ninety points. Miss Julia Tripp, three hundred and eighty points. Miss Gillian Potts, three hundred and eighty points. Miss Becky Carver, three hundred and sixty-five points. Miss Olive Silverton, three hundred and sixty points. Miss Imogene Wells, three hundred and thirty points. Miss Kate Harrington, three hundred and twenty-five points. And Miss Chloe Parker . . . fifteen points."

Mrs. Crescent patted Chloe's arm. Grace lifted her chin in the air.

The butler continued. "But it's only fair, considering we have a new guest, to even the playing field, especially as our guest has been a lady about the entire situation and not raised a complaint. As of tonight, everyone will start over with zero points."

The women, except for Imogene, gasped and stepped away from Chloe, as if this were her fault. Grace narrowed her eyes at Chloe, and all of them, Grace in particular, because she was in the lead, had real reason to hate her now.

"And in terms of popularity, according to our online audience ratings system, there is one woman who far outranks the rest at the moment."

The women all looked around at one another, except for Grace, who nodded and smiled at her chaperone.

"Miss Chloe Parker wins the week's audience popularity contest by tenfold," George said.

Chloe had never been superpopular before. But here, in England, in 1812, apparently they liked her, except for her fellow contestants.

"Now. The Invitation Ceremony. May I point out to you again the importance of the invitation in this era. Entire seasons, entire destinies are made or broken by invitations. If you are lucky enough to get invited to the right balls, the right dinners, you may meet the husband you are destined to be with. Without the invitations, you could become a spinster. Invitations are everything. Good luck," George said. He gave a nod and the footmen swung open the doors to a room swathed in crimson and lined with velvet curtains and velvet-stuffed chairs.

Sebastian stood next to a footman holding a silver salver stacked with five creamy envelopes, all with red W seals, no doubt. He stepped forward in his starched cravat, tailored black cutaway coat, off-white breeches, and stockings that showed off the muscles of his calves. He bowed, his dark eyes flitting from girl to girl. Chloe's white-gloved hands shook as if she'd had a round or two of triple-espresso lattes without the latte. Maybe what Grace said in the carriage was true. Maybe all that mattered to her was the money. But there was more to it than that. Mrs. Crescent nudged Chloe until she curtsied.

"Welcome to Dartworth Hall. So pleased to see you, Miss Parker."

Heat rose up her neck and into her cheeks. "Pleased to see you," she said, and curtsied again. She was more pleased than he could know.

The chaperones stood in a cluster off to the side, shifting their feet and adjusting their assorted headdresses and necklaces. The eligible women had been instructed to stand in a line straight across, arm's length apart, facing Sebastian.

"I just want everyone to know that this was one of the hardest decisions I've had to make." He looked down at his brass-buckled black shoes, reached for the first invitation, and looked straight ahead, then, after a pause, his eyes darted toward Chloe, then away.

"Miss Kate Harrington."

Kate stepped forward.

"Miss Kate Harrington, will you accept this invitation?"

"I will." She curtsied, went back to her place, and sniffled.

The blatant sexism that defined this reality show ate away at Chloe as she watched Julia, then Gillian gratefully "accept" their invitations. But George was right when he said invitations could make or break a Regency woman's future. It just never hit her until now, this pathetic aspect of being a woman in 1812. She tasted something sour in her mouth, but that could've been the tooth powder.

"Lady Grace d'Argent."

Grace sauntered forward with a smirk on her face.

"Lady Grace d'Argent, will you accept this invitation?"

"Absolutely." She curtsied, and slowly walked back to her place.

George stepped in front of the cameras. "Ladies. There is one invitation left." He paused for dramatic effect. "Mr. Wrightman, proceed."

Chloe felt nauseous, probably hungry. It couldn't be that her fantasy Regency world wasn't all she had cracked it up to be or that it was all crashing down around her. Mrs. Crescent crossed her fingers.

"Miss Chloe Parker."

Instead of looking at Sebastian, she looked at Mrs. Crescent, whose shoulders slumped in relief—she, who prided herself on her excellent posture.

"Miss Chloe Parker," Sebastian said again.

In a muddle of happiness and humiliation, Chloe stepped forward. This was what it felt like to be a woman in Regency England, waiting for men to determine your destiny.

Sebastian smiled. "Miss Parker, will you accept this invitation?"

The red wax seal looked like candy.

"Yes, I will." She hardly knew where the words came from. Glad to be asked, but mortified to accept, she curtsied, and on her way back, she noticed Imogene wipe a tear from her cheek. She, Olive, and Becky didn't have an invitation. Chloe's three favorites.

"Ladies," said George. "Mr. Wrightman has made his decision. You may say your good-byes."

Grace held her arms out to Imogene, who instead threw herself at Chloe. Abigail had cried like this when she finally understood that Winthrop wouldn't be living with them anymore. Chloe wrapped her arms around Imogene and realized that even Imogene could use a shower.

"I can't believe he chose Grace over me," Imogene whimpered into Chloe's neck. "I actually have feelings for him and . . . and I don't want to go."

"I know. I'm going to miss you."

Imogene was the closest thing to a friend Chloe had here, and Sebastian ripped her away. Who else would Chloe talk to? Paint with? Imogene stepped back and squeezed Chloe's arms. She lowered her voice to a whisper. "Good luck."

"That's quite enough now." George linked his arm in Imogene's, avoiding eye contact with Chloe. "Your carriage is waiting."

Chloe hugged Becky and Olive. They wished her well, even though, Olive said, Chloe seemed a mismatch for Sebastian. The audacity! Imogene threw Grace an air kiss. Sebastian said good-bye and thank you to the women. As Imogene walked out the double mahogany doors, her blue satin bow on the back of her gown drooped like a frown.

Sad as Chloe was to see her go, and embarrassed as she was to have participated in the ceremony, she thrilled at the thought of staying on, for the money and the man, and this mix of emotion made her uncomfortable. A torrent of lust and a wave of hope for love overcame her. Her mouth quivered into a smile as Mrs. Crescent congratulated her.

Sebastian turned and smiled at Chloe, but protocol dictated that he escort Grace. He took her arm and they both turned their backs on her. The other women and their chaperones followed suit, leaving Chloe in the back of the promenade alone.

George seemed to have vaporized and Henry appeared just as quickly and bowed to Chloe. He held out his arm and offered to escort her. "I'm sorry that Miss Wells was asked to leave. I know you'll miss her."

Henry was not only observant, but thoughtful. "Thank you, Mr. Wrightman. I *will* miss her."

"Someday, when we have a chance," he said, "I'd like to show you the library. I think you'd quite like it."

Chapter 8

From Chloe's vantage point in the back of the promenade, Sebastian looked hot and bulging in his "inexpressibles." His tight cream-colored breeches were revealed every time his coattails wafted open. With this potent cocktail of sexiness and intelligence that she had only ever seen on screen, she forgot everything else.

She felt compelled to reconnect with him as she had this morning, or next time around he could kick her off the show with his gold-buckled shoe. But she was at the end, the very end, of the line of guests walking through the mahogany-paneled hall toward the dining room at Dartworth. It made her jealous that he led the procession, arm in arm with Grace, and then it made her mad that she felt jealous. She was just getting to know him! Why was she crushing on him already? The rest of the party followed in order of rank with Chloe, the token poor girl (and come on, she had always thought of herself as decidedly upper middle class despite her current strife) bringing up the end.

Holding her chin high and her spine straight, she walked through the doors with Henry, the cameras all over her. Once she lowered her chin, she found herself standing in front of a long table bedecked in a white tablecloth, and she felt wistful now, on top of everything, because it was Wednesday night, her pizza-and-movie night with Abigail. The grand dining table in front of her stood resplendent with five-pronged candelabra and beeswax candles, silver-rimmed china bowls, and crystal wine goblets at each place setting. Pineapples and shiny red apple pyramids punctuated each end of the table. Fruit! She hadn't eaten fruit in days, as it was considered bad for a lady's complexion. Dainty desserts stood on silver epergnes, and five footmen in blue coats and gold waistcoats, all equally young and handsome, and all of uniform height, stood behind the Chippendale chairs, waiting to serve. And then she remembered pizza gave her heartburn and Abigail was probably having fun with her grandparents or, God forbid, her dad and stepmom-to-be.

"You were perhaps expecting a larger dining room?" Henry asked.

Chloe must've been frowning at the thought of Marcia Smith.

Henry smiled. "I do hope you find Dartworth Hall to your liking. You don't think it too ostentatious?"

"Ostentatious? No. No, not at all." She tried to remember the last time a man spoke to her using polysyllabic words like *ostentatious*. "I find it elegant."

"Allow me to escort you to your chair," he said.

Nobody had ever said *that* to her before. She took his arm. "Thank you." He was so nice she actually felt guilty for thinking maybe getting in good with Henry would help her score points with Sebastian.

Henry pulled out her chair and pushed her in next to him. Sebastian sat on the other end of the table, at the head, with Julia on his left and Grace on his right. He caught Chloe's attention and then rolled his eyes when Grace wasn't looking. Chloe shrugged. Next to Grace and Julia were Gillian and Kate, then Chloe and Henry, and all the chaperones.

"It appears that American heiresses don't pull much rank at the dinner table," Chloe said to Henry.

"Do you seek to improve your rank in this world, Miss Parker?"

"Oh no! I'm mainly here for the white soup."

Henry smiled. "Ah. You may not care about rank, but you do have expensive tastes."

Chloe had no idea that white soup was expensive.

"I'm sorry to say you're in for a disappointment. White soup isn't on the menu tonight."

Chloe eyed her empty wineglass. "Not to worry. The wine will more than make up for it."

Henry laughed as the footmen poured the claret. Chloe didn't think it was that funny—she hadn't had wine in days. Ladies didn't drink wine on their own unless they were "unwell," a stunt Grace had pulled every night since Chloe arrived.

"I propose—" Sebastian said, raising his glass, looking at Chloe.

Chloe raised her wine goblet, which was no bigger than a bud vase. A proposal already?

"I propose a toast to our new guest at Bridesbridge Court, who comes all the way from America. Miss Chloe Parker." He lowered his voice. "Welcome to Dartworth."

What class. What manners. What—luscious lips. Enthralled with watching him bring his wineglass to his mouth, she almost forgot to respond.

"Thank you," she said. "I'm thrilled to be here."

"May you find what you're looking for," Henry said.

Grace looked at Sebastian from behind her wineglass. "*I've* found what *I'm* looking for."

Thank goodness for the wine, because Chloe needed a drink. And with just a hint of oak and fruity notes, it went down smoothly. Henry looked at Chloe's empty wineglass, and almost as quickly, he emptied his.

The footman offered soup from a china tureen, and Chloe accepted two ladlefuls before she realized it was fish soup or bouillabaisse. No matter what kind of spin you put on it, she didn't like fish soup and neither did her stomach. She also didn't like the fact that she wasn't allowed to talk to the footmen and servants, that she had to forget they were real people. Even worse, the servants had actually faded into the background for her over the past couple days, and she, too, was beginning to treat them like the furniture, except for Fiona, whom she did her best to coddle. She stared at the cut-up fish flesh floating in the broth, stirring with her soup spoon. It didn't matter. She hadn't been hungry since the outing with Sebastian this morning.

Kate, who sat next to Chloe, scratched her bare arms. Under her caplet sleeves Chloe detected another outbreak of hives.

"Miss Harrington," Chloe asked Kate, "have you tried Gowland's Lotion? I've heard it's quite good."

Kate didn't get the obscure reference to the lotion mentioned in Jane Austen's *Persuasion*.

"Sir Walter highly recommends it," Henry said, completing the reference.

Henry—a Jane Austen fan? Just like his brother, as it had said in Sebastian's bio? Chloe did a double take. But then she remembered that it had been Henry who made the wet-shirt comment at the pond.

Kate tapped Chloe on the hand, her eyes already puffy. "Do you think there are any shellfish in this soup? I mustn't eat shellfish, or I'll blow up like a hot-air balloon."

"I can assure you there are no shellfish," Henry said. "Miss Parker. I hear you explored the old castle ruins today. Did you know it was built around the year 1130? Additions were made to it in the thirteenth century. Did you notice the herringbone pattern of stonework on the outer walls?"

"No. I'm afraid I didn't notice—that."

"It's too bad my brother didn't point it out to you. It's very rare to find that pattern of brickwork in a twelfth-century wall."

Sebastian had pointed—other things out to her.

Still, for a fleeting moment Chloe felt as if she had missed out on something. She could always go back to the ruins, couldn't she? "I did notice, though, that the archer holes were square and not narrow slits. That was unexpected."

Henry nodded in agreement and started to say something about how the castle was destroyed by cannonballs during the English Civil War, but Chloe turned away from him to make eye contact with Sebastian. She caught Grace's eye instead.

Everyone was talking with the person sitting next to them, and over the din of conversation, Grace raised her voice above them all. "This bouillabaisse is simply ecstasy. What a joy to have a French cook. I do so love French food and fashion. I would love to go to Paris again, wouldn't you, Miss Parker?"

This was some kind of trap. Grace must've known Chloe had never been to Paris. She'd been to Martha's Vineyard, Lake Tahoe, the Hamptons, but never Europe. Chloe opened her mouth and then shut it, like a fish. "I'm quite happy to be *here*," she said.

Mrs. Crescent nodded in approval from across the table.

Henry saved her butt. "Surely the Americans find France to be no place for a lady at the moment."

Grace sipped a spoonful of soup.

"Thank you for that," Chloe said to Henry.

"Thank Napoleon," he said, watching her play with her soup. "You're doing a wonderful job of not eating your bouillabaisse. Do you not like it? I can have Mr. Hill take it away and bring you something else. Mr. Hill? Mr. Hill—"

It was the first time she heard anyone refer to a servant with such respect. Everyone else just called the servants by their last names, without a "Mr." or "Miss" attached. "The soup is fine, really. Thank you." Chloe strained to keep eye contact with Sebastian even as she kept conversation going with Henry. She had to wonder why Henry was here, although she suspected he was supposed to help his brother scout out the women, and his latest assignment was to get the dish on her. It was obvious. So she thought she'd have some fun with it. It teetered on the edge of impropriety, but it didn't strike her as against the rules.

"Are you secretly engaged, Mr. Wrightman? Or otherwise spoken for?" Chloe asked.

Henry sputtered into his soup. "No. No, I'm not engaged, and have no prospects at the moment."

"Really?" Chloe was surprised. He seemed like the settled type. He didn't sport a wedding ring, or she might think he was married already.

"I'm taking a bit of a sabbatical from all that."

"By throwing yourself into a gaggle of eligible women in the middle of the countryside for six weeks?"

"Point well taken, Miss Parker. But you no doubt realize I'm here to help my brother find a suitable wife. He is ready to marry and settle down."

"And you, I take it, are not."

"I'm younger."

Not by much, Chloe thought. Maybe a year or two.

"My brother doesn't want to waste his time with anyone he can't envision as the love of his life. I'm here to help him in any way I can."

"A great sacrifice on your part."

"It is."

She turned to Sebastian. Once or twice he ogled down the table at her, steam rising from his soup bowl.

Sebastian wasn't very good in groups, Chloe decided. Shy. Darcy-like. Still, she suspected that he wanted to talk to her; he kept looking at her. But she had to admit, he was looking at the other girls, too, and she didn't like that. He was so gorgeous that his eyes gave her a rush every time she caught them. Made her hyperaware of everything. By the time the footmen cleared the soup bowls, Chloe determined he might well be her Mr. Darcy. When would she get him alone again? How would she possibly get to know him better? She conjured an image of them dancing, turning hand in hand, eyes locked in on each other—

"Partridge or fish, Miss Parker?" Henry asked.

A footman held a silver platter loaded with roasted birds and fish with the heads still on toward Chloe. A row of dead fish eyes gaped up at her and her stomach churned. She looked at the footman. "Are there any potatoes?" There were always boiled potatoes.

"I've been living on potatoes," she said to Henry.

"Suckling pig and cow tongue doesn't appeal?" Henry asked.

More than anything, the nineteenth-century presentation, where everything came with the head or the feet still attached, didn't work for Chloe. She had already lost some weight. She twitched her nose.

The footman nodded. "Just one moment."

She imagined the footmen and maids must have their own fun and their own pairing-off. She hoped so, anyway. It looked like she would, despite the abundance of food, leave the table without eating much, as was so often the case after a meal here in Regency England.

"I can manage almost anything, but not game birds," Henry said. His plate had a few fish on it.

"I can't eat them either," Chloe said.

"Does it have to do with your passion for birds, Miss Parker?"

How did he know about that? Chloe changed the subject to one of his interests—the frog hatchery. "And no doubt you avoid frog legs."

Henry smiled. "You're right."

"Tell me. Which one of the women are you currently recommending to your brother?"

Henry took a slug of his wine. "You are quite forward, Miss Parker."

"I'm just curious." She could see this line of conversation made him a little nervous, but a little intrigued, too. And she wanted to intrigue him—in order to intrigue Sebastian.

"I haven't recommended anyone yet. I have merely helped him discern some of the ladies' characters."

"And what have you discerned about my character?"

Henry refolded his napkin. "It's a little too early to judge. Although I have my theories." He smirked.

Chloe raised her eyebrows. Now *she* was intrigued. Unfortunately, during all this jabbering with Henry, Grace had managed to snare Sebastian into a conversation about hunting. "Oh yes. Last fall was my best season ever," she heard Sebastian say to Grace. He had picked two partridges clean and stacked the bones alongside a pile of fish bones on his plate.

Grace nodded with enthusiasm, her feather nodding with her.

Chloe watched Sebastian, who now seemed so animated, making hand gestures as he talked; he even smiled. The footman offered Chloe a platter of boiled potatoes and carrots, and with a pair of silver tongs, she plucked them from the platter, transferring them carefully to her plate.

Sebastian laughed. "I must've bagged fourteen grouse! Looking forward to the season. Grouse hunting in August. Partridges in September. Pheasants in October—"

Chloe turned her head to look at him and the potato she was lifting with the tongs broke and fell into her lap. "Oh—"

Henry offered his napkin to her. But before anybody noticed Chloe's faux pas, Grace squeaked like a mouse, and spouted a very deliberate "Oh, dear!" All heads and cameras turned to Grace as she squirmed, then shot up out of her chair.

One of her breasts had popped out of her low-cut gown!

At first, a wave of shock rolled through Chloe, and she would've stood up to help, but for the broken potato on her lap.

Grace paused for a moment, her hand over her pursed lips, looking down at her breast while the cameras jockeyed around her. Sebastian's eyes bugged out. He dropped his spoon. Henry sighed and looked away. Kate scratched at her arm furiously. Julia folded her arms.

And that's when it finally hit Chloe that Grace had orchestrated this stunt. Chloe kept reminding herself that a lady could never appear too angry, especially in public, but her hands shook and she wanted to tell Grace off. How dare she ruin Chloe's debut dinner at Dartworth!

"Oh my!" Grace squealed. As if in slo-mo, her gotta-be-a-fake boob stood there, erect, en plein air, until Sebastian burst out of his chair, ripped off his coat, and slid it over Grace's shoulders, carefully covering said breast.

Fish think, but not fast enough, Chloe thought. She plucked the broken potato from her lap. She whispered to Henry, "What do you think that reveals about *her* character?"

Henry didn't reply, but instead signaled one of the footmen over to help her clean up the potato. It was as if Grace didn't exist.

Grace hugged Sebastian's coat around her. She hurried behind a painted screen in a far corner of the room, and her chaperone joined her. Leave it to Grace to stage a strategic wardrobe malfunction that wouldn't soon be forgotten. All the women had, for days now, joked about their bodices slipping down, but it never did happen. Chloe shook her head. Grace had to have cut her corset to pull this one off. Everything put away now, Sebastian seated Grace at the table again.

Both Sebastian and Henry looked flushed and they talked about the wine from nearly opposite ends of the long table.

Gillian narrowed her eyes at Grace.

Grace held her wineglass up to the candlelight. "It has great body, don't you agree?"

Chloe raised her glass. "But a rather empty finish if you ask me."

Gillian smiled.

If only she could get that image of Grace's breast out of her head—and out of Sebastian's.

A footman brandished a platter with a pheasant, purple plumage still attached, encircled with roasted rabbits, their furry heads reattached.

"Any hope of what we in America call 'salad'?" Chloe whispered to Henry.

"You know full well that greenery is bad for your digestion, and tomatoes are poisonous."

Chloe didn't have a barb to fling back at him. She was surprised and impressed by his knowledge of Regency England. But maybe instead of picking up Regency trivia from Henry, she could glean information about Sebastian. "You're absolutely right about the salad. What was I thinking? Perhaps you can enlighten me on another subject: your brother. Does he *really* like to hunt?"

Henry set down his knife. "Most country gentlemen do hunt and fish, Miss Parker, for sport as well as for food. But my brother's bark is bigger than his bite."

"*Bon appétit,*" Grace announced. She helped herself to a slice of rabbit.

"Are you saying it has something to do with machismo? Is your brother overly concerned with his image?" Chloe asked.

"I didn't realize American heiresses were familiar with Spanish words like *machismo*, nor that they were trained in the wiles of journalism."

Chloe squirmed in her chair. Tapping Henry for information wouldn't be easy, but it was worth the effort. And it was fun to spar with him. Still, she felt comforted by the fact that Sebastian must've been overstating his hunting prowess to impress the women. He did have the reputation of a Regency squire to live up to, after all.

Sebastian stood, and all eyes moved toward him. "Yes, *bon appétit*, and, I'd like to invite all the ladies, and Henry, too, of course, to join me in a mock foxhunt on Sunday, nine in the morning. Ladies, we won't be pursuing a real fox, so not to worry."

Chloe looked toward the windows. Forget the fox. This meant she'd have to ride a horse sidesaddle. And, no doubt, this was another reality-show task with Accomplishment Points attached and nonparticipants asked to leave.

Julia practically bounced up and down in her chair and her chaperone glared at her until she calmed down.

"A hunt," Grace said.

Surely, Chloe thought, Miss Parker didn't have enough status to ride. Chloe hadn't ridden a horse since college. Could she still do it? Plus, here it would have to be sidesaddle.

Mrs. Crescent leaned toward Chloe and said across the table, "We'll spend the next three days riding, Miss Parker. Count on it!"

Chloe stared at the arrangement of small woodland animals in front of her.

"Miss Parker," Sebastian asked from the head of the table. "Are you quite all right?"

English men were so attentive. Chloe was about to respond when suddenly Mrs. Crescent pushed herself up out of her chair, her hands propped on the small of her back, sweat gathering under her curled bangs. "It's time!" she said, putting one hand on her belly. "It's time!"

Chloe's stomach tightened as she remembered the night she gave birth to Abigail. Abigail came a week early, and Winthrop was in Washington on business.

Chloe hurried over to Mrs. Crescent, but Henry was already there, guiding her to a fainting couch by the window. He took the watch from his watch fob and started timing the contractions.

Sebastian and Grace gawked. The chaperones and their charges crowded around Mrs. Crescent.

"Breathe. That's right," Henry said. He took her hand.

Mrs. Crescent did her breathing, stood, and paced. Chloe paced with her.

"We should call her OB," Chloe said to Henry. "An ambulance to take her to the hospital."

"Contractions are still well over three minutes apart." With his back to the camera, he spoke a mile a minute to Chloe. "We won't be calling anyone. She wants to have her baby here. Nineteenth-century style."

"What?! There is no way—"

"Perhaps instead of being so dogmatic, you could do something useful, Miss Parker?"

Chloe gulped and stepped back. Sebastian had disappeared and so had the all the footmen and servants. Grace took backward steps toward the door. Was Grace snagging some alone time with Sebastian—now? Chloe couldn't let it happen. But she also couldn't let Henry think she was a dogmatic idiot either. She released her arm from Mrs. Crescent's. "Julia, Gillian. Stay with her. I'm going to get the kitchen maids to boil some water." She dashed out the door and almost banged into Sebastian. Again.

Sebastian looked worried. "I—I'm not good in these situations. I'm an artist, not a doctor."

He was an artist? What kind of an artist? she wondered. Then Mrs. Crescent groaned. "Come help me boil some water," Chloe said. "I don't even know where the kitchen is."

Grace stood next to her chaperone at the dining room doors, her hands on her hips.

"We have to hurry," Chloe said. "Which way?"

"Follow me," Sebastian said.

Chloe was right on his coattails. She smiled to herself. She was chasing him—literally now. And all this dashing through the marble halls lined with antiquities would have been fun had it not been for the gravity of a woman giving birth without a hospital, without an epidural! After scrambling down the servant stairway into the kitchen, Sebastian stopped. Servants and footmen were bustling about, frantically boiling water on the old stove and in the kitchen fireplace. So this was where they had all gone.

"What can I do?" Chloe dove into the fray.

A kitchen maid scowled at her. "You shouldn't be down here!" She spotted Sebastian and curtsied. "Excuse me, miss, but we've got it sorted. Best if you get upstairs." She shooed Chloe out.

Chloe hurried up to the top of the stairs and Sebastian followed. "Now what?" she asked.

"I don't know." Sebastian rubbed the cleft in his chin. "I told you I'm not very good at this sort of thing."

Chloe snapped her fingers. "They'll need linens. Where's the linen closet?"

Sebastian smiled. "My valet takes care of everything. I hardly know where he keeps my boots."

He was sweet, really sweet. Like a boy. Chloe racked her brain, trying to figure out what they could do. She leaned up against a marble column and blew a strand of hair that had fallen into her eyes.

Sebastian moved closer, waiting for her to take the lead.

A camerawoman bounded toward them from down the hall. Footmen lumbered up the stairs with pots of boiled water and kitchen maids carried up stacks of white linens. All Chloe and Sebastian could do was follow.

When the entourage arrived in the dining room, Mrs. Crescent sat, fanning herself and smiling.

Henry stood with his hands on his hips, glaring at Sebastian and Chloe, who came in last. "False alarm," he said. "Her contractions have stopped." He pulled Chloe aside and lowered his voice to a whisper. "Well done, Miss Parker. You may be the smartest person in the room, but a lot of help you were, using this opportunity to take off with Sebastian. So glad I can count on you."

Chloe wavered, feeling dizzy, surprised by his snarky reaction, which complimented and scolded her in one fell swoop. It crossed her mind, but only for a moment, that he might be jealous of his own brother. "You—you can count on me."

Henry took off his glasses. "I hope so. Mrs. Crescent wants you to help me deliver the baby when it's time. Do you think I can rely on you, or shall I consider you otherwise engaged?"

Chloe was shocked. Whether it was because of Mrs. Crescent choosing her to help deliver her baby, or how good Henry looked without glasses, she wasn't sure.

"Can I count on you, Miss Parker?" Henry folded his arms.

"Of course."

*L*ater that night, in her boudoir, Chloe woke up to a nightmare of Henry asking over and over, "Can I count on you?" She got out of bed and stumbled to her chamber pot, sicker than a girl who'd drunk negus all night at her coming-out ball. She leaned over it, her stomach sloshing. Could have been that spoonful of fish soup, or the fact that she'd have to spend the next two days riding sidesaddle, and if she didn't ride, she'd be sent home. Would she still be able to ride after more than twenty years? As she hugged her chamber pot, she realized, though, she was sick over disappointing Henry. Ugh! She liked Henry, but—really! The fact that she cared so much about his opinion of her made her sick, literally. She felt overwhelmed and confused.

At home she could've turned on music, the TV—hell, even the computer to distract herself. But here? Her own thoughts could torment her relentlessly. Finally she decided to play the footage in her mind of her moments alone with Sebastian, and that made her feel better.

He felt the same way about her as she felt about him! She had to take the reins and come up with a plan that put her in control. She decided to host a tea after the foxhunt. It would take some doing, and she'd have to put aside her painting, but it would be her show and she could call the shots. Before she snuffed out her candle, she settled her eye on the stack of painting paper and tubes of oil paint that Sebastian had given her. He, too, was an artist. But what kind of artist? A vision of Dartworth Hall floated in front of her. Could he be the one? He was stacking up to be a most interesting man. Instead of snuffing out the candle, she blew it out and made a wish.

Chapter 9

Even though she'd only just arrived, every day Chloe asked James, the Bridesbridge butler, if there were any letters for her. She couldn't wait to hear from Abigail.

"Not today, miss," was his reply as he offered letters from his silver salver to the rest of the women.

Mail from overseas took at least a week, sometimes two, so how could she expect something in just four days? She spent the morning arranging the hunt-tea menu with Cook, thrilled that hosting the tea would bring her fifteen Accomplishment Points, and the afternoon working on mounting and dismounting sidesaddle, until she earned five Accomplishment Points for that. Grace and the other women earned ten Accomplishment Points because they were ahead of her, practicing their jumps.

James arrived at her side during teatime with the silver salver.

"Letter for you, Miss Parker."

The other ladies at the tea table set their teacups down and eyed the overnighted envelope with curiosity.

Chloe ripped open the cardboard envelope and almost bolted to the foyer, but then she remembered to ask first. "Mrs. Crescent, might I take this to the Grecian temple to read? I won't be long."

Mrs. Crescent, completely recovered from her false labor and feeling no ill effects, fed Fifi a lump of sugar under the table. "Go ahead, dear, but watch for rain. Soon as you're back, you must make your ink and start your needlework project."

Chloe's cameraman followed her as she trounced past the herb garden in her bonnet and walking gloves, parasol in hand, blue day dress flouncing at her ankles. Once under the green dome of the Grecian temple atop the hill at Bridesbridge, she sat on a stone bench and ceremoniously opened the envelope.

Abigail had painted the two of them surrounded by hearts and flowers. The painting had been wrapped around a plain white envelope, sent first-class mail, and addressed to her in care of her parents' house. Her mom had put a sticky note on the envelope: *We miss you. Write again soon! All's well here! This just arrived. We sent it off* ASAP . . . *Love, Mom.*

The cameraman knelt on the grass, probably to get a better angle at her smile. She opened the enclosed white envelope only to reveal a flimsy sheet of paper laser-printed entirely in Helvetica. The top of the page read: *State of Illinois Judicial Court,* and in bold: *Motion Regarding Custody.* It was a motion to change the custody agreement and it had been served to her on a silver platter.

Winthrop was prepared to show a substantial change in circumstances, as the motion read, to warrant increasing his rights in regards to legal and physical custody of Abigail.

From what she could tell, the attached list of circumstances included not only his impending marriage on July 15 but the fact that as the new senior vice president of PeopleSystems, he and his new wife would be moving to his company's headquarters in Boston. He would no longer be traveling for work. He was motioning to change his custody to summers and holidays.

In Boston.

The hearing was scheduled for July 30.

Chloe folded the painting, then the motion, and ran her fingers along the creases. She looked at her cameraman, who stood up now and backed away a bit. Her lips quivered. She swallowed. Off in the distance, Bridesbridge stood, as it had for the past two hundred and fifty years or so, stalwart and elegant. Its strong ocher-colored exterior had held up despite whatever untoward events had gone on within its thick, ivy-covered walls. Starlings crisscrossed in the cloudy sky above.

She couldn't go back to Bridesbridge just yet, despite the impending rain. She couldn't face the women and more cameras. The weather suited her mood, so she took a turn toward the deer park, where the leaves of the trees were fluttering in the wind. Her cameraman followed, and for once, his presence gave her a sense of security. The clouds moved quickly overhead, but they weren't ominous looking yet. She watched her brown lace-up walking boots move along the path, one foot in front of the other.

Winthrop couldn't possibly take Abigail for entire summers in Boston, could he? How could this be happening? How could she stop it?

A brown hawk circled overhead when she reached a grassy clearing. Then it tucked its wings, took a sudden dive, and flew just a few feet off the ground, fast and sure. Suddenly the hawk slowed, alighted on a man's outstretched, gloved left hand, and just as quickly soared overhead again, circling. The man wore a long, tan greatcoat and black boots. Was it Henry? It looked like him.

A servant stood by him, as did a cameraman filming. No sooner did he hold his arm out to the side than the bird dove and landed again.

Chloe had only ever seen falconry like this in the Andrew Davies TV adaptation of *Sense and Sensibility*. It wasn't in any Jane Austen novels, but it was historically correct. She focused on the exquisite choreography of man and falcon, and it took her mind off of her abrupt change in circumstances.

It began to rain, of course, sporadically at first, then steadier. Chloe opened her parasol, but the rain quickly soaked through. Water dripped from the edges of her bonnet, and raindrops rolled down her cheeks. Or were they tears? She could hardly tell.

The man in the clearing had turned with the bird on his arm. It was Henry. The falcon opened its wings to fly, and the wingspan had to have been three or four feet. The tips of the bird's wings brushed against his face, but Henry was unfazed. He handled the bird with complete mastery. The bird tucked its wings in, and that was when Henry saw her. He signaled to his servant, who gathered the bird's perch.

Chloe didn't know what to do. Was she on Dartworth property? Henry handed the bird off to the servant, who seemed dwarfed by it. While the servant headed in the opposite direction, Henry strode quickly toward her, his cameraman struggling to keep up. Finally the cameraman turned back. Chloe looked up at Henry. He seemed taller, somehow.

"Miss Parker. Whatever are you doing out here?" He took off his falconry glove and his greatcoat, bowed, and smiled. "Do you really need to go to all this trouble just to avoid your needlework?"

Chloe choked up with laughter and tears as he wrapped his greatcoat around her. The coat was heavy and warm and had a piney aroma.

"I hope I'm not on Dartworth property," Chloe said into the camera.

"Are you lost?"

"Kind of."

"You're not on Dartworth property. I'm on Bridesbridge land." He took her by the arm. "We're not far. I'll take you back." He looked at her carefully, even as the rain came at them sideways. "No harm done. No need to worry. Are you—crying, Miss Parker?"

The cameraman walked backward in front of them, filming.

"No." She laughed. "They're raindrops. It rains so much here in England." She wiped the tears with her wet gloves.

He lowered his voice as he handed her a handkerchief. "I certainly must apologize for my harsh words the other night at dinner. I was a little stressed by—well—the dining room was not where we planned to birth Mrs. Crescent's baby."

"No apologies necessary." Chloe blotted another tear from her cheek with the handkerchief.

"This is the wettest summer in three years," Henry said. "And the wettest summer before that was eight years ago, but, most interestingly, the summer with record rainfall previous to that was in the Tudor era. But enough about the English weather."

"Was that a falcon you were working with back there?" Chloe asked.

"That was King, my Harris hawk. Harris hawks are much more easygoing and sociable than peregrine falcons."

She always learned something from him. "I should've known it was a Harris hawk."

Henry laughed, but he looked away from her and at the cameraman. "My good man, would you quit your filming and fetch the lady an umbrella from Bridesbridge?! Much obliged!"

The cameraman, to Chloe's amazement, complied, and took off toward Bridesbridge as fast as he could. So many times the women had tried to get the crew to quit filming, but it never worked.

"Now, what is the matter?"

Chloe held back the tears. "I'd like to learn falconry. You're incredibly talented at it. Could you teach me? Would it be apropos?"

"As you know, Miss Parker, it isn't exactly a female pursuit. Perhaps if Mrs. Crescent joined us, but no, it's actually more appropriate if my brother gave you a lesson."

From a distance, the cameraman ran toward them with two umbrellas under his arm.

Chloe fell silent.

"But Sebastian—doesn't know much about falconry." Henry looked at her with intent. "Something has upset you. What is it? I'd like to help."

As they passed the Grecian temple on top of the hill, the rain tapered off.

"Do I have *any* chance here, Henry?"

Flecks of gold flickered in his brown eyes. "Personally, I think you have the best chance of all, depending on what you hope to gain."

She found this a little abstract, and wanted to press him about it, but settled for the fact that it sounded encouraging. The cameraman, breathless, handed off the umbrellas to Henry, who popped them open while Chloe closed up her parasol. They were nineteenth-century-style umbrellas, made of silk, and soon the silk had soaked through, too. They were at the kitchen garden now, and Chloe spotted several cameras on them from various windows in Bridesbridge.

"I'm going to be in so much trouble with my chaperone."

"No, you won't," Henry said as he led her down the stairs into the scullery, just off the kitchen. "I'll make sure of that." He opened the door for her and the scent of rosemary enveloped them. When Chloe closed up her umbrella, the painting from Abigail and the motion from the court fell from under the crook of her arm onto the stoop, and she froze.

Cook came to the door, hands on her hips.

"Not a word, now, Cook," Henry said as he picked up the papers and handed them to Chloe without so much as glancing at them. "I'm at your service, Miss Parker, should the need arise."

Chloe hesitated, then blurted it out. "Henry, I need George. I need to make a phone call. Something's happened at home."

"Of course. Say no more, it shall be done."

"Thank you, Henry. Thank you." She handed him his great-coat and looked down at her wet walking boots. When she looked up at him, wet, dark blond strands of hair had fallen into his caramel-colored eyes. His face was angular but inviting, with an alluring smile.

"Everything will be all right," he said.

He had draped his greatcoat over his shoulders and his white shirt and buff-colored breeches had entirely soaked through, making her entirely too aware of his sinewy body. She did, though, remember to curtsy.

He bowed, turned, and hurried off.

When she reached the top of the stairs, she noticed that the red paint on Abigail's painting had bled through.

To make the call sooner, Chloe had persuaded Mrs. Crescent to accompany her in the carriage to the entrance gate, where they would meet George.

Now that the rain had stopped, Chloe stood waiting at the iron gates while Mrs. Crescent eyed her pocket watch in the carriage. The gates stood some fifteen feet high with sharp points on top, and the black bars made Chloe think of prison. Or was it a sort of gilded cage?

She paced in front of the gates, the letter from court in hand. Beyond the gates was the real world, and she could even hear the sounds of cars driving on wet paved roads.

She had thought, long and hard, about going home and dealing with this latest stunt of Winthrop's. Was there anything she could possibly do before the hearing? That was the biggest question she had for her lawyer. Because if there were, she'd be on a plane tonight.

As the sun came out, George appeared on his ATV, and one of the crew unlocked the gates, setting her free from her thoughts.

George granted the call, Chloe got in touch with her lawyer, and no, nothing could be done until the hearing. Her lawyer advised her to stay on in England and make the best of it. That twenty-minute conversation alone would cost her $350.

As she headed toward the carriage, her head hanging, a glint of silver in the distance caught her eye through the trees, near the hitch post. It was a silver stirrup shining in the sun.

Sebastian cut a dashing figure on a horse. Unfortunately he was surrounded by a pack of barking dogs and two cameramen.

"Miss Parker!" He tipped his hat and waved it.

Mrs. Crescent stirred in the carriage. "Go ahead, go ahead." She waved Chloe on toward Sebastian. "Just stay in my line of sight. And we will be making that ink today!"

Chloe turned to walk toward Sebastian, but the dogs—foxhounds—spun and barreled toward her! She froze, Sebastian whistled, and the dogs circled back toward him. He dismounted. His face had tanned in the sun, and as he walked his white horse toward her, she wanted her camera to capture the moment. The tall grasses seemed to part for him as he walked toward her in his boots, riding crop tucked under his arm. His biceps bulged even under the riding coat. The dogs, panting and tired, lumbered behind. One of the cameramen focused on Sebastian, the other turned his camera toward Chloe.

Sebastian bowed.

Chloe curtsied. She stepped back from the whimpering hounds because she didn't like hound dogs any more than she liked pugs.

"Don't worry. I've called them off." He stood so close to her she could almost reach out and touch his designer stubble. "Henry tells me he thinks you've gotten some bad news from home. Is everything quite all right? Why are you out here by the gates? Not trying to escape, I hope."

Chloe clasped her shaky gloved hands in front of her. "No. I'm doing my best to stay!"

"Good. Good." He sighed at the cameraman.

There wasn't much hope for a meaningful conversation.

"The best way to guarantee your stay, Miss Parker, is to dedicate yourself to preparing for the foxhunt. It's a challenging task, but one I'm sure you're equal to. Do you have a sense of adventure?"

"Adventure? I'm all about adventure!" Chloe shot a look at the dogs out of the corner of her eye.

In his Hessian boots, he stepped even closer to her now, blocked the camera for a moment, and slid a note into her hand. She understood to hide it in her reticule.

"I'm glad to hear it," he said. "I would want a wife who enjoys adventure and games—a certain element of playfulness and fun. I think you have those qualities and so much more."

Chloe couldn't believe he'd said all this while surrounded by cameras and—dogs. Nor could she believe that he had slipped a piece of folded paper into her hands, unbeknownst to the cameramen.

A clipped bow, a tip of his hat, a bucking up of his horse, and he was gone, just as suddenly as he had appeared, his coattails flying in the wind and the pack of dogs hot on his trail.

When at last she closed her bedchamber door under the pretense of having to use the chamber pot, Chloe ceremoniously unfolded the note he had given her. The handwriting was old-fashioned, ornamental, and organized in stanzas. He had written her a poem! At thirty-nine years old, Chloe read the first love poem ever written for her:

As the sun shines high in the sky
Love blooms in my heart, I cannot lie.

To let our love grow
Is what is want, I know.
Still I cannot be convinced
Nay, I need more evidence
Of your intentions, are they true?
To convince me here is what you need to do:
As the clock strikes two you must find
Something in a garden where light and shadow are intertwined
Inspect the face in the garden bright
Then follow the line of light
Straight to a house without walls
Enter the door and go where the water falls
Extrapolate from this poem the puzzle within
Make a note of the six-word answer, write it, and you will win
Send your missive through the secret door and the answers you seek will
be in store!

She read it again. It wasn't a love poem. It was some kind of Regency courtship riddle turned reality-show task. She sighed. But she was up for it! It gave her insight into Sebastian's playful, romantic nature, and it cheered her as no other missive could at this point.

Did the other women get one of these? she wondered. But she couldn't ask them. Sebastian had expressly written that this task would be one for her to take on alone, without even her chaperone's knowledge.

What thing in a garden would incorporate light and shadow? The estate had acres and acres of gardens. Could the garden be in a painting? And what about the two o'clock reference? Could the answer be on a painted face of one of the grandfather clocks in Bridesbridge?

The joke was on her. She didn't get it. Not at all. And she couldn't ask Mrs. Crescent a thing about it.

* * *

*M*rs. Crescent had handed Chloe a recipe for ink, written by Martha Lloyd, Jane Austen's sister-in-law:

Take 4 ozs of blue gauls, 2 ozs of green copperas, 1 ½ ozs of gum arabic. Break the gauls. The gum and copperas must be beaten in a mortar and put into a pint of strong stale beer; with a pint of small beer. Put in a little refin'd sugar. It must stand in the chimney corner fourteen days and be shaken two or three times a day.

Chloe knew that "gauls" must be the "galls" she had collected from the oak trees. As for the rest, a pint of beer, even strong stale beer, sounded good right about now.

With Mrs. Crescent's help, she managed to get through the recipe, and restrained herself from drinking the beer, but had to remember to visit the parlor chimney two or three times a day from then on to shake her vial of ink.

"Not to worry," Mrs. Crescent had said. "I shan't let you forget."

With a total of ten Accomplishment Points now, Chloe faced two days of practicing riding sidesaddle on Chestnut, the nicest horse in the stable. In her spare time, she picked up as many of Fiona's chores as she could when the camera wasn't around, noting that her maid seemed sadder than ever. She also made a point of scouring the estate, tramping through gardens looking for shafts of sunlight and shadows, trying to solve the riddle from Sebastian. That was how she knew she was more than smitten. None of the paintings or clocks in Bridesbridge fit the description in the riddle, not even the pocket watch on Grace's chatelaine.

Her oil paints and stack of painting paper went untouched as Mrs. Crescent started Chloe on another task that would take more than a week: needlework. She had to embroider a fireplace screen for fifteen points when in fact the extent of her needlework skills were sewing on buttons that had fallen off. So much for her days of leisure.

When she scrambled down the servant stairs into the basement kitchen to help Cook do the baking for the tea, she found Cook standing at the pine worktable, beating dough with her fists. Flies buzzed around as a couple of kitchen maids, who seemed sixteen years old at most, stoked the fire in the open range, apparently to set something in the cauldron hanging above it to boil. A hare, dead and skinned, hung from the rafters, and all manner of tongs and knives and industrial-sized soup ladles hung from hooks on the walls. Black clothing irons stood upon a shelf, and everything reeked of onion.

Cook and the kitchen maids curtsied upon Chloe's entrance, and the formality flustered her. She rolled up the decorative, gauzy yellow sleeves of her overdress. "Do you have an apron? I'm here to bake for the tea party."

Cook shot Chloe a look with her icy blue eyes. "You can't possibly bake. You belong upstairs!"

Chloe snagged an apron from one of the wooden hooks near the copper pots and tied it around herself. "If you just tell me where the strawberry-tart recipe is, I'll begin with that. I just made my own ink, I'm sure I can get a couple of the items from the tea menu taken care of over the next two days."

Cook looked at the kitchen maids, who giggled. "If the lady insists. Here's the recipe." Cook opened a reproduction cookbook, called *A Propre new booke of Cokery*, and pointed with a finger tipped in flour.

....

To make a tarte of strawberries.

Take and strayne theim with the yolkes of foure egges & a little white brede grated/then ceason it vp with suger & swete butter and so bake it.

Short paest for Tarte.

Take fyne floure and a curscy of fayre water and dysche of swete butter and lyttel saffron, and the yolkes of two egges and make it thynne
and as tender as ye may.

....

"Well?" Cook asked. "Get to it. The scullery maid has gone to the
trouble of picking the strawberries. I'm about to fill the mincemeat
pies and the kitchen maids are in the midst of making the trifle you
requested. I'm afraid you're on your own for a bit."

Luckily, Chloe had made enough fruit tarts in her time that a
recipe wasn't even necessary, although she had never used saffron,
and washing the strawberries in a dry sink, without running water,
wasn't very effective, and then forcing them through the sieve took
infinitely longer than if she'd been able to use her food processor.

Considering that she rarely baked in her own modern kitchen,
her sudden enthusiasm for desserts and spearheading tea parties
could only be attributed to her overwhelming desire to impress Sebastian. What other explanation could there be for turning into a
Regency domestic diva?

When it came time to put the tart crust in the oven, Chloe was
stumped. The open range didn't have knobs, a touch pad, or a temperature gauge. In fact, the kitchen had no refrigerator, no running
water, and no disinfectant soap either. Not to mention a microwave
or coffeemaker.

Who knew that two centuries would make such a difference in
the kitchen?

She stood in front of the open range a good five minutes until
Cook stepped over, took the pie tin with the crust, and shoved it in
with a wooden oven handle.

"Keep an eye on it now." Cook shook a finger at Chloe.

After the crust browned, Chloe filled the tart and put it in the range. "What next?"

"You've done well," Cook said. "Can you help me gild these confections?"

"Absolutely." Chloe felt as if she had established some sort of relationship with Cook.

Cook brought a plate of handmade chocolates from the scullery and set them on the pine table along with a tin of edible gold dust.

"You simply dab them like this." Cook demonstrated.

She handed Chloe what at first seemed to be a cotton ball, but it didn't take long for Chloe to drop the thing on the table. The room began to spin around her.

"What—what is this, Cook? It's not a cotton ball, is it?"

The kitchen maids, who were beating eggs in a bowl, giggled again.

The scullery maid plucked feathers from a partridge, but didn't even look up from her work.

Cook left off from grating suet and came over to Chloe. "That, my dear, is a rabbit's tail, and it makes a wonderful brush, doesn't it?"

Chloe steadied herself against the table. She realized she hadn't eaten the pigeon pies and cold lamb for lunch, and she felt queasy. "I'd better check the oven—I mean range."

Thank goodness her strawberry tart needed to be taken out. She covered the tart with a cloth to keep the flies off. By the time she returned to the table, Cook had gilded all the chocolates for her with said rabbit tail.

"You've done a wonderful job helping us here." Cook turned to the kitchen maids. "Hasn't she, girls?" Cook asked.

The maids nodded in agreement.

"Now, I'm sure you have things that need tending to upstairs, like shaking your ink that's set in the chimney? And we'd best get started on dinner. There will be plenty more to do tomorrow." Cook patted

Chloe on the back as Chloe hung up her apron. "As for tonight, I sure hope you're hungry. We're making stewed hare and partridges for dinner!"

O n Saturday evening, after two full days of alternating between the riding field and the kitchen, Chloe collapsed in a settee in the parlor, wondering if massages had been discovered yet or not.

She'd gained ten more Accomplishment Points for riding, but the others had gained fifteen for more advanced riding and découpaging a box while she was in the kitchen.

"No rest for the weary, Miss Parker." Mrs. Crescent clapped and Fifi barked.

"I shook my ink vial three times today, Mrs. Crescent."

"No, no, it's not that."

"What, then? Darning a footman's stockings? Trimming Lady Grace's pantalets?"

Mrs. Crescent motioned her to get up. "Come here, dear, and you will see." She led Chloe to the drawing room, a footman opened the doors, and at first, all Chloe saw was the candlelight.

Sebastian rose from a high-backed chair near the fireplace, stepped over to her, and bowed.

Chloe wondered if she still smelled of mincemeat from the kitchen. She curtsied.

"Mr. Wrightman is here to take your silhouette."

"Only if Miss Parker wishes me to," he said.

If he only knew her wishes! "Yes, yes of course," Chloe said.

A candle burned in front of a large piece of paper attached to the wall and Mr. Wrightman escorted Chloe to the chair turned sideways in front of it. Chloe sat down, her back straight, thanks to the busk. He picked up a stick of charcoal.

Mrs. Crescent and Fifi sat on the far end of the drawing room, out of earshot, but not out of sight.

Mr. Wrightman put his hands on her head, then her shoulders, adjusting her until he achieved the desired effect, that effect being her whole body going aflutter.

"This may be a challenge for you, Miss Parker, as you cannot talk while I'm tracing your shadow."

Chloe smirked. "I can accept that challenge."

He started to trace. "Consequently, you'll simply have to listen. I must say, Mrs. Crescent is quite the taskmaster."

Chloe's eyes, not her head, turned toward Mrs. Crescent, who merely turned another page in her book and continued to pet Fifi.

"Ah, there, she can't hear me, so I can say what I came here to say."

Chloe couldn't imagine what that would be.

"You must know, Miss Parker, that I know significantly more about you than you know about me, and this puts me at a great advantage. I can confidently say we are ideally matched. Not only was I privy to your audition video, but to all the transcripts of your interviews with our producers."

He paused for a moment. "Certain strands of your hair simply refuse to be pinned in, and I find that infinitely charming and entirely indicative of your character."

Chloe didn't know how much longer she could remain silent. Her lips parted and her eyelashes fluttered.

"I also had the opportunity, since I knew your full name and the city you live in, to look you up on the Internet."

She gulped. This was exactly the kind of cyberstalking Emma would do. So much for a slow-build Regency courtship. He had TMI while she had—nothing.

"That's the advantage of the era we live in, that with just a few clicks we can learn so much."

That was exactly what she couldn't stand. A day after you've met someone, via Twitter or Facebook, you know what they ate for dinner last night. Where was the mystery? The romance? The *courtship*?

He paused again and stood back from the tracing, within her line of sight. He studied the shadow on the wall, not her, so her eyes were free to wander down from his broad shoulders in his tightly tailored cutaway coat, past his cravat, down the last two undone buttons on his waistcoat, to his suggestive white breeches tucked into boots with the tops folded over.

"Yes, I think I will continue past your slender neck and trace your bust, even though I am risking Mrs. Crescent's disapproval."

Chloe did her best to breathe slowly.

"Well, as it turns out, we have much in common, Miss Parker, perhaps most markedly in our charitable ventures and choice of entertainment. Architectural preservation events, the opera, theater, gallery openings, museum galas, gourmet restaurants, I see us together, you on my arm, perhaps even as my wife, in my London town house. Or my lodgings in Bath. Or here in Derbyshire, or all of the above."

Chloe did everything she could to keep her mouth from going ga-ga. She couldn't even imagine that kind of life.

"There." He stood back, hands on his hips, and stared at his work. "Not as good as the original, but—"

He could be a little too charming. "Really, Mr. Wrightman!"

He took the piece of paper down, picked up the scissors, pulled a Chippendale chair up across from her, and sat down, just looking at her. "But true, all of it true." He lowered his voice to a whisper. "Might I have a lock of your hair?" He held the scissors in his palm.

Was he for real?

"Go ahead," she said.

She offered some split ends to him, and, most seductively, he smoothed her hair, and slowly snipped about two inches off.

It was amazing how intimate an act it was, especially as he had to pocket it before Mrs. Crescent came over, rubbing her belly.

"A very good likeness, Mr. Wrightman, though I do find it a bit shocking just how low you've chosen to go. I daresay this needs trimming."

He rolled up the paper. "Not to worry, Mrs. Crescent. I shall trim it and lampblack it at home." He bowed. "I must let you both rest for the big day tomorrow. Until then!"

Chloe curtsied, and he left.

"Did he take a lock of your hair?" Mrs. Crescent asked.

Chloe didn't think she should say yes.

"You don't need to answer, I can see in your face that he has. Very clever of him to come under the pretense of a silhouette, with shears. It's a good sign, a very good sign!"

Sunday, the day of the mock foxhunt arrived, and everyone was excited except Chloe, whose sidesaddle riding wasn't exactly show quality yet.

Instead, she focused on the footman at the stable, with his blond hair tied back in a short ponytail and his taut calves that practically popped out of his tights. He took her tiny hand in his strong, white gloved one and helped her mount the horse for the hunt. She locked her legs into the stirrups and gripped the reins. Just a week ago, the prospect of an attractive footman would've enchanted her, but now more than ever, she wanted to win the fifteen Accomplishment Points and gain some more time with Sebastian.

Afraid she hadn't practiced enough, she mounted Chestnut with a show of bravado because horses, like dogs, sensed fear, and she had to be strong. She hardly recognized her shadow, cast on the fine gravel in front of the stable. It exuded confidence, from the tip of her riding hat with a ribbon underneath to her tight jacket, long riding habit skirts and crop tucked under her arm. The sun glistened on the Kelly-green hills, the hounds barked and horses milled about in the field, and—the stable stench snapped her back to reality. Where was Sebastian?

Her hands quivered as the footman carefully strapped the side-saddle belt across her lap. Her skirt seemed the size of a circus tent and she tucked in the heavy folds.

Grace trotted up on horseback. "Your skirt does look more un-wieldy than mine," she said.

The cameras weren't on them. "Thank you for that brilliant ob-servation," Chloe said.

"Perhaps the seamstress made a mistake on yours. You'd best not flash any leg while riding. That would be an infringement of the rules."

"And flashing a breast isn't?"

"That was an accident, Miss Parker."

"I'll say. I can only hope there won't be any accidents today." Chestnut started sniffing Grace's horse's behind. Chloe tugged at the reins, urging him to turn, and he would obey for a minute then turn his head again to sniff.

"I've spoken to Mr. Henry Wrightman about fixing your tiara. I would delight in undertaking a little project like that with him."

Chloe flinched. Now she was after Henry, too? "I'd prefer the jeweler it came from, Tiffany's, to do the fixing."

Grace seemed insulted. "I had very little to do with your tiara breaking, whilst you had everything to do with all of our Accomplish-ment Points getting wiped out. We worked weeks to acquire those points and making ink isn't exactly my forte."

"I'm sure it's not."

Grace kicked her horse and it trotted off—she was an expert rider. Chloe patted her horse's neck.

The master of the hunt, a red-faced man with a brass hunting horn tucked under his arm, headed over to Chloe. He took off his top hat and bowed toward her and the cameras.

"Our hunt awaits you, Miss Parker. Need I remind you that should you choose not to ride, you must go from whence you came?"

Chloe tapped the riding crop in the palm of her hand. The image of her whipping him with the riding crop flashed through her mind. "I do thank you for that gentle reminder," she said.

"Mr. Wrightman is quite keen on riding, and whatever woman he chooses should love to ride as well."

"Sir, I fully intend to ride. But might I ride western style?" she asked, trying to sound as 1812-ish as possible.

"I'm afraid not. Only a lady of title may choose to ride astride."

The footman led Chestnut toward the field where the rest of the riding party waited. The horse took steady, solid steps. Still, even this hunky footman couldn't hold a cheap tallow candle to Sebastian, who appeared on the field like the sun bursting from behind a cloud. There was something about a man on horseback—especially such a cultured, Oxford-educated man who also happened to be, well, a total hottie, as Emma would say.

She pictured herself and Sebastian in a white carriage festooned with pink peonies, pulled by white horses, riding off into the sunset together, he reciting poetry and—

Just then the hounds howled and Grace's gray horse sidestepped away from Henry's and toward Sebastian's. The tail on her horse whisked back and forth, brushing Sebastian's as if in shameless flirtation, as if even her horse were moving in on the guy.

Henry trotted over on his horse, and glad as she was to see him, he blocked her view of Sebastian.

"Will you manage, Miss Parker?" he asked.

What struck her was that he'd picked up on her fear.

"You have the gentlest horse in the stables."

"Let's hope he's not too gentle, I'll need some speed." She moved Chestnut backward to keep an eye on Sebastian, but Henry guided his horse closer, eclipsing Sebastian again.

"Just because he's gentle doesn't mean he's not powerful and fast," Henry said.

Chloe raised an eyebrow. "We'll have to see, then, what he's made of."

"I think you'll be quite pleased with his performance." Henry smiled.

Chloe wasn't quite sure they were sparring about Chestnut anymore, but she knew Grace was monopolizing Sebastian. Gillian, Kate, and Julia waited at the starting gate, doing the smart thing and resting their horses.

Chloe brought Chestnut forward again and stopped in full view of Sebastian. She waved good-bye to the footman, who, embarrassed, nodded awkwardly. She wasn't supposed to wave to the servants, and Henry chuckled.

"Just take it easy during the hunt, Miss Parker."

"Are you saying you don't want me to win? That ultimately you'd prefer your brother to end up with, let's say, Lady Grace, so you could spend all your holidays and birthdays with her?"

"How kind of you to think of me and my long-term happiness, Miss Parker. It's almost as if you're winning my brother over just to save me from a lifetime of misery. I'm much obliged."

"I'm always thinking of others."

"People who say they're always thinking of others are usually thinking of themselves."

Chloe sighed. As if she willed Sebastian to do it, he turned his horse away from Grace's and cantered toward her, tipping his hat. She went all aflutter, and certain swaths of her skirt unfolded.

"Have fun on the trail," she said to Henry. She brought her horse to a walk and left Henry in the dust. She patted Chestnut and gave a nod to Mrs. Crescent and Fifi under a tree on the sidelines.

"Ready for the hunt?" Chloe asked Sebastian. His designer stubble glistened in the morning sun.

He shook his head. "I'm not really a hundred percent. I've been rather out of sorts since the night of the dinner party. One of my French cooks kept the cream off the ice too long, and it went bad."

Chloe's mouth fell open. "I was sick the night of the dinner party, too."

"You were? I think we were the only two. I'm so sorry about that. It won't happen again."

"It only lasted a few hours for me." Chloe wanted to change the subject, and quick. "Perhaps you can inform me, Mr. Wrightman, what exactly it is we are hunting?"

He smiled. "It's only the smell of a fox we're after, not a real fox. The hunt master lays down the scent and trees it at the end."

"Trees the scent?"

"The hunt master will end the scent at a certain tree and the dogs will surround it, signaling the end of the hunt."

They trotted toward the gate, where the hunt master and the rest of the riders stood ready.

"I do so love the chase," Sebastian said as he adjusted his cravat. "Even if it is just a mock hunt."

"Do you prefer to chase or be chased?" Chloe asked.

"Why he prefers to be chased, of course," Grace butted in. "Isn't that why we're all here, darling? To chase you?" Sebastian looked out past the fence, toward the field. Henry slid his horse between Julia's and Chloe's.

The hunt master raised the horn to get attention and shouted. "I might remind everyone that fifteen Accomplishment Points are at stake in this race. Lady Grace, Miss Tripp, Miss Potts, and Miss Harrington lead with twenty-five Accomplishment Points each. Miss Parker has fifteen. Now, a scented trail has been laid out—along with some false leads and dead ends. Experienced riders may take the jumps. Others are advised to take the way around. Ladies are advised to keep pace with Mr. Wrightman and me if you can. Be the first to finish the race by finding the 'fox' and win. Everyone ready?" He brought the horn to his lips.

Chloe tightened her grip on the reins. "Let the chase begin," she said to no one in particular.

"I believe it already has, Miss Parker," Henry said.

"Tallyho!" shouted the hunt master. He blew the horn, the gate swung open, and the hounds came hurtling through, barking and yipping. A pounding of hooves sent a spike of determination up Chloe's back.

She gripped the reins, doing her best to stay on Sebastian's tail for what seemed like forever, until the hounds howled, the hunt master blew the horn, and the pace increased. Her riding hat flew off, and the ribbons chafed her neck, until finally she released one of her tight fists from the reins and untied the hat, letting it soar into the thicket.

Sebastian looked back at her and winked. He didn't have to ride sidesaddle, so he was able to go increasingly faster. Still, she gained on him with Chestnut. Grace's horse huffed and snorted right behind her, but Chloe knew better than to look back and lose any rhythm. The camera crew drove alongside them on ATVs.

Finally she caught up to Sebastian and leaned over, tapping him on the butt with her riding crop.

"Caught you!" she shouted.

He flashed a smile and spurred his horse to go even faster. Suddenly he turned, driving his horse off trail into the thick of the forest. Far ahead, the hunt master had stopped, his horse pointing in the direction of the yipping hounds, his hat signaling the turn.

Chloe hesitated just long enough for Grace to lunge ahead of her. Julia charged past, too. Kate and Gillian were still behind her, but Chloe realized she'd fall into second, then third, and then no place at all.

She kicked Chestnut, spurring him on, gaining on Grace, and finally passing her. But where was Sebastian? She saw his horse's backside way up ahead, and the horse seemed to be doing a jump. She couldn't do a jump, she'd have to go around, but she'd lose time. She leaned into the horse and squinted, making out a long tree trunk stretched over two stumps. Chloe's neck tightened as she bore down to steer him around it—but she had waited too long and Chestnut stumbled.

He regained his footing after they cleared the jump. Chloe inhaled as if she forgot how to breathe. Behind her, she heard Grace's horse knock the log off-kilter. Chloe almost stopped to turn around and help, but then she heard the stream of obscenities that confirmed that Grace had to be okay.

Her blood pumping, Chloe urged Chestnut on and caught up to Sebastian, but up ahead, in a ravine, she saw a black riding hat floating in the water, and it wasn't Sebastian's. She spotted Henry's horse rearing up, without anyone on him. Fear zigzagged through her. Henry was on the ground near his horse. He could get trampled. Was he hurt?

Sebastian mustn't have seen him. He clipped right by his brother.

Closer now, Chloe slowed Chestnut. Time froze as she looked to her left at Henry, who was struggling to sit up and rubbing his leg, then at Sebastian, who was galloping after the hunt master.

"Are you all right?" Chloe asked Henry.

"I'm fine! Go ahead!" Henry waved her on. "You're winning! Go!" He sat up, but didn't get up off the ground.

Chloe looked toward Sebastian. Clods of dirt flew from his horse's hooves. She frowned and brought Chestnut to a halt. The cameramen on the ATV switched their focus to Grace, who careened past and cracked her riding crop hard on her horse, spinning after Sebastian. The ATV drove alongside Grace and disappeared into the woods.

It took Chloe a while to dismount with her unwieldy skirt and Henry had meanwhile hoisted himself to his feet. He grabbed his horse's bit and calmed the horse.

Just then Julia galloped up and slowed her horse to a trot.

"Go, Julia, go ahead! Don't let Grace win!" Chloe said. "Hurry!"

Julia took off, with Gillian and Kate close behind. Kate looked back, but never said anything.

Chloe hurriedly tied Chestnut to a tree and hustled over to Henry.

"Is your leg all right?" She could see he was favoring it.

"I'll be fine. It's my horse's leg that's cut. No wonder he threw me. But it's not bad. Don't worry about me. If you go now, you still have a chance."

Blood was running from his horse's front leg. It looked like a deep gash. Chloe wasn't good with blood. The horse tossed his head up and down.

"I can't just leave you here," Chloe said. "You're both hurt."

"I can handle this. Go ahead or you'll lose! You want that money, don't you? Or Sebastian? Or both?"

It all seemed so crass, the way he put it. He whipped off his riding jacket, tossed it aside, pulled off his white muslin shirt, and ripped it into strips.

Chloe tried to avoid gaping at his abs, which also happened to be—ripped. She felt woozy, from the blood dripping down the horse's leg to his hoof, then curdling on the dirt, no doubt.

Chloe snapped to. She did her best to push up her tight sleeves. "You can't get rid of me that easily. Tell me what I can do."

Henry gave her The Look. As in The Look Mr. Darcy gave Elizabeth Bennet in virtually any film adaptation of *Pride and Prejudice* when he realized that he loved her. It was that Look along with the dive in the lake that typecast Colin Firth as romantic leading man for fifteen years, much to his chagrin. Chloe would know it anywhere, and it happened very quickly, but it was The Look.

She skipped a breath. Her riding jacket felt too tight and she stepped back.

"Here," Henry said. "You hold the bit and steady him while I wrap him up."

Henry expertly wrapped the strips of shirt like a bandage around the horse's leg, the horse whinnying and stamping as he tied it off. Blood saturated the shirt and it turned blood brown. He coiled the strips, but the blood soaked through everything.

Henry worked so quickly, so confidently, it impressed Chloe unlike anything she had seen before. He was a man who took action and took care of things, and people, and animals.

What was she thinking?! Her instinct had been to stop and help Henry, but had she made the right choice? She'd just sacrificed Sebastian, not to mention the Accomplishment Points. She thought about Abigail, the business, and her head began to spin. If she'd eaten that cow's tongue on toast for breakfast, she might have more strength—

"Miss Parker? Miss Parker?!" Henry was tapping water on her face with his hands, looking down on her from above, his face lit with a shaft of light coming through the canopy of trees. Her head was in his lap as he knelt on one knee. She heard the water lapping in the ravine. The bun of her hair rubbed right against his manhood, as they would say in the nineteenth century. Or was that just in romance novels? In a stupor, she turned toward his bare chest. His flesh felt warm against her cold, wet cheek. His pecs were impeccable. He had a pine scent about him. Or was that just the forest floor?

"Henry."

He leaned into her, she lifted her head toward him, and he kissed her with a hunger and a force that both surprised and excited her.

Just as suddenly he stopped, slowly releasing her bottom lip, and smiled. "Now you're going to tell me you didn't faint."

"I never faint."

"Clearly." He moved in for another kiss, and that was when Chloe noticed a cameraman sidestepping down the ravine toward them.

With Henry's help, she staggered to a standing position and turned to face the camera. Blood was rushing to her head. The cameraman hadn't got her head lolling in Henry's lap, had he? Henry, shirtless. Her, without her chaperone. Them kissing! What had possessed her? She broke into a shiver and her teeth began to chatter uncontrollably. This was not how she wanted it to end, not at all.

Chapter 10

"Welcome, ladies, to the second-to-last Invitation Ceremony," the butler said, rubbing his hands together like a seasoned gambler.

The cameras panned from him to the five women in gowns perched in front of the pianoforte in the drawing room at Bridesbridge Place. Their chaperones sat near the game table, fidgeting. Mrs. Crescent lowered her head to look at her locket portrait of William while Fifi twisted and turned at her feet, unable to settle down.

Even though Chloe had changed into a jonquil gown and put an ostrich feather in her hair, she still smelled of horse and muck, and she couldn't shake the thought of Henry kissing her. Okay, she was attracted to him for some reason, but what a mistake! She didn't think the cameraman had captured the kiss, or she would've heard about it. For four years she didn't have a man in her life at all and now she had two? That was one man too many. Kissing Henry? It never should've happened and she swore to herself that it never would again. Thankfully, she wouldn't have to see him tonight, because of the Invitation Ceremony. It would only be Sebastian. *Sebastian . . .* she smiled.

But it was Henry who set her, despite his hurt leg, back on her horse, and led both horses back to Bridesbridge, with a camera in tow. He got her back in time to change, wash up, and even attend to the last-minute details of the hunt tea she was hosting. If only it had been Sebastian.

Here she was dwelling on the men, and not the money!

She fingered the reticule she had sewn and trimmed herself during her sewing lessons, made of vintage maroon silk, embroidered with golden horses. It was barely big enough to hold a girl's calling cards—but able to carry a simple wish. A wish to stay.

"We have five ladies," the butler said. "And three invitations."

A footman promenaded into the room and set a silver tray on the marble table in front of the fire. Three crisp invitations lay fanned out on the tray, each sealed with a red wax W.

"Two of you will be sent home immediately." The butler looked Chloe smack in the eye.

Chloe looked down at her reticule. It was over. Tonight she'd be on her way back home, and the best she could hope for from this ordeal would be some PR for her business.

"Might I remind you," said the butler, "that Lady Grace won the foxhunt, Miss Tripp placed second, and Miss Harrington third."

Chloe sucked on her lower lip, which didn't matter because she had no lipstick on.

"The fifteen Accomplishment Points for winning the foxhunt will be awarded to . . ." He paused for dramatic effect.

Grace stood on her toes, ready to leap forward and accept her award.

". . . Miss Parker."

Chloe looked up.

"Miss Parker?" Grace whined.

The butler nodded.

All heads, with feathers and headdresses, turned toward her.

"Miss Parker wins the Accomplishment Points for making the most ladylike choice of all the contestants by stopping to help a wounded horse and Mr. Henry Wrightman, who had been thrown. Only one other lady considered helping, and that was Miss Tripp, who will be awarded five points for her considerateness. Congratulations, ladies."

Chloe smiled, Mrs. Crescent and Julia's chaperone clapped, and Chloe thought for a moment that there might be a glimmer of class in this circus of a reality show after all. She credited Sebastian, who had to be behind this turn of fate. He was a true gentleman.

"I wanted to stop, but—" Gillian started to say.

Grace gave Chloe an icy stare and whispered, "It's obvious that you care for Henry. Perhaps more than just as a potential brother-in-law?"

Chloe could feel her pinned-up hair practically standing on end. "I care for a lot of people," she replied. "But I'm here for Sebastian. I've put everything on the line for him."

The butler cleared his throat and looked into the cameras. "Before Mr. Wrightman presents these invitations, Miss Parker has arranged a posthunt tea in the back drawing room. This will allow all of you ladies to make any last impressions before he announces his decision. Best of luck."

The footmen opened the doors to the hall. Sebastian stepped in, radiating heat, and Chloe could feel herself gravitate toward him. His crisp white shirt and cravat enhanced the effect of his sun-kissed skin. He offered each of the women a red rosebud posy wrapped tightly with pink ribbon.

A certain hunger came over Chloe. In her best imitation English accent she asked, "Shall we go to tea?"

Grace locked her eyes on Sebastian, then took his arm and spoke over her shoulder to Chloe. "How did you ever manage to find the time to save the wounded *and* put a tea together Miss Parker? You are too *good.*" Her gaze shifted to Chloe's reticule. "What other tricks do you have up your sleeve—or should I say in your bag? Do tell."

Whatever did she mean by that? Even Sebastian looked confused.

Grace led Sebastian toward the hall, Kate and Gillian following in her wake. Julia took Chloe's arm and the chaperones and Fifi followed them into the back drawing room.

Hosting the tea was her way of taking control and flaunting her knowledge of Regency mores, and as far as she was concerned, a nineteenth-century aristocrat couldn't have pulled it off any better. A quartet of musicians in the corner played Mozart, the punch sparkled in a crystal bowl, and candles flickered around the silver epergnes stacked with slices of strawberry tart, rout cakes, sandwiches, a trifle, the gold-dusted confections, clotted cream, and apricot ice. Wedgwood china dishes crowned the table, a teapot warmed on the grate, and a whist table stood set and ready.

Sebastian looked impressed, or at the very least, hungry.

"I want to host a tea. Why haven't I hosted a tea?" Gillian asked her chaperone.

"You didn't think of it, dear," was the chaperone's reply.

Julia took a turn about the room with Kate.

Before anyone so much as touched a teacup, the butler suddenly announced a random reticule inspection.

So much for my being in control here, Chloe thought. "What is he talking about?" she asked Julia.

"This happened a couple weeks ago before an Invitation Ceremony," Julia whispered. "It's like a pop quiz. They want to make sure you've remembered to bring everything a lady might need at such an event."

Julia, Grace, and Kate all passed muster. They each had an array of the necessities: fan, smelling salts or vinaigrette, calling-card case. The butler opened Chloe's reticule last. He named each item as he pulled it out. "Vinaigrette. Calling-card case. Fan." Then he fell silent as he pulled something else from her bag, even though Chloe hadn't put anything else in there. It was a small, square black packet with serrated edges. At the sight of the glistening wrapper, horror flashed through Chloe. It was a condom! What was it doing in there? She had left the condoms in her valise back at the inn!

Grace gasped. "Oh my." She fanned herself.

The butler held the little packet up high so everyone could see it. It took a while for the crowd to make out what it was, then the room went abuzz.

Chloe squinted. It wasn't one of the strawberry-margarita-flavored condoms Emma had given her. This one had a black wrapper. She looked at Grace, who smiled. In an instant, she knew that Grace had planted it on her, and that was it. The end of ladylike behavior toward Grace.

"That's not mine," Chloe said to the butler. "Someone must've planted it on me. I'd never smuggle something like that in here, and even if I did, would I bring it to the tea party I myself am hosting? It doesn't make any sense."

The butler nodded in agreement. "Still, you have no proof that anyone 'planted' this on you, as you claim, Miss Parker. If you had proof, that would be a different story."

"Likewise there isn't any proof that it is mine," Chloe said.

"It was in your reticule," Grace pointed out.

Mrs. Crescent spoke. "I can attest to the fact that my charge did not smuggle any such thing in here. She has been set up. I stake my reputation on it." Fifi barked in agreement.

The butler looked stymied. "This item will be confiscated and we will determine how to proceed. For now, let the tea party resume."

Chloe frowned. She vowed to get proof—whatever that might be. Talk about awkward. Well, she'd wanted to make an impression on Sebastian, and she sure had.

Grace fanned her way to a settee, patted a cushion next to her, and urged Sebastian to sit. "I've never been to an American tea before, have you, Mr. Wrightman?"

Sebastian opened his mouth to speak, but appeared to have second thoughts on the subject and remained silent.

Grace had pushed Chloe too far. Chloe held up a punch glass. "Lady Grace, would you like a punch?" she asked ingenuously.

"How amusing. I prefer tea, thank you."

Chloe reached for the teapot on the grate, but the butler beat her to it. "Allow me," he said.

"If this is an American tea party, then I find it quite charming." It was Henry, interjecting from behind the fireplace screen. He rose out of a high-backed chair and bowed to the women and the chaperones.

"I—I didn't expect you to be here," Chloe said.

"Indeed you did not," he replied. "I had to ask the servants to bring an extra tea setting."

She couldn't look him in the eye, even as he came closer.

"Still, you seem to have thought of every other detail. Like you said, you didn't know I'd be here." Under his breath he said, "Did you think I'd miss your hostessing debut?"

Chloe cooled her sweaty palms on her punch glass.

"Mr. Wrightman," Grace said to Henry. She left Sebastian to take Henry by the arm. "I've been meaning to remind you about a little silversmithing project I have for us to work on together. You're so good with your hands, I thought of your talents right away. Might I have a word with you in private?"

She stole Henry away from Chloe while Gillian slid in next to Sebastian. Chloe stood alone with an empty punch cup in her hand. She didn't like Grace slithering away with Henry like that, but she set her sights on Sebastian.

Suddenly something brushed against her leg. Next thing she knew, something warm and furry was pushing against her calf. It startled her, and her punch cup slipped out of her gloved hands and crashed on the floor. It was Fifi—humping Chloe's stockinged leg with wild abandon. Chloe lifted her gown, trying to shake the dog off. The quartet stopped playing, but Fifi kept going. First the condom, now the dog? This was not the way her elegant tea party was supposed to go.

"Fifi," Mrs. Crescent yelled. "Come back here to Mother." She waddled over to her dog.

Fifi kept humping away with unusual tenacity even as Mrs. Crescent detached him from Chloe's leg. Chloe felt her cheeks flushing red with embarrassment and she swooped down to pick up the shards of glass.

Grace chimed in from across the room: "It seems everyone and his dog is attracted to Miss Parker."

"Poor Fifi." Mrs. Crescent held the quivering dog. "It's always the same this time of year for him."

A maid plucked the glass shards from Chloe's open hand and cleaned up the remaining slivers from the floor. Chloe could feel Sebastian staring at her while Henry looked politely away, and into the fire. She stepped backward. Somehow her gloved hand landed in the bowl of clotted cream on the tea table behind her.

Grace, moving closer for a better look, laughed. "Is this a typical American tea party?" she asked. "How provincial."

Chloe boiled over like a forgotten teapot. She imagined smearing the clotted cream all over Grace's face. Nothing would've made her happier. She edged closer to her rival.

"Miss Parker. Please, dear, protocol." Mrs. Crescent wedged herself between the women, but her belly ended up bumping Chloe's arm and the clotted cream smudged Grace's arm.

"I do apologize," Chloe said. "That was an accident."

Another cameraman rushed in from the hall and suddenly they were surrounded by three cameras. Grace lunged toward the table, reached for a miniature mince pie, and dropped it onto Chloe's shoe.

"Oh. I'm sorry. Really. That was an accident, too."

"Oh, dear Lord, another pair of shoes ruined," Mrs. Crescent groaned as Fifi, in an unexpected show of loyalty, growled at Grace.

Without even looking down, Chloe plated a slice of strawberry tart. "I see the mince pie does not appeal to you. Perhaps a tart would be more apropos?" She handed the plate to Grace, who did not take it. Eventually Julia took it and promptly ate it up.

Grace picked up a goblet of apricot ice. "Here's something even an ice queen like you might enjoy, Miss Parker."

Chloe plucked two gold-dusted confections from the sweets plate and set them on a small dish. "Perhaps the lady would like these? She seems to enjoy digging for gold."

Mrs. Crescent breathed heavily and began fanning herself furiously. "Miss Gately, the good Miss Gately would never, never behave like this," was all she could manage to expostulate.

Henry took a sip of his punch. "I daresay this is the most amusing tea party I've ever attended," he observed.

Sebastian turned to look at Julia.

Chloe smiled to herself. It was a smackdown, nineteenth-century style.

Kate sneezed three times. "Were there strawberries in those rout cakes?" she asked. "I must stay away from strawberries."

"There aren't any strawberries in the rout cakes! The strawberries are in the strawberry tart!" Chloe rubbed her forehead and signaled to the quartet to start playing.

Amid the cacophony of the musicians tuning up their instruments, Henry approached Chloe. "Are you all right?" he said with obvious concern.

"I sure didn't see that coming." Chloe glared at Grace.

"None of us did," Henry said. Under his breath he added, "But you have to realize we've all been here awhile, and some of us are on edge. They miss home. Family. Friends."

And Chloe didn't miss anyone? How could he say something like that? She thought about smearing his face with clotted cream. Getting him away from her would solve a myriad of her problems. He kept usurping time she should be spending with Sebastian, and with an Invitation Ceremony just minutes away, he was putting her position in jeopardy. She had to make it clear to everyone that she had no romantic inclinations toward Henry, and maybe she had to do it for herself more than for anyone else.

In a very calm, but firm and rather loud tone, she said to him, "You don't know anything about me, Mr. Henry Wrightman." Even as she spoke, the memory of his lips upon hers rose up in her mind. "*Nothing*. And I prefer to keep it that way, thank you very much." She ripped herself away from him, and practically fell into the hands of Mrs. Crescent and Fiona, who did their best to make her presentable again.

Sebastian, meanwhile, was leaning against the fireplace mantel, watching Grace's chaperone and maid rush to her aid. Fifi was wagging his tail while Julia looked out the window. But Grace wasn't finished with Chloe yet.

"Tell Mr. Wrightman what happened in the forest this morning with Henry, Miss Parker!" she said.

"Nothing happened, as you all well know." There was no proof— of anything.

Grace laughed. "Perhaps Miss Parker has designs on your younger brother," she said to Sebastian. "Perhaps she means to use the item found in her reticule after all."

Heat rose to Chloe's cheeks as an inevitable image surfaced in her mind's eye, of herself and Henry writhing together naked. She raged at Grace. "You're absolutely wrong, Lady Grace. I have no intention of the kind with *Henry!*"

Mrs. Crescent buried her head in her hands. Fifi whimpered.

Sebastian's brows came together. He glared at Chloe and Henry.

Sebastian oozed testosterone, and Chloe realized that he could probably beat the crap out of Henry should he wish to.

Henry paced the floor. "I think Miss Parker has made it quite clear that she has no designs on me whatsoever."

Chloe leaned against the tea table. She felt light-headed.

Sebastian crossed the room and glowered into the fireplace. If she didn't convince him that the condom had been planted in her reticule and that she felt no attraction to Henry, she'd be sent home knowing she hadn't given it her best shot. She followed Sebastian. "What I did for Henry during the foxhunt, I would've done for anyone here, including you, Grace."

Fifi barked in agreement. Mrs. Crescent rubbed her belly.

Henry buttoned his coat.

The cameras surrounded Chloe and Sebastian. The glow of the fire made his tanned face look even darker. Chloe plopped down in the settee near him, but springs hadn't been invented in 1812, and it didn't give, hurting her butt, already tender from the morning's horse ride. She was losing him, she saw it in his smoky eyes. Him, the man who had chosen her from so many thousands of other women, who had given her the gift of paints and paper, a poem even. Well, the closest thing to a poem any man had ever written for her. She gulped. "I hope you'll give me a chance. Get to know me a bit more."

Sebastian's eyes went glassy. "I believe I have gotten to know you more." He stared into the fire. He seemed to have made his decision.

"But you don't understand. If this is about Henry, you have to realize, I talk to him mainly to find out more about you. To get to know you better. He's a doorway to you." This was, of course, only partly true, and Chloe knew it.

"Speaking of doorways . . . if you will excuse me." Henry bowed and left before the ladies even had a moment to curtsy.

Chloe felt the emptiness he left behind.

"Time for the Invitation Ceremony," the butler announced.

Chloe stepped back toward the door, her bare shoulders cold.

The butler opened the doors. "Ladies."

Chloe had failed to get through to Sebastian. She hadn't gotten a chance to eat any of the delicious confections she'd made either. The bullet pudding had gone untouched, a symbol of the fiasco this supposedly festive occasion had turned into. And to top it off, she'd lost Henry.

The butler tapped the condom in his pocket. "After you, Miss Parker."

She was the last member of the party to leave. She needed a drink, and not just a lame two-hundred-year-old lemony-watery punch with a splash of champagne. What she needed was a massive modern martini.

No drinks and only a few minutes later, Gillian, Chloe, Julia, Kate, and Grace stood poised in front of the pianoforte, all cleaned up and smoothed over. While the cameras rolled, Sebastian paced on the far side of the room, and everyone tried to ignore the three cream-colored invitations on a silver tray.

In Chloe's imagination, Sebastian would see her innocence on all fronts, fling two invitations into the fireplace, waltz right up to her, and present her with the remaining envelope. "It's you," he would declare. "It's always been you. Take this invitation. *Take me!*" He would sweep her up off her feet and— But that wasn't going to happen. Not by a long shot.

Instead Sebastian cleared his throat. "Let me begin by saying . . ." He paused for the camera and lifted one of the invitations. "This was one of the most difficult decisions I've ever had to make." He shifted from one side to the other in his Hessian boots. "You are all very attractive women, with equally—interesting personalities." He looked right at Chloe.

Zing. Chloe felt that one. *Interesting* was never good in guy language, whether Regency or contemporary. She also became acutely aware of her pungent body odor. That was what no showers, horseback riding, and sweating bullets at tea-party debacles did to a girl.

Sebastian looked down at the invitation in his hand, his long, thick eyelashes practically brushing against his aristocratic cheekbones. The room was completely still, the flames of the fire providing the only semblance of movement, and it was so quiet you could hear a nineteenth-century needle drop. He looked up. "Lady Grace."

Voom. One video cam swung to shoot Grace sauntering up to Sebastian while another recorded the expressions on the other girls' faces.

Chloe clenched her gloved fists. In the corner of the room, her sewing box sat unlatched, the fireplace screen she had only just started seeming to mock her. She would leave so much unfinished here if she had to go now. It wasn't just about the money anymore, she realized that. She was willing to gamble it all—her business, her precious time with Abigail, and even her friendship with Henry—for this, for Sebastian, and all the possibility of him. His quiet dignity, his perseverance throughout this process, his romantic gestures with riddles and silhouettes and packages wrapped in gold in a castle keep.

"Lady Grace, will you accept this invitation?" Sebastian asked in an almost singsong voice.

"Of course." Grace slid the invitation from his hand, eyed him up and down, then curtsied.

He bowed and watched her butt as she walked back.

Chloe cringed. She blocked out any thoughts of Sebastian and Grace hooking up; the possibility made her nauseous.

Grace took her spot next to Chloe, pressing the invitation to her chest.

"Miss Tripp."

Of course he chose Julia, Chloe thought. Who wouldn't? Lithe, enthusiastic Julia deserved to stay on. Plus, she didn't have a scandal, real or imagined, attached to her name. Chloe looked straight at Sebastian now and rose on tiptoe in her satin slippers, on the edge of the carpet, on the edge of everything.

The butler lunged in front of Sebastian. "Ladies, before Mr. Wrightman presents the final invitation, it has been determined that, for hosting the hunt tea, Miss Parker will gain only ten of the fifteen Accomplishment Points, due to unladylike behavior. The reticule inspection adds five points to everyone's score except hers. Nevertheless, Miss Parker currently leads with a score of forty points, Miss Tripp with thirty-five, and the rest of the women are tied at thirty points each. Consider carefully, Mr. Wrightman, the behavior you've witnessed tonight. I can assure you that the ratings online indicate that Miss Tripp is the favored contestant, and in choosing her to stay on, you have chosen wisely."

The butler turned toward the women. "Mr. Wrightman will now present the final invitation. Two of you will be sent home tonight. Mr. Wrightman, if you please."

Chloe, Gillian, and Kate took a step forward together. Chloe could feel the beads of sweat running down her back and in the sour taste that filled her mouth, even though she'd brushed with her swine's-hair toothbrush and chalky powder less than an hour ago.

"Miss Harrington . . ." Sebastian said.

Kate practically skipped up to him. Chloe's neck went limp and her chin hit her chest. Of course it was Kate, who, despite her allergies, seemed rather sweet. Chloe had blown it. As recently as a few days ago, she might not have cared so much, but at the moment she felt completely devastated.

". . . and Miss Potts."

Chloe was confused. There was only one invitation.

Sebastian took Kate's and Gillian's hands in his own. "You both are wonderful, amazing women, and you will find someone who de-serves you. But I'm afraid I must ask you to take your leave of Brides-bridge Place."

Chloe lifted her chin. On their way back to their spots, Gillian sneered at Chloe and Kate looked dumbfounded.

Sebastian picked up the last invitation from the silver salver. "Miss Parker . . ." He extended the invitation toward her.

Chloe's shoulders slumped with relief. He got it, she realized. He got *her*. Maybe he even believed her story about the condom, and about her lack of feelings for Henry. She stumbled, but didn't fall on the edge of the carpet. Behind her, as she padded toward Sebastian, she could hear Kate blowing her nose.

Sebastian looked down on her with a half smile. "Miss Parker, will you accept this invitation to stay on?"

"I do." Chloe took the envelope. The heft of the handmade paper in her hand felt good and right. "I—I mean I will!" She laughed. He crinkled his nose, and remembering both her bad breath and nineteenth-century protocol, she fumbled a curtsy as she breathed out of her nose. He bowed. As much as she wanted to talk to Sebas-tian, to stay with him, she forced herself to turn and walk back to her spot. It was enough to know that he trusted her. Now that the trust was there, they could build on it—spires into the sky.

"Ladies," said the butler. "Mr. Wrightman has made his decision. You may say your good-byes."

This time, the good-byes were not as difficult for Chloe. Imogene had been her closest friend here, and she was gone. Gillian and Kate, by comparison, were easy to let go.

"Miss Potts, Miss Harrington, your carriage is waiting," said the butler.

Sebastian turned to Chloe, Grace, and Julia. "Good night, ladies. I look forward to our next encounter." With that, he escorted Gillian and Kate out the door.

Outside the sash windows, the afternoon sun was fading fast and maids began to scurry around inside to light the candles while footmen lit the torches outside. Grace sat down at the pianoforte and pounded out an English reel. A maid set a candelabrum on the piano and lit it.

Mrs. Crescent waddled over to Chloe, fanning herself from face to pregnant belly. The white ruffles of her cap wagged right along with Fifi's tail. "I don't know how you managed it." She squeezed Chloe's hand.

She'd managed it by sacrificing Henry, and already she began concocting ways to rectify that situation. He, and his good opinion of her, meant more to her than she had thought, and it made the victory bittersweet.

The carriage pulled away from the house, lumbering toward the road.

"Whatever could be wrong?" Mrs. Crescent asked.

"I'm missing—a friend," Chloe said.

"Miss Wells? She was never your friend," Mrs. Crescent whispered.

That wasn't who she'd been thinking of. Wait a minute. "She wasn't?"

Mrs. Crescent shook her head. "We're not here to make friends. Nobody's here to make friends. Nobody here is your friend! It's not about friendship; we're here to win. And we're on our way. Well done! Let's go. We have needlework to do." She nodded toward the hall.

"But it's Sunday—bath day, right? I've been looking forward to a bath!"

Mrs. Crescent shook her head. "No, dear, due to the foxhunt, bath day has been postponed."

"Postponed? Until when?! How much longer can a girl wait?" Chloe was beside herself.

"Waiting, dear," Mrs. Crescent declared, "is the name of the game."

Chapter 11

*C*hloe took a candelabrum into the dark hall, stopping by a painting of roses to wait for Mrs. Crescent and Fifi. The candlelight seemed to illuminate the thorns in the painting more than it did the roses, and Chloe felt a chill come over her.

The cameras weren't following them, so as soon as Mrs. Crescent and Fifi caught up to her, Chloe spoke quickly. "I was terribly rude and unladylike to Henry. I need to set things straight." She blew out a candle with her breath. A wisp of smoke curled between them.

"My dear Miss Parker, you won this round. Lord knows how, but you won it. With the new Accomplishment Points you've gained, you've earned another outing with Mr. Wrightman. You're leading the way with forty points. There's no need to talk to Henry."

"But Henry's an important ally. He could influence Sebastian against me. It's a delicate situation."

A footman sped by while she was speaking, his livery coat askew, cravat untied. He yanked on his drawer strings with one hand, sported a candlestick in the other, and then dropped his cravat in a wicker laundry basket at the top of the servant stairs.

Mrs. Crescent cleared her throat. "You must wait, like a lady, for Sebastian to make the next move. And forget about Henry. Put the notion of visiting out of your head, or you'll get us both booted out of here."

Candle wax dripped onto Chloe's thumb. "Ow!"

The footman returned to plunk his hat into the basket.

"That's it!" Chloe snapped her fingers. "What about—having a footman deliver a message?"

Mrs. Crescent stooped over to pick up Fifi and sighed on her way up the stairs. The candle flames in the candelabrum bent with her exhale and almost went out. "You know you can't write a letter to a man unless you're engaged."

"There wouldn't be a letter. I'd just have a footman deliver a verbal message. We have to—push the envelope. You know how Grace is. We have to bend the rules, not break them. You want us to win, right?"

"It's not proper."

Chloe knew Mrs. Crescent was right and she leaned against the cold wall. Her right to talk, to communicate, had been stripped away, and she stood helpless, imprisoned in a glorified prom gown. She was a modern woman after all, used to her freedoms of movement and expression. This was exasperating!

At that moment Grace, lips pursed and armed with her own candelabrum, swooshed by the two of them with all the attitude of a model in a Victoria's Secret commercial. She tugged at her bodice and smoothed her gown. "You're such a *good* girl with your chaperone," she sneered in Chloe's ear. Her berry-stained lips were smudged. Chloe's candelabrum went out completely as Grace turned the corner. Two cameramen trailed Grace's flowing gown.

"At least I won't get gonorrhea or—pregnant!" Chloe coundn't keep herself from muttering.

Mrs. Crescent shushed her.

Grace was, by Chloe's standards, a strumpet, and she had no doubt that the girl had just added another notch to her calling-card case by dallying with yet another footman.

But maybe Grace was right, after all, and Chloe was being too good. Despite Mrs. Crescent's advice, she knew she had to be proactive, aggressive. Grace had planted a condom in her reticule and gotten away with it, for God's sake! At the very least, she had to protect—herself.

With their candelabra snuffed out, Chloe and Mrs. Crescent had no choice but to feel their way through the hall, back to the drawing room. The fire in the fireplace and the candelabra in the room were flickering on the ornate gold frames of the paintings. Mrs. Crescent opened the walnut sewing cabinet, pulling out Chloe's floss and needles.

"Needlework? Haven't I endured enough punishment for one day?" Chloe asked.

Grace was sleeping with the footmen, and here she was, doing her needlework!

She fingered the irregular, loose stitches in her embroidery. Miss Gately's fireplace screen stood finished in the corner, a testament to her accomplishments. Uniformly stitched peonies blossomed on a red background, while the robins in Chloe's embroidery looked more like rats. But then again, she had just started to learn this craft, and she was here and Miss Gately—wasn't. Grace, though, was still here, too, and so was Julia.

The butler brought the tea things in and Chloe wondered what he had done with that condom anyway.

"Thank you," Mrs. Crescent said, "I'll pour." As soon as he left, Mrs. Crescent shot Chloe a serious look. "We made the cut. You deserve a cup of tea for all your efforts." She handed Chloe a teacup full of plain, room-temperature water.

"You forgot to run the tea leaves through it."

"No, I didn't, dear. Just try it before the cameras find us."

Chloe sipped and practically spit the liquid all over her embroidery. "Vodka?" she cried. "Vodka! Where in the world did you get it?"

"Ah, the benefits of doing one's needlework." Mrs. Crescent gestured toward a vodka bottle in the recesses of the locked sewing cabinet. She shut the cabinet door and collapsed on the double settee.

Chloe thought of adding a twist of lemon from her deodorant supply, then slammed the vodka and helped herself to two more, all just before a cameraman arrived on the scene. "Cheers, Mrs. Crescent. Here's to you. And needlework." She hadn't eaten anything all day, and the booze went right to her head.

Mrs. Crescent shook a finger at her. "You must drink your tea like a civilized lady. Slowly. And that's all the 'tea' you're getting—tonight."

Chloe tried to nurse her vodka as best she could. "Mrs. Crescent, is there a garden somewhere around here with something in it that casts shadows and light?"

Mrs. Crescent locked the sewing cabinet with a key she kept in her reticule. "I daresay I regret giving you that tea."

Chloe sipped from the teacup. "Or, perhaps there is a clock somewhere in this house with a garden painted on it?"

Mrs. Crescent shook her head and rubbed her belly. "Oh, dear."

The vodka warmed Chloe, raising her spirits and her confidence, and loosening her Regency restraint. She knew she needed to take action.

The clock in the hall struck eleven, the women's curfew. Only the men could be out and about at this hour. As Chloe looked out the window, a star-filled sky seemed to beckon to her. The vodka had dulled her rational side just enough for her to follow her impulses.

"Time for us to turn in," Mrs. Crescent announced.

Chloe moped toward the doorway, and being rather drunk, she accidentally kicked over the wicker laundry basket. As she put the laundry back in, it hit her.

She could go over to Dartworth, legally—dressed as a man! She hoisted the basket to her hip, balancing it and her candelabra, then leaped up the steps and clicked her door shut in a most ladylike way.

After she stirred the fire to warm up her room, the air of which felt brisk even on this summer night, she lifted a pair of footman's knee breeches from the laundry basket and held them up against her waist. She wouldn't really be breaking the rules if she were a "man." The trick was to bend the rules and not get caught, just as Grace did with drinking her nightly wine, shagging the good-looking footmen, and God only knew what else.

Maybe it was the vodka talking, but after she pulled on the footman's white stockings, snug-fitting breeches, and brass-buttoned jacket and tucked her hair into the footman's black hat, she cocked her head in the floor mirror and decided she looked like quite a hot little footman. After days of wearing dresses, the pants felt liberating, sexy even. Chloe smiled in the mirror. If Grace could have closed-door interludes with footmen at the drop of a tricornered hat, then Chloe could go for a walk after eleven o'clock disguised as a man.

She stuffed her bed with pillows, pulled the velvet coverlet over them, and snuffed out the candles. By the light of the fireplace she opened her window to the thick darkness outside. "This is crazy. I came here to win the money and I'm losing my heart to two men." She said it out loud. *There*. She'd admitted it. It had to come to this for her to realize.

Outside there were no streetlights, no lights on the front of the house—no wonder a girl wasn't allowed to roam at this hour. A few torches, though, burned in front of the main door. Opting not to break a leg, she decided not to jump out the second-story window. Instead she waited for all the women's doors to click shut, and stocking-footed, shoes in hand, she sneaked down the servants' staircase all the way to the basement kitchen. Cook's eyeglasses, she noticed, were lying on the pine table. Chloe put them on in hopes of bettering her disguise. For a moment the glasses blurred her vision, but then the fuzziness cleared. She slipped out the kitchen door without anyone noticing. Once she was outside, the cool evening air sobered her, but only for a minute. She pulled on her shoes and groped her way toward the torches.

As she followed the stone wall of Bridesbridge Place, feeling her way toward the light, she saw a candle appear in a window on the second floor, then the window opened, and *whoosh*—a chambermaid dumped a washbasin of water out the window. Chloe jumped back, but it splashed on her calfskin walking shoes. Dots of mud sprayed onto her white tights. The window slammed shut.

"Damn!" Chloe whispered to herself. "Talk about getting cold feet." She stepped around what she'd bet was the cold water Grace had just washed her face in. "Forget this." So much for bending the rules. She decided to shelve this idea.

"Who's there?" A night watchman raised his torch, pacing atop the steps of the main entry.

Too late to go back now.

Chloe lowered her voice. "Hullo! Just a footman out for a walk." She yanked on one of the torches, and finally, like the sword in the stone, the thing came out of the ground. It was taller than she was, and heavier than she thought. She almost fell over.

"Here now!" the watchman called out, squinting his eyes to see her better. "Since you're out, you may as well deliver this to Mr. Sebastian Wrightman." He handed her a letter and a lantern, and took the torch. Now she had a mission and she considered this to be a sign.

As the watchman came closer, he screwed up his mouth and

squinted at her. "Promise me you'll bring it directly, no stopping for a thimbleful of drink along the way?"

"Promise." Chloe spun around, wanting to say as little as possible, and headed toward Dartworth before the watchman had a chance to question her further.

Her shoes sank into the mud as she pointed herself toward the flickering torches in front of Dartworth Hall far off in the distance. Her shoes made a slight squishing sound in the mud. Despite her nerves and her shaking hand, she tried to enjoy her newfound freedom without a chaperone. And she was out after dark. She hoisted the lantern high, but it didn't feel right. She wasn't like Grace. She couldn't break rules any more easily than she could break hearts.

The lantern helped her see, but the light it cast was limited at best. She'd never take streetlights for granted again. She almost turned back because the darkness scared her, but she knew that the night watchman had his eye on her and there was no going back. Trees creaked, owls hooted, and something rustled in the woods along the path. The footpath to Dartworth Hall certainly was a lot longer than it looked from her bedchamber window. Just then a nearly full moon burst from behind a cloud and shed a blue light on everything.

When she looked back over her shoulder to see how far she'd gone—*wham!* She slammed right into a panel of glass and her tricornered hat almost fell off her head. Her shoulder hurt, but at least the glass wasn't broken. She raised her lantern and discovered she'd bumped into a greenhouse, a massive greenhouse from the looks of it. The glass felt warm and moist on her palm. She wiped away the condensation and shone her torch on strawberries growing on a vine inside. Standing back, she looked up, hoisted her lantern, and made out leaded-glass windows.

After days of forcing down mutton, rubbery little potatoes, and peacock presented with the head still on, she'd been craving fruit. Forbidden fruit!

She heard hurried footsteps and a night watchman from Dart-worth Hall came running up with his lantern. "Hullo there," he called. "What is it, boy? Come from Bridesbridge at this hour? On foot?"

Chloe bowed her head, lowered her voice, and presented the let-ter. "I—I have a letter for Mr. Wrightman, sir."

"Do ya now?" The watchman looked at her askance. "You don't look familiar to me, boy."

"I'm new at Bridesbridge."

"You'll have to bring the letter in yourself. The front-door foot-men have gone to bed. He's in the billiards room. Catty-corner from the main dining room. Follow the large hall and stay right."

Chloe's shadow, with her thin legs and ankles, did look rather boylike and the coat hid her hips better than any slimming under-wear ever could, although, as a result of the rigors of a Regency diet, she'd already lost the seven pounds she'd been needing to lose for quite some time.

She set her lantern down and bounded up the marble steps—the hundreds and hundreds of steps shining in the blue moonlight. It was too delicious to be true. She'd have Sebastian all to herself—dressed in her cute little footman outfit! And as an added bonus, she could find Henry and apologize to him. She skipped through the open doorway and into the foyer, dimly lit by a few sconces on the walls. The candled chandeliers were out for the night, but a candelabrum stood on the foyer credenza and she picked it up.

She hurried past the dark library, dining room, and drawing rooms and followed the sound of men's laughter in the distance.

As she approached a brightly lit doorway in front of which a foot-man sat slumped in a chair, apparently sleeping, Chloe saw a massive mahogany pool table. Sebastian was sprawled in a chair, cognac in hand, smartphone in his lap—smartphone!? Henry was reading a book. George paced back and forth with his hands on his hips.

She lunged toward the door, hoping to hightail it out of there, but the footman chose that moment to wake up and blocked her with his arm. "What do you want?" he demanded.

Chloe handed him the letter, but he didn't take it. "Delivery from Bridesbridge."

"Sebastian, finish tweeting!" George commanded from behind the doors.

The footman shoved Chloe back into the dark hall and into his wooden chair, where she couldn't see anything. He clicked the double doors shut behind him and left her in the dark.

She heard muffled voices. What the hell? She didn't even have a toilet and they were tweeting?

One of the double doors suddenly swung open, casting light on Chloe's mud-spattered tights.

"You may come in," the footman announced, and he spun off. Like in a bad dream, Chloe wanted to move but couldn't. Finally, she took a deep breath and stepped into the room. The stench of snuff filled the air. Under a high rococo ceiling, a claw-footed pool table dominated the interior. The side tables were littered with wine decanters, snuffboxes, and chocolates. Her eyes scanned the room for the phone and George, but both were gone.

"Well, my boy," Sebastian slurred as he leaned against his pool cue. "What brings you here at such an ungodly hour?"

The vodka, Chloe realized, was starting to wear off, and goose bumps were beginning to pop up and down her arms. Thank God there weren't any cameramen around. Maybe the camera crew had turned in for the night.

Sebastian's eyes looked a little glassy. He had been drinking, and this bolstered her courage. "A delivery." Chloe handed him the letter.

Henry closed his book and furrowed his brows at her.

Chloe stepped back, wary.

Then Henry's lips curled into a smile. If he'd seen through her disguise, he didn't seem upset at her. "What is your name—boy?" he asked.

"Charles—sir." Chloe bowed her head and pushed Cook's glasses up the bridge of her nose.

"Charles. Right. Do take off your hat, Charles."

"No—no, thank you, sir, I cannot stay."

"Fancy a drink?" Henry asked.

Chapter 12

Sebastian bent over the red-wool-covered billiard table. While his leather-tipped cue stick thrust toward the eight ball, he leaned forward and his tight "inexpressibles" left Chloe unable to express—anything. The floor-to-ceiling Merlot velvet draperies provided a stunning backdrop for his unruly black hair, crisp white shirt, and tanned face. "You cannot offer a servant a drink, Henry," he said, and with a click, the eight ball sank the seven into the right corner pocket.

Chloe locked her knees to keep them from turning to white soup in her footman stockings.

Another footman unglued himself from the wall next to a flowery tapestry to pour more red wine into Henry's and Sebastian's depleted glasses.

Henry set his book aside, stood, and chalked his cue stick. "True. Personally, I would not want Charles to be sent packing." He looked Chloe up and down, head to mud-splattered toe. "All for a mere moment or two of immediate gratification."

Chloe tugged at her cravat; she must've tied it too tight, it suddenly seemed. She tried to clear her head, then her throat, and lowered her voice an octave or two, directing her words to Sebastian. "I most certainly do not want to be sent home, sir," she said. "I am quite honored to be here. It is such a—stimulating—experience." She wanted his attention, after all.

Sebastian stared at the pool table, not at her.

Henry scoped out his shot. "Have you had many similarly stimulating experiences in your young lifetime, Charles?" He looked up at her with mischief in his eye.

"This definitely ranks as one of the most stimulating."

Henry raised an eyebrow, then made his shot. The resounding clunk reminded Chloe of her impending doom should Henry decide to rat her out.

Two balls sank in the left corner pocket. Henry wouldn't expose her before she had a chance to apologize, would he? She'd have to pack her trunks tonight if he did. Her livery coat felt heavy.

Sebastian slid dangerously close to Chloe, reaching above her head for a tin of snuff on a high shelf. The seam of his shirtsleeves fell just below his broad shoulders and his undone cravat hung carelessly around his collarbone. "My foot hurts, for some reason or another." He kicked his boot up onto a chair.

"Gout," Henry said. "Too much red meat and red wine, Sebastian."

Sebastian shot a fleeting glance at Chloe. "What is it, my boy?" He looked good even when shoving snuff up his nostril and sniffing into his sleeve.

Chloe swallowed, pushing Cook's glasses up the bridge of her nose, careful to lower her voice to the proper level. "I have it on good authority, sir, that the item found in Miss Parker's reticule was planted there and I vouch for her innocence. It's not in her character to do such a thing."

Sebastian was stalking the billiard table, hunting out his next move. "Of course we know that. We're not taken in by the ridiculous shenanigans that must go on among those women at Bridesbridge Place."

This was a revelation, although a bit derogatory toward the women.

Across the room, near the fire, Henry again raised his wineglass, breathed in the bouquet, and set it aside. Chloe could practically taste the wine rolling past her tongue, down her throat . . . If only she could have another drink to steel her nerves.

"Exactly what *is* Miss Parker's character?" Henry asked. He walked toward her, leaned on the edge of the billiard table, and looked her straight in the eye.

No guy had ever asked her that kind of question before. A lightning bolt of fear cracked through her as Sebastian took his shot, and a ball ricocheted off the side of the table, but missed the pocket.

"Do tell, Charles," Sebastian said. "I'd quite like to know myself."

Henry took off his glasses, folded them, and placed them atop the mantel. "I assume you're around her enough to know the answer." He smiled, and for the first time, Chloe noticed a dimple on the left side of his clean-shaven cheek. And his sideburns were cut so perfectly.

She spun to face Sebastian, who was chalking his cue stick. Now was her chance to lay it all out on the neoclassical mahogany billiard table. "Miss Parker, from what I can tell, seems fabulous. She's the living embodiment of all the best old-fashioned values." Chloe folded her gloved hands behind her back. Candles were suspended from some kind of contraption above the billiard table, their wax dripping into the tray underneath; she noticed that the fixture didn't provide much light, and breathed a sigh of relief.

Sebastian walked over to his empty wineglass. "I'm not sure I believe all this balderdash."

Henry spoke from behind her. "One of those values being—honesty? Another being—loyalty to her friends?"

Chloe again pushed Cook's glasses up the bridge of her nose. "Yes and yes. She seems very honest and good to everyone around her."

"Of course, dear Charles," Henry said, "you've only just arrived at Bridesbridge. What would you know?"

Chloe sucked in her cheeks.

Sebastian held his empty wineglass out to the footman, who filled it, and almost as quickly, Sebastian drank it.

Chloe put her hand to her heart.

"Sebastian, no more wine for you," Henry said. He slid the glass out of Sebastian's hand. "Will that be all, Charles?"

Did Chloe just hear a shuffle in the hall? She'd better be quick. Sebastian was tipsy, and now was her chance, so she leaned in toward Henry and whispered, "Miss Parker wants to apologize to you for her harsh words during the tea party," she blurted out. "She values your friendship very much and sincerely regrets what she said."

Sebastian slumped into a chair.

Henry gave his brother a sidelong glance. "Sebastian's had a rough day," he observed.

Chloe spoke faster. "May I tell Miss Parker that you accept her apology?"

Henry was silent.

"Consider the pressure she's been under. She's quite a nice person and deserves a second chance."

Henry cracked a smile. "Coming from you, Charles, that's a very objective endorsement, and one to be taken quite seriously."

Chloe unlocked her knees and couldn't help but laugh.

Sebastian sank deeper in his chair, barely awake.

Henry stepped right up to Chloe and leaned on his pool cue.

Chloe wanted this kind of attention from Sebastian, not from him.

Henry smirked. "Pray tell Miss Parker I will consider her apology.

I appreciate the trouble she has gone to in order to express her sentiments. She put herself quite at risk by sending you here, Charles."

Chloe realized she'd just prioritized Henry over the money, and it shocked her almost as much as it apparently shocked him.

Henry eyed her up and down. "I have to say, though, Charles, you are the most adroit little footman I've ever seen. I'll inquire if we can hire you here at Dartworth. It just so happens that I need a new valet. Would you be interested in the position?" He almost brushed his hand against her cheek.

A valet dressed—and undressed—his master. Chloe stopped herself from mentally undressing Henry right then and there.

"I'm quite happy at Bridesbridge at the moment," she replied modestly.

"I understand. Just let me know if you change your mind," Henry said.

As he was speaking, the doors behind him opened and a videocam crew came filing in. Henry guided Chloe toward the door. "Now, Charles, you had best get back to Bridesbridge." He spoke so quickly, she hardly understood him. "It's getting late. Did you ride here on horseback at this hour?"

"No, sir." Chloe pulled on her coattails. "I walked."

A look of astonishment and what could only be termed affection flitted across Henry's face. "Charles. I insist you take a gig. It's too late to walk. I'll ring to have one readied for you."

Chloe took a shallow bow.

"Now—run along, Charles!" Henry planted the candelabrum in her hand, propelled her into the hallway, and made a point of blocking the cameras from filming her.

Another video cam popped out from round the corner just as she broke into a jog, doing her best to keep the candelabrum alight. With the cameraman hot on her coattails, and Henry behind him, she hurried through the labyrinth of dark halls as if she were being chased through a museum at night. Before she shut the great doors behind her, she passed off the candelabrum with only one candle alight to the night watchman, who told her a gig was waiting for her out front.

Once outside, she stopped only for a moment at the top of the wide, palatial stone staircase glimmering in the moonlight. Just the other night a footman had handed her out of a chaise-and-four and she'd waltzed up these stairs in her gown, gloves, and dancing slippers. Down she went now, taking three steps at a time. One of her calfskin shoes fell off, but she didn't stop. Stockinged foot and all, she hopped into the gig and looked around for the driver.

She could almost hear the proverbial crickets.

The stable boy handed her the reins, because there wasn't a driver.

"Damn! Of course there's no driver! I'm a footman! *I'm* the driver!" Chloe whispered to herself.

The stable boy cocked his head at her, like a dog who knew he was being spoken to but was unable to understand the words. He hung two glowing oil lanterns on the front of the gig. "Just have it sent back in the morning," he told her.

The seat felt cold and hard. The stable boy stuck the whip into her hands. The horse breathed out of his nostrils and snorted. Terror whipped through her. She'd never driven a horse and buggy! She looked back toward the blazing torches flanking the great front doors at Dartworth Hall. The doors swung open. Two video cams and a boom boy appeared. Henry sidestepped down the stairs and swooped down to pick up her shoe as one of the cameramen barreled down the steps.

"Can you, would you, drive me back to Bridesbridge?" she asked the stable boy. "I'm new and not used to these gigs."

The stable boy shrugged his shoulders and hopped in next to her. With a flick of his wrist the horses lurched forward, and it wasn't long before the camera crew was well behind them.

The moon was floating high in the night sky now, in what would've been a perfectly romantic night if she weren't crouched in front of a horse's butt dressed in men's clothes. She was torn between men and money, past and present, bending the rules and breaking them.

They approached Bridesbridge in silence.

"Thanks for the ride. I really appreciate it."

The stable boy shrugged his shoulders again, but as soon as Chloe climbed out, she saw the camera crew catching up to her on an ATV.

Just as she thought her little venture in deception was about to blow up in her face, the scullery door creaked open, Cook held a candlestick into the night, and called out, "Come in, footman! Teapot's on!"

Cook held the door open wide and Chloe stumbled toward the candlelight and the vague thought of hot tea. She slunk into the kitchen, where a teapot was steaming on the range. The smell of potato peels and yeast enveloped her.

"Nothing to see here," Cook told her, bolting the door so the camera crew couldn't get in.

Chloe collapsed into a chair at the pine table. In her wet stockinged feet, the stone floor felt cold.

Cook grimaced at her. Her face looked as ruddy as a new tomato, and Chloe knew she was about to get grilled but good.

"I should blow the whistle on you right now." Cook yanked the glasses off Chloe's face. "You stole my spectacles. Do you know how much spectacles cost an underpaid cook like me?" Chloe's eyes slowly readjusted to being without the glasses. "Do you know how long it takes to have spectacles made? I'm sure you don't. And I'm sure you don't care. You're just an uppity Yank without a thought in the world—"

"I am not!" Chloe interrupted, sinking in her chair. "I'm sorry about the glasses. Really. It's just—"

"You don't fool me for a minute." Cook popped up and, with her bare hands, pulled the steaming kettle from the range and set it on the table. The rising steam helped clear Chloe's head. Cook reached up to retrieve a wooden box of used tea leaves from a shelf, which she had to do because only Grace held the key to the caddy with the fresh tea leaves. Servants had to use sloppy seconds. She darted a blue eye at Chloe. "You don't fool me, dressed up as a footman either." She mixed the tea leaves, set them in a perforated spoon atop a ceramic teapot, and poured the boiling water over them. "And you don't fool me when you're upstairs dressed in your gowns and gloves and baubles."

Chloe bowed her head. Cook was right, she was a total fake and could never be an heiress, not even an industrial heiress, from America.

Cook plopped a teacup on the table in front of her. "You're just un upstart Yank with lots of silly ideas and no right. No right to an English blue-blood fiancé."

Why was this woman talking to her like this? she wondered as Cook took down another locked wooden box from the shelf. With another key hanging from her apron she opened this box to reveal a large, cone-shaped loaf of light brown sugar. Dartworth Hall had highly refined white sugar, the most expensive of the times, while here, at Bridesbridge Place, it was light brown. She took the sugar nippers and clipped off two lumps, dropped them into the cup, poured the tea in, and stirred. "Do you know how long the kitchen staff and I slaved over those confections you and Lady Grace bandied about the drawing room like so many tennis balls?"

"It wasn't exactly like that. And, yes, I do know how much effort goes into the cooking here. I made the strawberry tart and the syllabub, remember?"

Chloe sank lower in her chair. Even the used tea and not-so-refined sugar smelled fabulous. "I didn't think—"

"No, you didn't think, did you, now? If you were my charge, I don't know what I'd do."

Slowly, guiltily, Chloe stretched out to cup her hands around the warm tea but Cook suddenly whisked the cup away.

"What makes you believe I made this tea for you?" She plunked the teacup down on her side of the table. Her icy blue eyes scanned Chloe's face for a response. "You used to help us servants out, but now you've gotten used to being waited on hand and foot. You feel entitled."

"That's not true."

Cook slammed a cloth bag of flour onto the table and a puff of it rose like a storm cloud. "Do you know that I prepare the dough at this hour for your breakfast toast?"

"I didn't realize—"

"You don't realize plenty of things. More than eight thousand proper English applicants. And he turned them away for the likes of you."

Chloe needed to get out of the frying pan here. "I really am sorry about the trouble I've caused. I blew it by dressing up like this. I just wanted to clear everything up with—Henry." She looked at the tea caddy and sugar box as if for the last time.

Cook plunked a big ceramic mixing bowl on the table and sent a puff of yeast into the air. "What do you care about Henry?"

"I don't understand why everyone keeps treating him like a second-class citizen. He's a great guy. There, I said it. I was rude to him earlier and I just wanted to apologize, so I dressed up in footman's clothes, because women aren't allowed out after eleven, and I couldn't write a note—or call, e-mail, text, tweet, or send a Facebook message! If wanting to apologize is a crime, then I'm guilty, so turn me in." She held her wrists out to Cook, as if Cook would handcuff her.

Cook poured some flour and water into the bowl and mixed with a big wooden spoon. "I should turn you in, but I won't. I, too, have a soft spot for Henry."

Chloe stumbled toward the door and looked away from her disheveled reflection in a row of copper pots and pans. She'd said too much.

"You'd best go to bed," Cook told her, taking a tin of salt down from the shelf above the washbasin and prying the lid open with her thumbnail. "Just do me a favor."

"You name it."

"Remember the cook."

Like she could forget.

"And remember one more thing. I'm on your side."

She was?

For a long time, Chloe lay in her canopied bed and tossed in her nightgown, unable to sleep. She thought she heard a mouse scuttle from the floor mirror to the writing desk, but there couldn't possibly be mice running around her bedchamber, could there?

She wished she didn't care about Sebastian or Henry, but it was too late for that. She moved over to her half of the bed—making room for—someone.

The next morning, she woke, unable to do anything except sit on the edge of her bed, even though it was Monday and there might be mail from Abigail. Fiona worked around her while a cameraman filmed. She must've been quite drunk to dress up like a footman and go to Dartworth! The very thought of it made her paralyzed with fear.

"This is how it should be, mum," Fiona said as she brushed Chloe's hair with a large, heavy, gleaming silver brush in front of the French bombé dressing table. "It's much better when you just let me take care of everything like this. 'Tis my duty."

Chloe wanted to be brushing Abigail's hair, braiding it, getting her ready for the day.

Fiona twisted Chloe's hair back so tightly that Chloe winced. But she always did a great updo, and when Chloe looked in the mirror, she had to admire the sexy way her hair spilled out from the knot atop her head.

"James told me to bring this up to you, miss."

It wasn't mail, but something wrapped in a blue silk scarf that turned out to be her shoe from last night. She sighed. It was a nice gesture on Henry's part, and as far as that went, her mission had been accomplished.

Fiona was pulling back the draperies and sunlight was flooding into the room when suddenly Mrs. Crescent and Fifi came bounding in.

Mrs. Crescent was almost breathless. "You missed breakfast, Miss Parker. The butler announced that your outing with Mr. Wrightman has been bumped by a group competition at the hedge maze. Can you fathom why?"

"I can't." Chloe was shaky, and needed to eat something.

Two plump strawberries from the Dartworth hothouse waited in a mortar and pestle bowl to be crushed and made into rouge for Chloe. Red, ripe strawberries. Overcome with desire, Chloe snatched them up and ate them both at the same time. What did it matter if her cheeks had no color today? After last night, she'd surely be sent home, anyway.

Mrs. Crescent shook a finger at her. "I daresay it's no wonder Lady Grace always looks so much more polished than you. You've gone and eaten your cosmetics again!"

Chapter 13

Being a corn-fed girl from the Midwest, Chloe had seen corn mazes, but never a maze sculpted from eight-foot-tall yew trees. Ever since she arrived, she'd been enticed by the prospect of the hedge maze, and now, it seemed, was her chance to see it, although it did sting that the visit to the maze had trumped her scheduled outing with Sebastian.

The women and their chaperones were gathering around the entry to the maze while Sebastian and Henry came riding toward them on their horses.

Chloe had imagined running along the narrow, pebbled paths between the high hedges, dropping red rose petals behind her, Sebastian at her heels. They would meet in the pagoda in the center to kiss, his lips finally touching hers, her fingers finally grazing his squared-off sideburns, nothing but green all around and blue sky above—

The butler interrupted her reverie. "This morning the three of you will be competing for fifteen Accomplishment Points. Mr. Wrightman will be sitting in the pagoda in the middle of the maze.

You will all be sent off into the maze at the same time, and the woman to reach Mr. Wrightman first wins the points and time alone with him until the other ladies catch up."

Chloe almost groaned out loud. This, of all the competitions so far, seemed the most demeaning. She crossed her arms and kicked the dust with her walking boots.

Just then, out of nowhere, George came zipping up in an ATV. George!? Was he here to send her packing?

Janey was sitting next to him, sipping coffee from a white cardboard cup.

Chloe had given up drinking coffee here in England. Regency coffee tasted horrid, and the weak tea proved only marginally better.

George swung his blue-jeaned legs out of the cart and pushed his sunglasses up the bridge of his nose. A Bluetooth was stuck on his ear. Chloe couldn't stand those things; Winthrop used to wear his all the time.

"Girls." He made guns with his fingers and aimed at Chloe and Grace. "A word?" He whipped off his Bluetooth and raked his hair. The air around him hinted of shampoo and toothpaste. His hair must've been loaded with product. How else could it have smelled of shampoo and looked so much like bed head?

"Over here." When he grabbed them by the elbows, their parasols tipped to the sides. Regency men didn't call women "girls" and they didn't yank women around by the elbows. After weeks of Sebastian's and Henry's gentlemanly behavior, even Grace seemed shocked at such treatment. In addition to bowing, Sebastian and Henry always stood when a lady entered the room, and a lady could get used to such things.

George led them, faster than their calfskin boots could carry them, toward the topiary arch at the entrance of the hedge maze. Overhead, clouds were rolling in.

"No cameras," George barked at two of the crew, and they backed off.

Moments later, Sebastian and Henry arrived and tied their horses to a tree.

Grace's chaperone looked intent with concern and Mrs. Crescent sent Fifi on to be with Chloe.

"Listen, ladies," George began ominously, "I can be the king of grouchy Brit reality-show judges, you know."

Grace folded her arms just under the hem of her spencer jacket, which so nicely accentuated her boobs and tiny waist. "I don't see what I have to do with all this."

Chloe stooped down to pick up Fifi's leash.

George flashed a frown and pointed his iPhone at Chloe. "Officially, Miss Parker, you're on probation. You haven't gotten caught on camera, and your antics are great for ratings, and those are just two reasons why I'm not getting rid of you here and now." He paced around the soft grass, checking his phone.

Chloe picked up Fifi, who began pushing at her arm as if he wanted her to rub his neck, or what would be his neck if he had one.

"Suffice it to say that both of you are here, for the moment—with warning. Mr. Wrightman wants you both here because somehow he can picture you both as wife material, although I can't say I agree with his judgment. Then again he doesn't know everything I know, although I am tempted to tell him. Condoms appearing in reticules, shagging every footman in sight, going out after curfew—these are serious infractions." He keyed something into his phone.

Chloe tipped her well-coiffed head, which, at the moment, was covered in the unfortunate poke bonnet. "Did you know that the condom was planted on me?"

"We have no proof the condom was planted on you, Miss Parker, and unless you can produce proof, the jury's still out on that one." George's phone rang and they were saved by the bell.

It'd been a while since Chloe heard a phone ring and it actually sounded pleasant. For the first time in a long while, she didn't cringe at the sound. She watched George as he talked on the phone to someone far away, to people other than this small crowd, and she marveled at it, as if she really were from 1812. She felt a sudden urge to snatch the phone from him and call Abigail, just to hear her voice.

Chloe watched George slide the phone into his back pocket. She just wanted to hold it, really. Okay—she wanted to check her e-mail! Surf the Web! Buy toilet paper online! My God, what was happening to her? She clutched Fifi.

"Now, Miss Parker, we're on National Trust property at Bridesbridge Place—the key word being *trust*, okay? Respect it. The clothing, the grounds. Mr. Wrightman would be none too pleased if any damage befell his ancestral home or belongings."

"I would never damage anything on the grounds!" Chloe swore off sewing-cabinet vodka right then and there.

"You must have the common decency not to destroy our English heritage, Miss Parker," Grace said. When she tossed her head a few of her blond sausage curls fell out of her turban. "You of all people should be concerned for the grounds, what with your last name."

Chloe put her hand on her hip. "What is that supposed to mean?"

"I'll tell you what it means," Grace returned. "The surname 'Parker' originates in the Old French, meaning 'keeper of the park.' Your ancestors, Miss Parker, were groundskeepers and gamekeepers. It's a most dreadfully common last name."

Fifi nuzzled under Chloe's arm. "And your last name means 'money' in French, perhaps because your ancestors, not unlike yourself, I might add, were overly preoccupied with it."

George took his sunglasses off. "Ladies. I blame you both. Equally. For everything."

Grace pouted. For some reason, her lips seemed plumper than they had been yesterday.

George's phone rang again. He smiled and talked as if nothing were the matter. He was the British version of Winthrop. She wondered if he, too, would make the crucial mistake of e-mailing his wife "Happy 35th Birthday" from across the country, without sending flowers, a present, or even bothering to call.

George wrapped up his conversation and set his sunglasses atop his head as the sky began to darken. "You've both been duly warned."

Fifi growled and Chloe forced herself to pet him, just to calm him down.

George raked his hair. "God knows nothing can happen in a silly hedge maze, but we have an archery competition slated for tomorrow if the weather holds. Aim for the targets. If so much as an apple gets hit by a stray arrow, the game's over and you'll be replaced with two beautiful, smart, and eager prospects."

"You wouldn't!" Grace practically popped out of her spencer. "After all the time I've invested in this? Leaving all my clients high and dry? Really! When you know very well that all this is Miss Parker—Chloe's doing!"

Fifi quivered in Chloe's arms, and at first Chloe thought it was from the rain, the first drops of which had started coming down, but then he snarled at something that looked like a weasel. It was burrowing under the hedge. All of a sudden Fifi lunged from Chloe's grip, flinging his hot little body into the gargantuan maze with his leash trailing behind him.

Chloe held out her arms, as if she somehow expected him to come bounding back. "Fifi!" she cried, clapping as the dog squeezed under the hedge. "Come back here!"

"Fifi! My Fifi!" yelled Mrs. Crescent, cradling her belly and waddling over. "He'll get hopelessly lost in there!"

Chloe tossed aside her parasol, hiked up her gown, and sprang into the maze.

"Cameras! Get on this!" George whistled with his fingers, and the cameras rolled behind her. "That girl's golden," she heard him say. "Wherever she goes, drama follows."

Grace laughed and George's ATV spun off.

Fifi growled somewhere within the maze, but Chloe couldn't see him. She ran toward the spot from where the growling seemed to be coming. Her walking boots were so thin she could feel the gravel under the soles of her feet.

"Fifi! Fifi! Come here!" Her bonnet fell to her shoulders. Her white shawl snagged on a yew branch.

"Miss Parker! Miss Parker!" Mrs. Crescent called from outside the hedge maze. "Save my baby Fifi! Hurry! Before he gets hurt! Oh, Mr. Wrightman—thank goodness you're here!"

Sebastian? Great. He was supposed to be chasing *her* through the maze, and here *she* was chasing a droopy-eyed pug. She heard more growling and shuffling.

"Fifi! Fifi!" Chloe found herself bumping into dead end after dead end as larger and larger raindrops began to fall faster and faster.

"Yip! Yip!" Fifi yelped, and Chloe spun, sprinted, took a sharp turn in the hedge, and barreled right into—Mr. Wrightman—the younger, the penniless.

"I've been meaning to run into you," he quipped, offering her a hand to steady her. "But not quite like this."

That sounded like something she would say, or did say, to Sebastian.

The rain was falling even harder now.

"Listen, I'll get the dog. You head back," Henry said.

"Yip! Yip!" Fifi yelped again, and Henry marched off.

But Chloe couldn't leave Fifi. She clambered behind with a broken shoelace and her flimsy boots soaked through. Deep into the maze, she finally caught up to Henry and watched him throw his jacket on a tangle of pug and weasel and somehow magically extract the dog from the pile. He tucked Fifi under his arm like a football while ribbons of blood and mud trickled down the dog's back. Fifi was yipping and crying.

Chloe felt as if the seams of her corset were showing through her white dress. Her gown clung to her legs, revealing her garters at midthigh.

Henry's eyes roamed from her face to her neck, her breasts, her legs—then he turned to head back. "Follow me for the way out," he said in the pouring rain as he led the way. "If you lose sight of me, keep your left hand on the hedge. I've got to hurry and get the dog cleaned and bandaged before infection sets in. He's covered in mud."

Henry didn't know her lace was broken. As she followed him, her cameraman followed her, rain running down her face, over her lip, and into her mouth, tasting sweet and salty at the same time. The sky flashed lightning.

In a matter of moments she lost sight of Henry and could no longer hear his boots crunching in the gravel. She placed her wet glove on the hedge to her left. Fog was rolling in among the hedge-rows, and all at once the vivid green hedges seemed grayer, taller, woodier. What kind of mother would let herself get lost in a hedge maze in the middle of nowhere in England, during a thunderstorm?

"Hand on the left. Hand on the left."

Rain dripped down from her fingertips to her elbow as if she were a human gutter. She felt as if she'd been in this very spot five minutes ago. Did she just make a big circle? It occurred to her what a brilliant invention the GPS was, and she determined that as soon as she got home and could afford it, she'd buy one, because she hated being lost and alone. But, as it turned out, she wasn't alone.

She turned and looked right at the cameraman. "All right. How do we get out of here?"

He didn't respond, he just kept filming.

"You don't have to say anything. Just lead the way. I'll follow you."

He stayed put.

"Ugh!" Exasperated, Chloe threw her arms up.

Thunder rumbled and the hedges seemed to grow taller. *Left hand. Left hand against the hedge*, she reminded herself. Her gloves went translucent on her fingers. Tufts of fog blew through the hedgerows, obscuring the path. She kept bumping into the same dead end over and over. When the rain began to let up, she stopped shivering. Her hair had gone wild and windblown around her shoulders and the bottom of her white gown was brown with mud.

Finally, she saw an opening in the distance. It was the exit! She did it. She'd made it! All by herself. Something moved toward her, ran toward her in the fog. It was Sebastian come to save her, a little too late, unfortunately. She shook off the disappointment, but not the cold and rain.

"Miss Parker! Are you all right?" Sebastian called out.

"I think so, Colonel Brandon," she replied.

He smiled at the Austen reference and opened his arms to her. Did he forget he couldn't touch her? She was too cold and wet to care about protocol or the camera. He held out his arms to her and she had no resistance left. She buried her head in his wet, white ruffled shirt, taking in his wine-barrel, snufflike aroma. He, too, had been soaked through and his body felt chilled.

"I think we make a pretty cool couple." She shivered and whispered in his ear, alone with him at last.

Sebastian didn't have an umbrella or a coat to offer her, but in an instant he swooped her up in his arms.

She locked her arms around his strong neck, and he carried her toward Dartworth Hall. Now, where were all the cameras when she needed them?

"You are Colonel Brandon after all," Chloe said.

Sebastian smiled while his Hessian boots trudged on. He seemed an enigma to her, but the scent of spongy grass filled the air and being in his arms made her feel safe and taken care of.

His dark eyes looked straight ahead at the doors of the hall, his nostrils flared slightly. The rain had stopped, but it had made him slick back his black hair, as if he'd just stepped out of the shower. His cheekbones were so chiseled a girl could go rock-climbing on them. The moment was right out of a movie, until he lost his footing, slipped in the mud, and Chloe slid out of his arms and landed with her feet on the ground.

He caught her, helped her regain her footing, and their hands touched for the first time. "So sorry," he said, with his incredible English accent.

"I'm not." She melted faster than a chocolate molten lava cake. "Maybe you're falling for me."

He laughed and there they were, face-to-face. "I am—falling for you. I've never met anyone like you. You're a rarity." He moved closer as if to kiss her, and her lips parted. She resisted taking his designer-stubbled jawline in her hands.

His lips were almost pressing against hers and his arms had almost gone around her waist when they heard twigs snap behind them, reminding them that Chloe's cameraman was still there, and now another cameraman had appeared as well.

She stepped back. She couldn't help but notice Sebastian's very revealing breeches, so she tried instead to focus on the wet shirt clinging to his muscled torso—and that was certainly no punishment. Their bodies quivered to be together, and for the first time, Chloe felt for Regency women who weren't allowed to act on any of their impulses, or, if they did, they'd suffer life-altering consequences.

Chloe needed more time with Sebastian, preferably not in a thunderstorm and surrounded by cameras, and perhaps not in the nineteenth century, for that matter. She had to admit that in the modern world, they'd have slept together already! Their relationship would've been so much further along by this point. How could you get to know a man when you were surrounded by chaperones? When you couldn't talk to him, be alone with him—or rip off his ruffled shirt and breeches?! Did Regency women really know who they were marrying? How could they have?

Chloe could learn more in a single weekend away at a beach cottage with him than six or even twelve more weeks of this. And, if she really wanted TMI, she could've done what Emma did with men she's just met, and Google them, check out their Facebook page, follow them on Twitter. Just a few minutes of cyberstalking would've revealed more than she'd learned about Sebastian in two full weeks!

The hedge maze was far off, and however enticing it had once looked, Chloe couldn't be happier than to be free of it.

At that moment a footman came running toward them. "Mr. Wrightman, we need you in the stables. Do you have a moment?"

Sebastian looked at Chloe. So much for their romp in the hedge maze, she couldn't help but think. "Go ahead," she said. "I'm fine. Is everyone inside? Do you want me to just—head into Dartworth?" It was awkward asking if she should just drop into his sprawling estate or what.

"Yes, I'm sure everyone's gathered in the music room. The competition will be postponed."

"I'll escort you," the young footman offered.

Sebastian bowed, she curtsied, and he headed toward the stable.

She tied off the broken lace on her waterlogged boots and noticed that one of her white stockings had gone shocking pink at the ankle. Mrs. Crescent would never approve of pink stockings. It seemed she had cut her ankle on the hedge and blood had turned the stocking pink.

On her way toward Dartworth, she and the footman stepped over a little creek that had swelled up during the storm. She stepped on a wide rock in the middle of the creek to get to the other side and noticed how two streams of water flowed on either side of it. This divergence weakened the streams, until they trickled off into nothingness.

She never imagined she'd fall for two so very different men, brothers no less, so quickly. The money and the winning got washed away, and too often, she forgot all about them. She had to stay focused, follow ridiculous Regency protocol, and not allow her resolve to weaken any more. No more getting lost. She'd set her GPS for Sebastian, and that would be it.

Chapter 14

"Well, well, look what the pug dragged in," Grace said. She cast a crisp silhouette against the floor-to-ceiling windows in the music room at Dartworth.

The windows in this room offered the best view of the hedge maze. Julia and her chaperone were playing cards in front of the fire. Mrs. Crescent had dozed off on a Grecian sofa.

Chloe clenched her fists. It took all of her willpower not to rail against Grace.

Chloe had to remind herself of how her feelings for Sebastian had been growing steadily stronger. She forced herself to think, too, of the money, of how it would save her business and might even save her from having to sacrifice Abigail to Winthrop every summer.

At that moment Fifi appeared, trotting in from the hallway, his rib cage wrapped in linen bandages. The yellow room dripped with white flowered molding like frosting on a wedding cake, while rainwater dripped from Chloe's hemline to the floor. The fireplace crackled and the shadows danced on the gold-leaf harp in the corner. She wiped her face with her wet shawl and the white fabric turned gray with grime.

Grace, in her shimmering gold silk gown, circled Chloe like a lioness assessing her prey. "It's not about how shocking you look, Miss Parker." Her voice rose up to the domed ceiling. "It's about how hopelessly blind you are to the fact that you just don't belong here."

A cameraman angled in and Chloe imagined balancing a book on her head, chin up, just like Mrs. Crescent had taught her.

"Fifi! Miss Parker!" Mrs. Crescent hoisted herself out of the chaise. "Thank God you're both all right." She bent to pat Fifi delicately on the head.

"Whatever did you do with poor Mr. Wrightman, anyway?" Grace asked as she floated back to her window.

"Wouldn't you like to know," Chloe muttered. She clenched the sage silk draperies.

Abruptly, Grace came slithering up from behind, startling Chloe with a click of a bronze telescope, which she promptly extended to its full length and aimed toward the maze.

Mrs. Crescent, with one hand on her belly, took Chloe by the arm and whispered, "We must go, dear, before Mr. Wrightman sees you in such a state!"

"He has already seen me—aaaachooo—" she sneezed. "Excuse me." She covered her mouth a little too late. There was enough dirt on her hands to confuse her with the gardener . . . or one of her alledged groundskeeper ancestors.

Lady Grace raised an eyebrow.

Chloe lowered her voice to a whisper as she spoke to Mrs. Crescent. "I just need more time. Things are—heating up."

"Then let's keep the teapot boiling," Mrs. Crescent whispered back. "Let's get tidied up." She took a deep breath and lifted Fifi as if he were a swaddled newborn. "Jones!" she called out.

In a blue liveried uniform, one of the footmen scurried over to Mrs. Crescent and bowed.

"Ready one of Mr. Wrightman's carriages, if you please. Miss Parker and I must return to Bridesbridge. Immediately."

"I won't go unless Lady Grace, Julia, and the chaperones come with us," Chloe said.

"I'm certainly not leaving." Grace stifled a fake cough. "Humph. All that muck." She waved her hand dismissively. "Mr. Wrightman invited us to stay until the rain subsides. I wasn't aware of his inviting *you*, Miss Parker, or am I mistaken?"

Chloe felt a draft coming from behind. "We didn't spend much time—talking."

Grace snapped the telescope closed and picked up a book from a large table draped in an Oriental rug, thumping it with her long, slender fingers.

A housemaid, on her hands and knees at Chloe's walking boots, was wiping up the wet trail of mud and grass she'd left behind her on the wooden floor. Without thinking, Chloe stooped to the floor. "Let me help you." She took a rag from the bucket.

A portrait of some eighteenth-century Wrightman women above the fireplace seemed to be looking down their English noses at Chloe, their silver gowns glistening, their faces and hair powdered white, each of them forcing an ever-so-slight painted smile.

Mrs. Crescent yanked Chloe up and the rag went *splat* on the floor. "A lady doesn't—that's servant work." She bobbed her head toward the camera. "Against the rules," she whispered.

"But I'm responsible for this—" Heat rose up Chloe's neck, her head throbbed, and she wiped her dirty hand on the back of her gown, leaving fingerprints.

Grace laughed, covering her pouty mouth with her glove. "I'm glad to see that she at least knows her place. She should've been cast as a scullery maid."

Scullery maid happened to be the lowest ranking of the maid hierarchy. Chloe knew this now, after working in Cook's kitchen.

"Carriage is ready," Jones announced.

Mrs. Crescent tucked Fifi under her arm.

"The storm's passed!" Henry announced as he trounced in with his medical bag. Chloe noticed that something salty was dripping into her mouth and realized that her nose was running. She knew better than to wipe it with her cap sleeve. Before she could do anything, however, Henry pulled a handkerchief with *HW* embroidered on it out of his pocket and, without a word, wiped her runny nose then put the thing right back into his pocket. Just like her grandpa used to do when she was little.

"Thank you." Her eyes followed him even as she stepped away from him.

"Ugh," Lady Grace groaned, tossing a book that she hadn't even cracked onto the table. She plopped down at the pianoforte and shuffled the sheet music like cards.

"Miss Parker, whatever happened to your leg?" Henry asked.

Mrs. Crescent gasped. "I had no idea! Dear Lord!"

Grace pounded on the pianoforte, sending Beethoven resounding throughout the room.

"I'm fine. It's just a little cut." Grace was banging the pianoforte so loud that Chloe had to practically yell. She wanted as little interaction with Henry as possible, so she looked into the fire in the fireplace and fidgeted with her gown.

"May I take a look at the cut?"

Grace moved on to Bach's "Toccata and Fugue in D Minor."

Chloe decided that she had to stop giving Henry mixed messages. "I said I'm fine, Mr. Wrightman!"

Fifi whimpered.

"Oh dear, oh dear, oh dear," Mrs. Crescent singsonged forlornly.

Henry persisted. "I recommend you bathe and replace the bandage in the next twenty-four hours. I also recommend a dram or two of spirits."

That got her to smile, although she had sworn off that sewing-cabinet vodka . . . and off Henry as well.

"And, of course, I'll need to check on your progress tomorrow."

"That won't be necessary."

Just then Sebastian walked in to see Henry and Chloe together—again.

This was exactly what she didn't want to happen! She turned to Sebastian. "And thank you, Mr. Wrightman, for rescuing me in the hedge maze."

Sebastian merely nodded.

Henry had ruined her progress with Sebastian again!

Grace and Julia chose that moment to swoop in on Sebastian, each vying for his attention, each beautiful, glittering, and—dry.

Chloe decided that Mrs. Crescent was right, she looked a mess and was in no state to compete with Grace and Julia, certainly not physically, and maybe not mentally either! She should listen to her chaperone more often, really.

"Well, Mrs. Crescent and I must go." Chloe curtsied, the men bowed, and she shuffled toward the foyer, Mrs. Crescent following.

In the marble-tiled foyer, Chloe caught a glimpse of herself in a full-length gold-leaf mirror, and thought she looked more like a mad-woman locked in the attic than an Elizabeth Bennet who had just muddied her petticoats running all the way to Netherfield. Regard-less, petticoats were hopelessly out of fashion in 1812. She pulled a twig out of her tangled hair.

What had made her think she was worthy of an Oxford-educated aristocratic hottie anyway? She used to think she belonged here in England, and now, it seemed, Grace might be right. She didn't be-long here, or anywhere else.

She hesitated before stepping into the carriage, a hard-topped black chaise with a gold W emblazoned on the door. The four black horses tossed their manes and stamped their hooves.

"To Bridgesbridge Place," Mrs. Crescent told the driver.

Fifi tugged at his bandage by Chloe's side and nuzzled his head under her hand. Chloe petted him, he licked her arm, and this time she didn't wince. The carriage lurched forward, the back of her head hit the leather tufts of the carriage seat, and the next time she looked out the carriage window she saw the vine-covered walls of Brides-bridge Place. She must've fallen asleep.

Mrs. Crescent put her hand on Chloe's knee and smiled. "Well, we missed the opportunity to score Accomplishment Points in the hedge-maze competition, but you will gain the bath you've been wanting. And I'm pleased to hear that things are going so well with Mr. Wrightman."

They had been going well . . . until Henry intervened.

*L*ater that afternoon, Fiona summoned Chloe to the bath, and Chloe was more than happy to leave her embroidered screen behind.

"Let's put on your bath gown." Fiona reached into Chloe's Chippendale wardrobe and pulled out a thin sleeveless white cheesecloth type of thing.

"There's even a gown to wear to the bath?" Chloe asked. The gown brushed against her ankles as Fiona led her into a stone-tiled room.

"You'll see, miss," Fiona assured her. She rolled up her sleeves and Chloe spotted the Celtic tattoo she had noticed more than a week ago.

Linens the size of sheets hung from pegs and a large copper tub full of water gleamed in the sunset that was streaming in through the window. The skies had cleared. Candles flickered in the sconces on the wall, and a silver pitcher full of fresh lavender stood on a wooden table near the tub. The only thing missing? A glass of wine. Chloe could almost hear a choir of angels singing "Hallelujah" in her head. A bath! After more than a week now? In a gorgeous copper tub! What joy, what bliss— "What's this?" Chloe picked up what looked to be a brush with a handle that was used to scrub floors.

"That's the brush I'm going to clean you off with," Fiona said.

A camerawoman stood in the corner, on an upturned wooden bucket, filming.

"You will stop filming now, right?" Chloe asked the camerawoman, who didn't respond. No matter how desperately she wanted a bath, she refused to be filmed naked and have such compromising images of herself blasted all over the Internet. She wouldn't be naive about this!

"Get in the tub, please, Miss Parker." Fiona hovered over Chloe with the scrub brush. "We haven't all day, other people in the house are waiting their turn."

Chloe lifted the bath gown up to her thighs to take it off, but couldn't go any higher. How could they do this to her? Show her a tub full of water after seven days without a shower or bath and then expect her to be filmed naked? "You know what? I can't do this. Any of this. Anymore." She turned on her barefoot heel, but Fiona was blocking the door, scrub brush in hand.

"You're to keep the bath gown on while you bathe," she said. She put the hand with the scrub brush on her hip.

"I'm supposed to keep this on?"

"Yes. It would be unladylike to do otherwise."

For the first time in her life, Chloe thought to herself: *Regency England sucks.* Who could bathe with a gown on?

Worse, she didn't want to be filmed in the tub, with or without the gown. But then Fiona sprinkled fresh lavender sprigs into the water, and the bath looked more tempting than ever.

"It's either this or no bath at all," Fiona said. She took Chloe by the hand and led her toward the tub.

"Everyone else has bathed in their gowns."

Chloe folded her arms. "They have? Who?"

"Let's see, Lady Grace, Mrs. Crescent, Mrs.—"

"All right. I'm in." Fiona handed Chloe in and she sank into the water as the gown billowed out around her.

Within seconds, her butt had gone numb. "This water is f-freezing!" She popped up out of the water like a piece of toast from a toaster, only not as warm.

"It's colder out of the water than it is in," Fiona observed tartly, and pushed Chloe's shoulders back under. Brush in hand, she scrubbed her mistress's neck, hair, and shoulders. "You'll get used to the temperature."

Chloe cringed. The brush hurt and the wet gown clung to her ribs. "Why is the water so cold?" Her teeth were chattering.

Fiona scrubbed a little harder. "You really don't know, do you?"

"No." Goose bumps on Chloe's arms and knees were showing through the gown. She brought her knees up to her chest and eyed the camerawoman who was filming discreetly from the side.

Fiona ladled water the temperature of frozen vodka over Chloe's head. "First, the footmen had to pump water from the well," she said. "Then they had to carry it up two flights of stairs, with wooden yokes on their backs, until they dumped it in here. The two of them had to go up and down about fifteen times."

Sorry as she felt for the footmen, Chloe touched her lips and wondered if they'd turned blue yet.

"That work alone took the better part of the day. Then, of course, we started the bathing in order of rank. Lady Grace went first, then her chaperone, then yours, then Julia's chaperone, then Julia, and now you. After you, it'll be the servants' turn, starting with Lady Grace's maidservant."

Chloe saw that a long, curly blond hair was floating in the water along with some of the froth from the raw egg shampoo and she pulled it out, draping it on the side of the tub.

"After a few people have been in the water, it gets colder, it seems." Fiona rinsed the egg out of Chloe's hair with the ladle. "Best to be first."

Chloe froze, if an already frozen person could freeze any more. She shot up out of the water and splashed both Fiona and the camerawoman. "What?! I'm taking a bath in *used* bathwater?!" She grabbed her elbows to hide her hard nipples from the camera.

Fiona looked up at her. "Well, yes, of course. Only the titled ladies get fresh water. But you knew that, didn't you?"

"Ugggh!" Chloe vaulted out of the bathtub, knocking over the silver pitcher of lavender, which clanked to the ground. While Fiona bent to pick it up, Chloe whisked a linen sheet from a peg, wrapped herself up, and squished down the hall in her wet feet.

"Does this mean you're finished with your bath, then?" Fiona called out after her.

Chloe had climbed onto her sagging mattress and lay shivering in the linen sheet, which didn't work anything like a terrycloth towel.

"A lady doesn't scream in her bath," Mrs. Crescent declared as she lumbered into the bedchamber, Fifi and Fiona right behind her.

"I know," Chloe said while Fiona rubbed her hair with the linen towel. "Tell me. How does a Regency lady quit being on a reality-TV show? I want to go home."

Fifi chose that moment to bound onto the bed and wag his curl of a tail at Chloe. Someone had removed his bandage and there was only a scrape on his back.

"Quit?" Mrs. Crescent settled into the mahogany chaise with the gorgeous scrollwork at each end. She rested her head on a tasseled cylindrical pillow, closing her eyelids. "You can't. You told me your-self things are heating up."

Although Fiona had laid out an amazing blue gown, Chloe pulled on her nightgown.

Fiona folded her arms. "What about your dinner gown, miss?"

"I'm too tired for dinner. Tired of suckling pigs and quail. Tired of a cesspool instead of a bath. Tired of chamber pots. I'm tired of Lady Grace's attacks both by bullet, mince pie, and barely minced words. I quit."

Mrs. Crescent shook her head. "But you look gorgeous, dear. I believe you've lost more than a few pounds. You're not a quitter."

"Oh, yes I am. If you only knew!"

She'd quit her marriage for one thing. She was the one who left Winthrop. He didn't have the guts to leave her.

As these thoughts swirled through her mind, the camerawoman opened the door and continued filming.

Mrs. Crescent leveraged her pregnant self off the chaise and clapped for Fifi to follow her. "Sounds like you need some rest. Just ring if you want a tray brought up to you, dear."

Fiona stoked the fire, drew the drapes, and snuffed out the candles.

Chloe fell asleep to the scuttling sounds she had been hearing every night now. She hugged her elbows and tucked her knees to her chest. She could no longer deny it. There was a mouse in her room!

*T*here is a mouse in my room," Chloe said to Fiona the next morning. She had been here a week and a day, and hadn't had a serious issue with the accommodations until now.

While Mrs. Crescent and Fifi looked on, Fiona laced Chloe's stays and pulled at the laces as if they were reins.

"Mice are all over the house. The kitchen's got black flies and a hornets' nest hangs outside the drawing room. Haven't you noticed?"

She hadn't. Rose-colored glasses again. "I hate mice. I need to get rid of them."

"Does this mean you're staying after all, miss?" Fiona tied off the stays and pulled the most amazing pomona-green gown over Chloe's head. She slid an almost translucent sleeveless dress over the gown. Chloe looked down at her knees where the dress floated and fluttered.

"What do you call this—this confection?" she asked, turning to admire it in the mirror. It was the first morning she had woken and not immediately hoped for a letter from Abigail.

Fiona tied the dress in the back, cinching it just under her boobs. "It's an organza overdress."

"Mmm," Chloe mused while she sat down at the vanity for Fiona to do her hair. Fiona fastened an amethyst necklace around her neck.

"Can't imagine leaving all this, can you?" Fiona asked. "And you have a chance at another five Accomplishment Points with the bonnet-trimming session today."

A footman arrived at the door with a knock and silver tray. "Miss Parker?" He bowed down to Chloe and held the tray in front of her. "Letter for you."

At last! Chloe hoped it was from Abigail. Or Emma. Or her lawyer—or all three.

"A letter! How exciting!" Mrs. Crescent was instantly at the heels of the footman. "Who from?" she asked as she wiped Fifi's drool off her arm.

"Don't get too excited. It's postmarked Chicago."

"Oh." Disappointed, Mrs. Crescent waddled out of the room.

There were several pages of computer-generated art from Abigail wrapped around a letter.

Chloe sank down onto her bed, and made a resounding crunch. "What did the chambermaid stuff my mattress with this time?!"

"I think it's cornhusks, Miss," Fiona said. "And sawdust. Seems we're fresh out of hay."

Chloe sighed. Grace, due to her higher rank, had a feather mattress.

The letter was from Emma and she read it while Fiona brushed her hair.

Dear Chloe,

We're all so jealous. Are you having fun in your ball gowns swooning over that young Colin Firth look-alike or what? Nothing but same-old same-old this side of the pond. (Yawn.)

You'll be happy to know we did get an order for some poetry chapbooks.

On the bright side, we've been following Twitter, Facebook, and the blog for the show, and your Mr. Wrightman has great things to say about you—but I'm sure you already know that! Have you tagged and bagged him yet? From the online video, it looks like his brother is a hottie, too—more my type than yours, though. Save him for me?! Everyone's e-mailing and Facebooking about you. Even Winthrop came by the shop asking about you. Someone wrote up an article in Chicago magazine and you're all over the alumni website. Lots of buzz. I'm taking the opportunity to do some viral marketing for Parker Press based on all this publicity you're getting. Thought I'd strike now rather than wait till you get back.

Hope you're doing us all proud.

I call Abigail almost every day, just like you wanted. She loves getting your daily letters. She's been painting something on the computer for you every day. I included some of them here. She's so proud

of you. You're providing her with such a great role model—a woman
who follows her dreams! Come back with the money, honey!

Miss you,
Emma

Chloe slumped down in her bed. She knew she couldn't quit.
Aside from all the buzz, and Abigail's good opinion of her, she was
too invested, at this point, to leave Sebastian in favor of a warm
shower. If she did, it would leave her with a big "what if?" that she'd
never be able to get past. Besides, Abigail sounded fine. But why
was Winthrop asking about her? As for the rest of the letter, it was
all the things she didn't want to hear, and very little about what she
did: the business.

After Fiona curtsied and left, Chloe tucked the letter into the
secret drawer in her writing desk, where she found the poem from
Sebastian. She reread the poem, tucked it into her reticule, and
grabbed her bonnet, parasol, and walking gloves. At long last she had
the time, and the determination, to work on solving this riddle.

The lady needed a good run anyway—or at least a walk. Ladies
were not supposed to exercise. Who knew Chloe would miss working
out, of all things? The cameras weren't on her, so she leaped at her
chance. Quietly, quickly, she sneaked down to the kitchen door,
where the stench of roasting mutton hit her hard. Regency life was
turning her into a vegetarian. She'd never be able to eat the picturesque English sheep that grazed in the hills just beyond her window.
She slid the cold iron latch, the scullery door opened a crack, and a
slice of sunshine appeared.

"I hope you're not going beyond Bridesbridge propery unchaperoned!" Cook's voice boomed out behind her.

Chloe held a hand to her pounding chest. Cook's blue eyes
emerged from behind the copper pot rack. Four dead, skinned rabbits

were hanging from a rafter above her, cabbage heads were lined up next to a cleaver as if for execution, and she was swatting a fly away with sprigs of mint leaves.

"Cook! You scared me. Of course I'm staying within bounds."

Cook smiled and offered her a few mint leaves to chew on. She stripped the rest of the leaves from the stems and piled them next to a half-dozen cabbages that sat on a wooden table in front of the fireplace.

The mint freshened Chloe's mouth and the taste reminded her of Henry, but she didn't want to go there. "I need to get some air."

Cook pulled a large knife from a drawer and set about chopping the mint leaves methodically, quickly, and thoroughly. Within seconds she'd quartered all six cabbages. "Well then, you had best hurry along. I'll cover for you for an hour—no more! Be back by twelve-thirty luncheon."

That would all be fine if Chloe carried a little watch on her chatelaine like Grace did.

Cook stabbed the knife right into the wooden table, where it gleamed like the sword in the stone, and Chloe chose to get out while the getting was good.

Cook shut the scullery door behind her, and Chloe heard the latch click closed. Cutting through the kitchen garden, where the aroma of basil swirled in the summer sun, she lifted her gown and overdress and hopped the lavender border. She followed the footpath to the deer park, on the lookout for a house without walls, something with a face in a garden—maybe a statue? Julia's energy might've rubbed off on her, but Chloe just wanted to trounce around and figure out this riddle. Julia was continually seeking out creative ways to replace the daily jog she had taken in her real life, but somehow Chloe couldn't move fast enough in her bonnet, parasol, shoes without any support, and stockings that kept sliding down.

The path twisted to the edge of the deer park, where nothing matched the cryptic description in the poem. As much as Chloe had looked forward to slowing down her fast-paced life, even she had to admit her impatience with Regency-era pursuits such as this one, for people with too much time on their hands. Snail-mail letters had gotten to her, too. The immediate gratification that computers and cell phones brought couldn't be denied. No matter how gorgeous and physical a letter was, it never arrived soon enough and never communicated enough.

She heard some kind of bird cry high in one of the trees. It sounded as if it were laughing at her, and the mocking sound echoed in her chest. She shaded her eyes, looked up at the cotton-candy-blue sky, and her bonnet fell to her shoulders. Still looking up, she hoisted her dress and overdress, and wandered into the grove. From here, she could hear the bird better. The sunlight through tree canopy, so high and dense, created a dark, dappled effect on the forest floor even on this bright day. She looked up, and there was the bird she had heard, a bright green-and-yellow bird with red plumage on the top of his head, and as it flitted among the branches, it laughed at her again.

Horse hooves were pounding nearby, she caught a blur of black threading through the trees, and the galloping stopped just as the bird, which had grown silent, started up again. Chloe moved toward where she heard the horse. Twigs crunched under her walking boots, and then, in a clearing just ahead, she saw Henry sitting astride a black horse.

Why always Henry? Why didn't she run into Sebastian more often? Henry was holding binoculars in his hands, and was focusing on the bird. She thought Sebastian was the bird-watcher—but then again they were brothers, and brothers that seemed to share the same pursuits. Perhaps they even shared the same taste in women? Another twig crunched underneath her boot. Henry heard it, put the binoculars down, and saw her. His horse stepped backward, as if even he sensed the surprise and awkwardness. They shouldn't be together unchaperoned.

"Miss Parker." His horse advanced. "I didn't expect—"

The bird laughed again and they both looked up. Chloe didn't want to risk being caught alone with Henry; she needed time alone with Sebastian. Even the damn bird was laughing at her hard luck.

"It's a green woodpecker," Henry said. "They love this grove. The trees here are more than three hundred years old. This one is six." He pointed to a tree with his riding crop. "Green woodpecker calls always sound like laughter. It's unnerving."

Chloe's father used to take her bird-watching when she was little, and the quirky hobby had stuck. She admired men who appreciated nature, but there would always be something special for her about an ornithologist.

Henry dismounted, tied his horse to a younger tree, and walked toward her, offering the bronze binoculars.

"I—I really need to go back," Chloe said.

The woodpecker started calling again. "Have a look." He handed her the binoculars. "I was just on my way to check up on you, but considering you're out scrambling in the woods without a chaperone, I trust you're feeling better."

She stepped backward without taking the binoculars. "I'm feeling fine. But I never did get those 'spirits' you prescribed."

Henry laughed. "Then I'll prescribe some more."

"And I didn't sleep very well because there are mice in my bed-chamber."

Henry rubbed his chin thoughtfully.

Chloe curtsied. "If you'll excuse me, I'll see you—at the archery meet?"

"You're going to walk away from a green woodpecker? To my

knowledge, you don't have them in America." He offered her the binoculars again. The woodpecker stopped calling.

"I don't think it's proper."

"I'm amazed, and impressed, at how loyal you are to a man you haven't even really gotten to know yet."

She squirmed, as if she were again under Henry's mental microscope.

"Here." He stretched the binoculars in front of her eyes and slid behind her. His buttons grazed the small of her back. With his arms brushed up against hers, he adjusted the focus for her. "Do you see him?"

She saw a lot of things, including the fact that she liked Henry a lot more than a girl was supposed to like a potential brother-in-law. "Yes. He's—he's beautiful." She watched the woodpecker as he turned his green head topped with red feathers, and she handed the binoculars back. Her eyes fell to the forest floor littered with leaves. "Thank you. The most common woodpecker back home is the downy woodpecker. He has red plumage on the back of his neck. He's much smaller, though."

She smoothed down her overdress. Mrs. Crescent had told her that a lady must never reveal her full intelligence to a man, and this she found exasperating. She stepped into the breezy clearing, and away from him. Anyone could see them here. She had to get away, but didn't want to leave.

He moved toward her. "By the way, would you like me to fix your tiara? I'm afraid, though, it's too late to repair it before the ball."

It was enough to stop her for a moment longer. She had to think about this one.

"I can come by later to look at it. I'll be able to tell you if I can fix it as well as any jeweler would." He pulled an apple out of his pocket and shined it on his coat.

Chloe licked her lips at the sight of the apple. A breeze wafted through the trees and the dappled light flitted around them like sparkles from a disco ball.

She had to get out of here. "Yes, that's fine," she said absentmindedly. "I—I need to head back."

"Absolutely. I would escort you—but . . . we shouldn't be together." Henry bowed and fed the apple to his horse.

The horse crunched on the fruit. Chloe was ravenous, especially for fruit. She'd slept right through the mutton dinner last night.

Henry raised his eyebrows. "Unless you'd like me to escort you back to Bridesbridge after all?"

"No, thank you. But might I ask if you have any more of those apples?"

A shaft of sunlight came down on him through the trees. "You do realize how bad they are for your complexion, right?"

She smiled. "I'm willing to take that chance."

"I don't have any more, but the one my horse is eating was barely fit for consumption, human or equine. If you want fruit, I have something better." He smirked.

Chloe folded her arms. "I'm sure you do. But that's not what I had in mind." She curtsied and turned to go. Much as she enjoyed the repartee with Henry, she needed to be bantering with Sebastian instead.

"I'm talking about the fruit growing at the Wrightman hothouse."

Much as the hothouse sounded—hot—she knew better. "I can't risk it and I don't have the time."

"How much time do you have?"

The woodpecker started laughing again.

"Considering I'm not of high enough rank to carry a chatelaine, I never know what time it is. But I only have until twelve-thirty."

Henry checked his watch fob, and Chloe checked her thoughts of the two of them in a "hothouse."

Even though she'd kill for a strawberry, it had to be nearly twelve-thirty and she had to hurry back, so she curtsied. "Good day, Mr. Wrightman."

With that, she left him, and didn't look back.

*O*nly when she got back to the scullery door did she realize she'd forgotten to look for clues to the riddle—that was what she'd gone out to do! Cook scanned Chloe from head to toe and yanked her inside. She shut and locked the door behind her. "You're late." A butcher knife flashed in her hand.

"I'm sorry."

"Were you with Mr. Wrightman?" Cook sneered.

Chloe swallowed. She never lied to Cook. "No—no. I just ran into Henry."

"Taking a fancy to the penniless one? Tossing your fortune to the wind?" Cook chopped a carrot.

"It's not just about the money!" Chloe blurted out.

Cook raised an eyebrow. "Humph. What about Mrs. Crescent's little William?"

"You know about him?"

"Of course." A cauldron on the range bubbled over and dripped into the fire with a sizzle. Cook swung the pot hook out and let the cauldron hang, cooling.

Four dead, skinned rabbits lay on the table. "He doesn't have a hope without that prize money." Cook raised her knife, chopped the heads off each rabbit, then stood the heads up on a platter in a neat row.

Chloe looked at the decapitated bunnies and tried not to gag at the sight of their bloodied blue neck bones. "I want to help him. I have someone the money can help, too."

"You need to be pursuing Sebastian." Cook put her finger to her lips. "Shh. Someone's coming." She pushed Chloe toward the dead-bunny table and stuck the butcher knife in her hand. She flung two decapitated, plucked chickens on the table. At least they looked like chickens. "If it's a cameraman, you're going to chop the feet off. Right? That's the plan. Just follow my lead."

It was a camerawoman. Chloe touched a rubbery yellow foot. She much preferred to see poultry and meat wrapped in cellophane on Styrofoam trays, another perk of modern living. One of her silk stockings fell to her ankle. Why couldn't it have been a potato or an onion? Why was Cook helping her, anyway? And why did the room keep spinning?

Wham! Chloe brought down the butcher knife on the chicken's feet, but she missed and chopped part of the legs off, too. Blood spattered onto her gown. The camerawoman got it all on film.

"Miss Parker!" Cook yelled from the other end of the kitchen, near the second stone fireplace. She ran past the camera and pulled the knife from Chloe's sweaty hand. "You're doing it all wrong. Now you've gone and chopped the legs!" Her blue eyes rolled from the camera lens to Chloe. "And spoiled your gown. How many times do I have to tell you to get out of my kitchen? I have maids for this work." She waved the butcher knife around like a flyswatter. "Run along now. You belong upstairs!" She shooed Chloe away, but Chloe could barely walk for thinking that she just chopped the feet off a—bird.

Still, Cook's plan worked, and the camerawoman followed her up the kitchen steps to the breakfast room, where the maids were stacking the sideboard with sandwiches and cakes.

Julia sat at the table, tipping her chair back on two legs. Her chaperone tapped her shoulder to quit. "Miss Parker, where have you been? I was hoping we could go for a walk."

Mrs. Crescent clasped her hands together when she saw Chloe. "I had the servants looking all over for you. You had a caller." She handed Chloe a creamy calling card with the upper-right corner folded down. *Mr. Sebastian Wrightman* was letterpressed into the card in a distinctive, but not overly ornamental font. The folded corner indicated that he had come in person, and the fact that he came "calling" at all pointed to a new level of intimacy in their relationship. Chloe held her palm against the wall. To think she had missed Sebastian all because of Henry!

Mrs. Crescent stood back to inspect Chloe's gown. "My, you look a fright."

Grace waltzed in, making even a check print look sexy with its scoop neck and her bare arms. She gave Chloe a sidelong glance. "You realize you look like an absolute serial killer. Honestly." She turned her blond sausage-curled head to the sideboard.

And, just as a joke for the camera, Chloe pretended she had a knife in her hands, Norman Bates style, and she acted as if she were stabbing Grace repeatedly in the back. The camerawoman did her best not to laugh.

Grace stood at the sideboard, hands on her hips. "Ah. Cold mutton and cow's tongue. My favorites."

Chloe remembered Sebastian's calling card fluttering to the floorboards, but she didn't remember fainting. Really.

Chapter 15

Chloe was hoping that the top half of Grace's boobs would get good and sunburned, because of course, sunblock didn't exist in 1812.

Her bonnet trimmed and five Accomplishment Points garnered, Chloe pretended to do her embroidery as she spied on Sebastian and Grace through the casement window in the drawing room at Bridesbridge Place. The couple bobbed up and down in the rowboat on the reflecting pond.

Since Chloe had been MIA while out bird-watching with Henry, and Grace had finished embroidering her fireplace screen and had more than enough points for another outing, she was granted the time with Sebastian. Julia, too, had finished her screen and was slated for an outing with him before the archery competition that afternoon.

Julia had fifty Accomplishment Points, but Grace and Chloe only had forty.

"Lady Grace isn't using her parasol," Chloe reported to Mrs.

Crescent. "And where's her chaperone, anyway?" She pricked her index finger with the needle. "Ouch!" A drop of blood bubbled up. She flung the needlework to the table and sucked on her fingertip.

Mrs. Crescent was lounging on the settee with Fifi at her side and a leather-bound book in her hands. "You have less than two days to finish that fireplace screen." She closed the book. "You won't get any Accomplishment Points for it and you'll get another, worse task, like mending stockings and stays."

Chloe stomped over to the pianoforte, where she banged out a few notes. Then she trudged over to the globe, lifted it from its wooden stand, and turned it. She found England, traced the outline of the tiny country with her pricked finger, and set the globe back in the stand.

Mrs. Crescent rubbed her belly. "What you need is to win the archery competition this afternoon. Then we'll all be on our way."

"Oh, I'll win all right. I have to!" She needed more time alone with Sebastian.

"That's the spirit. Now finish up the screen."

Chloe pressed her nose against the window. "They're supposed to be bird-watching. Why aren't they bird-watching?" She picked up her needlework. She set it back down.

Mrs. Crescent stood and rubbed the small of her back. "Lady Grace has no interest in birds. You know that as well as I do."

Chloe cut a deck of historically accurate oversized cards at the game table, which was draped in a maroon silk tablecloth.

Mrs. Crescent picked up Fifi. "I'm just glad to see you're back full force. We need to stay focused."

The cards fell from her hands in a spray on the floor.

Fiona knocked. "Delivery for Miss Parker."

It looked like some sort of a picnic basket. Fiona set the basket down on the game table and gave Chloe a note, sealed with a blue wax W.

"Thank you," Chloe said, holding the note in her hand as if it were a winning lottery ticket.

As Fiona curtsied and left, Fifi leaped out of Mrs. Crescent's arms, jumped up on a chair at the gaming table, and began sniffing the basket. Mrs. Crescent leaned toward the letter.

Chloe broke the seal and read aloud:

"Dear Miss Parker,

Please accept this mousetrap with my regards. I do hope it will catch the mouse in your bedchamber. Looking forward to time together again soon.

Yours,
Mr. Wrightman"

"Mousetrap?" Mrs. Crescent looked sideways at the basket. Fifi started growling.

Chloe thought she saw the basket move, but then again, it could've just been her excitement.

"Henry must've told him about the mouse." Chloe held the note up to her nose and breathed in. She showed it to Mrs. Crescent. "Look. He signed it 'yours.'" She hugged the note close for a moment. No mere e-mail could ever surpass a handwritten note.

Mrs. Crescent rubbed her belly and swallowed. "He quite fancies you, doesn't he."

Chloe unhooked the basket lid and a young tabby cat peeked out.

"Oh!" Chloe held her arms out to the cat, but Fifi barked and the cat sprang to the writing desk, almost knocking over an ink jar. Fifi hurled himself at the desk in a barking frenzy. The cat arched his back and hissed at Fifi, who snarled and scratched at the desk leg.

Mrs. Crescent scooped up her dog. "Shush, Fifi!"

Chloe whisked the ink jars from the writing desk, but the cat snapped the quill pen in his mouth and held it there like a rose between his teeth. Chloe had to think of Abigail, who loved cats, but never had one as a pet. Chloe missed Abigail so much she had to steady herself against the desk for a moment.

Fifi growled from Mrs. Crescent's arms as she waddled to the door. "I'm going to rest before the archery meet this afternoon. Now, I suggest you take your mousetrap to your bedchamber, inform Fiona of the new arrival so that she can provide food and a litter box, and use this time to complete your needlework. Enough dawdling!"

Chloe rolled her eyes. "I'm no good at needlework."

Mrs. Crescent pointed a finger at her. "To win this competition, you need to do more than *act* like a lady. You need to *be* one." With that, she took off.

Chloe picked up the cat and slid the quill from his teeth. She thought about sending Sebastian a thank-you note, but she couldn't write to a man unless they were engaged. Or could she? Marianne Dashwood in *Sense and Sensibility* did.

She took the cat up to her bedchamber, shutting him in the room with her. She'd never had a cat before. And no man had ever given her anything with more of a pulse than a potted petunia. He must've really trusted her; after all, he had no idea that an eight-year-old girl thrived under her care.

She plopped herself down on the red velvet-cushioned stool at her writing desk and ceremoniously lit a tallow candle with a piece of kindling from the fire in her fireplace. The cat paced near the door. She took a piece of thick writing paper from the shelf and it felt almost like cloth. Seizing her bottle of rose water from the dressing table, she sprinkled a couple droplets onto the paper. Mmm—text messages never smelled like roses!

She plucked the goose quill from the penholder, and—was it her sex-starved imagination, or was this pen totally phallic? She touched the hand-cut nib, which was spliced up the center, and ran her hand all the way up the bare shaft to the few feather barbs left at the top. Henry had told her most quills came from the gray goose, and "pen" derived from *penna*, Latin for "feather." They were made from the stiff flight feathers on the leading edge of the bird's wing. Henry, schmenry. The only reason why she thought about him at all was that she spent the most time with him by default, and that had to change.

She flipped the silver top off the crystal ink pot, dipped the quill into the ink, and wiped the shaft of the pen on the rim, as Mrs. Crescent had taught her. The ink permeated the nib and she'd just written the word *Dear* when the ink ran out and the cat jumped onto the paper. Paw prints and ink were smeared all over. At least she no longer got ink up to her elbows like the first time she tried to write with a quill. She started all over again, with fresh paper, and wrote in a most ladylike tone:

Dear Mr. Wrightman,

Thank you for the mousetrap.
    It was a most thoughtful gesture and I'm hoping the cat will catch the mouse sooner rather than later.

Yours,
Miss Parker

After rolling the blotter over her words, she folded the letter and dipped a black sealing-wax stick into the candle. Smoke uncoiled into the air. The melting wax perfumed the air with sweetness. The wax dripped slowly onto the paper, forming a liquid circle. Brass seal in hand, she pushed the letter *P* into the soft wax. It was much more satisfying than clicking the send button!

"Fiona," Chloe called out down the hallway. Fiona was never far. "Please have this delivered to Mr. Wrightman immediately."

Fiona took the letter and curtsied.

"Wait. No. I can't do this. Please give that back to me, Fiona. Sorry to have bothered you." It was the ladylike thing to do. She'd have to thank him in person, the next time *he* chose to see her.

Fiona handed the letter back, and without a second thought, Chloe tossed it into her fire. With that, she closed her bedchamber door, stripped off her silk gown, donned a lacy dressing gown, pulled all the pins out of her hair to let it down, and stood at the window.

Her eyes went all glassy as she imagined Sebastian serenading her. He would toss a bouquet of red rosebuds up to her and she would catch it—

An hour and forty-five minutes later, she sat at her open window, flicking her cheek with the quill pen. She couldn't see Grace and Sebastian anywhere anymore. The hall clock had struck one ages ago. Two o'clock and it was archery time.

She watched a footman and driver mount a carriage below and drive it off toward Dartworth Hall in the afternoon heat. Footmen dressed in long-sleeved coats and wigs carried big wooden tables and wooden chairs out to the lawn for the archery meet while the maids balanced wooden trays loaded with pitchers of lemonade and raspberry puddings ringed with rose petals.

Well, some music would've been nice. She didn't realize how much she'd miss the radio, her CDs, her LP collection, and yes, even iTunes. Sometimes it was just so—quiet here. And the fact that Sebastian had sent her a gift of a cat put her in a celebratory mood. He must have some feelings for her!

She sauntered over to the four-poster bed, vaulted onto the mattress, and swung around one of the bedposts. A song popped into her head. She hadn't heard anything other than the pianoforte and harp in a while now, but she started singing and swinging her hips to the thumping bass in her head. Soon she was swirling around the bedpost in her corset and stockings, pulling white gloves past her elbows, dipping her head back and letting her hair sway, tickling her legs with her quill pen, cavorting around like a pole dancer, when outside her window, down in the semicircular drive—something moved. She squinted. It was Sebastian! He was in his top hat, gazing up at her with his binoculars.

"Oh God." She froze for a moment, her stocking leg wrapped around the bedpost.

She heard something trickling—water. The cat was peeing near her evening shoes!

Sebastian stepped forward and back, adjusting the focus on his binoculars. She unwrapped herself from the post, slipped off the bed, and whipped the velvet curtains closed, like a bad puppet show. A pole dance wasn't exactly what she'd had in mind. Something just slightly more ladylike was on the agenda, like flirting from the open window with her hair down, because she looked good with her hair down, much better than the Regency updo Sebastian had associated her with, and she wanted Sebastian to see her that way. Finally, she opened the curtains to say, "It's huge in America, you know, pole-dance exercise classes."

He smirked. "I can see why. Please, don't stop on my account. I find it most—diverting. Carry on."

Chloe just laughed. "I have to get ready for the archery competition now."

"You are on my list, Miss Parker. I will be calling on you and you'd best be at home when I arrive!" He bowed and left.

Chloe sank down on the mahogany chaise, putting her head in her hands. Hard to be a lady when the lady was a tramp!

Someone knocked on her door. She snatched her chocolate-colored archery gown from the bed and held it up against herself as if she were sizing it up.

It was Fiona, and Chloe breathed a sigh of relief.

"Time to dress for the archery competition," her maid said, then gasped at the sight of Chloe's hair. "Why did you take your hair down, Miss Parker? You know full well it will be half an hour to pin it up again."

*F*iona pinned up Chloe's hair so quickly and so badly that, right in the middle of the archery competition, when Chloe was already down several points and trying to focus on the red bull's-eye in the middle of the target, she felt the updo going down.

She kept dwelling on the pole dance. A section of hair fell on the nape of her neck. It startled her into releasing the bowstring sooner than she wanted, and just like that, another arrow bounced off the outer edge of the target and fell to the grass. No doubt the fifteen Accomplishment Points would be going to Grace or Julia at this rate.

"Concentrate!" Mrs. Crescent mouthed to her from a wooden chair on the grassy sideline. And then she mouthed something else, but Chloe never could read lips. Sebastian, Henry, and the chaperones sat under the shade of an old beech tree, watching Grace, Julia, and Chloe face off. Fifi and two greyhounds were asleep under the wooden table where Fiona and some of the other servants were pouring lemonade and stacking Bath buns.

Chloe propped up her lancewood bow, almost as tall as she was, next to her, while she avoided eye contact with Sebastian. She tightened the laces on her brown suede archery gloves. A servant gathered up her misfired arrows and handed them to her like so many broken dreams.

Grace readied her bow.

"Ladies . . ." The butler stepped in front of the camera. "May I interrupt for a moment?"

Grace sighed, relaxed her stance, and scratched her collarbone.

Sunburn, Chloe thought. Soon it would be peeling!

"I'd like to remind you," he said, looking first at Chloe, then at Grace. "This is the final round of our archery competition today—"

A mosquito buzzed around Chloe's eyes. She snapped her eyelids closed for a minute, brushed it away, and when she opened them again, she accidentally looked straight at Sebastian, who winked and smiled. At least, it looked like he winked. Anyway, he was smiling—at her. He had this way, even with the gorgeous Grace and alluring Julia around, of making her feel as if she were the one. The only one. She swung her lancewood bow at her side.

"Ahem . . ." The butler cleared his throat. "The winner of today's competition will not only earn fifteen Accomplishment Points, but will also win an exclusive outing with Mr. Wrightman. Let the games begin." He raised his arm for the competition to continue.

Chloe's hands shook.

Grace flashed her white teeth in a fake smile, and Chloe noticed that her teeth somehow seemed whiter than they'd been yesterday. "Another excursion with Mr. Wrightman? I'll shoot for that." Grace pulled her bowstring back, and with a snap she nailed it, another bull's-eye.

Chloe's hands began to sweat in her suede gloves.

"Miss Parker, may I ask you a question?" Henry bowed in her direction. Mrs. Crescent was standing right by his side.

Chloe didn't want to get sidetracked by Henry. Not now. "We can talk after the meet, I'm sure, Mr. Wrightman." She curtsied to soften the blow of her refusal.

"This might help you, Miss Parker. Come over here with us," Henry said. He guided her toward the lemonade table and handed her a glassful. Her hands shook and when she took a sip, the glass clinked against her teeth. Henry politely ignored this blooper, but the camera got it. She took a big gulp, thinking that what she really needed at the moment was a vodka lemonade.

Henry looked her straight in the eye, as if she had a speck of dirt or something in it. "Miss Parker, do you wear glasses back home?"

She almost sprayed her lemonade all over him. "What?!" She wiped her mouth with a cloth napkin from the table. "Um, I mean, excuse me. Pray tell, what kind of question is that?"

Henry took off his glasses and looked into her eyes while Mrs. Crescent and even Fifi seemed to stare at her. "Have you had your eyesight tested recently?"

Chloe laughed. "Are you saying I'm blind, Mr. Wrightman?"

"It's your shot, Miss Parker," Grace called as she slipped her arrows into her tin quiver with a loud *ker-plunk*.

Chloe put her hands on her hips. "I can see perfectly, thank you very much." She could see that Sebastian was standing in the background, his arms folded and his brow furrowed as he watched her once again engaged in conversation with Henry.

Mrs. Crescent tapped Chloe's cap-sleeved shoulder. "Henry has observed, dear—you squint every time you shoot."

She narrowed her eyes at Henry. What was he trying to do? Break her concentration?

Her thought was interrupted by the butler, who stepped in front of the camera again. "Miss Parker, you must take your turn now. Or do you forfeit?"

The nerve! A lady would never articulate what Chloe was thinking, so she spun away from the lemonade table, plucked a wooden arrow from her tin quiver, grabbed the green velvet grip, raised her bow arm, and kept it locked. Slowly, she drew the twisted linen string back until her thumb hit her jawbone and her index finger almost touched the corner of her pursed lips and—she squinted. There. Now she saw the center circle clearly. She aimed, held her breath, and thought all those archery lessons at summer camp all those years ago had to pay off. She released the arrow but kept her shooting position until she heard the arrow hit the target. *Wham!* The arrow bounced off the edge of the target and to the grass. She wanted to throw her bow to the ground, but instead she leaned on it and frowned.

Grace mouthed something to Sebastian from across the field. Sebastian mouthed something back, but Chloe had trouble seeing his lips from a distance. Was Henry right? She needed glasses? Was this an approaching-forty thing that had crept up on her so gradually she hardly noticed? She had five arrows left in her quiver. She turned to Henry, who was sitting on the edge of his chair.

"Mr. Wrightman—Henry?" was all she said, and he came right over.

He didn't say a word. He took off his very clunky nineteenth-century spectacles, with lenses almost as thick as quizzing glasses. A chunk of his hair fell into his light brown eye and he swished it away. He wiped the lenses clean with his cravat and slid the glasses onto her nose as if he were sliding an engagement ring onto her finger. At first she saw nothing but a blur, and she raised her hand to take them off, but then, suddenly, she saw it clearly: the red circle in the middle, the outer rings . . . Wait—now she was seeing the individual leaves on the trees instead of green clumps. She saw peonies in the gardens rather than a blur of pink. Even from this distance, she saw Sebastian's watch fob dangling from his pants!

She took her stance, held her breath, and shot. Bull's-eye! She breathed in.

"You'll need five more of those," Grace mumbled, leaning nonchalantly on her bow as if it were a streetlamp.

Four bull's-eyes later, Sebastian, Henry, and Mrs. Crescent clapped and stood. Grace slung her arrow case over her shoulder and folded her arms. Julia folded her arms, too, and drummed her fingers on her taut biceps.

Chloe held the last wooden arrow in her gloved hand. She visualized herself as Cupid, with curly hair and wings as she nocked the arrow in the center of her bowstring and readied herself to take aim, but Grace chose that moment to step none too gently on Chloe's foot, and Chloe's fingers released, even though she hadn't even raised her bow arm. The arrow spun from her bow, as if in slo-mo, and spiraled toward Henry.

Chloe squeezed her eyes shut for a second. Cupid fantasies or not, she certainly hadn't wanted to shoot an arrow at Henry.

Grace did her best to appear to swoon. "Oh my." She fell to the grass. "I can't stand the sight of blood," she cried, then pretended to faint.

"Blood?!" Chloe ran to Henry's side. He was already opening up his jacket, looking for the wound.

Chloe's heart pounded.

"It didn't hit me," he said.

Chloe sighed. "Thank God," she breathed.

Henry looked at her for a moment, then turned away and scrambled to get up. "I think it just hit my watch fob and bounced off."

Chloe saw that with the fainting, Grace had conveniently managed to land in Sebastian's arms. He tried to revive her, as if she needed reviving, with her vinaigrette and her fan, and the sight of her in his arms sent chills up Chloe's corseted spine.

Chloe found the arrow and picked it up, examining the tip. "No blood on the arrow either."

"It really didn't hit me," Henry said, buttoning his coat.

At that moment Grace seemed to miraculously awaken from her fainting spell. "Of course it hit you," she said from the crook in Sebastian's arm. "I saw it hit you. You went down because it hit you."

The butler glared at Chloe.

Out of nowhere, George zoomed in on his ATV in his sunglasses and blue jeans. "Stop the cameras."

Chloe was taken aback. She'd forgotten that men in the real world didn't bow when they saw a woman.

George slid his sunglasses down the bridge of his nose and stared at Chloe. "You got lucky," he said sharply.

Chloe looked down at the arrow in her hand. She did get lucky. If it hadn't bounced off Henry, she'd be bounced out of here.

"I'm going to be watching this time. Because I don't want any messing around. Lady Grace, I want you far away from any archers. Take your final shot, Miss Parker," George said as he moved to the side. "And, Henry, I'd advise you to stop putting yourself in Miss Parker's path. She tends to attract trouble."

"Thanks, George," Chloe muttered. "Don't forget I happen to be armed at the moment."

"Take your shot, Miss Parker. Cameras—roll it."

Sebastian escorted Grace to a wooden chair on the side and then headed back toward the lemonade table.

Henry's spectacles slid down Chloe's nose and she pushed them up with her suede gloved finger. She took her stance, drew the string back, and visualized the money, Sebastian in her arms, everything. She raised her bow arm, kept it locked, and drew back the string until her thumb touched her jawbone and her index finger reached the corner of her mouth. She took aim at the red center of the buck-skin target, took a breath, held it, breathed out, and released the arrow. *Thunk!*

"It's a bull's-eye!" Mrs. Crescent shouted. Fifi, who'd been fast asleep in her arms, woke up and began to wag his tail.

A servant plucked the arrows from the center of the target and carried them over to Chloe as if they were a bouquet of long-stemmed roses. Triumphantly, she slid them back into her tin quiver, while on the sidelines, Grace's fan dropped with a faint *thud* into her lap.

Chloe slid the glasses down the bridge of her nose, and the target blurred again. The leaves and the flowers became fuzzy clumps. Yes, she needed glasses all right. She hurried over to Henry, wanting nothing so much as to throw her arms around him. But instead, she said coolly, "Thank you, Mr. Wrightman, for your observations and for the loan of your gl—er, spectacles."

He bowed, and as she took in his minty scent, she saw Fiona smile as she poured Sebastian's lemonade. He smiled back, stirred his lemonade with his finger, and leaned over to whisper to her. Fiona whispered back.

George slipped in between Chloe and Henry. "Miss Parker, I'm sorry to say that you lost the competition by a single arrow." He signaled the camera crew and hopped in his ATV.

Chloe clicked her heel-less walking boots together. "Thank you again, Henry. I did much better because of your—foresight."

Henry smiled and flicked the hair out of his eye. "You flatter me. Anyone with any medical experience could have guessed the problem. Eyesight can change rapidly when one approaches—"

"A certain age?" Chloe interrupted.

Henry nodded.

Grace popped out of her chair so fast she knocked it over. "Such an unladylike display of affection," she announced. "Running over to Mr. Henry Wrightman and thanking him so fervently!"

A blush washed over Chloe's face. Henry's glasses slid down her nose. She took them off and folded them up.

"Ladies, gather round," the butler announced as he stepped in front of the cameras. He opened his notebook.

Julia, Grace, and Chloe encircled him, and their chaperones stepped forward.

"Third-place winner is . . . Lady Grace."

Grace put her hands on her hips.

"First runner-up . . . Miss Chloe Parker, who forfeits the first dance at the ball due to an arrow gone awry. And, finally, Miss Tripp wins the archery competition, bringing her total to sixty-five Accomplishment Points. Lady Grace and Miss Parker stand tied at forty points. Both Miss Parker and Miss Tripp, however, are due an outing with Mr. Wrightman."

Chloe handed Henry his spectacles.

"Keep them," Henry said, and gave them back to her. "Until we get a ladies' pair made for you."

"Thank you." She tucked the glasses into her reticule. "But will you be able to manage without them?"

He nodded.

She curtsied. Mrs. Crescent patted her on the arm, and together they turned toward Bridesbridge Place.

"Did you happen to notice," Mrs. Crescent said, "just how sun-burned Lady Grace's bosom was?"

True, Grace had been burned, but that didn't change the fact that Chloe was going to have to sit out the first dance at the ball. And was Fiona flirting with Sebastian? Beads of sweat trailed down her back. It was too hot for this heavy archery gown. For once, she was happy to change for dinner.

When she opened her bedchamber door, she saw that the cat had knocked over her rosewater bottle and the ink bottles, and shredded some of her blotting paper, and she suddenly remembered that she was supposed to shake her ink vial in the chimney. But just when she was ready to reprimand the cat, he stepped out from behind the drapery with a dead mouse in his mouth, hanging by its pink tail.

Chloe screamed, and as if in obedience to some ancient instinct, she leaped onto a chair and hiked up her archery gown.

Sufficient screaming and shrieking prompted a footman to do away with the remains of the mouse. It was then that Chloe noticed pink petals scattered on her pillowcase. The petals surrounded a letter addressed to *Miss Parker*.

Her cameraman filmed her as she opened the note.

Dear Miss Parker,

I do believe the cat is doing his best to catch the mouse.
   Looking very much forward to a picnic at the Grecian temple,

Mr. Wrightman

Chapter 16

As Emma would've put it, Chloe had one chance to snag, tag, and bag Sebastian. It was Wednesday of week two, and she only had nine more days to get Sebastian to propose. So she decided—not to wear Henry's spectacles on her date.

Even though she fully intended to appeal to Sebastian's intellect and his noble upbringing, she figured whatever she could do to further her cause wouldn't hurt. So she selected her flimsiest gown with the neckline that didn't quit and the stays that turned her boobs into the uniboob—a force to be reckoned with. She shaved her legs for the first time in almost two weeks, illegally albeit, at her washstand, with a razor stolen from one of the footmen, even though she knew Sebastian wouldn't be seeing her legs. She chose a necklace that had a slightly damaged clasp in the hope that the emerald it contained might slide right into her cleavage at an opportune moment. Mrs. Crescent doused Chloe's muslin gown with water as any wanton, but still respectable, lady would do under the circumstances.

And, as predicted, as soon as she hit the cooler summer air on this increasingly cloudy day, her nipples went hard.

Sebastian handed her up into his curricle, the sports car of the early 1800s. They were going for a turn around the estate and then a picnic and a bit of nature sketching at the Grecian temple, where Mrs. Crescent awaited them. Chloe couldn't have planned a more romantic outing herself. Neither Mrs. Crescent nor the cameras could fit into the curricle, so she and Sebastian were filmed from an ATV shadowing them alongside the road.

Unfortunately, Sebastian had a toothache, and as he drove the horses, he sucked on cloves to help with the pain, because aspirin hadn't been invented yet. Chloe broached subjects she knew interested him from the bio she'd read: architecture, poetry, painting, astronomy, even bird-watching, but he just rubbed his jaw in reponse. He was clearly in a lot of pain. But the last thing she wanted him to think about was a toothache. She had to distract him, but how, without breaking the rules?

They passed the grotto in silence. She wanted to know his favorite movie, his favorite restaurant, where he liked to travel, his hopes, his dreams, even his fears, his failings. She wanted to learn everything about him, but all efforts seemed so forced, and he was consumed with pain. What a far cry it was from yesterday's pole dance at her window, when Sebastian had eyes only for her.

The pressure mounted. The time would go quickly. Certainly Lady Grace was sexier than she, and Julia, no doubt, had youth and exuberance on her side. This called for drastic measures, something Emma, her employee, not Jane Austen's Emma, might concoct.

She thought about tossing the ladylike approach out the carriage window and throwing herself around him and his double-breasted riding coat, which stretched tautly across his chest. She imagined untying his cravat, tearing off his shirt, and crushing her breasts up against him like a common trollop. Instead she demurely tucked a stray hair under her bonnet. "Mr. Wrightman," she said, "I wanted to let you know that your cat has caught the mouse."

"It has?" He shifted on the carriage seat and raised an eyebrow at her. He took his hand off his jaw. The horses shook their manes and their nostrils flared.

"Absolutely."

"That was certainly quick."

"Well, your cat has great instincts."

He almost dropped the reins as they clipped along past the deer park. "Thank you."

She became acutely aware that she didn't have so much as a thong on. He was so close, so—hot. These sudden urges made her uncomfortable. It went against everything she believed to lust after a man she'd met just a couple of weeks ago, but then another image of her and Sebastian flashed through her mind. They were parked behind the stables in the back of the carriage and the hemline of her gown was up to her ribboned Empire waist. She was raking her fingers through his thick, dark, tumbling hair as his hands cupped her breasts—

"Are you—enjoying your time here at Bridesbridge, Miss Parker? Is it everything you hoped it would be?"

"Yes, I'm having a fabulous time, and it's beyond what I had hoped. But what about you? Are you getting closer to making your final decision?"

"Yes, every day. It hasn't been easy—but it has led me here, to this point, with you. You're so different from the others."

She'd heard this before, and it was beginning to sound a little stilted. "You keep saying that, Mr. Wrightman. But what, I wonder, does it mean?" He looked pained again, so she lightened up. "Good different, I hope?"

"Yes. Good different."

"It's hard to tell—sometimes—exactly how you feel," she ventured.

"I don't really like all the attention I'm getting as the host of this thing. With the chaperones, so many people I don't know well, it's hard to relax and be myself."

That must be why his behavior seemed at times so contradictory. This reality show was putting strange pressures on all of them. But her mind kept turning to his skintight breeches tucked neatly into his shapely riding boots. "I feel for you," she said.

She'd like to feel him, period, she thought. She could hardly contain her physical attraction to this man, and from the way he looked at her when they were alone, it seemed as if he felt the same way. They had chemistry all right—on steroids. The force of the attraction, she reasoned, was probably made all the more powerful by the restrictions of Regency etiquette. She couldn't touch him, kiss him, or even hold his hand until he asked for her hand—in marriage. A flash of her untying his breeches came into her head. She would take hold of him with her leather-gloved hand and he would throb with need—

"I hope you'll like the afternoon I've planned for us."

"I'm sure I will." He could be so thoughtful at times, so considerate of her feelings and her pleasure.

He slowed the horses to a trot and they stopped at the Grecian temple. Chloe began to feel another urge rising up in her. It was the simple urge to pee. It happened to her every time she was out in the middle of nature, it seemed.

When he offered his hand to help her out of the carriage, she cast an eye toward the weathered green dome of the Grecian temple on the hill. Behind the temple's fluted columns, a picnic blanket had been laid out and sprinkled with red rose petals.

She reveled in the beauty of the scene. She never wanted to forget it. But one of the horses chose that moment to make a loud farting noise and a wave of the most disgusting-smelling air rose up around them. Just at the wrong moment, Sebastian whisked his hand away to cover his nose with his arm. "Arrgh," he muttered, wincing.

Chloe made a move to lean on his hand that suddenly wasn't there and stumbled out of the carriage. Meanwhile, the horse lifted its tail and dumped on the road. The pile stank and steamed. Both Sebastian and Chloe gagged.

Such were the hazards of driving by horse.

Sebastian escorted her toward the temple. Heavy clouds began to gather in the sky. Chloe needed to go to the bathroom, but didn't want to leave.

A basket overflowing with dainty sandwiches, buns, and grapes anchored a corner of the picnic blanket. Grapes! And not a mutton leg, cow's tongue, or pig's head in sight. A stack of reproduction first-edition William Cowper and Wordsworth poetry books and a box of charcoal sticks and sketchbooks weighed down another corner.

"Well, what do you think of what Mr. Wrightman has arranged for you here?" Mrs. Crescent asked. She clasped her hands in obvious satisfaction.

"It's perfect," Chloe said, trying not to think about her bladder.

"Lemonade?" Mrs. Crescent asked as she held up a corked bottle.

Chloe leaned in to whisper to her. "I need to dash off to the ladies' room."

"You do? How unfortunate. Well, one never thinks of such a thing out here on a picnic. You'll have to go in the woods—or walk over to Dartworth Hall. And remember, ladies don't run, even to the ladies' room."

"If you will excuse me, Mr. Wrightman. I need to use the—facilities." Under her breath she said to him, "Or lack thereof."

He bowed. "Of course. I recommend Henry's lab."

Henry had a lab? As in science lab?

"See it right there?" Sebastian pointed to a little brick building that stood beneath a clump of trees. "It's a lot closer than Dartworth.

And he happens to have one of those newfangled water closets all the way in the back of the building. Don't be long. I'll be waiting for you." He popped a grape in his mouth and plopped down on the picnic blanket. "Ugh, my tooth." He started rubbing his jaw again.

Chloe knocked on the door of the lab, but nobody answered. When she opened the door, light from floor-to-ceiling windows spilled into the room, shining on a neatly organized wall full of books. A large telescope on a tripod stood in a window. Wooden plank tables had centerpieces of test tubes in wooden racks, a primitive stethoscope, a camera obscura, and pieces of what looked like a gas lamp. A journal stood open on one of the tables, and next to it a volume of Shakespeare's sonnets. Everything, every single thing, piqued her curiosity.

It was like a snapshot of the inner workings of Henry's mind. If only she could get such a glimpse inside Sebastian's. She spotted the initials WC on a door in the back and stepped onto what seemed like a back porch. There it was, a sort of wooden toilet, the first toilet she had sat on in almost two weeks. Who knew that the sight of a toilet could make her so happy?

Chloe was straddling the primitive-looking toilet bowl, hoisting her gown, when suddenly she heard boots clomping on the floorboards in the lab. "Mr. Wrightman?" She searched for the toilet paper. There wasn't a basket of rags anywhere either. When someone pushed the door open, she put her hand up to stop the door from opening fully. "I'm in here!"

Whoever it was pulled the door shut again. "Miss Parker?"

It was Henry.

"So sorry. I had no idea you were in there!"

"It's all right, Henry. But—do you have any . . . toilet paper?" she squeaked.

Chloe heard him scrambling, and what sounded like a tin of

something fell to the floor. A moment later he handed her a bucket of rags.

Chloe used one of them. *Now . . .* Another nineteenth-century conundrum. What to do with it? None of this was in her rule book. She couldn't exactly flush it down whatever this thing was. She pulled the handle, but it didn't flush.

"Just bring them out here, Miss Parker. I'll take care of everything."

Chloe's head pounded with embarrassment. She creaked the door open.

He held out a cloth sack to her.

Without looking at him, she stuffed the rag in the bucket and he took it outside to a tin trash container.

She followed him. What a gentleman to deal with all this! "Um, to make matters worse, the water-closet thingamajig wouldn't flush."

"I know! I've been working on it every spare minute, and still haven't perfected that part of it yet. Here's a washbowl for your hands." He guided her toward an outdoor washbasin and handed her a large ball of what she recognized as very good soap. He wasn't wearing a riding jacket, his waistcoat was unbuttoned, his cravat untied, and his shirt, a pullover white muslin with a long V neck, hung open. His hair was disheveled.

"Thank you for helping out a damsel in distress." He had a delicious scent about him, an aroma of oil paints and turpentine, something only an arty girl would know and love.

"You're welcome. I hope you'll excuse my appearance," he said as he raked his fingers through his hair. "I just came from doing some painting in the field."

"Hmm," she said out loud. "I—I mean, hmm, your lab looks interesting." She peeked back into the building. "But I have to get back to my chaperone and your brother."

"Of course."

"Speaking of which, do you have something other than cloves for a toothache? Your brother's in a lot of pain."

He eyeballed a row of bottles from the doorway.

"He keeps rubbing his jaw."

Henry stepped into the lab, then returned with a tiny bottle in his hand, containing a scant amount of liquid. "Two drops of this, mixed with a non-alcoholic drink, should help. But no more than two drops. It's laudanum, and it's powerful."

"Thank you, Mr. Wrightman. I'm much obliged!" She took a few steps backward, turned toward the hill, and squirreled the laudanum in her reticule. "Why don't we have a water closet like that at Bridesbridge?"

"The Bramah water closet? Chiefly because I haven't figured out how to make it flush yet. As soon as it's ready, I'll have one installed at Bridesbridge. It's taken me this long to work it out. Along with the shower."

"Did you say 'shower'?" She stopped.

"I didn't realize that the subject of plumbing would cause you so much excitement. Have a wonderful time with Sebastian." He bowed.

Chloe curtsied.

She must've lost almost twenty minutes of her time with Sebastian by now. The breeze picked up, and then, *BANG!* A gun went off in the field behind her. She froze, her ears ringing and her heart pounding with shock. Turning and squinting, she caught sight of Grace, who was within shouting distance. She was practicing with her revolver and target. Damn her! Chloe stomped toward her, then stopped. *Wait.* That was exactly what Grace wanted her to do, to waste her alone time with Sebastian arguing with her about gunshots. Chloe spun around and made a dash for the Grecian temple, where Sebastian had dozed off and Mrs. Crescent was munching contentedly on a cucumber sandwich while reading a book.

"A lady never runs, Miss Parker. How many times do I have to remind you?" Mrs. Crescent said. "Sandwich?" Fifi wagged his tail as he chomped on a miniature mince pie.

"No, thank you." Chloe was too discombobulated to eat.

Just then, Sebastian, who was lying on the picnic blanket, propped himself up with his elbows. His jaw looked a little swollen. "Finally. You're back. I missed you." He stared at her without flinching.

It was as if she could dive into his eyes and float. She flashed him a smile. How was it he always knew what to say and do to make her feel like—well—a hundred thousand dollars?

She wanted to tell him about the laudanum, but that would bring up the impropriety of her having been with Henry unchaperoned. Hoping he'd forget about his toothache so they could get on with this date already, she decided to just spike Sebastian's lemonade with the stuff and be done with it. This proved easy enough to do. Sebastian had closed his eyes to sunbathe and Mrs. Crescent was deep into her book.

Chloe turned her back to the cameras. The size of the "drops" she was supposed to add to the lemonade, however, was clearly open to interpretation. She slipped two rather smallish ones into his drink, not wanting to give him too much. Then she read a Cowper poem to him aloud, the verse punctuated by gunshots, until he finished his lemonade.

Plucking a blade of grass to use as a bookmark, she asked him, "What did you think of that poem?"

He rubbed his jaw, contemplating his response. "I must confess. I was paying more attention to you than to the poem. I couldn't take my eyes off you, and I guess my mind started wandering."

Chloe looked at Mrs. Crescent, who winked and stuffed a Bath bun into her mouth. Off in the distance, she saw Henry walk out of the lab, mount his horse, and gallop off toward Dartworth. A cool breeze fluttered the corners of the picnic blanket.

Chloe picked up a sketchbook and charcoal sticks. She wanted to sketch Sebastian—his tousled black hair, his dark eyes and chin with that perfect little cleft in the middle. But a lady would never be so bold. She worked on a beech tree in the distance instead.

"Mr. Wrightman," Mrs. Crescent said as she handed Sebastian a second sketchbook. "I'd like to see you do a portrait of Miss Parker. I know one of your pastimes is sketching."

"It would be my pleasure." Sebastian sat up, placed the sketchbook down in his lap, took a sidelong glance at Chloe, and immediately put his hand on his jaw. "Ugh. This tooth is killing me." He rubbed his jaw again. "And these cloves aren't helping." He tossed them over his shoulder.

Chloe hoped the laudanum would kick in soon.

Mrs. Crescent took a sandwich from the basket and looked up at the darkening sky.

BAM! BAM! Two shots in a row got Sebastian's attention, and he put down his blank sketchbook to stand and make sure everything was all right in Graceland. And of course it was.

"I truly don't know how you tolerate her, Miss Parker." He sat back down. "Is she always like this?"

She smiled, because a lady would never articulate what was swirling around in her brain after a comment like that. She had to bite her lip to keep herself from saying exactly what she thought of her competitor.

He began rubbing his jaw again.

Chloe closed her sketchbook. "Mr. Wrightman, I do believe I'll go for a turn around the hill," she said.

"May I escort you?" He stood and straightened his cravat.

"Please do," Chloe said. She disappeared behind a fluted column and stepped into a grassy patch that was covered with orange and red poppies.

BAM! Another gunshot rang out.

The cameraman followed them, but Mrs. Crescent started talking to the camera, apparently with the goal of furthering Chloe's cause of getting Sebastian alone. The cameraman stayed with the chaperone for quite a while.

A ring-necked pheasant landed on a rock in front of them. Chloe stopped to watch it.

"What a beauty," Sebastian said as he eyed the bird.

A wave of warmth came over her.

"I can't wait until hunting season!" *What?* He pretended to hold a gun and shot at the bird.

The pheasant flew away.

"Excuse me?" Chloe's hands shook, along with, for a moment, her resolution. She thought he was an ornithologist!

"I'm kidding, really. I don't know what's gotten into me."

It was, no doubt, the laudanum, and that was, without a doubt, all Chloe's fault.

When they reached the grotto, she looked back toward the Grecian temple, but she couldn't really see it that well. It was fuzzy. She did need glasses! But it couldn't have been that far away. She wasn't allowed to be out of Mrs. Crescent's line of sight, although she was the most forgiving of chaperones when it came to anything to do with Sebastian. The breeze felt cooler now, and almost damp.

"Let's give the cameraman the slip," Sebastian said as he took her hand and led her into a thicket of trees, then through an opening in a huge hollow oak tree. He jumped down a giant hole and landed just under the tree roots. "Follow me down the rabbit hole, here." He held out his arms.

"That's not a rabbit hole," Chloe said as she peered down at him.

He laughed. "Of course it isn't. It's a secret entryway to the grotto.

Come on." He held his arms out and she slid down into them. The red poppies she had picked scattered at their feet.

For a moment they stood there, pressed up against each other in the grotto, listening to the water from the reflecting pond lap against the rocks. He slid the bonnet off her head and his hand traced her spine, then moved down to her thighs. His touch sent tingles up and down her.

"I'm feeling much better now," he said as he lifted her chin with his hand to kiss her.

It suddenly occurred to the lady that drugging her suitor might not have been a good idea.

BAM! What sounded like another gunshot echoed through the grotto, but this time it was accompanied by a flash, and both Chloe and Sebastian startled, looking toward the opening of the grotto. Rain was gushing down.

"We've got to go—" Chloe stepped toward the entrance, but Sebastian grabbed her by the waist and smiled, pressing her against the mossy wall. Lightning flashed again. Well, she'd gotten herself into this rabbit hole. Now how the hell was she going to get out of it?

The prospect of being in the grotto had been so intriguing to her—the rocky walls covered in moss, a table and two chairs chiseled into the rock. Now it seemed nothing more to her than a dank cave, where, even if she screamed her loudest, nobody would hear her.

Meanwhile, Sebastian was nibbling on her neck and pressing himself against her.

Much as she wanted him, and wanted to give in to her increasing desire for his increasing hardness, she knew that Mrs. Crescent would not approve.

"I thought you had a toothache!" She tried to pass the situation off as a joke, to push him away, but he just reined her in closer.

"I have to get back to Mrs. Crescent!" Her necklace chose that moment to stage its fall into her bosom and Sebastian promptly fished it out, letting his fingers delve into her cleavage. Then he flung it toward the grotto opening. The rain pummeled down sideways.

This was all her fault, the drug was too much for him. "Sebastian! Let's go!" She raised her voice, but he locked her against the wall of the grotto with his arms and stifled her with a kiss, which, under normal circumstances, might have been exciting. But by nineteenth-century standards, such behavior was beyond shocking. So she did what any lady would do in her situation: she hiked up her gown, raised up her knee with superhuman force, and decked him. But good.

"*Owww!*" He doubled over in pain.

Chloe dashed toward the grotto opening—looking back at him— and *wham*—she collided right into Henry, who happened to be barreling through the entrance at that very moment. This time she was thrilled to see him.

"Excuse me, Miss Parker," a soaked Henry said as he bent down to pick up her necklace and hold it up, the emerald dangling.

She reached out for it. "Thank you. I'm so glad to see you. I'm afraid I may have overmedicated your brother. He's breaking all the rules!"

Henry shot a glance at Sebastian, then glared at her. "How much did you give him?"

"Two drops—that was it, Henry."

Henry's brows furrowed. "I never should've given you that laudanum. Come on, Sebastian. Get into the carriage. It's pouring."

Henry held his greatcoat over Chloe as she stepped into the rain and into gooey mud.

Drenched, she bent to step into the carriage, where Mrs. Crescent was already sitting, and slapping her closed fan in the palm of her hand like she was holding a constable's nightstick. Sebastian lumbered in and promptly fell asleep. A raindrop slid down his nose and hung, poised on the tip of it.

Well, it was sure to be a date he'd never forget. Or had he already forgotten? Why did she give him that laudanum? It was a drug, after all. She had brought out his dark side, and now what? She couldn't deal? Considering the fact that she managed to drug, and then deck, the bachelor heir, she'd surely be on the next plane out of here.

These questions taunted her that night as she thrashed around in her bed. Her flimsy mattress made crunching noises every time she moved. Instead of getting her beauty rest, she was agonizing over what to do next, until finally she determined to solve that damn riddle of a poem and search Grace's room for items that she'd smuggled in. She needed proof if she was going to outwit Grace and win the money. Or was it to win over Sebastian? And maybe Henry's good opinion?

The money. The man. The men! Would she consider stealing something from someone else's room for money alone? She really didn't want to fall for Sebastian or Henry, or worst of all, for both of them. That would complicate everything, her entire win-the-money-and-run plan.

Her last lingering thought before she fell asleep was to remember to have her chambermaid add more straw to the mattress. It felt like she was sleeping on a board, which, essentially, was exactly what she was doing.

The next morning, after Chloe once again inquired about any letters, hoping for news from Abigail, and after all the women had won five Accomplishment Points for painting a footstool, Grace was out horseback riding with Julia. So after taking her usual romp around the grounds trying to solve the impossible riddle Sebastian had given her, Chloe snuck into Grace's very red, walnut-paneled, and humongous room, and rifled through the table in her dressing room. She wanted to find condoms and nail Grace with the evidence.

The room, with its wooden-beam ceiling and lead-paned casement windows, seemed more Gothic than Regency in style. A small fire glowed in the fireplace, and even though it was the beginning of July, the room was cold. But she had to find proof of Grace's cheating, because this morning, as she put extra butter on her roll, the butler announced that there would be an Invitation Ceremony that very night at Dartworth after the women displayed their musical talents.

Her hands shook as she rummaged through Grace's drawers, because she never did this kind of thing. Really.

When she used the bathroom in other people's houses, she never even peeked in their medicine cabinets. She would feel guilty just opening the sink cabinet to look for toilet paper if it ran out.

She tugged at the lion's-head pull to open the top drawer and it made a scraping noise. Her heart throbbed and she checked the door—still closed. Grace's dressing table, capped in Italian marble and nearly twice the size of Chloe's, had not only a bottle of rose water on it, but lavender water and orange water, too, plus a vase of fresh cabbage roses.

As her hands felt their way around in the drawer, she found all the expected things: hair ribbons, hair combs, and a—curling iron? She pulled it out. It wasn't a curling iron. She pressed the "on" button. It started vibrating. It was a vibrator!

"Yuck!" She dropped it to the ground. It fell with a loud clunk, but kept vibrating right near the dressing-table leg carved into the shape of a lion's paw. Chloe froze. Only her eyes jumped to the beaded silver doorknob. Nothing—yet.

Looking down at the flesh-colored plastic thing pulsing on the hardwood floor, she got the willies. How gross to know that she had turned on Grace's vibrator!

Thank God she had her walking gloves on. She swooped down to pick the thing up and shut it off. How did Grace smuggle that in here? Chloe didn't want to know.

With her gloved hand gripped around the vibrator, she looked in the ornate gilded mirror, about the size of a plasma TV, tilted on top of Grace's dressing table. Henry's spectacles, which she wore now whenever Sebastian wasn't around, made her look like a spinster on steroids. And maybe she was. She didn't own a vibrator. She didn't even know how to hold it, exactly. It looked totally out of place in her hands—period clothing or not.

Her hazel eyes looked browner than ever, and under the thick glass of Henry's spectacles, they appeared wider apart. Somehow, in the mirror in her room, as small and oval as her face, the glasses seemed okay. The poke bonnet with a straw crown and ruffled white trim completed the old-maid look. She frowned. Grace had already gotten a good laugh out of the glasses, and now Chloe could see why. She pulled the bonnet from her head, held it upside down, peeled back the ruffled cotton liner, and tucked the vibrator in. The poke bonnet had an extended crown, almost like a stovepipe, and quite a bit could fit into it. She opened the other two side drawers and found half a pack of cigarettes, teeth-whitening strips . . . eureka! The condoms! She tossed it all into the bonnet and eyed the doorknob.

Of course, the dressing table was way too obvious. Was there more? She peeked behind the tilted mirror, and something silver caught her eye. Reaching behind the mirror with her arm, she pulled out a foil packet of pills. Xanax? Weren't those antianxiety pills? What could a beautiful, titled lady possibly have had anxiety attacks about? *Please*. She put them back, not wanting to see Grace off her meds. Sheesh!

She looked under Grace's palatial canopy bed. Nothing. Chloe turned to the washstand, snooping around the linens. Grace had five walnut-sized soaps on her washstand. Five! Chloe pilfered one and stuck that in her bonnet, too. In the mahogany wardrobe that happened to be three times as big as Chloe's, she found enough gowns to make a princess swoon and it was no wonder Grace never wore the same thing twice. She closed the wardrobe door and turned the ornate bronze key in the lock.

She opened each little drawer in the hutch above the writing desk and found a pink MP3 player! She popped that into her bonnet, too, then carefully squished the bonnet on her head, tied the ribbons under her chin, and glanced in the mirror. Amazingly, it didn't look any clunkier on her than it had before she stuffed all those things in it. She scanned the room one last time before she turned to the door to go, but she heard Grace talking in the hallway.

Her knees went weak. *Damn!* Where could she hide? Her eyes ricocheted from the wardrobe, to the open casement window, to the bed. Grace's bed was high off the ground, even though that had gone out of fashion by the Regency, but it was, in the end, her only option. Her bonnet just made it under the heavy wooden bed frame, and it was too risky to reach for Henry's glasses, which had fallen off under the bed, near the edge of the Oriental carpet. The floor was dusty and her nose itched. She had about a foot-high field of vision from under the bed frame. Grace's boots and riding habit train came by first, followed by her chaperone's boots and riding train.

Chloe's bodice was smushed against the wooden floor. When would she be able to get out of here? Grace's chatelaine hit the dressing-table top with a clunk, like a key ring.

"I got a letter from my new lawyer," Grace said to her chaperone. "And?"

"He, too, claims the land's been with them so long that nothing can legally be done about it."

Grace's maidservant came in; Chloe saw her feet. She couldn't hold her straining neck up any longer so she set her chin on the dirty floor to rest. Grace walked toward the bed and her boot tips almost kicked Chloe in the nose. With a creak, Grace sat down on the bed, and the bedboard groaned above Chloe's bonnet. The heels of Grace's boots were practically in Chloe's face.

The maidservant knelt down to unlace Grace's boots. Chloe held her breath, as if that would help. Finally, the maidservant slipped the boots off Grace's feet, stood again, and Chloe exhaled.

Grace's chaperone walked to the other side of the room. "Well, then, you only have one choice, as I see it." She always spoke as if she had an English muffin in her mouth. Stuffy.

The maidservant must've been helping Grace out of her riding habit. A slight ruffling noise and the skirt and train disappeared. Chloe looked away, even though she could only see up to Grace's skinny calves. Chloe just wanted out of here.

The chaperone interrupted by clearing her throat, a not-so-subtle signal that the hired help might be listening. "We must get everyone else out of the picture. Out of your picture. No matter what it takes."

Chloe knew what they were talking about, so she was pretty sure the maidservant knew, too. Her chin hurt, and she turned her face the other way, to keep her neck from cramping up.

The maidservant's feet came into view. "Would you like to wear this gown, my lady?"

"No. No. The iridescent square-necked one." Both the maidservant's and Grace's feet walked away. Chloe heard splashes coming from the washstand where Grace must've been washing her face.

Grace's chaperone walked toward the door. "You know what needs to be done. This isn't just a game anymore. It's about the land. Dignity. Rightful ownership." The maidservant came back in and the door clicked shut.

Grace sat on the edge of her bed again—*oophf*—while the maidservant slid indoor shoes on her mistress's feet. Her gown seemed gorgeous to Chloe, even if she could only see it from the calf down.

"If that'll be all, my lady . . . ?" The maidservant's feet moved as if she was curtsying.

"That's all."

The door opened and shut again. Grace's shoes nearly stepped on Henry's glasses.

Blood rushed to Chloe's head, causing a colossal headache. Someone tapped on the door.

"Finally!" Grace whispered. "Get in here, quick." She closed and locked the door. Chloe's spirits sank.

A footman's buckle shoes and white tights came into Chloe's line of sight. Footman? Locked door? *Uh-oh.*

Giggles and kisses and little moaning sounds got Chloe's skin crawling. The footman and Grace scrambled to whip off their shoes and stockings, flinging them to the floor, and then—*thud*—the bedboard really sank down on Chloe. Oh God, no. She had to get out—now! But how? She grabbed Henry's glasses and wriggled her way toward the edge of the bed closest to the door.

Chloe squeezed out, pulled herself up to standing, and bolted for the door. Her hands quaked as she turned the lock. She couldn't look back, even though Grace yelled from behind her. "Just WHAT are YOU doing in here?!" She wouldn't turn around.

If only she had a camera phone, she'd have proof of this, too.

Chloe opened the door, and without looking back, she spoke. "I—I was looking for something. But I caught you with your pants down—I mean your gown up."

"How dare you hide in my room! Shut the door!"

"I would say you're in no—position—to do anything about me being in your room." Chloe leaped out into the hallway and clicked the door shut behind her.

Grace must've thrown a pillow at the door, because something hit it and slid down to the floor.

Where was the camera crew when she needed them? She ran down the hall, down the winding staircase. If she had a cell phone, she could've just called them.

Chloe had never run around so much in her life as she had in the past couple of weeks. As she ran down the gallery with one hand on her bonnet, she bumped into a footman carrying a silver salver.

"Miss Parker, you had a gentleman caller. We couldn't find you anywhere. He waited for upward of half an hour. He left his card." He held out the salver toward her. But she spotted a camerawoman heading into the parlor. "Wait! Cameras!"

She snapped up the card. It was Sebastian's calling card, with the corner folded down. She had missed him again! If she had a cell phone this would've been easily rectified.

"Hurry!" Chloe ran after the camerawoman, grabbed her by the arm, and tugged her toward the stairway. "You need to film something upstairs—"

Chloe tugged her up, through the hall, and right outside Grace's door. She ignored the woman's efforts to try to say something.

"There's no time to talk!"

The camerawoman turned to Chloe with an annoyed look. "My camera needs to be recharged. Portable battery's out."

Chloe's dust-covered chest sank. "What?! Well—stay here. You can be a witness." She swung open the door with triumph—and there was Grace, sitting fully clothed, alone, and reading on the bed. A maroon drape flapped in the open window.

The camerawoman rolled her eyes at Chloe.

Grace closed her book. "Miss Parker, I do wish you wouldn't barge in without knocking. It's not polite. It's just not done. Don't they teach any manners in America?"

Chloe leaned her square-cut back against the doorjamb and really looked at the calling card. On the back Sebastian had written, *I wanted to talk with you in person. But this will have to do. My sincerest apologies for my forward behavior.*

Why was he apologizing? Didn't he realize she had drugged him? Still, the two of them had upgraded from calling card to handwritten message on the calling card, and that was good.

"Miss Parker." Fiona bounded up the steps. "Mrs. Crescent wants you in the rose garden immediately."

"I'll be there in a minute."

"She said you'd say that. She wants you 'immediately.'"

"Is she having contractions?"

Fiona shook her head no. "But she said you'd ask that, and I'm to tell you that it is a matter of equal importance, with all due respect, miss."

Chapter 17

In the rose garden, the summer sun warmed the roses and perfumed the air around Chloe. This moment would've been bliss if her bonnet were not loaded with cigarettes, a pink MP3 player, condoms, and a vibrator.

Mrs. Crescent and Henry were discussing the upcoming birth. Henry straddled a wicker chair.

"You asked for me, Mrs. Crescent?" A bead of sweat slid down from under Chloe's heavy bonnet, past her brown tendrils, and onto her brow, where she wiped it with her walking glove.

Mrs. Crescent scowled at Chloe. "Whatever happened to your gown this time?" She brushed something off Chloe's capped sleeve with one hand and rubbed her belly with the other. Fifi circled around them.

Chloe looked down at her dress, and the vibrator slid to the other side of her bonnet, throwing it off-kilter. She steadied it with her hand as she noticed that her gown was flecked with dust and cobwebs.

She slapped at her skirt, brushing off the gown with her gloves.

"Do you need—a hand?" Henry asked as he squinted at her in the sunlight, the corner of his mouth turning up.

"No! No—thank you." Chloe said, finally settling back down on the settee with a squeak from the wicker. Her bonnet slumped to the other side, nearly falling off. Fifi lifted up his head.

She retied the bonnet ribbons tightly under her chin.

Mrs. Crescent collapsed in the padded chaise under a shady bower across from Chloe and Henry. "Miss Parker, I've told Mr. Henry Wrightman that I'd like your assistance during the birth," she said. "Will you agree to helping?"

Chloe gulped. She was no nurse. It would be the first home birth she'd ever witnessed. "Of course."

Henry shaded his eyes from the sun with his hand. "Ah. Here comes Mr. Tanner, the footman, one of Bridesbridge's most loyal employees. Let's hope he made good on my special request."

Mr. Tanner had worked up a sweat in the heat. He set a large wooden crate at Henry's riding boots.

"Toys," Henry said with a smile as he looked at Chloe.

"Toys?" Mrs. Crescent sat up and stared at the crate.

Henry lifted the lid off the crate. "I have arranged a surprise for you, Mrs. Crescent." He looked up at her with a smile and brushed the hair out of his eye.

Mrs. Crescent fanned herself. "If it is a toy, I am not amused."

Henry stood up and put the crate on the wicker table in the center of the parterre. "I've arranged for your boys to visit at three o'clock and—"

"My boys! Oh, Mr. Wrightman!" She dropped her fan, and he picked it up for her. "All of them?" She put her gloved hand on her heart. Fifi wagged his tail and jumped up and down.

"The entire brood."

Chloe's eyes welled with tears. "I'm so happy for you, Mrs. Crescent. To see your boys after all this time!"

Mrs. Crescent flapped her fan as if it were a wing and Fifi ran up and down the length of the parterre.

"Hence—the toys. But Miss Parker and I must test the toys first, of course." He pulled a wooden sword from the box and tossed it to Chloe, who caught it.

It had been weeks since she'd held one of Abigail's toys. A wave of sadness came over her.

Henry brandished a toy sword at her. *"En garde!"*

Chloe, with a hand on her bonnet, jumped up and pretended to duel with him. Their swords clashed and they both collapsed in the settee laughing.

Mrs. Crescent lowered her eyes at Chloe. "A lady would never—"

"Ah. But a lady would catch butterflies." Henry pulled two butterfly nets out of the crate and handed one to Chloe.

Chloe smiled. She looked at Mrs. Crescent.

Mrs. Crescent continued fanning herself and Fifi. "How can I refuse? My children are coming! I miss them so much—"

She did? Except for little William, Mrs. Crescent didn't talk about her children much, but then again, Chloe didn't talk about Abigail at all.

"I know you've missed them." Henry surveyed the lawn. "Mr. Tanner. Please have the canopy set up on the clover patch. I'm sure the boys will want to play ring toss and lawn bowl."

The footman dashed off as Henry unpacked the crate, stacked with historical reproductions of children's books, a flower press, sketchbooks and charcoal. He pulled out a pair of binoculars and set them on the wicker table.

"Do you have any bird-watchers in the family, Mrs. Crescent?" He winked at her.

Mrs. Crescent shook her head. "No. No bird-watchers. Too many other gizmos at our house, if you catch my drift."

Henry laughed, closed up the crate, and took one of the butterfly nets from Chloe. "I'm afraid bird-watching is terribly out of fashion—almost as démodé as catching butterflies." He picked up a huge jar and a piece of cheesecloth from the crate and headed out to the lawn with the net propped on his shoulder like a fishing pole. He stopped and turned, scanning Chloe from bonnet to boots. "Come on, Miss Parker. Let's see what you can catch." He headed for the hollyhocks.

Chloe looked at Mrs. Crescent, who turned her chaise to face the lawn. "Just remember." She pointed a finger at Chloe and lowered her voice. "The one thing you're supposed to catch—is Sebastian."

Chloe watched Henry as he set the jar down under the sundial. "I'm beginning to think they're both quite a catch. That was so thoughtful of Henry to invite your children."

Mrs. Crescent picked up Fifi. "Think again. You're here to win, and so am I. Do you want to be seen on the telly all across America as a failure? As the poor sap who fell for the penniless younger brother and lost out on a hundred thousand dollars?" She petted Fifi and looked out toward the side gate where the children would come spilling through. "We need to finalize the details of your gown for the ball before my baby comes, which could be anytime now. I'll give you a few minutes. No more."

Normally, Chloe would've been all over picking the trim for her ball gown and choosing just the right shoes. Instead, she scampered under the pink rose arbor with the butterfly net, hurrying toward the sundial. The only thing dragging her down was her bonnet.

Henry had already caught a butterfly, and after setting the jar on the stone ledge of the sundial, he slipped in a few hollyhocks for it to feed on.

The shadow on the green sundial showed that it was almost two-thirty. *Wait a minute. Sundial!* Chloe propped her net against the sundial and dug into her reticule for the poem. She turned her back on Henry and read the pertinent lines again:

As the clock strikes two you must find
Something in a garden where light and shadow are intertwined
Inspect the face in the garden bright . . .

After folding the poem back up and putting it back in her reticule, Chloe bent over the sundial's face. It had a green patina, and the dial itself stood in a formal knot garden. Why hadn't she put it together before? She had seen the sundial several times already. She studied the green patina on the face. She almost forgot that Henry was there until he cleared his throat.

Henry raised an eyebrow at her sudden fascination with the sundial and handed her the butterfly net. "If you see a dark brown butterfly with a red splotch or orange bands on each wing, it's a *Vanessa atalanta*. Better known as a red admiral. Oh, and I'm sure you'd recognize the orange-and-black one. *Cynthia cardui*."

Chloe grinned. "Of course I would. I go around spewing the Latin names for butterflies all the time." Her eyes followed the trajectory of light from the sundial, but of course, it was past two o'clock, and everything would be slightly off. She had memorized the next three lines of the poem:

Then follow the line of light
Straight to a house without walls
Enter the door and go where the water falls . . .

Chloe lifted her butterfly net. "I'll go this way." She padded in the direction the sundial pointed, until Henry began pontificating like a professor. As a proper lady would, she felt obliged to stop and listen, even though she could hardly wait to figure out where the shaft of light would lead her.

"Are you in a hurry for any particular reason, Miss Parker?"

"No. I'm just anxious to catch a butterfly, that's all." She swung her butterfly net like a golf club.

"Look," Henry said. "This one's a painted lady." He held up the jar in the sunlight.

She really didn't want to hear his nature documentary narration, but there was something about the way his large hands wrapped around the jar, something to the way he turned it while the butterfly flitted around, that stopped her. Suddenly she had a vision of him as he held her in her ball gown and turned her on the dance floor. She tried to shake it. She even shook her head, but the vibrator shifted, and the bonnet almost fell off. She tensed up and tightened the ribbons again. Really, she should've gone inside and emptied out the bonnet, but she had to solve the riddle now, and given all that she had to deal with at that moment, the last thing she needed was to fall under Henry's spell.

"You think you have it rough." Henry pointed to a butterfly in the hollyhocks. "Look at this green-and-white one. See the orange marking on the top of its wing?"

"Yes. It's beautiful." She watched as the butterfly lowered and raised its antennae at her as if it were trying to communicate.

"It's a male *Anthocharis cardamine*."

She smirked.

"All right, he's an orange tip. It's unusual for him to be around this late in the season. They only have eighteen days to find a mate."

"And then what?"

"They die."

Chloe picked up her net and aimed for the orange tip, but it flew off. The net billowed in the air. "That's harsh. If I don't find my mate, I just lose out on a hundred thousand dollars."

"You don't care about losing out on the money?"

"Well . . ." Chloe didn't know what to say. It must've been a trick question. "This may sound like a cliché, but to me, it's not about the money." And it wasn't, anymore.

A cloud floated in front of the sun and the shadow on the sundial disappeared.

"Oh no!" Chloe lowered her butterfly net.

"What is it?"

"I—I see some butterflies over there." She hurried in the direction the sundial had pointed.

Henry followed. "We'll see what kind of nineteenth-century botanist you really are."

The trajectory led more or less right into a thick hedgerow, and Chloe stopped at the dead end. Now what? Butterflies flitted around her. She looked at her net, then back at Henry, who leaned on his butterfly net as if it were a walking stick. He was watching her. "I've never caught butterflies before," she said.

"Really? What about when you were little?" The cloud passed, and the sun beamed down on them again.

Chloe stood back to see if there was a way around the hedgerow. She laughed as she pushed her fist into the net, straightening it. "I spent most of my childhood being shuttled between ballet, piano, and voice lessons. I hardly had time for catching butterflies." And she shouldn't be taking the time now either, but Henry was on her. She better just catch one and be done with it. She raised the net and aimed for the blue one.

"Wait." Henry reached from behind her and clasped her fist.

Her blue butterfly flew away. "Hey! I could've had him."

Henry bent her arm and lowered the net. "Did your mum have you take tennis lessons, too?"

"How did you know?" She stepped back and looked at his hand wrapped around hers.

He put his other hand on her shoulder.

"You're holding the net like a tennis racket. We're not out to kill. Think of it as netting a fish out of a fishbowl. Like this. Gently."

He guided her arm in slow, swishy, underhanded swoops. His minty breath felt cool on her warm neck. She shouldn't be here, like this, with Henry, when the riddle needed to be solved. The sun shone in what had become a Tiffany-box-blue sky, the birds sang overhead, and she was, of all things, chasing butterflies with a captivating man. How a guy could've made catching butterflies look manly, sexy even, blew her mind.

"There. That's better. Just relax."

Easy for him to say, he didn't have a stolen vibrator rattling around in his bonnet and a burning desire to find something that matched the description of a house without walls.

He released his hand from hers, and even in this summer heat, her hand suddenly felt cold. "Mr. Wrightman, would you be so kind as to fix my tiara? I'm quite sure you could do it, after all."

"I'm happy to do the smithing, but there isn't enough time to have it ready for the ball."

"That doesn't matter. I'll have a footman bring it to you before you leave. Please, though, don't let Lady Grace help you with it."

"Did Mr. Darcy allow Caroline Bingley to mend his pen?"

Chloe laughed. Did this mean he saw Grace as a Caroline Bingley type?! Chloe knew she couldn't be the only one who'd noticed a similarity between Grace and the Jane Austen character.

He pointed to a couple butterflies across the lawn in the lavender, and motioned her toward them, but then stopped and squinted toward the rose garden. "You're wearing my glasses and I'm nearsighted—is Mrs. Crescent trying to get your attention?"

"No. Not really." Chloe pretended not to see Mrs. Crescent, who stood now under the shady bower of roses, and waved Chloe in like a jumbo jet on a foggy runway. As Mrs. Crescent waddled toward them, Chloe's arm went limp and the net fell to her side. She didn't catch a single butterfly and she wasn't able to go beyond the hedgerow. She took a step back and crushed a clump of lavender behind her.

Fifi trotted up to Chloe as Henry bowed to Mrs. Crescent. "Thank you for releasing your charge for a few moments, Mrs. Crescent." He reached for the butterfly net in Chloe's hand, but she moved it behind her back and pushed it into the lawn as if she were staking her claim.

The servants had set up a green-and-white striped canopy above the clover patch.

Mrs. Crescent wiped sweat from under her cap with a lace-trimmed handkerchief. "Miss Parker, the mantua-maker is here to work on your gown." She lifted her watch from her chatelaine and tapped on it. "I would've sent a servant to tell you, but I thought I'd deliver the message personally, so you understand the sense of urgency."

Chloe looked back at the hedgerow. "Mrs. Crescent, Mr. Wrightman, you must excuse me. I'll be right with you. Just wait here!" She curtsied, held on to her bonnet, and ran all the way to the end of the hedgerow.

"Obstinate girl!" she heard Mrs. Crescent say.

"Is she, really?" Henry asked.

"I implore you, Mr. Wrightman, to please get her back here immediately."

Chloe heard all this, because she was on the other side of the hedgerow, exactly where the shaft of light would've pointed, and she found herself looking at a gazebo she had never noticed before.

"A house without walls," she said to herself.

By the time Henry caught up with her, she had discovered a fountain on the other side of the gazebo. It was in the form of a statue, a merman tipping a seashell, but the fountain was dry. She looked frantically for a secret door of some kind, but the fountain was solid.

"What are you doing?" Henry asked.

"Admiring this fountain," Chloe said. She was still looking for some kind of secret door when she stepped on a small metal square with a green patina. It must've had something to do with accessing the plumbing for the fountain.

"Your chaperone is growing very impatient. I think you've pushed her to her limit."

Chloe yanked on the weathered ring that was set into the metal until the small square creaked open. There, just under the lid, was a basket with a note that read, *You have found the secret door outside the house without walls, but have you solved the puzzle in the poem? If so, you may place your answer here. If not, then you must go back and begin again.*

Henry walked over, but Chloe slammed the lid shut just in time.

"Mrs. Crescent is waiting."

Chloe sighed. He escorted her back to Mrs. Crescent, who stood with her hands on her hips. Fifi whimpered at her feet. Chloe stopped and stood, statuesque, near the lavender, because a bumblebee had buzzed onto her bonnet and she hadn't solved the puzzle in the poem. She did a sort of whiplash move with her neck, the bee flew off, and the bonnet went toppling. It crashed to the lawn, rolled over, and the vibrator spilled out. It landed just in front of a marble statue of a naked nymphet smelling a marble rose.

Her first coherent thought was to thank God that the camerawoman who was following Henry and her had had to sneak off to go to the bathroom. The rest of the camera crew was off filming Julia and Grace horseback riding.

Mrs. Crescent and Henry gawked at the fleshy-looking object in the grass.

As Chloe watched a blue butterfly float by, and noticed how lovely the green-and-white striped canopy looked in the clover patch, she thought how perfect the moment would have been if not for that monster vibrator lying in the grass. She wanted to run, but everything, the canopy, the sundial, the secret door, the unsolved riddle, started spinning around, and she grabbed onto the butterfly net for support.

Fifi trotted over to the vibrator and sniffed it. Then he picked it up like a bone, carried it to Mrs. Crescent, and dropped it at her swollen ankles. Mrs. Crescent, with a hand on her belly, looked at Chloe.

Chloe clung to the butterfly net and swallowed. "It's not mine."

Mrs. Crescent's eyebrows furrowed.

"It's Lady Grace's."

"Of course it is," Henry said, unhooking his arm from Mrs. Crescent's. He pulled a handkerchief out of his pocket, bent over, and wrapped up the vibrator. He seemed to be stifling a laugh.

"I'm all for practicality, but it's hardly historically appropriate." Mrs. Crescent turned to Henry. "It—it's a—"

"A neck massager." Henry stood up with the wrapped vibrator in his hands.

"It is?" Mrs. Crescent turned her head to look at Henry, but because of her chaperone's poke bonnet, Chloe couldn't see her face.

"Absolutely."

"Well, you're the doctor. The neck massager should be confiscated."

Chloe's gloved arm swung out, knocking over the butterfly net. "No!"

Henry, who was cracking up now, turned his head away and pretended to cough. The white roses behind him swayed in the wind like little white surrender flags. Maybe she should've told them about the stash from Grace's room. They were on her side, weren't they? Chloe opened her mouth, ready to confess all.

Henry interrupted. "Here, Miss Parker. Take it." He held the sheathed vibrator out toward her.

The stretch of grass between them seemed to go on forever. Her cheeks flushed with heat.

"Take it back—to Lady Grace, of course." Henry smiled.

"See the mantua-maker immediately after that," Mrs. Crescent said.

"You have to believe me." Chloe studied his eyes. "It really is Grace's." She took the thing in one hand, still unsure how to hold it. She swung her bonnet up off the grass by the organza ribbons and plopped the swaddled vibrator in it, holding her chin high and her back straight, as if she had a book on her head, and sauntered toward the parterre.

Henry followed her. "I daresay, Miss Parker, it certainly doesn't surprise me that you have more than a bee in your bonnet."

Could he see the cigarettes and the MP3 player? Chloe eyed the bonnet swinging at her side. No. She whipped her head back at him and narrowed her eyes. Her hair spilled down around her sweaty neck and forehead. "Better to have a bee in my bonnet than nothing at all—like some of the ladies around here."

"Touché." Henry laughed, and Chloe cracked a smile, even as she looked straight ahead at the mantua-maker waiting near the partarre.

Chloe spun toward the kitchen door, where, on a wooden table outside, the scullery maid gutted fish. The fish skins shone in the sun and the stench almost made Chloe lose it.

"Not the servant door, Miss Parker—" Mrs. Crescent said in an annoyed-as-ever voice. "Take her through the main doors."

She had to walk past Henry, who politely bowed as she escorted the dressmaker to the main doors. As soon as the footmen closed the doors behind them, Chloe excused herself for a moment, and before the exasperated woman could protest, Chloe was up in her chamber. She stashed the vibrator, the MP3 player, the whitening strips, the condoms, and the cigarettes under the rags in the basket next to her chamber pot. Only the poor chambermaid touched that. She rang for a footman to bring her tiara to Henry.

In the parlor, as Chloe stood on a cushioned stool, the dressmaker pinned her dress for final alterations. The satin drapes had been drawn, and Chloe could see clear through to the parterre, where five boys spilled through the wrought-iron gate in the east garden wall. Each one of them wore knickers and a vest and looked straight out of a costume drama. Mrs. Crescent must be pleased at the historical accuracy.

"Turn, please," the mantua-maker mumbled with a mouthful of pins.

Chloe turned, and saw Henry playing with one of Mrs. Crescent's older boys. Which one was William? Mrs. Crescent hugged two of her littler ones, and they patted her pregnant belly. Henry gathered the boys around him and showed them the jar with the butterfly in it. They all looked, even the oldest one, wide-eyed, with tiny hands on the jar. Chloe thought only of Abigail. She would've enjoyed all this.

Henry held up the jar, pulled off the cheesecloth, and the butterfly flew up and around the boys, who clapped and jumped up and down.

The boys hung on to Henry, laughing and smiling, and Chloe got butterflies in her stomach. He was so good with kids. And, she couldn't help but think, he would be good with Abigail, too.

The dressmaker tugged on Chloe's gown to get her attention.

"Would you like a Greek-key trim or tattered lace?" Chloe tried to focus on the two snippets of trim the seamstress handed her. "Oh. Um. Greek key."

"Turn, please."

Chloe turned again and this time she saw herself in the full-length gilded mirror. The peach-colored silk gown glimmered in the summer sun that streamed through the windows. Was it just the light or did she lose about ten pounds? For the first time ever, she wanted to hop on a scale. Even with the glasses, she looked—like a lady.

Henry had a toddler in his lap and he was reading aloud from one of the children's books. A wave of warmth washed over her.

"You have lost inches since I was here last, Miss Parker."

Chloe heard the dressmaker, but she sounded far away, as if she were in another room.

Grace, in her low-cut white gown, sauntered over behind Henry and put her arm around his chair as he continued to read. She seemed to be reading it aloud with him to the boys. Henry looked up at Grace and smiled as they mouthed the words together.

Chloe's fingers clenched like claws. *Et tu, Henry? Wait a nineteenth-century minute.* She was getting jealous over—Henry.

Then Julia romped onto the parterre and set up the ring toss for the boys, and the boys left Henry and Grace alone with the book.

"Miss Parker?" A gorgeous footman, maybe even Grace's most recent conquest, held out a silver salver with a handmade envelope on it addressed to her. Chloe picked up the thick note and the footman bowed and left. It was sealed with a red wax *W*.

"Now for your pelisse, Miss Parker." The dressmaker held out the thin, floor-length tailored jacket for alterations. Chloe broke the seal and opened the note.

Dear Miss Parker,

I am hoping to see you at the upcoming ball. If you come to the ball, I would like to meet you at the ice house just past the stables after the last dance. I have something to ask you, so please arrive alone. Hoping you do not disappoint.

Yours,
Mr. Wrightman

Even with the tight-sleeved pelisse covering her arms, she got goose bumps. Of course, meeting Sebastian at the ice house alone would be against the rules, but it sounded like he was going to propose. He had something to ask her!

But didn't most Regency proposals take place in the daytime? In a parlor or drawing room, after all the sisters and nosy mothers had been whisked away? At least, that was what happened in the novels and costume dramas. This meeting had to be aboveboard. Sebastian wouldn't jeopardize her position on the show, would he?

Chloe repeated the poem again in her mind. She still couldn't decipher it.

As the mantua-maker cuffed the sleeves of the shimmery silk pelisse, Chloe watched Grace, Julia, and Henry play "London Bridge Is Falling Down" with the littlest boys. She could see them mouth the words: "Falling down. Falling down. London Bridge is falling down. My fair lady."

That was the problem with wearing glasses. You began to see things clearly.

Chapter 18

*L*adies, there are two invitations and three of you," said the
butler in the music room at Bridesbridge on Friday evening.
The women had displayed their talents on the musical instrument of their choice. Grace played the harp, as it was the most
expensive instrument, and it accentuated her higher-class status. Not
to mention the fact that harp players had the added bonus of being
able to flash some ankle while they performed. Julia played a complicated Regency piece on the pianoforte. Chloe attempted a Mozart
selection on the pianoforte—one that she'd played at a Christmas
piano recital when she was twelve.

Grace and Julia garnered fifteen Accomplishment Points while
Chloe earned five for effort.

She had to admit to herself that some time-management software
might've come in handy for such ongoing projects as the piano practicing, the needlework, and remembering to shake her vial of ink
three times a day.

Chloe stood between Grace and Julia, who tapped her toe on the

Aubusson carpet. Grace feigned a yawn. Chloe felt flushed and fanned herself. Mrs. Crescent, who lounged in a green tufted Grecian couch, looked down at Fifi and petted him.

The butler looked straight into the cameras. "Before we proceed, I would like to remind Mr. Wrightman that Miss Tripp has ninety Accomplishment Points, Lady Grace seventy, and Miss Parker forty-five. Mr. Wrightman has to take into account that Miss Parker failed to finish her needlework task even after a request to extend the deadline was granted."

Chloe felt the sting of that failure and she really cringed to know that the public announcement of it was being filmed. She didn't want Abigail to see it, for one thing.

"All three of you have gowns for the ball already made and fitted," said the butler. He rose up on his toes in his gold-buckled shoes. "But, only two of you will be invited to attend. If you are not chosen, you must immediately pack your trunks and you will be sent home tonight. The two that remain will be attending the ball tomorrow."

More than ever, Chloe wanted to stay. Surely, Sebastian wouldn't have sent her that note if he didn't want her to stay.

"Mr. Wrightman, if you please."

The butler stood aside, and Sebastian came forward. He looked elegant in his dark coat and breeches and a white cravat that showed off his tanned face.

Sebastian lifted an envelope from the salver. "Lady Grace."

It was like a guillotine slicing down. Chloe's chances were suddenly cut in half. It was going to be Julia or her. Even though the note he'd given her had raised her hopes, this had all occurred before her pathetic pianoforte performance, and anything could happen now. Fear of being sent home ripped through her. She realized the worst had happened: she was falling for Sebastian!

Grace curtsied as Sebastian bowed, and the ostrich feather in her turban brushed up against him. *Why her?!* Chloe fumed internally.

Sebastian gazed at Chloe and Julia, as if even at that moment, he hadn't yet decided which one of them he would choose. Chloe imagined having to go home to Abigail. Abigail would be thrilled to see her, but also crushed to know that her mother had been sent home. She'd be even more crestfallen to know that her whole life would have to change. They'd have to downsize, move out of the city, and Winthrop, being in a better financial situation, might even be granted the holiday and summer custody he wanted.

"Miss—" Sebastian paused for the cameras. He glanced at the envelope with the red wax W and then at the two women. "Miss Parker."

She could almost hear the French horns blaring triumph in her head. She felt tantalizingly close to victory, despite her pianoforte fiasco, because she was to meet Sebastian at the ice house. She said her good-byes to Julia, incredulous that Sebastian would let her go and Grace stay.

"Ladies . . ." The butler looked at Chloe and Grace. "Mr. Wrightman will see you at the ball tomorrow night."

Sebastian bowed, Chloe and Grace curtsied, and Chloe watched Julia as she didn't bounce, but shuffled into the foyer on Sebastian's arm.

"Good riddance to her," Grace said, and brushed her hands off as if she'd just gotten rid of an annoying fly.

The final task was the ball, and Saturday morning, Chloe put herself in the capable hands of Mrs. Crescent, Fiona, and even her chambermaid and a few random servants to help dress her, arrange her hair, fasten her jewelry, and make her up for the evening. She was as diligent as a bride dressing for her wedding, and it took a village.

Mrs. Crescent, alas, would not be going to the ball. She had to stay at Bridesbridge for fear of slipping in the mud and a superstition that a full moon might induce labor. Chloe would be under the dark wing of Grace's chaperone for the night, but even this didn't daunt her. Finally, the anticipated moment arrived.

Lit by the moon, the remaining ladies of Bridesbridge Place, Chloe, Grace, and Grace's chaperone, stepped out of their carriage in front of Dartworth Hall. Dressed in their silk gowns, ostrich feathers, and elbow-length white gloves, they stepped into mud thick as chocolate frosting from the day's rain.

The rain and mud, combined with the lack of Julia's sporting presence, not to mention Mrs. Crescent's, conspired to dampen Chloe's spirits, but she smiled in anticipation of her first ball in England, surrounded by English people with their English accents. And she quickened at the prospect of dancing with Sebastian even as she wondered at what to expect at the ice house.

After Grace and her chaperone were helped out of the chaise, the footman handed Chloe out and helped her balance on the steel platform pattens strapped to her pale pink ballroom slippers.

Chloe looked back at Bridesbridge Place. She missed Mrs. Crescent, however pregnant and persnickety she might have been. How could she pass this final test—the ball—on her own?

Cameras were everywhere and it made her uneasy. Granted, going with Grace meant she got to ride in the chaise-and-four. Still. Still, she was going to the ball with one of Cinderella's evil stepsisters, and she knew it.

Grace, in her wedding-white gown, looked down on Chloe from the first landing on the stairs. Chloe stretched her bejeweled neck toward the bright open doors of Dartworth Hall. She lifted her silk gown and pelisse and took a deep breath. Back home, everybody was eating cheeseburgers because it was the Fourth of July, but she got to go to a ball in one of the grandest country estates in England.

She teetered her way to the palatial staircase a good four inches off the ground in her pattens. They made a sucking sound every time she took a step in the mud. Everyone laughed as a footman's shoe stuck in the mud and he had to hop around in his stocking foot. How would she trek to the ice house in all this? And who knew it rained so much in England?

The maids ushered the women into the ladies' cloakroom, where one of them took off Chloe's Greek-key-trimmed pelisse and her pattens. The maid even retied her ballroom slippers, fastening the spaghetti-thin pink straps around her ankles a little too tight, but Chloe didn't complain.

She looked in the same mirror in which she had beheld herself after the hedge-maze debacle and hardly recognized what she saw. This time, instead of seeing a madwoman, she saw a peach-gowned princess with a tiny Empire waist trimmed in sparkly gold. Her arched eyebrows, blackened with ripe elderberries, beckoned. Candle-soot eyeliner brought her bright eyes to life. And this time she hadn't eaten her rouge. Was it the strawberry stain, or did she actually have cheekbones now? The weeks of not eating haunch-of-venison soup, raised giblet pie, and Florentine rabbits had paid off. She could market this Regency diet when she got home. She wished Abigail could see her now!

She smiled at her stick-straight hair that Fiona had transformed into a splendor of curls. But the pin curls and yellow beaded silk ribbon that swirled around her hair reminded her of—question marks. Were her feelings for Sebastian real? Or was she just projecting her idealized vision of Mr. Darcy onto him? Did she know him well enough to even say yes to a made-for-television marriage proposal?

"Miss Parker!" Lady Martha clapped her hands at Chloe.

Grace's chaperone always clapped at Chloe, as if she were a dog or circus animal.

Lady Martha put her hands on her silver-spangled hips. "Are you *quite* ready?"

"Really." Grace rolled her eyes.

Chloe was incensed, and with a huff she spun and led the way through the foyer. Video cameras rolled and cameras clicked away as she marched through the gallery, past rows of oh-so-serious Wrightman family portraits, toward an archway at the end of the marbled foyer that was flanked by two footmen and two candelabra. But, when Henry stepped out from behind the arch in a black cutaway coat, gray knee breeches, white stockings, an elegant ruffled white shirt, and gray gloves, she came to a screeching halt. He bowed. Then, from the other side of the arch, Sebastian appeared, looking as dapper if not more so in his black coat and buff-colored breeches. He bowed, too.

The only thing better than one gentleman was two.

Once again imagining a book on her head, Chloe floated along with video cameras at her side, her gown flowing at her ankles. She glided toward both Henry and Sebastian, who stood waiting in the anteroom. She was ready to glide, on both of their arms, into the pale yellow ballroom bedecked with gilt floral molding and sparkling with candles reflected in gilt mirrors when Henry, with his eyes, and a flick of his gloved hand, signaled her to step aside. She slowed her pace. She had forgotten to let Grace precede her. How could she have forgotten that?

Suddenly the ball of her right foot stuck to the ground, her heel lifted out of her slipper, and she stumbled. Grace had deliberately stepped on the back of Chloe's slipper!

She felt her face flush with color. Of course the cameras got that.

"Ballroom blunder number one," Grace whispered out of the side of her mouth as she slithered past Chloe.

Chloe shot a look at Lady Martha, who just lowered her eyelids in disdain. "You must enter the ballroom in order of rank. You must always remember your place, Miss Parker," she sneered.

Chloe leaned back on her heel and crushed the back of her slipper.

A cameraman cut from Lady Martha to Chloe as she watched Sebastian and Henry bow to Grace.

Grace's chaperone looked over her capped-sleeve shoulder at Chloe. "That would mean you come in behind us." She glanced at Chloe's slippers. "Go to the cloakroom and have a maid repair your lace. You cannot enter the ballroom looking like *that*."

A group of people dressed in ballroom attire sauntered past Chloe. One of the pink ribbons strapped around her ankle had broken. She looked up and saw Sebastian leading Grace and her chaperone into the glowing ballroom. Henry greeted the crowd with a smile and a handshake.

If she went back to the cloakroom now, she'd miss the opening minuet, and that was probably exactly what Grace and her chaperone had planned, even though Chloe, as she knew full well, had to sit out the first dance in punishment for her mishap at the archery competition. She ducked into an alcove, knelt down to fix the lace, and the camera was on it. Or was the camera on her cleavage? *There*. She'd fixed it. She stood up and flashed a fake smile at the camera. But she couldn't enter the ballroom without a chaperone—she knew that.

The footmen stood like soldiers guarding the archway. The cameraman filmed her biting her lower lip. Another crowd of ball goers passed by. Who were these people? Townfolk? Actors?

She stood awkwardly and pretended to check for something in her reticule when a whiff of garlic hit her. It was Cook dressed in a high-cut green silk gown and white gloves, her silvery hair held in place by a peacock-feathered hair band. Her blue eyes twinkled. "What's the belle of the ball doing out here?" She held out her arm.

Chloe took it in her own. "You don't want to know. I'm so happy to see you here. You look—gorgeous."

"Might I be your chaperone for the evening?"

Chloe beamed. Together they headed toward the anteroom.

"Tonight, at least for a little while, I'm a card-carrying member of the well-to-do Ton. You know. Society with a capital *S*."

"I know what the term *Ton* means," Chloe said. "And you more than qualify, as far as I'm concerned."

Cook patted Chloe's hand with her fan and lowered her voice to a whisper. "George had everyone at Bridesbridge dress as society for the ball. It's fabulous, but sad, in a way, too. The show's almost over."

"The show?" Chloe was always surprised when Cook stepped out of her Regency character. She wasn't at all like Mrs. Crescent in that regard. Then again, this could be another test.

"The reality show. The little charade."

Chloe just smiled.

Henry and Sebastian both turned toward them. Henry flicked the hair out of his eye and Sebastian adjusted his cravat.

Both men smiled at her. It had started out as a show. A way to score some money. But what was it now? Chloe's heart was on the line and it felt as fragile as a Regency-era Wedgwood teacup. First Henry bowed, then Sebastian. Sebastian escorted Cook into the anteroom, and seemed to slight Chloe. But why? Had her eye lingered too long on Henry when he bowed?

"So glad you could join us, Miss Parker." Henry offered his arm. "Before I escort you to the ball, would you like to see the library here at Dartworth—just for a minute? It's right over there. You don't need a chaperone with all these people milling about."

Chloe hesitated. "I don't want to miss the minuet, even though I have to sit it out."

"You won't. I promise."

As excited as she was about the ball, this might be her last chance to see the Dartworth library. She stopped. "This isn't code for showing me your etchings, is it?"

"Maybe."

"Is this some kind of test? Because I won't do anything to put my relationship with your brother in jeopardy. You must know, Mr. Wrightman, where my affections lie."

"I do."

Once Chloe walked into the library, she had to catch her breath. Hundreds and hundreds of candles had been lit and carefully placed around the room. The leather-bound books with gold- and silver-embossed titles on the bindings glistened in the candlelight. And, in tiny vases everywhere, were flowers from the heirloom cutting garden at Dartworth. Larkspur, snapdragons, bachelor's buttons, lilies, and foxgloves perfumed the air and seemed to sprinkle their colors against the dark wood paneling.

"It's—it's amazing. Did Sebastian do this?"

"I did."

"You did?"

Henry nodded. "I did it for you. And this is for you, too. I'll have a footman run them over tomorrow."

He placed three leather-bound books in her hands. Jane Austen's *Sense and Sensibility* in three volumes.

She ran her gloved fingers along the letterpressed title.

"Someday our kids will laugh about these things called 'books.'"

Chloe got stuck on his saying "our kids."

"Good thing we're both wearing gloves. It's a first edition," he said.

Chloe handed the books back to him. "I can't accept them. They're worth a fortune. I can't accept *any* of this."

"The books may be worth a fortune, but I never planned on selling them. I don't think you will either."

He looked at her with so much passion in his eyes that she— she swooned—and had to lean against the writing desk. "Henry. You have to stop."

"I must warn you that this goes against all the rules, but some things are better expressed without words." He gently but firmly nudged her against the bookshelves, the section labeled FANTASY, and he trapped her there with his arms. Their bodies crushed together as he kissed her deftly and deliciously. He stopped for a moment, and desire ricocheted through her.

"You really are quite accomplished, Miss Parker," he said. "Very talented."

He rendered her speechless. He cupped her cheek in his hand. "You don't have to say anything. I just wanted you to know how ardently I admire you."

The room spun a little around her, but the light-headedness could've been due to a lack of oxygen. She hadn't been kissed like that in a long time. Why was he doing this to her? Was this another test?

He checked his watch fob, which happened to be dangerously near his bulging breeches. "The minuet will be starting soon."

Chloe's mouth dropped open a little. He didn't want anything more than a kiss? Surely she did. But "Miss Parker" did not. Miss Parker had already gone too far.

"Perhaps, sometime, when there isn't a grand ball going on, you would like to accompany me back to the library?"

Chloe looked around at the candles, the flowers, the books, drinking it all in. All of it was slipping away already, like a good dream you only remember pieces of when you wake.

"You don't have to answer. I've read it all on your face."

She buzzed into the ballroom on Henry's arm. She felt as if she'd drunk a couple of glasses of wine. People approached Henry with smiles and swarmed around him. The height of the room, the gilded ceiling, the candlelight, orchestra, and gowns intoxicated Chloe even more than she already was. Cook made her way toward them.

Henry pulled out chairs for the two women. He motioned a flourish with his hand for them to sit. "Ladies, if you please?"

"I'm much obliged. Thank you, sir." Chloe sat, her vision of the evening torn asunder. She was bedazzled and bewildered all at once.

Henry said something about supper at midnight, lemonade, tea, coffee, and even wine, which, God knows she would've given her last soap ball for a glass of. She half expected to see Colin Firth or Hugh Grant mingling in the crowd. Chloe caught a sudden whiff of beeswax and a drop of something from above fell into the crook of her arm just above her glove. It hardened into a warm white circle. She rubbed it off with her gloved finger.

Henry pointed to the ceiling. "Wax from the candles."

She squinted up at a gold chandelier hanging high above her like an oversized halo. The ceiling itself was painted in a skyscape of white clouds, sunshine beams, and golden-haired cherubs.

"The candles melt quickly in all this heat. It takes an army of servants just to keep the place lit. Which reminds me. Mr. Smith?" He signaled a servant. "Please snuff out the candles in the library. Thank you."

The candles that hung above her had already melted to half their height. She wasn't ready for all this to melt away. She didn't want the candles in the library to be snuffed.

Her eyes welled up with tears. At least she wasn't wearing any mascara, but the candle-soot eyeliner might smudge. She dabbed the corners of her eyes with her glove.

Henry, of course, offered her a handkerchief. He always had a handkerchief. It was so old-fashioned.

An older woman, doused in Chanel perfume and draped in layer upon layer of silk, broke into their little threesome. "Mr. Wrightman—" She spoke to Henry, but looked down at Chloe, then deliberately turned so that her butt was in Chloe's face.

Cook squeezed Chloe's hand.

The woman hooked her arm in Henry's. "I simply must introduce you to my niece who's in from London. She's a doctor, just like you. You will absolutely adore her."

Who were these people? And why were they mixing with the unwashed from the reality show?

Henry bowed. As the woman led him away, he looked back at Chloe over his shoulder. "Save two dances for me."

"Of course." Chloe bowed her head, and when she lifted it, Henry and his companion had already disappeared into the crowd. *Poof.* It felt as if someone had doused the lights. Her eyes scanned the room for him.

"So." Cook tapped her on the knee with her fan. "Mrs. Crescent tells me you're really taken with Sebastian—I mean Mr. Wrightman."

Chloe opened her mouth to speak and looked at Cook, her familiar face, her smile as warm as plum pudding, and she realized she didn't even know her name.

"Here you've cooked every meal I've eaten since I got here—and I don't even know your name."

Cook crossed her legs under her glistening gown. "It's Lady Anne Wrightman."

Chloe opened up her feathered fan. "Your real name."

Cook smiled. "It's Lady Anne. I'm Henry and Sebastian's aunt."

It crossed Chloe's mind that this was a show, after all.

"Oh! I'm *so* sorry." Embarrassed, she started to sweat. She fanned herself frantically. "I just assumed you were, uh—"

"Not titled? It's understandable. I've spent the past month or so in the basement kitchen." Lady Anne laughed.

Chloe tried to reconcile this Lady Anne with the woman she knew as Cook.

"Don't worry, you were always very kind to me—and all the servants, for that matter. And I really put you to the test! But you'd best be careful with how you manage your fan." She looked at Chloe's fan.

"With that kind of fluttering, you're sending a message to all the men that you're engaged."

Chloe snapped up her fan and held it in her left hand, at the angle that meant "desirous of acquaintance." Lady Anne nodded in approval.

It hit Chloe like a ton of stale Bath buns that not only was she sitting next to the aunt of the two men in her life, but that the room was swarming with beautiful women in gowns with plunging necklines, and neither Sebastian nor Henry was anywhere to be seen.

The orchestra, discreetly hidden behind topiaries and shrubbery, struck up and everyone stood.

"Lady Anne." Chloe had to raise her voice loudly so that her companion could hear her over the music. She practically shouted. Unfortunately, though, at the very moment that she yelled, "Who are all these women?!," the orchestra took the liberty of stopping.

All the faces in the crowd turned toward Chloe, who fumbled with her fan and unwittingly sent all kinds of mixed messages around the room, from "kiss me" to "I hate you" to "you are too willing." She couldn't breathe.

"Play on!" Henry said from the top of the ballroom, and the orchestra started up again. And she breathed again. But she still couldn't see Henry.

The crowd circled the dance floor, and Chloe and Lady Anne nudged their way to the front, where Grace and Sebastian, as the couple of the highest status, opened the ball with a perfectly danced minuet.

Grace lived up to her name on the dance floor, and the minuet seemed to last forever.

Finally, the dance ended and Chloe craned her neck to see over and around everyone, and wished she was wearing a pair of heels instead of flats. Heels have their purpose, after all, just like so many things from the modern world that she missed. She managed to get a glimpse of the archway, but Henry wasn't there either.

"May I have the pleasure of this dance?" Sebastian bowed as he stared into her cleavage. Well, the pleasure was hers, really. On the ballroom floor, the women lined up on one side and the men on the other. For Chloe, one of the most elegant and joyous parts of the dance was this, the beginning, the anticipation, when the line of women faced the line of men and bowed and curtsied simultaneously.

Chloe looked forward to talking with Sebastian. Regency dancing offered a rare opportunity for a couple to speak privately.

Sebastian's black jacket was so beautifully tailored that Chloe did all she could do to keep herself from hanging on to his coattails. But she had to keep her hands to her sides now and during most of the dance. As with all Regency dancing, touching was minimal.

The orchestra struck up the first chords of "Mr. Beveridge's Maggot," the very song that Mr. Darcy and Miss Elizabeth Bennet danced to in the 1995 adaptation of *Pride and Prejudice*. They turned by right hands, touching for the second time, their hands low, each of their eyes locked into the other's. They turned by left hands and she felt the heat surge between them, but then again it was a summer night, there was no air-conditioning, and there had to be sixty some dancers on the floor. Despite the heat, it was a fantasy of hers come to life. She was dancing to "Mr. Beveridge's Maggot" in a gown, in a ballroom, in England, with the most attractive, most mysterious, and richest man in the room! She talked about the dance, but he didn't reply. She wondered if he was in one of his brooding moods, which she found both sexy and exasperating.

She smirked. "It is your turn to say something now, Mr. Wrightman. I talked about the dance, and you ought to make some kind of remark on the size of the room, or the number of couples."

He smiled. They came together and they parted, and doubt crackled through her. She almost forgot to cross and cast down the line.

Had he really caught the Austen reference she'd just made? She wasn't sure.

When they met again, she watched him as if he were a science experiment about to bubble over. He seemed to be concentrating on the figures, counting his steps. He looked so preoccupied that Chloe began to doubt that he'd even heard her Austen reference.

Toward the end of the dance, at the point where they faced, met, and led up, Chloe finally broke the silence. "I want to thank you for the apology you left about our outing, but really, I'm the one that should apologize."

He looked straight at her, and not at his feet, with his intense black eyes. "I'm so glad you brought that up. I can only say I wasn't myself—"

"Because of laudanum I put into your lemonade," she blurted. "It was all my fault!"

He looked incredulous. "You put *what* into my lemonade?"

"Laudanum. I gave it to you for your toothache."

Now he looked confused.

"It's some sort of a painkiller. I didn't give you much, but it was enough to push you over the edge, I guess."

"I don't understand why you didn't just tell me."

She sighed. "It's complicated." There was no winning this one. She was wrong for not telling him and wrong for being alone with Henry to get the medicine in the first place. He looked deep into her eyes, and she felt herself falling down that rabbit hole again.

She didn't want to disappoint him—but she needed to win the money. For some reason, though, she kept forgetting about the money. No doubt about it, her priorities had changed. She was actually putting Sebastian first and the prize money second.

Luckily, the dance was over. He bowed, and when she looked up from her curtsy, she finally saw Henry. He was pacing in front of a floor-to-ceiling window like a caged tiger. The rush of air behind him blew out candles as he walked and an annoyed-looking servant had to relight them in his wake.

"Can I interest you in some negus, Miss Parker?" Sebastian asked. He slid his arm in hers and guided her away from Henry, toward the top of the ballroom, where the orchestra sat behind the topiaries. The lively English reel they were currently playing grew louder as they approached, and they couldn't hear each other talk, so there was no point in saying anything. Chloe linked her arm in his as they headed toward the refreshment tables in the conservatory, where a crush of people gathered under palm trees in huge ceramic pots.

Just as they were about to cross into the room, where the wine that Chloe was craving awaited them, Grace and her chaperone suddenly appeared, barricading the entry.

"I've been looking all over for you." Lady Martha scolded Chloe like a child. "A girl is not allowed to be alone at a ball. This could be reason enough to have you sent back home." She put an indignant hand on her hip.

"I'm not alone," Chloe answered her coolly. "I'm with Lady Anne Wrightman."

Grace and Lady Martha looked at each other. Lady Martha looked back at Chloe. "Lady Anne would not associate with the likes of—"

"Miss Parker is with me." Lady Anne—aka "Cook"—appeared as if magically conjured, and linked her arm in Chloe's.

Clearly suppressing their frustration, Grace and her chaperone curtsied.

Sebastian took Lady Anne's hand, and he kissed it. "How nice to see you again."

Lady Anne smiled at him, but turned to Grace's chaperone. "I need to go back to Bridesbridge soon, and at that time I will return Miss Parker to you."

"Very well." Grace and Lady Martha curtsied again to Lady Anne and made their way back to the ballroom. Chloe had to laugh at the sight of their fawning behavior toward someone whom, when she was merely known as "Cook," they wouldn't have deigned to look at.

Sebastian brought Chloe and her companion a goblet of negus.

Just as Chloe raised the goblet to her lips, Lady Anne turned toward the ballroom. "I need to sit down. Let's go." She took Chloe by the arm and Chloe, who didn't even get to taste her drink, handed it to Sebastian, who downed her glass as well as his own.

When Lady Anne found a seat, Chloe found that Sebastian had disappeared, and as she smoothed the bottom of her gown to sit, she saw both Sebastian and Henry on the dance floor. Sebastian was dancing "Upon a Summer's Day" with Grace and Henry was paired with someone equally beautiful and intelligent looking, probably the doctor from London he'd been fixed up with.

Chloe tapped her fan in the palm of her gloved hand. She watched the red-haired London doctor, who had no doubt showered, brushed her teeth, and put on real makeup today. But more than her looks, Chloe watched the way she and Henry talked and nodded and laughed through the dance. Sebastian and Grace just stared at each other.

Chloe stood, sat again, and smiled a zigzag smile at Lady Anne, who patted Chloe on the knee.

The dancers formed a circle for "Sellenger's Round." They circled to the left, then to the right. Sebastian and Henry and their respective partners, like distant planets, traveled in an orbit far, far removed from Chloe's universe.

She didn't even belong as a guest in this ballroom. How could she have dreamed of being the mistress of an estate like this? She didn't know how to care for two-hundred-year-old painted ceilings or gold chandeliers that hung fifty feet off the ground. How did you clean two-story floor-to-ceiling silk draperies anyway?

She felt herself shudder and tried to watch Sebastian, but her eyes kept gravitating toward Henry.

"Henry really knows these dances," said Lady Anne.

Chloe agreed. He moved through the dances with such ease. His doctor friend kept screwing up, but somehow he corrected her and made it look like she knew what she was doing. Fascinating as it was to watch just how he did this, Chloe just couldn't watch him arm in arm with another woman. She had to turn away.

Finally the dancers formed a circle again, and everyone's backsides swirled in front of Chloe, including that of the blue-gowned London doctor.

Lady Anne pressed her hand on Chloe's knee just as the music grew louder. "You haven't taken your eyes off Henry the entire time we've sat here, do you know that?"

"I haven't? I keep looking at Henry?" Chloe forced a smile. "Well, I can hardly see a thing. I don't have any glasses on. And neither do you, I might add!"

Lady Anne laughed.

The dance ended and Sebastian asked Chloe to dance once again. She accepted. He seemed to want to be with her.

They danced "Le Boulanger" and this time Chloe had to concentrate to remember all the figures and steps. Another thing she hadn't practiced as much as she should've!

Sebastian seemed to know this one and kept talking as he danced. He told her about the sixteen-inch fish he caught fly-fishing the other day. And the regimen of log lifting and a red-meat diet his trainer was putting him through to prepare for a boxing match. Then he recounted the moment he first saw her, their time in the castle ruins, and how he carried her from the hedge maze, all in incredible detail. "The best memories I have of these past six weeks are of moments I spent with you. Only you."

As she counted her steps, his eyes began to wander, and as they were waiting their turn to dance up the line, he stared at a certain woman who leaned against a column. Chloe squinted. It was Fiona, dressed up in a golden gown with a white plume in her hair. It looked as if she'd just arrived. How could Sebastian be wooing her and scoping out Fiona at the same time? Then again, she had just kissed his brother in the library, not more than an hour ago. Although technically, he had kissed her.

Chloe spotted Henry, arms folded, blond brows furrowed, and hair fallen into one eye. He glared at her and Sebastian from across the room.

Something raced through her.

Henry was smoldering!

She danced up the line opposite Sebastian with renewed energy. When she reached the top of the line, she looked back toward Henry, but he was gone.

"May I have the pleasure of one more dance?" Sebastian bowed and his biceps bulged under his tight jacket. A man asking to dance with the same woman twice in a row was a strong signal that he was serious. Anyway, if she refused him, according to manners of the day, she'd have to sit out at least two more dances. That was an entire hour.

"You may." She curtsied.

But before the orchestra started in, she heard a familiar voice above the din. "Attention! Attention!" George, all suited up in Regency attire, stood on a wooden platform and the crowd gathered around him. George looked like he was dressed for Halloween; the breeches, coat, and cravat didn't mesh with him at all. Still, Chloe was happy to see him. So much had happened this evening that the concerns of the modern world seemed to have disappeared.

"The next dance will be a waltz," George said. The crowd clapped and he nodded.

A cameraman jockeyed for a better angle at George, who raised his voice. "Which, the participants in our show know full well, was very controversial in 1812." The beautiful people looked at Sebastian and Chloe.

"The waltz, first introduced during the 1800s, allowed a couple to touch in a slight embrace. And in 1812, it caused quite a scandal."

The crowd laughed.

"You laugh, but the participants in our show have hardly touched each other during all the weeks of filming."

If he only knew.

"Unlike the present day, touching actually meant something during the Regency. It was a sign of commitment. Now, without further ado, I present to you what is sure to provide one of the most risqué endeavors of our entire stay . . . the waltz."

Chloe licked her lips.

George raised his arms and the orchestra struck up.

Just as Sebastian's gloved hand was about to encircle Chloe's Empire waist and her gloved hand reached out for his shoulder, Fiona, white plume pumping, slid between the two of them.

"Miss Parker." Her eyes widened and she wrapped her gloved hand around Chloe's arm. "Mrs. Crescent has gone into labor and she's absolutely begging for you to come to her side!"

Chloe's heart skipped. "Wh-what?" she stuttered.

"Mrs. Crescent wants you—now—it's time!"

Chloe's arm, the one she almost wrapped around Sebastian's shoulder, went limp. Her bare shoulders slumped.

Sebastian squeezed his fist, then relaxed his arm. The dancers twirled around them, a blur of color. Chloe felt the cameraman zoom in on her face—not one of her best cinematic moments, she was sure of that. Her mouth felt funny, like after a shot of Novocain.

"Hurry!" Fiona shouted above the music.

Chloe turned to go, but Sebastian reached out and squeezed her arm, pulling her back.

She shook her arm loose. "I have to go. Fiona—is that where Henry is?"

"Yes—that's where he is," Fiona said.

It made sense.

Sebastian retracted his arm and bowed.

"Tell Lady Anne!" Chloe shouted over her shoulder to Sebastian as she dodged as many waltzing couples as she could, like a pinball on the dance floor. She collided right into the London doctor, who sneered and still smelled of Chanel.

At the edge of the dance floor Chloe took a deep breath, and drank in the room and the waltz music as if to sustain her. That was when she saw Fiona and Sebastian waltzing.

But instead of throwing a fit or even feeling jealous, Chloe felt— nothing. Sometimes, though, as she knew full well, in moments of great shock, numbness set in, to protect a fragile heart.

She did feel the camera on her face as it panned from her to Sebastian and Fiona dancing, and back again. She spun on her heel-less slippers and hightailed it through Dartworth Hall. At least this time she wasn't dressed as a footman! She cut through the library, thinking it would lead to the gallery, but this wasn't the library. It had a bed in it . . . this had to be the biggest bedroom she'd ever seen. The room, lit on either end by two dwindling fires, seemed wallpapered with books. Two butterfly nets stood propped up against a writing desk. She turned around and a cameraman was right behind her. Without thinking, she asked him, "Where are we?"

The cameraman didn't answer. But she knew.

A sword and mesh fencing mask lay on the writing desk, along with a *W* wax stamper. A pile of handkerchiefs stood on the washstand. *HW* was embroidered in the corner. This was Henry's room. And was that a jockstrap hanging from the chair? It seemed rather— large. Ladies didn't lurk in gentlemen's bedrooms, examining their protective gear, especially not while their chaperones were in the throes of childbirth. Her face flushed.

She hurried out the same door she came in, retraced her steps, and finally found her way back to the portrait gallery.

She lifted her gown, scurried down the marble stairway, grabbed her pelisse from the cloakroom, and scampered out the front doors into the night. At the bottom of the palatial steps she saw the footman.

"I need a carriage and a driver!" She was out of breath. "Mrs. Crescent's having her baby!" She pulled her pelisse on.

The footman looked out toward the stables where the carriages were parked. "It'll take half an hour to ready a carriage."

Chloe paced on the bottom step. "Half an hour! I can't wait that long—"

"Here." The footman untied a horse from a horse post. "Take a horse. It'll be much faster."

She took a step backward.

The footman took her gloved hand with her fan and reticule hanging from the wrist and he lifted it. "I know it's saddled western-style, and not for a lady, but I'll help you up. You should be all right."

"No! No, thank you." Chloe pulled her hand back. "I'll sprint over there." And she sprang off the bottom step right into the pasty mud, where her ballroom slipper promptly got stuck. When she tried to lift her foot out of the glop, the lace almost broke again. She looked up at the footman, who smiled and extended his hand to help her out of the mud.

Okay, okay, so she missed cars, and taxis, and buses, and maybe even Harleys.

Chapter 19

The footman flirted with her. The guy couldn't be a day over eighteen and might even be jailbait. But Chloe didn't want to waste a minute, no matter how flattering the situation.

Finally he slid her muddied pink ballroom slipper into the stirrup.

Shaking, Chloe hoisted her gown up to her knees and flashed her silk stockings at the footman as she swung her leg over the horse.

The cameraman came closer to her, and she knew she was breaking every rule in the book by riding western style in her ball gown, but—Mrs. Crescent was having her baby! Her gown had ripped, but she clenched the reins and squinted, barely able to make out the torchlights in front of Bridesbridge. She brought the horse to a gallop as she hunched down low, near the horse's warm neck.

The horse seemed to go nowhere, like in a nightmare in which you're running and running but not moving at all. She had to get to Mrs. Crescent. She had to! Her hands sweated in her dance gloves and her calves cramped up as they squeezed the horse's sides.

The moonlight cast an eerie glow on the muddied road, and the dark trees seemed foreboding. When she finally arrived, she patted the horse on the neck with her quivering hand. Her reticule and fan, intact, swung from her wrist.

"You did it, boy. Good job. Good job." There was no footman, nobody at Bridesbridge, so she tied the horse to a tree.

Her hair and ribbons had tumbled to her shoulders and she wiped sweat from the back of her neck as she took the steps at Bridesbridge Place two at a time. Even the night watchman was missing in action.

A single candelabrum, with stubs for candles, burned in the dark foyer. How was that for a fire hazard? Did the place even have smoke alarms? Why didn't Chloe see these hazards before?

She scampered out of her totally ruined slippers, chucked them under the neoclassical credenza in the foyer, and grabbed the candelabrum. She slid a hand along the mahogany railing, padded up the staircase, and stopped at the landing, where, if it weren't dark as hell, she could see the lineup of casement windows.

Okay, so if Mrs. Crescent was giving birth, why was it so quiet and dark?

The soles of her feet flattened against the warm Oriental carpet at the top of the stairs. She felt her way to Mrs. Crescent's door and opened it a crack. A flicker of candlelight leaked out and spilled onto the threshold.

"Mrs. Crescent?" Chloe knocked on the doorjamb.

"Come in."

Chloe nudged the door open with her hip. Mrs. Crescent, propped up with plum-colored pillows in her great sleigh bed, dropped her nineteenth-century newspaper on her nightgowned belly like a tent. The headline read: HUNDREDS OF BRITISH SOLDIERS FALL IN FRANCE." She wiggled her bare toes. "Can the ball be over already?"

Panic seared through Chloe. She thought about Fiona, in her gold gown and white plume as she urged Chloe to leave. "You're not—having the baby?"

Mrs. Crescent was petting Fifi, scrunched on the edge of the bed. "Oh, I'm having the baby all right. Just not right now, dear."

Fiona had lied to her.

Chloe steadied herself with a hand on the Chippendale bookcase, sending her reticule and fan swinging. But why? Was she after Sebastian?

"Did you know that Lady Grace finished her fireplace screen? You'll have stockings to mend tomorrow. And how did you rip your gown?"

Chloe fingered the rip in her dress, took a step back into the dark hallway, and creaked the door closed.

"Miss Parker?" Mrs. Crescent struggled to sit up in her bed. Her voice sounded muffled, as if Chloe were hearing her from deep underwater. Her reticule and fan slid off her wrist to the floorboards. She swooped up both, grabbed her walking boots from her room, yanked them on, and headed for the front doors, where she swapped the candelabrum for an oil lantern abandoned by the night watchman.

"Miss Parker! Chloe!" Mrs. Crescent called after her.

Chloe finally stopped running when she felt the ground under her rise up in a mound. Then *wham*—she stubbed her toe on what felt like a huge rock.

"Ouch! Damn flimsy boots!" She dangled the lantern at a brick chimney capped with a wooden hatch door protruded out of the ground in front of her. Last week she might've thought the chimney was part of a picturesque little summer home with an earthen roof, but now she figured it was probably a smokehouse. Pig carcasses hanging from meat hooks flashed through her brain.

Flat-footing her way down the slippery side of the earth mound, she breathed deep and held back the tears. She should've known that Fiona was conspiring against her. That line about her fiancé being on military duty was, no doubt, a lie. Her pelisse trailed in the mud behind her while the moonlight sparkled kaleidoscope-like in her teary

eyes. Fiona couldn't win any of the money, though. Only the contestants could. What would Chloe do without that cash infusion?
She and Mrs. Crescent needed that money more than anyone. And
just because Fiona was after Sebastian didn't mean the feelings were
reciprocated.

Down at the bottom of the mound, wooden double doors stood
tucked into the earth, each with great iron hinges pointy as daggers.
She pressed up against the doors and buried her face in her arm. The
wood felt cool against her shaky hands.

Back home it was seven hours earlier, and it was the Fourth of July.
Abigail would be in the bicycle parade and everybody was playing
badminton and croquet and packing the lemonade and buttermilk-
fried chicken in picnic baskets for the fireworks. Here—there were no
fireworks to speak of. Not even a spark.

Something crunched on the forest floor behind her.

"Miss Parker, is that you?"

The lantern almost slipped from her hand. Henry swooped down
from his horse as if out of nowhere. "I didn't mean to startle you.
What are you doing here?"

"That's a very good question. Good question!" She sniffled. "I
suppose I might ask you what you're doing here! Anytime I'm where
I shouldn't be, you show up."

He smiled. "The footman at Dartworth informed me you'd taken
one of my horses to Bridesbridge. When I got to Bridesbridge, Mrs.
Crescent told me you thought she was having her baby, and stormed
out. I saw the lantern light from the road."

He guided her over to an old tree stump and she sat down, unable
to talk. In the flickering light of the two lanterns, he looked concerned. Worried, even. "Are you quite all right?"

"Not really." Chloe looked down at her ripped gown, collapsed in
the middle like a popover that didn't pop. The tips of her boots
pointed in at each other. She clasped her hands between her knees

and squeezed her fingers against her knuckles as if that would stop the tears. She and Henry shouldn't be here together unchaperoned in the dark, but nobody else seemed to be playing by the rules, why should she?

"Well, for one thing, I'm a little homesick. Today is—" She bit her lip and looked up at the stars. Red, white, and blue stars.

"Your Independence Day."

Another chunk of hair fell from her updo. "Ha! My Independence Day. Hardly." A white star shone brighter than the rest. "I hardly feel independent."

Henry gathered stones into a circle and marked the beginnings of a fire. "I disagree."

"Please." Chloe stood up and picked up sticks for the fire. "I'm in a gown I didn't even put on myself, chasing around some guy I thought I knew, thinking he's going to be my happy ending and solve all my problems. When am I going to learn?" She tossed the sticks into the stone circle.

He lit a fallen branch with the flame from Chloe's lantern. The dry branch sputtered and sparked. "I think you're quite independent. Here you are halfway around the world. On your own. In another culture—and navigating another time really." With the flame on the stick, he lit the fire in the stone circle and flames danced up all at once. "All this during a national holiday that marks your country's break from ours. It's got to be difficult."

"It's not difficult." She poked at the fire with a stick. The aroma of a campfire brought back memories of all those summers at camp out on the East Coast. She lifted her stick from the fire and watched a flame flicker around the end of it. "I never liked hot dogs. Or baseball. I liked my grandmother's crumpets. She was from England, you know. I liked the song 'God Save the Queen.' As for fireworks—well—"

Henry tossed a small log into the fire and it crackled and snapped.

"I love them. You can never have enough fireworks."

"It must be a little conflicting to be an American and an Anglophile all at the same time. Is that why you're here at the ice-house at this hour?"

Chloe's legs turned to white soup. She stood up and leaned against the wooden doors of what she thought was a smokehouse. "Ice-house?"

Henry kicked mud on the fire to put it out. "Yes. Whatever are you doing here? I didn't even get a chance to dance with you."

The fire dwindled under clumps of mud. Chloe looked behind her at the hinged wooden doors. Her torn ball gown and muddied boots flashed in the last flickers of firelight. Sebastian might show up any minute. "This is the ice-house?"

"Yes. Yes. Now, why not go back to the ball?"

Chloe stepped back from the wooden doors and picked up her lantern. Limestone blocks surrounded the wooden doors.

She caught her breath. "I thought this was a smokehouse."

Henry lifted his lantern and splashed the ice-house doors with light. The doors shone a lacquered red that Chloe hadn't noticed until now. He pulled a ring of keys from his coat pocket, unlocked the doors, kicked them open, and a wave of cool, earthy air spilled out and over Chloe. What was he doing with the ice-house keys, anyway?

"Come and see," Henry said, his voice echoing.

She looked over her shoulder into the forest, but Henry's words lured her in.

"Look, they built the inside with laced brickwork more than a foot thick." He held the lantern up to the ceiling and Chloe could suddenly see him, years from now, decades even. He'd point out things like the friezes at the Parthenon or baguettes in a Parisian bakery window to his wife, somewhere in the fuzzy future.

As Chloe ventured into the domed, beehivelike cove, the sad smell of melting snow enveloped her.

Henry tipped his lantern toward great, huge blocks of ice covered in straw. A trickle of water went down a drain somewhere within. The cool floor penetrated her calfskin boots and her legs grew cold.

Henry nudged the wooden doors nearly closed. "You would think they'd have used the ice-house to keep their meat and fish, but they didn't. They would cut ice from the ponds in the winter, cover it in straw, and then use it to make ice creams, cool drinks, and syllabubs during the summer. If a house could offer such luxuries during the summer, it raised the owner's social status—"

And this little history lesson would've been interesting if Chloe weren't wondering when Sebastian would show up. She pushed the wooden doors back open and Henry dropped his arm, his lantern falling to his side.

He cleared his throat. "Sorry to bore you—"

"No—no—you're not boring me. Not at all! It's just—"

"Allow me to escort you back to Bridesbridge." He held the doors open for her, then locked them behind her and slipped the keys back in his greatcoat pocket. He untied his horse and walked him over to her. "Let me help you up on the horse." He bent down and laced his fingers together, offering her a step up. The horse bent his head down, and his mane flopped into his eyes, as if he, too, agreed she should go back.

But Chloe didn't step up. "No! I mean—no, thank you." She curled her fingers around the lantern handle.

She thought she heard the sound of hooves in the distance. The fire barely glowed now. Henry bent to pick up his lantern and held it up to the dark forest. He heard a horse, too. He mounted his horse and looked down on Chloe. "You're meeting Sebastian here, aren't you?"

A breeze rippled around her. She looked into the orange-and-black embers of the fire. She had to think of Abigail and William.

"Why didn't you tell me?"

The hooves sounded close now. A lantern bounced behind the trees.

Henry yanked the reins on his horse, turned him, and looked back over his shoulder, bowing his head, his eyes looking past her, at the ice-house. "I bid you farewell."

She licked her lips to speak, but his horse spun, its tail swished as if Chloe were a fly that needed brushing away, and the horse carved up clods of mud as he galloped off. Henry was gone—*poof*—into the blue moonlit darkness.

Much as she wanted Henry, she couldn't have him! She was meant to have Sebastian.

She pressed her back against the cool wooden ice-house doors and goose bumps raced up and down her arms. In one fell swoop, Sebastian entered her circle of flickering lantern light, dismounted, tied up his horse, approached her fast and sure. He cupped her face in his warm hands, but she turned away.

"What is it?"

It was only everything. But she did have something to hang her bonnet on. "It's Fiona. Is there something going on between you and Fiona?"

Sebastian laughed. "She's only a kid. I think she has a little crush on me. I just danced with her. That's all."

"That's not all."

"So I flirt with her a little bit every now and then. I could say the same—or more—about you and Henry."

Touché. She didn't want to blow this chance with him, and a squiggly smile skirted across her lips.

"I'm so glad you joined me here." He kissed her, and kept one hand on her neck while another hand expertly reached down—into his pocket for keys.

His mouth tasted like hard liquor. A flickering of tongue, a clinking of keys, and she practically fell backward into the ice-house. Her reticule and fan fell to the brick floor.

He ringed her waist, steadied her, and set her down so gently, so gallantly—on an ice block covered in straw. A chill penetrated her thin silk pelisse and gown and her butt went numb.

"This is so hot," Sebastian whispered into her ear as he dug in his pocket for something. "Isn't this hot?"

Chloe nodded, feeling rather chilled. How naive of her to think he would propose. She looked up at the laced brickwork, remembering Henry's strong fingers laced together. Mostly she remembered the look on his face when he realized she wouldn't be going back to the ball with him. She winced.

Sebastian's fingers glided down her stocking and he slid her gown up to her thighs. And it would've been hot if it weren't so damn cold! His other hand slipped out of his pocket, and in the faint lantern light, Chloe caught a glint of silver, heard a click, and a knife blade flashed dreadfully near her neck.

She sprang up and catapulted toward the doors. He beat her to them, barricading them with his wide shoulders.

She froze. She already was frozen, but she froze some more.

He smiled. "It's just my penknife." He held the knife in the palm of his hand and it did look small, now.

Chloe stepped back until her calves hit the block of ice. She grabbed her elbows, pulling her pelisse in around her.

"Relax." He spoke and his voice was as soothing as cough drops. "I have a great idea. You're going to love it."

She leaned on the ice block, clenched her fists, and wondered how far this would go. No matter how attractive Sebastian was, and how he held everything she wanted and needed in the palm of his hand, she felt as if she were forcing herself. Danger, too, rippled through the air.

Sebastian edged in next to her and massaged her neck with one hand. She had to admit, it felt good. He chipped off a piece of ice with the knife in his other hand. He flung the knife to the door, where it stuck like a dart.

"Bull's-eye!" He looked at her with smiling dark eyes and she could see the little boy in him. Playful, but playing with things he shouldn't have been, like knives.

"Now, where were we?" He turned her face toward him with a brush of his finger along her cheek. The piece of ice dripped in his hand.

What was she so afraid of?

He traced her jawline down to her neck with the ice. He licked his lower lip, glided the ice along the crescent moons of her breasts, which peered out from her bodice. Her nipples hardened and she began to grow warm.

He kissed away the melted ice in her cleavage. He slipped off her pelisse. Puh-lease. He was smooth, she had to grant him that.

She melted. She combed his tussled hair with her fingers. With every lick of his lips, her breath grew shorter, shallower.

He was adept at unbuttoning her gown, unlacing her stays.

She untied his cravat, unbuttoned his waistcoat, and feverishly untied his breeches.

The drop-front pants took her by surprise. She didn't realize Regency men didn't wear underwear.

She was horizontal on the ice block. *Drip, drip, drip* . . . the melting ice trickled down a drain somewhere in the darkness.

Her shoulder blades stung from the ice. She propped herself up on her elbows.

"Wait a minute." She pressed her hands into his muslin shirt and felt the throbbing of his heart, or at least the bulging of his pecs.

"I have protection," he said.

"I hope it's not made of sheep's gut."

He looked confused. Very confused.

"You knew Regency condoms were made out of sheep gut or fish membrane, didn't you?"

He shook his head. "No. I really don't care—" He slid her gown higher up.

The bricks. The straw. The ice! What kind of a sadist would've picked a place like this for a tryst, anyway?

"This just isn't right. I can't do this. A Regency lady would never find herself in this position." She looked him straight in the eye.

His hands gave up on her back laces and he looked hurt. "What position?"

"The horizontal one." She pulled herself up to sitting and straightened her stays. "In an ice-house. Like a common trollop."

He tenderly leaned over and devoured her with a kiss that could make a trollop forget everything—almost everything.

He whispered just under her earlobe. "You're so excited you've got gooseflesh."

"They're goose *bumps*. And I've got them because I'm freezing. Now stop!" She pressed her hands against his shoulders and stood up. The laced brickwork closed in on her. It smelled like dank dog. "This is not how it's supposed to go." She picked up the lantern.

He yanked his shirt down over his rapidly shrinking shaft. Still, he managed to look somehow manly in his long white shirt, bare legs, and riding boots. "How what's supposed to go?"

"You. This. Everything." She thrust her arm up at the arched brick ceiling and paced the cold brick floor in her boots. She felt her torn gown billow behind her; the lantern swung and tossed light randomly around the dark brick like broken glass.

"Wait!" he said just as she aimed for the doors.

He was down on bended bare knee, his shirt, and everything else—dangling. He stretched out a hand toward her.

She stopped, set the lantern down, took his hand, and put her other hand on her hip. "This better be good."

He kissed her hand as if it were about to disappear forever and looked up at her.

Something as warm as oil burning in a lantern came over her.

"Miss Parker, will you marry me?"

"What?" She laughed and one of the ice-house doors swung open with a breeze, sending in a pool of moonlight.

"Don't laugh."

She bit her lip.

He pulled her closer, taking both of her hands. "I do believe I've fallen in love with you. I don't know why I haven't asked you sooner. Will you marry me? It'll be the perfect ending. The perfect television ending to our real-life beginning."

A white gown, flashbulbs flashing, and a carriage festooned with white flowers paraded around in her brain. Did the Regency Anglican church allow divorced mothers to wear white?

He pulled her closer, leaned his head in toward her hips, and wrapped his arms around the small of her back. "You don't have to answer right away. Just let me know you'll think about it."

"I will. Think about it." She thought about Abigail, the money, her business, William.

His knee must've been frozen.

He kissed her hip bone, moving slowly across her pelvis, where she felt the warmth of his lips through her crepe-thin gown to the other hip bone, and a tingling like she hadn't felt in years sparked all over her. She lifted off his shirt and laid it on the ice block where he flopped down. He pulled her on top of him.

"Say yes," he murmured as his fingers worked the buttons on the back of her gown. "Say yes."

She closed her eyes. She'd gone from something close to a governess to a temptress in a moment's time, and he'd taken her there. "Yes." She closed her eyes and kissed him with hungry lips and tongue. "Yes!"

And she would've said yes again, but he ripped her bodice open and a lantern appeared at the ice-house doors.

She almost fell off him. What if it was Henry?!

"Excuse me, sir—Mr. Wrightman!" Thank God it was just Sebastian's footman who shone the lantern on them. Sebastian palmed her breasts to cover them as the lantern light swung away.

"Oh—so sorry—ehm—sir."

"That will be all, Smith. Thank you."

Henry called all his servants "Mr." or "Miss" and then their surname.

"It's Mrs. Crescent, sir." Mr. Smith turned around and spoke toward the forest.

Chloe tucked her breasts back into her torn bodice, buttoned up her pelisse, and swung her leg off Sebastian for the dismount.

"She's having her baby, sir," Mr. Smith said.

Chloe turned toward the footman. The shadow of his ponytail and wig appeared in the moonlight at the door.

Sebastian propped himself up on his elbow and grabbed Chloe with his other hand just as she moved toward the doors. "This is of no concern to me. Now be gone."

"Yes, sir." The footman bowed his head and closed the ice-house doors.

"Mr. Smith! Wait!" Chloe smoothed down her pelisse and tossed Sebastian's breeches over his midsection. "Is it true? Is she really having the baby right now?" She tugged a boot on.

"Yes." Mr. Smith looked away, into the moonlight, confused about the question. "Of course. I heard her myself from downstairs. She sounds in terrible pain."

Chloe lunged toward the door, but Sebastian grabbed her arm and snapped her back.

"Ouch!" Her arm smarted.

Chapter 20

"Be gone, Smith!" Sebastian sat up on the ice block and yanked his breeches on with one hand and clamped Chloe's arm with the other.

He sneered. "How the devil did he know we were here anyway?"

Chloe turned toward the laced brickwork around the ice-house doors, and tried to wriggle her arm free.

She had totally messed up everything. Her fan splayed across the brick floor. Her yellow-tasseled reticule, flung near an ice block on the other side of the lantern, sat in a pool of melting ice. The outline of Henry's glasses showed through the silk.

She couldn't see much beyond Sebastian's lantern, but heard Mr. Smith's horse gallop off. His lantern bounced away like Tinker Bell disappearing into the night.

Sebastian finally released her arm, combed his hand through his disheveled hair, and took up the lantern. "I didn't want the hired help to know you've been alone with me. You understand, right? I didn't want to compromise your reputation. You'd get booted off the

show. Or we'd be forced to marry. But then you had to—talk to him."
He threw his arms up in the air, Italian style.

"Right." Chloe tightened her pelisse around her like a second
skin. Hypothermia set in. "I need to go." She shivered uncontrollably
and picked up her fan and her soaked reticule.

A real gentleman would've never strong-armed a lady. Then
again a real lady would've never found herself in an ice house at midnight with Sebastian the bodice ripper. What was she thinking? He
only had one proposal in mind, and that didn't involve any kind of
church ceremony. Is that all he wanted from her? Sex? Is that why he
always seemed to say exactly what she wanted to hear?

She stepped into the moonlight. The sudden brightness made her
squint. With a clink of the keys, Sebastian locked the ice-house
doors behind them. "I'll escort you back."

He was hot, he was cold. He could be decent. He could be an ass.
But he wasn't the one.

"Did you really mean it when you said you had fallen in love with
me?" Chloe asked.

"I think so. But this has all been very difficult for me—"

That was all Chloe needed to hear. George must've written up
Sebastian's bio, because the man described as Sebastian Wrightman
was not this Sebastian Wrightman. She'd thought this whole thing
was real, and that's where she had gone wrong. She was channeling
Mr. Darcy when she should've been paying more attention to what
was right in front of her.

He helped her up onto his horse. In silence, he led the horse toward Bridesbridge Place. She looked up at the moon as the horse
loped beneath her. She had just narrowly escaped, and she had the
full moon to thank for inducing Mrs. Crescent's baby.

When the moon was full in England, was it full at home, too?
Chloe wondered. Abigail loved the full moon. Chloe used to be
Abigail's moon, orbiting around her day and night, year after year,

never faltering. Now? Now she didn't think she could ever fall happily back into that eternal elliptical path without feeling alone and cold. Still, the moon called her home like a force stronger than gravity.

On their way to Bridesbridge, they passed the castle ruins. In the moonlight, Chloe could see how the castle had been pummeled by cannonballs. She could see the holes in the walls so clearly now. Why hadn't she seen them before?

Still, she had to win the money. Otherwise it wouldn't have been worth it to leave Abigail.

What was going to happen now that they got caught with Sebastian's breeches down?

At the bottom of the stairs at Bridesbridge Place, she buttoned her pelisse up to her neck. A candelabrum dripped on the griffin-footed table near the banister. A sudden howl from Mrs. Crescent rang out, and it echoed throughout the foyer. Waves of fear and memory crashed through Chloe. She'd never forget that peppermint-green birthing room, the thirst, the pain, the joy of childbirth. Slowly, she slunk up the steps, candelabrum dripping in the one hand, reticule and fan drooping in the other.

How could Mrs. Crescent have a baby here? Without electricity? Without phones? Without relaxation music? And—why?

It was almost as crazy as thinking you could find true love on a TV show.

The closer Chloe got to Mrs. Crescent's room, the more intense the breathing sound became. Chloe had to change her gown. What did a lady wear to a birthing room, anyway? She tiptoed past Mrs. Crescent's half-opened door.

"Miss Parker!" Nothing escaped Mrs. Crescent, even when she was giving birth. "Come here immediately! *Owww!*"

Henry's low voice, like water over river rocks, calmed and comforted Mrs. Crescent . . . and Chloe. She inched the door open. Mrs. Crescent groaned in pain. Chloe couldn't bear to look at the birthing bed—just yet. Instead she focused on their shadows, larger than life on the blue wall. Henry's shadow, Mrs. Crescent's shadow, and—the camerawoman's shadow all flickered in the candlelight like a pantomime play. Would this surreal night never end? And did this, too, need to be filmed?

Mrs. Crescent's shadow rocked back and forth, her knees up, her hair down and scraggly. Chloe squeezed her eyes shut and buried her nose in the silky sleeve of her pelisse. She might need her vinaigrette. She set the candelabrum on the dressing table.

Henry's shadow reached out and massaged Mrs. Crescent's back. "Push. Gentle now. We're almost there. One, two, three. Right. Stop pushing. Breathe. Excellent."

His shadow turned toward Chloe and bent to check his pocket watch. "How kind of the lady to pull herself away from her diversions to help us."

"It was hardly a diversion. It was enlightening. And I would've been better off here." Chloe still couldn't look at either of them. She curled her upper lip and talked to Henry's shadow on the wall. Mrs. Crescent grumbled in pain.

Nothing else might have been real, but this was. Chloe pulled off her gloves, rolled up her sleeves, and looked down at her hands.

"Scrub up, Miss Parker!" Henry nodded toward a washbowl across the room.

Henry wore a billowing shirt with the sleeves rolled up and the collar open. A slight tension pulled the shirt across his broad chest and she could see the curve of his muscles. With his cutaway coat off, his tight drop-front breeches revealed a body more enticing than Sebastian's, if that was even possible. But she was done with men in ruffled shirts and breeches, wasn't she?

"What are you waiting for, Miss Parker? Wash up, please."

My God, Mrs. Crescent was having a baby, and Chloe's mind was in the gutter, even after a scrape in the ice-house with an absolute rake.

Mrs. Crescent started her breathing, and Chloe hustled to the wash table.

"Do put on a pair of latex gloves," Henry instructed.

"Latex gloves?" The hot water scalded her hands and the soap-suds felt—real. She snapped the gloves on. She whispered to Henry, "When were these invented? Not during the Regency, I'm sure."

Henry lowered his voice. "If you must know, Miss Parker, it was 1964. Now please come and help Mrs. Crescent relax."

Relax? Nothing could've prepared Chloe for what she saw when she turned around, except gory hospital and crime shows that she never watched because she didn't have cable.

Chloe rocked back on her boots, reaching behind her for some-thing to lean on. Her hand awkwardly bumped Henry right on his tight ass. All manners, he pretended nothing happened.

"I offered her a sheet for modesty as they would've done in the Regency, but she refused."

Chloe knew there was no modesty in childbirth. She watched Henry unroll a suede package on the dressing table.

"Obstetric kit."

It was an obstetric kit from the Regency era. The instruments, tucked in the suede kit with a strip of leather, looked more like prun-ing shears, great big tongs, some sort of a spatula, and the biggest fishhook she'd ever seen.

One glance would've been enough to get anyone—maybe even Grace—to sign on for a life of spinsterhood and celibacy. "You're not really going to—"

"To use these? Hardly!" He lowered his voice to a whisper as he pulled out the wooden forceps. "But this is what the OB or 'accouch-eur' would've used. We've come such a long way in just two hundred years. No wonder one in three women died in childbirth."

"What?! One in three—"

"Ugggggggggggh!" Mrs. Crescent's face contorted into a grimace. Red splotches and sweat covered her face and neck.

Henry handed Chloe a stack of cool, damp washcloths. She hadn't known that one in three women died during childbirth in the Regency. It was hard to reconcile the gowns and the glitz and the romance with this horrific statistic.

She scissor-stepped over to the bedside and dabbed Mrs. Crescent's forehead with a washcloth. Her voice wavered. "Just think, Mrs. Crescent, soon you'll be holding your beautiful, healthy, happy baby. Your baby will know you just by your heartbeat, your voice. It'll look up at you—"

"It's a wonder you know so much about childbirth!" Mrs. Crescent exhaled deeply, focusing on Chloe's torn gown barely covered by a hastily buttoned pelisse. "Whatever happened to your gown *this* time? It's a fright. An absolute fright! And your hair is down!"

A warm and glowing feeling came over Chloe, just knowing that Mrs. Crescent was still herself. She brushed Mrs. Crescent's hair out of her face.

Henry scanned Chloe from her slightly askew amber necklace to her muddied hemline.

Chloe looked away and her eyes fell on her fan and reticule at the washstand. "Mrs. Crescent, you'll be happy to know I remembered my fan and reticule."

Mrs. Crescent clenched the stiff sheets on her sleigh bed.

Chloe's knees went wobbly. She couldn't do this. She wasn't a nurse and this wasn't a hospital.

"Time to push again," Henry said with the utmost calm.

Mrs. Crescent banged her fists on the bed. "Ugh!"

Chloe let go of the wet washrag.

"One, two—" Henry counted, easing Mrs. Crescent into a more comfortable position.

Chloe's head throbbed and she couldn't breathe, she couldn't take it anymore. "Henry! We need to get her to a hospital. It's not really 1812 here, you know. She needs an epidural—now. Who the hell has a baby without an epidural?"

The cameraman aimed at Chloe. Henry dropped his watch and it dangled from his watch fob.

"Sorry. That was very unladylike."

Henry looked with affection and sympathy at Mrs. Crescent. "Three. And breathe."

Mrs. Crescent could breathe, but Chloe couldn't. She broke out in a sweat.

Henry massaged Mrs. Crescent as he glared at Chloe. "Miss Parker, this is what Mrs. Crescent wants. A natural birth. It's too late for the epidural now. Please. Get ahold of yourself. You'll upset our rhythm."

She gulped. She didn't know Henry could've been so—type A.

Mrs. Crescent leaned over and picked up a brown medicine bottle from the night table. "Should she have a dram?"

Henry shook his head. "If you don't need it, she doesn't. I just concocted it for fun in my lab."

Chloe straightened and clenched her Empire waist. "What is it? Maybe I could use it."

"It's laudanum, and no, you can't have any. You don't have any medical reason." Henry handed the bottle to a servant. "Take it away." The servant hid it behind Mrs. Crescent's dressing-table mirror and then hurried to change Mrs. Crescent's bed linens.

Mrs. Crescent huffed and puffed. "It's an opiate."

Chloe tilted her head. "As in opium?" *Great.* She had drugged Sebastian with opium.

"Yes." Henry continued to massage Mrs. Crescent's back. "It's used for everything from headaches to liven up an evening in a drawing room. It's a sort of cure-all."

Chloe put another cool washrag on Mrs. Crescent's forehead.

"Look." Henry reached for a shelf above Mrs. Crescent. He lowered his voice. "We have a mobile phone in case of emergency. An ambulance is at the ready." The phone glistened in his latex-gloved hand. Without thinking, Chloe took it from him. She squeezed it in her hand, held it close to her chest. If only she could call Abby. Emma. But knowing she or Henry could call the ambulance made her feel better, and she put the phone back on the shelf.

Henry's valet burst into the room. "Ice shards, sir."

"Set them near Miss Parker. Thank you."

The valet took one look at Mrs. Crescent and bolted out the door.

"Miss Parker, please give Mrs. Crescent an ice shard—"

Mrs. Crescent opened her dry mouth and Chloe put a piece of ice on her tongue. The ice brought it all back to her. So much swirled around her. Birthing Abigail. The ice-house. Sebastian. The look on Henry's face before he rode off.

Henry looked at his watch. "In just a bit, we'll push again."

The camerawoman readied for another dramatic scene.

Mrs. Crescent pushed, exhaled deeply, until at last the baby crowned.

"My baby!" Mrs. Crescent sweated and squealed with joy.

Chloe's eyes teared up, remembering her first sight of Abigail's face. She'd do anything for Abigail. Anything. Even this. Even marry the on-again off-again Sebastian in a fake ceremony.

Henry turned to Chloe with a list of instructions as he supported the baby's head and eased it into the world. He lowered his voice to a whisper. "A shoulder is stuck. I need to guide it out. Here. Hold the head."

Hold the head?! Chloe cradled the baby's head with her slippery gloved hands.

"Should I call the ambulance?" Chloe cringed as she watched Henry work the tiny shoulder out.

"We'll be fine. We can do it."

A split second later he slid the shoulder out and the hot little baby slipped into Chloe's hands. Her heart throbbed.

Henry swooped in, wiping the baby's mouth and eyes clean. Then he lifted the baby like a prize for Mrs. Crescent to see. "It's a girl! A girl, Mrs. Crescent!" The baby cried.

Chloe would never, ever again romanticize the Regency. Every single love that culminated in marriage would end like this: with natural childbirth. Because there wasn't any reliable birth control. The mother would be lucky to survive, and probably become pregnant within a year, and every year thereafter. No wonder all of Jane Austen's novels ended with the wedding!

Mrs. Crescent quivered with happiness and exhaustion. Chloe covered her with a blanket. Mrs. Crescent held her arms out for the baby.

"You'll have her in a minute. Just a minute," Henry said. "Miss Parker, I need you to hold the baby now."

Chloe took the baby in her arms. She looked away as Henry cut the umbilical cord.

"Well done, Miss Parker." He took the baby from her, and his face beamed. The room seemed to light up. "Go soothe her. Give her water. I'll clean up the baby. Unless you want to, of course."

Chloe laughed. "I'll let you do that."

Mrs. Crescent gave Chloe a little squeeze.

"Thank you, Miss Parker. You were wonderful—"

Chloe shook her head. "No—you were. The baby's perfect. She's beautiful. It's the girl you always wanted." She pulled off the soiled latex gloves, washed her hands, and poured Mrs. Crescent a glass of water. She couldn't believe they did it. Without a hospital. Without an epidural. But she'd never want to help with a nineteenth-century birth again, that was for sure.

Henry brought the cleaned and swaddled baby toward Mrs. Crescent. But before he handed her to her mother, for just a moment, he put his arm around Chloe, and she leaned against him. She saw their shadows, the two of them, together, and a tiny profile of a baby reflected on the wall. Then he stepped away and handed the baby to Mrs. Crescent.

Henry stood right near Chloe, their arms brushed up against each other.

"Mrs. Crescent, we need to do a little stitching," he said. "Please give the baby to Miss Parker for a moment."

Chloe couldn't believe it. Stitching? Without painkillers?

Mrs. Crescent kissed the baby and handed her off to Chloe, who rocked her like an old pro. Because she *was* an old pro! For the first time in a long time, Chloe knew where she belonged, and that was at home with her own daughter, in the land of cell phones and ambulances, hospitals, painkillers, computers, and e-mail.

"You look like quite a natural," Mrs. Crescent said to Chloe. "You'll be a great mum someday."

The baby's eyes closed tight, like little crescent moons.

Chloe shot a look at Henry, who had been watching her.

Henry smiled at Mrs. Crescent. "I've gotten word that your husband and children are on their way. They'll be here soon."

Then Henry snapped on a fresh pair of latex gloves and threaded a needle. Chloe's stomach lurched. She handed the baby to a servant girl behind her. "Excuse me, I need some air." She lunged for her fan and reticule and ran out.

When she stopped running, she was outside, and breathed the early-morning air in heavily. She collapsed on the steps in front of the semicircular gravel drive, under a lit torch. She fanned herself frantically. She untied the hospital gown and it fell in a heap at her boots. The clock in the foyer behind her chimed three times.

Someone came and put an arm around Chloe. It was Fiona.

"I didn't mean to hurt you," she said.

Chloe couldn't look her in the face. She just stared at her Celtic tattoo. "You lied to me. Just so that you could dance with Sebastian?"

"Sebastian's a terrible flirt. He danced with me for one dance and he had promised me at least three."

"What's your deal, Fiona? Are you after him, too?"

Fiona hung her head. "I wanted to be a contestant. Like you. But I didn't make the cut."

That explained a lot, and Chloe had suspected it all along. "I don't get it, though. Aren't you engaged?"

"It's been on and off. We'll figure it out when he gets back."

"Sebastian's a lot like you, Fiona. He doesn't know what he wants." Chloe waved Fiona off. "Go to bed. It's late."

She curtsied and sauntered off. This gave a whole new spin to the issue of finding good hired help.

Chloe sat for a long time, until, off in the distance, on the way to the reflecting pond, she saw something move on the lawn. It was probably a deer. She opened her silk reticule, slid Henry's glasses out, and put them on. It looked like some kind of animal out there, all right. Actually, it looked more like two animals—one of which was humping the other. She looked away.

Even the animals were getting more action than her around here. She buried her head in her arms until she heard a loud moan. She lifted the torch out of the ground and carried it to the edge of the gravel drive. Soon after the moaning stopped, a lantern lit up on the lawn. A lantern? Animals with a lantern?

She squinted through Henry's glasses and clearly saw a shirtless Sebastian pulling up his breeches. Grace hopped into her ball gown.

No wonder Sebastian brought up Grace in conversation so much during their time alone. He wasn't protecting Chloe from her. He was trying to find out as much about Grace as possible.

He was an ass! He was a player!

He was most definitely not Mr. Darcy.

Chloe just stood there. And held the torch.

Where was that laudanum?

Chapter 21

*Y*ou're drunk!"

It had taken a few days to find the laudanum, but she managed to find it despite her busy schedule of wedding-gown fittings and trimming her wedding bonnet. Chloe and Sebastian had been caught together in the ice-house, and just like in the Regency era, they were forced to marry. It was to be a rushed wedding on a Tuesday morning.

So, when Chloe poured more than a few drops of laudanum in her tea this morning, it made it taste like sherry.

Mrs. Crescent leaned over in the chaise-and-four to get a whiff of Chloe's breath.

"I'm not drunk." Chloe rubbed her forehead under her white bonnet. These carriage rides always undid her updo, but today horse's hooves seemed to be clomping on her brain. Hungover? Yes. Buzzed? That was earlier this morning. She looked out of the carriage window at the hedge maze, wondering how she'd ever get out of this.

Mrs. Crescent tightened the pink bonnet ribbon under her chin and narrowed her eyes. "Did you get into the sewing-cabinet vodka again?"

"No. No. Just took a drop of that laudanum at dawn to calm my nerves. One tiny drop! As any Regency lady would do under the circumstances."

Mrs. Crescent slapped her hands on the leather-covered bench. "What? Opium! On your wedding day—"

"This is *not* my wedding day."

Chloe looked down at her white pelisse, white muslin wedding gown, and white calfskin pumps. Her wooden trousseau trunk had been filled with all sorts of frills and Belgian-lace gowns, and strapped to the back of the carriage, in anticipation of the honeymoon. Packing that trousseau was an exercise in humility, preparing for a honeymoon that would never happen after a wedding she didn't want.

She came across Henry's handkerchief in her washstand drawer, the handkerchief he gave her on her first day at Bridesbridge, and she decided to pack that as well as her vial of ink that had only just congealed to perfection.

Mrs. Crescent fumbled around in her reticule. "You *are* getting married today. Here." She pushed fresh mint leaves into Chloe's gloved hand. "Where did you get laudanum?"

Chloe popped the mint leaves into her mouth, then pointed at her closed lips as she chewed. A lady would never talk with her mouth full. Finally, she swallowed. "I got it from your room. I relieved you of it."

"You stole it."

Chloe sat up straight, pinning her shoulders against the upholstered black leather seat back.

"The night you gave birth to Jemma. I added it to my stockpile." She folded her arms over her bodice.

"Dear Lord! What are you stockpiling?"

The carriage passed the hollyhocks where she and Henry had caught butterflies. The pink flowers swayed in the breeze.

"I've been stockpiling things that Grace smuggled onto the show to prove that she planted that condom on me, and that although I bent a few rules, she broke so many of them."

Mrs. Crescent grabbed Chloe by the arm, the same arm that Sebastian had grabbed only a few nights ago. "Listen, dear, we've been over this a thousand times. You were caught. You have to marry him." She lowered her voice to a whisper. "It's what would've been done in 1812."

As soon as those drop-front pants came down, the deal was sealed for Chloe because she got caught by the footman, who told. Grace didn't get caught by anyone—except Chloe.

The carriage, with its wooden wheels, jostled on the crusty road and seemed to punctuate Mrs. Crescent's words. "Be glad he wants to marry you. Not all Regency girls are so lucky. Anyway, it's just for the telly. You're not really marrying him. By hook or by crook, this is what we wanted. We've won!" She clapped her gloved hands joyfully.

But she stopped when, in a clearing alongside the road, she saw cameras filming a throng of servants gathered around a—gallows? A noose swayed, and a girl appeared to be hanging from it. A girl about Abigail's age. Chloe's gloved hands shook. "What—what's going on?" Waves of horror crashed through her.

"It's a hanging. They're hanging that orphan girl." Then she whispered, "A mock hanging. It's a dummy, not a girl."

The dummy twisted on the noose in the sunshine and turned toward Chloe, who cringed. "Ugh. That's horrifying. Why?"

"She stole a loaf of bread."

Chloe didn't mean why did they hang her, but why stage a mock hanging at all. "But—wait. That little girl was hanged for stealing bread?"

Mrs. Crescent nodded.

"That seems a little medieval to me."

"It's very Regency. Typical Regency."

"She's just a schoolgirl."

"Girls don't go to school, you know that."

Chloe did know. Girls weren't educated. They couldn't go to Oxford or Cambridge. And ladies couldn't choose to work. They had to marry. Chloe looked down at her white reticule. A mock hanging on her mock wedding day. How appropriate. The shadow of the girl as she twisted toward Chloe stayed with her long after they'd passed it. And even though the execution wasn't real, it rattled Chloe to the core.

Regency life was grim for women, very grim, and this, too, had been one of Austen's messages, just not the one Chloe had wanted to acknowledge.

The carriage came to a jarring halt in front of an old limestone church that looked to have come straight out of a fairy tale. Bay-leaf garlands draped the stone gateway to the churchyard. A round rose window adorned the front of the church. A fuzzy figure stood in the doorway, holding open the door for guests. If she would've just worn the glasses Henry made for her, she could've seen it all clearly.

"Anyhoo, it's a beautiful morning for a wedding," Mrs. Crescent said for the video cam as she looked out of the carriage window at the blue sky frosted with white clouds.

Chloe slumped back in her seat. "Morning. Who gets married in the morning, anyway?"

Mrs. Crescent frowned. "We do, dear, here in the Regent's England. Have I taught you nothing?"

A footman opened the carriage door to hand her out.

"I won't marry him." She turned to Mrs. Crescent, who, short of breath, stepped out of the carriage with the footman's help. She had left the baby with the nursemaid and her husband and children, all at Bridesbridge Place, so she could be Chloe's matron of honor. Chloe had one and only one bridesmaid: the breast-feeding Mrs. Crescent. The bride herself? A divorced single mom with a child nobody knew about and a tryst everybody knew all about. It was warped.

Together, bride and matron of honor walked under the bay-leaf garland and into the churchyard. Tombstones, old crumbling tombstones, littered the green grass around the little church. Chloe couldn't do this, no matter how fake the ceremony.

"Who dreams of getting married in a white bonnet trimmed with white lace, anyway? I want a tiara, a veil—an engagement ring, for God's sake." She stuck out her left hand. No ring. Regency couples rarely marked their engagement with a ring, and certainly, this debacle allowed no time for a ring.

A camera swung toward her as her white shoes navigated the cobblestone path to the church door. An older man in knee breeches and a black coat with tails cut a familiar figure at the door. He took off his black top hat, bowed to Chloe, and opened the church door.

Chloe practically tripped over a loose cobblestone. She gripped her nosegay of pink rosebuds tightly. It was her dad.

She stopped. "Dad?!"

"I believe that would be 'Father,'" he corrected with a smile. "You look beautiful, Princess." He held out his arms. He came forward, the church door closed behind him, and they hugged as if she were five years old all over again.

"Oh my gosh! How's Abigail? Does she miss me? Is she here?!"

Chloe pulled away. He smelled of too much Ralph Lauren aftershave.

"Of course she misses you. But no, she's not here. She's at Ned's. She's happy to be with her cousins. She's fine. We came for you. Our little princess."

Chloe sighed. Happy as she was to see him, she wanted to see Abigail more than anyone back home.

He held her hands. "Someone has to give you away. Right?"

Her mother appeared at the door in an appropriate mother-of-the-bride beige silk gown, a color Chloe knew her mom would never willingly wear, topped off with a poke bonnet. The churchyard, tombstones and all, spun around her. She was getting married. All over again. Her parents were mother and father of the bride. All over again. A dummy girl was swinging from a noose. She shuddered.

Her mother gave her a Chanel-lipstick kiss. How they still managed to afford their little luxuries on their reduced income was beyond Chloe. How did they afford to fly over here? "Darling. You look as if you've seen a ghost. And wow. You've lost weight! But really, we're so proud of you, sweetheart."

"You are?" Chloe linked arms with her dad for support. Did they realize why she was getting married?

Her mother crinkled her nose. "I'm afraid you do need a shower."

Funny, but Henry had installed a primitive shower at Bridesbridge just yesterday and she'd used it today. But it was hardly a shower, more like a cold sprinkle of water from a bucket for a total of one minute.

Chloe's mom waved her hand in front of her face. "Have you been drinking, Chloe?"

Chloe breathed through her nose.

Her mother leaned in and whispered, "Your betrothed paid for our plane tickets. He's quite the gentleman. He deserves better than to have his bride inebriated at the wedding ceremony."

Mrs. Crescent made her way up to the church. She cleared her throat. "Ahem. I'm Mrs. Crescent." She held out her hand and Chloe's father kissed it.

Mrs. Crescent blushed, because, of course, this behavior would've been de rigueur back in the eighteenth century, but in the nineteenth, kissing a woman's hand meant much more. But how was he to know?

Chloe's mother noodled between her husband and Mrs. Crescent, even though there was plenty of room on the landing. "So pleased to meet you. I'm Mrs. Parker." She extended her hand. "My grandmother was a titled English lady, you know."

Heat rose from Chloe's chin to her forehead.

Mrs. Crescent seemed unimpressed.

"Perhaps your family knew her. Lady Blackwell?" Mrs. Parker waited a moment. "Lady Anne Blackwell?"

Mrs. Crescent checked her chatelaine for the time. "No. I'm afraid I don't know the family."

Chloe's mom tossed her head, but when you have a poke bonnet over your hairdo, such gestures lose their effect. "Well. Our little Chloe is quite the celebrity back in Chicago."

"I am?" Chloe opened her silver vinaigrette and took a whiff. She was feeling faint.

Chloe's mom directed the entire conversation to Mrs. Crescent. "Everybody's been following the blog, the twittering—"

Chloe stomped her calfskin pump on the church step, but it didn't make a sound. It just hurt. "Blog! Twitter! I knew it! Who's been blogging?"

"Why, your betrothed, dear—"

"He's not my betrothed!" She popped out her hip and crossed her arms, while her mom, suddenly aware of the camera, oozed like a jelly donut.

Her mom smoothed down her gown, smiled, and spoke right to the lens. "We're so excited she's marrying a landed English gentleman. Imagine." She clapped her gloved hands together. "An English gentleman choosing an American—"

"Imagine," Chloe interrupted, swinging the camera toward her. "I haven't had a toilet for three weeks and he's been tweeting—" She whipped the nosegay against the church door, but at that moment the door opened, and the curate ended up with a bunch of flowers in his face.

"Oh! Excuse me, sir, uh, Father—I apologize."

When her dad bent to pick up the nosegay, her mom rushed to the curate, apologizing in a hushed voice.

Her dad put his arm around her and nodded his head toward the video cam as he whispered, "The cameras, Chloe. They're filming. Think about your reputation. Abigail. Our family. The family's reputation. Previews of the show are all over the Internet in order to promote it. In a month it'll be on international TV. We came here thinking this is what you wanted."

"I thought it was what I wanted," Chloe said. She turned her back to the church and the camera. "England. Manners. A gentleman. Eighteen-twelve. The most romantic time in history." Not to mention the money. But the past few days, while she struggled to prepare for this sham of a wedding, had given her time to think about the money and she realized that she had the power within herself to turn her business around. She'd taken copious notes with her quill, planning just how to go about it. She looked down at her white pumps on the gray stone.

The church bell tolled out the time. One, two, three— Her dad talked louder now, and the bells drowned out his voice. The boom boy jockeyed around them with the mike.

"Let's just have some fun with this, okay? Your mother and I came all this way."

Chloe sucked on her strawberry-stained lower lip.

"It's just a game. For TV. This isn't real. Pretend you're an actress. A movie star. Think of all the buzz this show will generate about you. You can do anything you want after this. I was against this when you found out it was a reality show, but it's very tasteful."

Chloe smiled. "It's just like I wrote to you. Not a hot tub in sight."

Seven, eight, nine gongs. She looked up into a lime tree. She knew about lime trees now, because of Henry. A bird bounced among the branches. The bell rang ten, and the last gong echoed. The ceremony was supposed to begin at ten. She opened her white silk reticule and pulled out the glasses Henry made, hooking the silver over her ears.

Her mom scurried over and took Chloe's gloved hand in hers. "If you're disappointed about the wedding party itself, angel, well, so was I. Really. I mean who wants to settle for a wedding breakfast for eleven people instead of a steak dinner for four hundred with a live orchestra? When I found out there won't even be a wedding cake, I . . ."

Her mother kept talking, but Chloe focused on the bird. It was a green finch.

Her mother patted her back. ". . . but I guess that's how they did it in 1812. Sad, really. When you two really do marry, you'll have a real wedding. I'll see to that. Let's go, dear. It's time. Do take off those glasses. Since when do you need glasses? They look so—horsey."

Chloe kept the glasses on. Her dad stuck the nosegay in her right hand and linked his arm in her left. Just as they stepped over the threshold of the church door, she heard a finch call out.

The church felt twenty degrees cooler and smelled—like churches smell everywhere, all over the world. Vaulted ceilings and carved stone moldings added to the chill. Candles flickered in the drafts. With his perfect profile, Sebastian stood at the altar, waiting.

For a fake wedding, it sure felt real. She leaned on her dad. Henry wore a bottle-green cutaway coat and practically paced in his pew.

She wanted to wrap her arms around him, or at least catch his eye. But he was the only one not looking at her, the bride, as she made her way to the altar. Even Grace glared and drummed her gloved fingers on the scrolled pew railing in front of her. Immediately after the wedding, Grace would be sent home. She had lost the competition. But of course, filming her watch the wedding made fabulous drama, so she had to stay.

For a minute it did seem like a movie and not like the real thing.

Chloe felt like she was looking down on herself getting married—again. The first time around, sixteen years ago, it seemed exactly the same. Movielike. Unreal. An out-of-body experience in a white dress. Back then, of course, the white dress was appropriate. As a thirty-nine-year-old divorcée with an eight-year-old stateside, not to mention her ice-house moment, it seemed downright scandalous.

Sebastian, the cad, in a tight black cutaway coat, white breeches, and black shoes, looked the part he was playing. Chloe could tell he didn't like the glasses. He kept squinting and clearing his throat as the curate spoke.

She looked around the rim of her bonnet for Henry.

The curate had already started the ceremony. ". . . and therefore is not by any to be enterprised, nor taken in hand, unadvisedly, lightly, or wantonly, to satisfy men's carnal lusts and appetites, like brute beasts that have no understanding . . ."

How could you take this lightly? She looked up at the rose window.

". . . but reverently, discreetly, advisedly, soberly, and in the fear of God; duly considering the causes for which Matrimony was ordained."

She was sober all right. A lot more sober than she was hitting the laudanum at the crack of dawn this morning. Two video cams turned in on her.

". . . if either of you know any impediment, why ye may not be lawfully joined together in matrimony, ye do now confess it . . ."

Chloe looked up at the curate, and opened her mouth, afraid that nothing would come out, but it did.

She let her rosebud nosegay drop to the stone floor. "I can't marry him."

"Pardon me?" The curate's book slid down from his chest to his side. A great rustling and shuffling and whispering came from behind her.

"Well, that's a relief!" Grace stood up. "It saves me from having to announce an impediment—or two."

Chloe's mother stood, too, and leaned on the pew in front of her, apparently for strength. And Henry—where was Henry?

Chloe looked straight into Sebastian's eyes. "I can't marry the wrong Mr. Wrightman. Even if it is just for TV." Her eyes darted around the church. Henry was gone.

Whispering rose up to the church's vaulted ceiling.

Sebastian grabbed her by the arm. "What are you doing?" He lowered his voice to a whisper. "You can't do this to me in front of everybody."

Mrs. Crescent stepped up to the wedding group. "She can't mean it, Mr. Wrightman. She's just nervous. Let me talk with her."

The curate furrowed his brows.

The cameras stayed on Chloe.

"Let go of me," she said to Sebastian, and yanked her arm away from him. A ray of sunlight shone through the rose window. "You're no gentleman. And you never will be. You're not the brooding, silent type. In fact, I don't know what you are, and you don't know what—or who—you want. I don't care how much money you have—you can take it and stick it into your breeches for all I care!"

Sebastian stepped backward, his perfect jawline askew.

Cook—Lady Anne—made her way up to the altar. "Miss Parker—let me explain."

"No, let me explain." Chloe stood next to the marble altar draped in a maroon sash. Her voice echoed throughout the pulpit. "The real gentleman here is Henry, who stands to win nothing and gain nothing. The rest of us are just modern-day screwups in gowns and cutaway coats. Pretending. Grace is pretending so she can win back her family's land that her great-great-great grandfather lost gambling. I'm pretending I'm not divorced, with an eight-year-old daughter at home waiting for me."

The small crowd gasped. Henry was still nowhere to be seen.

"I thought this was real. It isn't. Everyone's pretending—except of course, for Lady Anne, who, as far as I can tell, is the real deal. But the rest of us? We can't even act like Regency people. We know too much, we've done too much, and said too much to even pretend to live in the nineteenth century. Here, Grace." Chloe tossed her nosegay to Grace, who caught it. "You marry him. For TV or real life or land or money or all of the above. I don't care."

Chloe untied her wedding bonnet. Her dad tried to pull the cameramen away. She dumped her bonnet upside down on the altar, where the cameras filmed a vibrator, a pink MP3 player, whitening strips, a pack of cigarettes, and condoms wrapped in black foil tumble onto the maroon altar cloth.

"Dear God!" Mrs. Crescent gasped. "Don't throw it away now, Chloe. We've won. Don't."

"We can't live like it's 1812. Not even for a few weeks. Come and get your stash, Grace. I'm going home. Back to my daughter, where I belong."

The curate stepped up to her and put his hand on her shoulder, but she shrugged it off.

Grace stepped up to the altar. "I have absolutely no idea what you're talking about. These aren't mine."

"Don't be stupid, Grace. This is the twenty-first century. I had my gloves on every time I handled them. A simple dusting for thumbprints will prove they're yours, and if that doesn't work—there are always DNA tests."

Chloe's mother barreled up to the pulpit. The cameras loomed in on Chloe from the front. She felt hunted. Her dad clenched his teeth. Her mom's manicured nails clawed at her even through her gloves. She had to get out of here.

She hoisted up her gown, dodged them all, and ran all the way down the aisle, out the church door, down the steps, past the tombstones, and right smack into the white wedding carriage, an open barouche covered in pink peonies and pink ribbons. Not just one, but four horses turned their heads. She untied them from the hitching post, clambered up to the driver's perch, and with a shaking hand, flicked the reins. The horses lunged forward. When she looked back she saw everyone had spilled out of the church, past the stone fence, but nobody else had a horse. They had all walked to the wedding in their finery! She brought the horses to a trot. The great carriage rattled along, peonies flew off, ribbons flapped, her updo collapsed.

When she finally reached the iron gates that marked the end of the deer park and the beginning of the real world, she stopped the carriage. The gravel road ended. A paved road intersected it. She hadn't seen blacktop in weeks. It looked so unnatural, yet so promising. The open road. It was the American in her, all right, thrilled to hit the open road.

A red Jaguar whizzed by on the wrong side of the street, because of course, this was England, and it startled the horses. She couldn't exactly ride a barouche into town, now, could she? She stepped out of the carriage, guided the horses to a wrought-iron hitching post on the edge of the deer park, and tied them to it.

She stood on the edge of the blacktop, looked east and west, followed the road with her eyes. Thanks to the glasses, she could actually see the road twist into the distance. Which way to civilization? She went west. She bunched up her gown to jog, and tried to run, but her shoes didn't cooperate. They had even less support than her stays. Who knew she would actually miss her harness of a sports bra and running shoes? She slowed to a walk, letting her gown fall back to her ankles.

She passed English farmland pungent with manure and grasses. A hawk circled overhead and she thought of Henry. Her thoughts always circled back to Henry. Sunshine poured down on her and she felt naked without a bonnet and, for once, she could actually use a parasol and fan. Sweat dampened her silk stockings and her lower back, so she stripped off her pelisse and gloves. Those lemons she rubbed under her underarms this morning were not exactly meant to hold up under a power walk in nineteenth-century wedding attire.

And she would feel better about all this tramping about the English countryside without knowing where she was really going if she had a cell phone. Or a portable GPS. Or at least a damn plastic water bottle. How irresponsible it was for a mother to fling herself into the countryside on the other side of the earth without even knowing where she was going? What if something happened to her and Abigail ended up getting raised by her ex? In Boston? With the fortunate Marcia Smith?

By the time she reached the top of the third hill, she didn't have to shield her eyes from the sun, because a battalion of rain clouds had floated in. The breeze, cooler now, dampened her skin, and she could tell that it was going to rain. How could it rain on her almost-wedding day? She pulled her pelisse back on even as she licked her dry lips. The sight of a church spire and slate-roofed red-brick houses in the distance helped spur her on.

Someone in a passing car tossed a white cardboard coffee cup out the window and over a hedgerow. The blacktop turned to cobblestone as she crossed what must've been a stone bridge from the Roman era. Normally, Chloe would've loved this quaint village with its cobblestoned main street and whitewashed, half-timbered cottage storefronts where cars seem oddly out of place. As she read the sign at the end of the bridge, HUNTSFORDSHIRE, she walked right into a woman pushing a jogging stroller in her workout gear and talking on her cell.

"So sorry," the young mom said. The baby looked up at Chloe with big blue eyes.

She had to get back to Abigail. What was she doing?

"Are you quite all right?" The young mom took the cell from her ear.

Chloe nodded yes, even though she really wasn't.

"Sorry again." The mom pushed the stroller on.

Chloe, out of habit, curtsied. She curtsied!

The mom's eyes narrowed and she looked Chloe up and down, navigating her precious baby around in a wide circumference as if Chloe were some kind of lunatic.

Her head throbbed with the onslaught of car engines, a train, honking horns, voices, and car radios. Raindrops fell, and umbrellas of all different sizes and colors popped up all around her.

None of the men bowed to her. The women didn't curtsy. Nobody even looked at her, or if they did, they quickly looked away out of politeness. She was the raving lunatic homeless woman on the street.

Pelting rain dripped down her face and neck and probably by now had smudged her eyebrow liner made from candle ashes. Even in the rain, though, the aroma of scones spilled out of a bakery. She stood in front of a tearoom and coffeehouse under a dripping awning, looking at a reflection in the window of her sodden self. The antibride with a child hidden in her attic.

She pressed her hand to the window. She needed a plane ticket home, but first—coffee. It didn't even have to be a double espresso latte, but she didn't have any money. For the first time in a long time, she ached for a credit card, and couldn't believe she cut up all her credit cards in a fit of rage all those years ago.

A young man sat inside the tearoom, holding a bouquet of flowers wrapped in white paper. For the first time in forever, a man with flowers didn't make her moon over Winthrop. She smiled. They were better off, the two of them, without each other. She had left him for good reason, and now she finally felt the strength to fight him in the upcoming custody trial. She could do it—and win.

The young man in the tearoom gave Chloe a hostile glance; no doubt she looked crazy. She stepped back and the rain from the awning dripped heavily on her. He was waiting for someone, because he had a life, a real life, with real people in it. All these people had a life. She had nothing. Except for Abigail, who counted on her for everything. And as far as that went, she had blown it. She'd be coming home without the prize money. What she *would* be coming home with, though, was a resolve to leave the past behind—all of it—even the nineteenth century, and that was worth a lot more than a hundred grand.

She darted under a covered bus stop where an old woman sat in her green trench coat with a cloth market basket full of lettuce, tomatoes, and cucumbers. Lettuce! Green lettuce helped digestion. She craved lettuce. She'd trade the gown off her back for a chopped salad.

She sat on the bench next to the woman, wiped her glasses with her wet gloves, put them back on, and looked up the street, where, high atop a hill in the distance, Dartworth Hall stood. It would've made a great postcard. Hell, it probably was one and probably was sold in the shops along this street.

"I can't believe—" she said out loud, like a homeless woman.

The old woman looked at her, then quickly looked at her watch.

"I threw it all away."

The woman pushed back her plastic rain scarf. "Threw what away?" She eyed Chloe up and down; she was curious.

"Dartworth Hall. The prize money. Everything."

The woman gave Chloe a tissue from her trench pocket, which only reminded Chloe of Henry and his handkerchiefs. Chloe wiped her dripping nose.

"Are you part of that film going on up there?"

Chloe nodded. "They wanted me to marry him. But I couldn't. Even though it was just for TV. I couldn't."

The old woman had kind green eyes. "Marry who?"

"Why, Sebastian, of course. Sebastian Wrightman."

The old woman looked confused. She stood up. "Who? Ah. Here's my bus. But Dartworth Hall doesn't belong to anyone named Sebastian." The bus lumbered up. "Henry Wrightman is the master of Dartworth Hall."

"What?" Chloe clenched her pelisse around her chest; her lips quivered.

The bus doors opened and the woman stepped up the first step in her black flats. "I would say it's a good thing you didn't marry that Sebastian—"

"Door's closing!" the annoyed driver yelled, and the doors snapped closed.

Chloe stepped out from under the Plexiglas bus stop, into the rain, to watch the woman take her seat and wave.

She collapsed back down on the bench under the covered bus stop and buried her head in her hands. Maybe that old woman didn't know what she was talking about. Maybe she had Alzheimer's or dementia or some sort of addled-brain disease that Chloe was convinced she would get someday, too, if she didn't have it already. She better start doing crossword puzzles or something—and soon. *Wait a minute*. Crossword. Acrostic—she opened her wedding reticule and pulled out the well-worn folded-up poem from Sebastian. The acrostic jumped out at her now:

As *the sun shines high in the sky*
Love *blooms in my heart, I cannot lie.*
Let *our love grow*
Is *what is want, I know.*
Still *I cannot be convinced*
Nay, *I need more evidence*
Of *your intentions, are they true?*

To convince me here is what you need to do:
As the clock strikes two you must find
Something in a garden where light and shadow are intertwined
Inspect the face in the garden bright
Then follow the line of light
Straight to a house without walls
Enter the door and go where the water falls
Extrapolate from this poem the puzzle within
Make a note of the six-word answer, write it, and you will win
Send your missive through the secret door and the answers you seek will
be in store!

The first letter of every line was to be read down, and it spelled out *ALL IS NOT AS IT SEEMS.* She squeezed her eyes shut and heard something familiar in the din of gushing rain and cars. The sound of hooves clomping on the cobblestone.

It was Henry on a white horse. On Sebastian's white horse. Rain dripped from his wide-brimmed hat and nineteenth-century great-coat as he rode right smack down the middle of the road and ignored the chaos he was causing. Two hunting hounds nuzzled up to Chloe and slipped their soaked heads under her hands. Never in her life had she been so happy to see a dog, not to mention two sopping wet hounds. She rubbed their bony heads. But Henry? If he was really the master of Dartworth Hall, he had lied to her. And who the hell was Sebastian, then?

Henry slowed his horse right in front of the bus stop, tipped his hat, and held out his hand to her. "Miss Parker, your conveyance has arrived."

She folded her arms and the dogs wagged their tails against her wet gown. The lady was not amused.

His lips curled into a smile as he eyed her up and down. "I must say that your dramatic exit from the church was better than any production crew could dream of. Even now they're salivating over the prospect of skyrocketing ratings. Well done."

Traffic wove around the horse. Chloe looked up the street, and half expected to see the camera crew. A small crowd under umbrellas gathered around them.

"And where are the cameras now? I'm sure they'd love to get me on film looking like this."

"No cameras. I lost them in the deer park. And as for your looks, well, I've never been happier to see you."

"I wish I could say the same." If what that woman said was true, then he'd been lying to her for weeks! Chloe took off her glasses and tucked them into her soaked white reticule. She looked away from Henry and toward Dartworth Hall, where a patch of blue sky had broken through the clouds.

Henry dismounted, tied his horse to the bus-stop sign, and sat down next to her on the bench. She slid over and looked the other way.

"Can I buy you a cup of coffee? How about a double espresso nonfat latte?"

How did he know what kind of convoluted coffee she drank? The rain made a soft splashing sound on the cobblestones, the breeze picked up, and she shivered. Across the street, people darted into the red-brick pub with leaded windows. A sign swung on a wrought-iron post that read THE GOLDEN ARMS in forest-green letters. She'd been in England for almost three weeks and hadn't even been to an English pub.

Henry slid closer. "Or maybe a pint sounds better?"

There he was, reading her mind again.

"If you bought me a pint, I'd probably dump it all over you."

He looked confused. "Lady Anne informed me that you pontificated to no end about my merits."

A young pierced-nose couple in wet leather jackets came into the shelter, his arm around her shoulder, hers around his waist. They were taking pictures of Dartworth Hall with their cell-phone cameras. Chloe realized they were trying not to stare.

She stood up and the dogs did, too. "Forget the coffee or Guinness or whatever you people drink. I want the truth. Can you give me that? That would be good right about now. Let's start with this simple fact: Are you the owner of Dartworth Hall or not?"

He stood and took his greatcoat and hat off, a lock of hair falling into his eye. "Oh. Someone told you."

"Yes."

The pierced couple and several others were outright gaping. But Chloe and Henry were used to being watched by cameramen, by George, the hidden production and editing crew.

Chloe paced in front of the bus-stop shelter in the rain, her hands clasped behind her. "It pays to get out into the real world and talk to real people and find out what the real deal is—"

He draped his greatcoat around her. "I understand you must be upset but—"

"Upset? I wish I were merely upset. I'm freakin' furious!" Though the greatcoat did feel warm and dry around her. "I thought you were a gentleman. No—first I thought Sebastian was a gentleman, possibly even someone I could love. Took me a while, but I figured that one out. Then I thought you were a gentleman. Ha!" Suddenly the rain stopped. "You're both fakes."

"I see your point." He linked his arm in hers. "I'm going to buy you a coffee." He guided her toward the tearoom.

"I don't want you to buy me any coffee. You can't buy me with your money."

He opened the tearoom door for her. "As you wish, my lady. Please just step in to warm up. They have a fabulous hearth."

When the door opened, the smell of coffee and tea and cream hit her with a jolt. The fireplace, flint stone all the way to the ceiling, lured her in with its warmth. Various dogs rested inside, at their owners' feet. The English loved their dogs. Of course, the dogs could hardly wait outside, in the pouring rain. The hounds followed Chloe in.

A sideways glance in a silver platter hanging from the wall along with other tea accessories proved to Chloe that she really did look like the Bride of Frankenstein. She fumbled with her hair while Henry removed the greatcoat from her shoulders and hung it near the door.

The hostess signaled a busboy. "Clear that table by the hearth for Mr. Wrightman." The busboy scurried off, and in no time they were at the best table in the house, in front of a sizzling fire.

"What can I get you?" a waitress asked Chloe, clearly trying not to stare at her ruined gown.

"A double espresso nonfat latte. To go."

"To go?"

Chloe imagined that book on her head. She straightened her spine and spoke in her best English-ese. "In a takeaway cup, please."

The waitress raised an eyebrow.

Henry ordered a pot of Earl Grey and a plateful of scones and clotted cream. He smoothed his napkin in his lap. "Just where are you planning to go with your coffee?"

"Home."

"I see. Are you planning to walk to Heathrow in the rain? And then board a plane without a ticket, passport, or credit card?"

She folded her arms and scowled into the fire.

"Allow me to rescue you. I've even brought the white horse."

"That's Sebastian's white horse."

"It's my white horse."

"Whatever. I don't need to be rescued anymore. I just need one thing from you before I go."

"Ah yes. I should've given it to you sooner. If you will excuse me a minute."

He stood, bowed, headed over to his greatcoat, pulled out a maroon velvet drawstring bag, opened it, and revealed Chloe's tiara. He set it on the white tablecloth.

Chloe cupped her hands around the tiara. He really knew how to throw her off guard; she had actually forgotten all about her tiara. "Thank you. Really." She ran her fingertips along the diamonds and rubies. "Did you really fix it yourself?"

"Yes. With nineteenth-century silversmithing tools, no less. It was a bit of a challenge to get it right."

She couldn't even see the seam where he'd welded it together. "Thank you. You are—talented." She tucked the tiara back into the velvet bag and steeled herself. "But this isn't what I need from you."

The waitress brought a fragrant pot of tea, a plate of sliced lemons, sugars, and a pitcher of cream. The stack of scones came next and a dish of clotted cream so thick it took everything in Chloe's power not to scoop it up like ice cream. She was famished. The waitress set Chloe's white paper cup of coffee with the familiar plastic lid right where her plate should be.

Henry swept the blond hair out of the corner of his eye. "Please bring the lady a plate for the scones. Perhaps a paper one, if you have it. Pity, but she's not staying."

Chloe held back a smile. After all that weak tea and coffee that tasted as if it really were hundreds of years old, this coffee tasted amazing. Still, jokes and good coffee aside, she didn't want to get sidetracked. "The truth. Spill it."

Steam from his tea rose out of his cup. "It's true that I'm the heir of Dartworth Hall. I'm a doctor, but I don't need to work for the money. I do it because I enjoy helping people. I'm forty years old. My friend George came up with this crazy idea for a TV show because women kept coming after me for my money. But you—you forfeited the money. A hundred thousand dollars. For me, it was a game until you came along. I've wanted to tell you for so long that the bio you read about Sebastian back in Chicago? That profile was—me."

"All of it was you? All this time, you were behind every little—"

"Detail. Not only do I love art, I own a few galleries. You already know I'm a Jane Austen fan and a bird-watcher. I'm also an avid traveler and architecture buff."

"Everything was a lie," Chloe said, shaking her head.

"It wasn't a lie—it was all me. There were clues everywhere. All laid out for you."

"What clues? I didn't see any clues."

"No, you didn't. The poem, for example. That was a clue."

"If that's your idea of a clue, then you're clueless. I'm not Sherlock Holmes here. I'm just a girl. A girl who's been played by Sebastian. Ultimately, though, I hold you responsible."

Henry looked down.

Chloe clenched her fists. She wanted to swear at him up and down, but the Regency Miss Parker kept the modern Chloe's mouth in check. "This was all an experiment of some kind. I was right about you when I first met you. Who do you think you are that you can just put people in a petri dish and watch them squirm under a microscope?"

"It was an experiment, of sorts, and I realize now it was wrong of me."

"I'll say! Hearts were broken! Dreams were dashed!"

"You've taught me. I was wrong."

Chloe shook her head. "Another thing I don't get: Why keep Grace? Why send Julia and Imogene home?"

Henry looked into her eyes. "George had me keep her on. For production value."

"Is that why you kept *me* on?!"

"No—no, not at all."

She didn't believe him.

"I just wanted to find a loyal and true love, a kind of modern-day Anne Elliot, if you will. But it was a crazy idea."

The waitress brought a Wedgwood china plate rimmed in gold.

Chloe slathered clotted cream on her scone and not even the cream at the Drake could compare. She dabbed her mouth with her napkin and calmed herself. "So. If Dartworth is yours and Sebastian's profile is yours, then who is Sebastian?"

"A distant cousin. Who wants to break into the film industry."

Chloe looked up from plastering another scone with two inches of clotted cream, and looked at Henry.

"He's—an actor?"

"Well, he wants to be, but—"

"That explains his lines. He always knew exactly what to say. He's a damn actor. No wonder he never told me what kind of an artist he was. He's a scam artist!"

"Those lines were true—they were coming from me—Miss Parker—"

Chloe took the scone dripping with clotted cream and pushed it into his face, turning it a few times just for effect.

The tearoom went silent while Henry wiped cream from his face with his napkin.

"I deserve that, I know. But do you know that I love you? It's not a game anymore. There's more. I want to tell you everything. Your 'Cook,' Lady Anne, is my mother—"

Clotted cream covered his eyebrows and Chloe got a flash of him, decades from now, as an old man with white eyebrows.

"So *she* lied to me as well? Guess what? I lied, too. A lot. I'm divorced. I have a little girl at home. How's that for a deal breaker?"

She put a hand on her hip.

He wiped the clotted cream from his eyebrows. "I know about your daughter. And your divorce. They're not deal breakers."

She took a long, slow sip of her coffee. "I need to go. I'll be taking your horse."

Henry bowed. "Of course. Because that's what you do best. You run away."

If her coffee didn't taste so damn good, she'd pour the rest of it on him. Her hand quivered with the thought.

"I'm not running away. For once I'm running to something. My real life. In the real world. Where people are—real!" She stamped her calfskin pump to no effect.

Coffee in one hand, tiara in the other, she burst into the . . . sunshine? How dare the sun shine now?

Henry stood in the doorway, his greatcoat draped over his shoulders. "Despite everything—I think what we have is real. It's a real beginning—"

In half a second she untied the horse, tied the velvet bag to the saddle horn, and mounted western style, her gown hiked up to her thighs, coffee cup still in hand. The wet saddle chafed against her legs.

"You're no more real to me than a character in a Jane Austen novel—no—a character from a bad film adaptation. You played me. I played you. We never had anything real."

She tossed her empty coffee cup into a trash can on the sidewalk and tossed her head. "And we never will." If only all this could've been caught on camera.

Henry moved closer to her. "I'm not a character from a book. I'm a real person. Who makes real mistakes. And so are you. But look what came out of it—we've found each other—"

"I don't think I found anybody—except, as the old cliché goes— myself."

She pulled on the reins to turn the horse around. After starting up the street, she took one last peek at Henry, who was running after her in his riding boots. She brought the horse to a canter. She didn't need Sebastian or Henry or Winthrop or any man. She was going home—home to the twenty-first century, where she would ramp up her letterpress business with Web capability. Ideas on how to bring the business into the modern world tumbled around in her.

She soon realized she was cantering up the wrong side of the road. Once on the left side of the street, she brought the horse into a brisk gallop. Cars and trucks swerved around her, some drivers honked, others stared, and still others swore, but she had her plan. She couldn't wait to put it all into action.

Without looking back, she galloped out of the only English village she'd ever been in, without even a souvenir T-shirt for Abigail that said ENGLAND on it, without having had a pint in the local pub, and without a clue as to what she would do once she got back to Bridesbridge.

Chapter 22

The headlights from the black English taxicab bounced up the gravel drive in front of Bridesbridge. Its rubber tires made a determined crunching noise in the dark. Chloe had called herself a cab on her dad's BlackBerry.

George had tried to stop her. "You outed us. You found Mr. Wrightman. Henry wants to grant you the prize money. You earned it."

She looked down on George from her high horse. The cameras were rolling. "I don't want Henry's money, George. Give it to Mrs. Crescent for William."

"You have got to be kidding."

"I'm not."

George looked at her as if she were from another planet. And maybe she was. Clearly, George would've taken the money. George was all about money. He was a cad, just like the rest of them. Probably sleeping with his assistant while his wife and kids were in London.

"You can't leave like this."

"I can."

"You have to take the money. Those are the rules. We're going to have it sent to you. We can't keep it."

"If those are the rules, then make sure William gets the best treatment he can with the money, and I'll consider taking what's left over. If I end up using any of it, I'll pay it back within the year. With interest."

"We won't take it."

"Then I'll make a donation—to the National Trust. To the Chawton House Library!" It felt so good to be free of the lure of the money, to finally see how her business could be propelled into the future without a rescue from anyone or anything but herself.

Chloe sat on the steps of Bridesbridge Place in the new blue jeans her mom brought from the States, and checked her e-mail. She had 4,623 unread e-mails. She stood when the cabbie stepped out.

"'Ello, there." The young cabbie loaded her carry-on and suitcase into the trunk.

The double doors to Bridesbridge Place swung open behind her. "Miss Parker—Chloe—wait!" Mrs. Crescent, dressed in her real clothes now, too, looked—almost hip. Her baby slept in a carrier strapped to her chest. Chloe curtsied out of sheer instinct, then laughed and hugged Mrs. Crescent and the baby.

"I'm going to miss you—both." Chloe kissed baby Jemma on the head.

Mrs. Crescent put her arm around Chloe. "Please don't go. Stay just for tonight. After all, you won! You figured it all out! And you really don't want to forfeit the prize money, do you?"

"I'm just happy that William has enough money to get his operation. As for me, I have a few irons in the fire. What I learned here, in these few weeks, is worth more than any prize. I have a real life. In the present. And there's no time like now to start living it."

"Please join us. We're having a farewell party on the veranda at Dartworth Hall." She eyed Chloe up and down. "You do look fabulous."

"So do you."

"I don't think this whole thing has changed me as much as it has you. Anyway, you and your parents must come."

Chloe took in Bridesbridge for the last time. "My parents are too busy sucking up to Lady Anne right now—"

The cabbie interrupted. "I'm afraid you're on the ticker, miss."

"Don't call me 'miss'—please."

He almost dropped his cigarette. She hadn't seen a cigarette in weeks.

"Be there in a minute." She turned back to Mrs. Crescent. "Did you know that Lady Anne is really Henry's mother!"

"And she absolutely adores you. I didn't know anything. None of us did. Only Lady Anne, Sebastian, Henry, and of course George. But, Chloe, you must realize that Henry's world is full of phony people. Girls that just want his money. His title. With George's help, he created this game to find a woman who could love him for who he is."

Chloe got a lump in her throat. She headed into the cloud of cigarette smoke the cabbie just exhaled. She tried not to breathe in. "I have to go, Mrs. Crescent. I'll e-mail you. I have your address."

"But you hate e-mail."

"Not anymore." Chloe flashed the BlackBerry with a smile. "I can't wait to buy one of these for myself! Here, you can give this back to my dad for me."

The cabbie opened the door for her and the light went on inside the cab. The first electric light she'd seen in weeks. Electricity. It was like a miracle. No more drippy candles. The cabbie waited to close the door for her.

"I can close the door myself. Thank you."

She looked up, beaming, at Bridesbridge Place, awash in floodlights, fluted columns under the portico. As she was about to close the door, a familiar hand stopped it from closing. It was Henry, dressed in jeans and a button-down shirt. He had a trench coat draped over his shoulders, and was wearing hip glasses. He looked amazing.

Chloe raised an eyebrow.

"I have a delivery for you, Miss Parker," he said. "Excuse my reach."

He set some sort of blanketed box on the other side of her.

"Thank you, Henry, but whatever it is, I really can't accept it."

"It's yours, Miss Parker. It's not mine. And please do me the honor of reading this."

He handed her an envelope sealed with a red wax W. He looked at her as if he were about to say something important. "Safe journey." He tapped the door shut and bowed. He bowed!

Chloe leaned forward so the driver could hear her over the radio he just turned on. "Please, hurry."

The cabbie peeled out of the drive, leaving Henry, Bridesbridge, and Chloe's English life in the dust. The radio newscaster rattled on in his British accent, a blur of bombings in the Middle East, a murder trial in London, a hurricane off the coast of Florida, the horrific state of the economy. It was like she never left. The pace of it dizzied her.

Still, she didn't look back. She only looked forward, into the darkness.

"Heathrow, right?" the cabbie asked.

"Yes." Chloe peeked under the blanket draped over the box. It wasn't a box but a green plastic crate with holes on the side. She turned the thing around, but just as she was about to look under the blanket again, something exploded and flashed behind them. Henry's letter slid out of her lap and onto the floor of the cab.

The cabbie braked. Chloe put her hand out in front of the crate, keeping it from rolling to the floor. The cabbie shifted the car into park and hopped out. There was another explosion. A bolt of fear seared through Chloe. She popped out of the cab. *Bam!* Still another explosion rumbled through her. She couldn't see anything. With a shaking hand, she fumbled for her bag and pulled out the glasses Henry made for her and put them on askew. Just then, the biggest, reddest fireworks she'd ever seen lit up the sky and cast a silhouette of Dartworth Hall with its classic, symmetrical facade. Two more fireworks, blue and white, exploded in the darkness. She heard more fireworks launch, and the anticipation of their size and their colors made her giddy.

The cabbie turned to her. "Just fireworks. They had me going there for a minute, they did." He got back into the cab and shut his door.

Chloe was transfixed. Henry did this for her. She bit her lip. Another round of fireworks melted in the sky. Then another and another. They were all red, white, and blue.

The cabbie rolled down the window. "Best be going now. The meter's running."

"You're right. Let's go." Chloe took off the glasses, slid back into her seat, and shut the door. Flashes of colored light appeared in the cabbie's rearview mirror, but she looked at the floor of the cab, where Henry's letter had fallen.

"Meow." The crate started meowing. Chloe sighed. "Meow." She lifted the blanket and saw, now, that it was the tabby Sebastian had sent her. *Wait a minute.* It was Sebastian who sent the cat, right? Or was it really Henry? Anyway, how the hell was she going to take a cat on an overseas flight? "Meow." She let the blanket drop. A cat?

She'd always liked cats, but there was something about a thirty-nine-year-old single woman with a cat. She'd be a cat lady. She'd end up eighty years old, in a dilapidated house with a thousand cats. She had to get this cat back to its home. *Wait.* That was exactly what Henry wanted. He wanted her to turn the cab around and bring the cat back. He wanted her to come back. To miss her flight.

The cat meowed again. *Ha!* Well that wasn't going to happen. She'd just pay the cabbie to take the damn cat back. Chloe bent down to pick up Henry's letter. For a long time she just held it and rubbed her thumb over the sealed wax *W*. Nobody had ever put on a fireworks show for her before.

Was Mr. Wrightman so *wrong* after all?

She broke the seal with her fingernails, freshly painted orange, a color she borrowed from Fiona. Outside the window, one quaint English village after another blurred by in the night.

"Can you turn on the light back here, please? I need to read something."

The cabbie turned on the light and raised the volume on the radio. The rap music that was blaring out of it gave Chloe a headache. Certain words floated to the surface: *ho* and *butt* and *bitch*, and *nasty*. She sank down into the seat and held the cream-colored letter in front of her.

He had written it with ink and quill.

Dear Chloe,

I haven't much time to write, as you've ordered a cab and it will soon be here, so this missive will not be as polished as I would like.

Do consider staying on a bit longer. If not for me, then for your friends, such as Mrs. Crescent. If not for Mrs. Crescent, then for yourself, to really see England. I can arrange for a private tour guide to show you the sights of London. How can you leave without seeing London Bridge? Buckingham Palace? Windsor Castle? I just can't bear to have you leave our country in this manner. I can't bear to have you leave at all.

*I apologize for deceiving you. I don't blame you for being upset. It
was a damn ridiculous thing to do to a woman like you.*

*Still, I find it comforting to know that, even if you are half a world
away, a woman like you exists. I had quite given up. You see, I, too,
fell in love with you on paper, when I read your profile and all the
transcripts of your interviews months ago. I asked for you to be the
first chosen. But George didn't want you on the show until the final
weeks—for drama's sake. He told me you had been contacted but
were engaged to be married. I was taken by surprise when you arrived.
Truly, I let Sebastian go a bit too far, and he, too, seemed to fall for
you. But he's not ready to settle down, as you well know.*

*What I do know is that my feelings for you are real, and al-
ways will be. When you get back to the real world, I hope you
will think of me. And when that day comes, please contact me by
e-mail, post, telephone, or smoke signals. I'll have both you and your
daughter flown over here in a heartbeat. I'd like to propose a secret
correspondence and we can get to know each other better—the old-
fashioned way.*

I will be waiting.

Sincerely yours,
Henry Wrightman

*P.S. Take good care of your mousetrap. I've known Alistair since he
was a kitten. All the paperwork required for travel is enclosed. And
yes, I named him after Alistair Cooke.*

"Departures. American Airlines. We're here," the cabbie said. He
went around to the trunk, or the "boot" as the English called it, and
started unloading. Chloe shoved the letter in her bag. The American
Airlines logo shone in her face. She slid out of the cab, grabbed her
bag, and looked back at the crate.

She handed the cabbie his fare. "And here's full fare back. Please take that cat back to Dartworth Hall."

The cabbie looked at her as he lit up another cigarette. "I'm not going back. I'm staying in London tonight." The smoke made her nauseous.

Rap music rumbled from the inside of the cab, the bass throbbing in her brain. "Then take it back tomorrow. Next week. I don't care." She handed him the money, but he pushed it away.

"I don't like cats."

Chloe looked around. "How about another cabbie, then?"

Near the curb a couple kissed good-bye. The woman started crying. She stood alone for a minute to watch her man run through the automatic doors to catch his plane.

The cabbie handed the crate to Chloe. "Thank you very much. I've got a pickup." He left her there on the curb, loaded with baggage, meowing crate in hand. And he didn't even bow.

Alistair turned in his crate and scratched on the door. She lumbered over to a line of cabs. She knocked on every window, but nobody wanted to drive out to the country at this hour. Did these people want to make money or what?

Finally, she gave up. It was time to check in. The overhead announcements, flashing computer screens, ads, and throngs of people dashing around made her queasy. She leaned on the metal stand that marked the end of the long, mazelike check-in line for economy class. Crying children clung to their parents. Some people carried suitcases and cardboard boxes wrapped in duct tape. She glanced over to the business-class check-in. Two men in suits and a woman with a laptop floated to their respective check-in desks.

Her check-in guy didn't even smile. He just handed the crate back to her. "All animals need to be brought to the international cargo desk." He did say this with a charming, posh English accent, though. "Four hours ahead of departure."

Chloe's passport shook in her hands. "What? But my flight leaves in an hour!"

He gave her a blank stare. The man behind her bumped into her with his rolling carry-on and didn't even apologize—or stop.

"Can the cat go on the next flight, then?"

No response.

"Without me?"

"I do believe that's possible."

An hour later she was in the boarding line, half expecting Henry to burst through the crowd and give it one more shot. But he didn't.

If she weren't so hungry, she might've thought the empty feeling inside was something like regret. She was so hungry she might've even eaten a rabbit with head and furry ears still intact.

"Second row from the back, middle seat," said the flight attendant on board. She had an American accent.

The person behind Chloe pushed into her. Chloe took her ticket from the flight attendant.

"Um. Just a question. If I've changed my mind, can I go back now?"

The flight attendant smiled. "No." She nudged Chloe along. "Second row from the back, middle seat."

Chloe wedged herself between a sprawling teenager playing video games on his phone and a pregnant woman breathing heavily and spilling over two seats. A child behind her kicked her seat incessantly. Nobody taught manners anymore. Mental note: buy iPad with earbuds as soon as possible.

She covered herself up in a blanket up to her chin, and decided to rid herself of all vestiges of her English fantasy world. It was over. So over. Still, she hoped Alistair was okay. And Abigail. She couldn't wait to see her!

Chapter 23

Ten minutes with Abigail and it was as if Chloe had never left. They quickly settled back into the strong mother-daughter team they'd always been and Chloe served up pasta for nights on end. But it took weeks to deprogram Abigail out of the princess mode that Grandma and Grandpa had gotten her into, despite their current lack of cash. Chloe packed away the pink dress-up trunk full of shiny gowns, magic wands, and plastic tiaras for good. She donated the books of fairy tales to Goodwill and put Abigail on a strict diet of nonfiction because she didn't want to perpetuate the myth of charming princes on horses and happily-ever-after.

"Grandpa still calls me his princess," Abigail said days later as Chloe brushed her long brown hair for school. "And he said he's the king."

Chloe looked at the two of them in the bathroom mirror and pointed with the pink brush for emphasis. "Have I taught you nothing? Remember? They're not royalty of any kind. And neither are we."

Abigail frowned and looked down at her new cowboy boots.

"You're not a princess. You're a very smart girl who's going to go to college and live in an apartment and work in a big city. It's so much better than being a princess."

Abigail looked up with her long lashes. "So—after I work I'll meet the prince?"

Chloe sighed. This could take a while. "You might meet a smart man, and if you love him a lot, you might just ask *him* to marry *you*. Now come on, it's time to go to your sleepover."

Abigail went to a party that happened to have a princess theme and Chloe was having Emma over to watch the grand finale of what ultimately became *How to Date Mr. Darcy* on cable. Emma said she was bringing "a friend," which usually meant a blind date for Chloe, and they arrived before she could pour the appletinis and mojitos.

"Hi. I'm Dan." Dan didn't bow when he met her. He wore a Cubs hat and brought his own nachos with microwavable orange cheese. "It's so cool to meet a reality star."

Chloe shot a look at Emma as soon as she could, but Emma just shrugged. "He's supernice," she whispered. "Just give him a chance."

"What's for dinner?" Dan asked.

"Salad," Chloe said.

Every episode of *How to Date Mr. Darcy* was like nails on a chalkboard for Chloe. She didn't like seeing and hearing herself on TV, especially her little freak-out over the confiscation of her cell phone that George had allowed to be plastered all over YouTube, the program's website, everything.

Worse, she saw now how Sebastian charmed his way into every woman's heart on the show—not just hers. He even seduced one of the chaperones, fifteen years his senior, in the weeks before Chloe joined. If anyone was "accomplished," it was him.

"You kick ass, Chloe." Dan ate with his mouth open, and talked with it open, too, so she could see the neon-orange cheese and tortilla chips mashed together in his mouth. "You're number one!" He'd brought an oversized foam finger and brandished it every time Chloe did something "cool" like leave Sebastian at the altar, dumbfounded.

In this final episode, after Chloe left in the taxicab, George announced that the tallied Accomplishment Points were deemed irrelevant due to unforeseen circumstances. He'd done exit interviews with Grace, Fiona, Mrs. Crescent, and Sebastian. After each interview, the screen went black and a little update paragraph about each person appeared. Grace was back to work at her trading firm and dating a British politician. Fiona had set her wedding date with her fiancé, who had come back ahead of schedule from his tour of duty in Afghanistan. Mrs. Crescent's William had a successful operation and the lump was benign. Sebastian, thanks to the reality show, had accepted the leading role in a show called *The Libertine* set to be filmed by England's Independent Television, and, it turned out, was dating one of the milkmaids from *How to Date Mr. Darcy*. He shouldn't have even been talking to the milkmaids. Then a photo of Chloe appeared on-screen and dissolved. The white type on the black screen read:

> **Chloe Parker returned home to Chicago, where she turned her business around to solvent. The court did move to modify custody of her daughter, but only granted her exhusband custody for one month per summer. And the National Trust thanks her for her generous donation to help restore historic properties throughout England.**

The show ended with a short clip about Henry. Chloe sucked down her drink.

"Miss Parker, I know you're out there watching," he said into the camera.

Chloe, in her faded blue jeans, propped up her knees and hid her head.

"It was a great pleasure to get to know you and I do hope that you and your daughter consider visiting Dartworth Hall sometime very soon. I quite miss you. You pierce my soul—and all that."

"Aww," Emma said.

Dan took a slug of beer and burped. "What was that supposed to mean?"

It seemed forever until they left. Chloe stood looking out the third-floor window of her brownstone. It was Saturday night and fireworks were going off at Navy Pier. Red, white, and blue lit up the night sky.

She'd been thinking about Henry a lot lately. About England. The fireworks dripped in front of her like falling petals, or tears.

Alistair sat on his haunches in the living room with his back to her, surrounded by the white, brown, and black feathers from a down pillow he had just shredded. He was a mouser cat, and unless Abigail was home, he was bored.

"Alistair!"

He didn't flinch; she clenched her fists.

"Alistair Cooke!"

He slowly turned around and his green cat eyes stared at her as if he knew all. He had a long white feather in his mouth.

Chloe's heart pounded. At first she actually thought it was a quill pen. She released her clenched fingers and he dropped the feather at her lime-green painted toenails. She stepped on it with her stiletto heel, then sank down into her once shabby-chic couch that she had since reupholstered in black leather. The leather wasn't as comfortable. Neither were the stilettos. And lime green was never her color.

"Meow."

She slipped off her sandals and tiptoed to her desk. The embossed letters on the spine of her Volume I first-edition of *Sense and*

Sensibility gleamed in the moonlight. She pulled out a sheet of thick writing paper, then put it away and turned on her laptop instead. She clicked on her e-mail and adjusted her horn-rimmed glasses.

Maybe you could mix e-mail and etiquette. Business and bird-watching. Nineteenth-century courtship and modern-day feminism. The best of Austen and the worst of our reality.

Maybe she and Abigail could find a way to live in both worlds.

Dear Mr. Wrightman,

I have been thinking of you.

More importantly, Abigail and I need to bring Alistair back home to you. He has not been acclimating to urban American life very well, I'm afraid. And aside from the hot showers, it's been a rocky adjustment for me, too. May we come visit Dartworth Hall before summer's end? I would particularly love to see the library again. And you still owe me a falconry lesson.

Sincerely,
Miss Parker

Her cursor lingered over the send button for a long time, but finally she clicked the mouse. And once you hit send, there's no going back.